Praise for
World Fantasy Award Winner
Jeanne Cavelos
and *Babylon 5:*
Casting Shadows

"It is the rare book that not only matches the quality of the material it is based upon, but surpasses it. . . . Events range from falling-out-of-your-chair laughter . . . to ripping-your-heart-out sadness. I have heard people talk before about books they just couldn't put down . . . but I had never experienced that feeling. Until now."
—*The Zocalo Today*

"Well written and evocative."
—*Science Fiction Chronicle*

"The beginning of an epic. . . . If the writer set out to prove that media tie-ins could fulfill the demanding art of original storytelling and not just capitalize on a brand name, then she's succeeded brilliantly here."
—*Wigglefish*

"The best *Babylon 5* book to date. . . . Doesn't deserve to be classed as a mere 'media novel.'"
—About.com

"A revelation. . . . Not 'television episodic' in look and feel. They are truly novels in their own right."
—*Science Fiction Weekly*

Published by Ballantine Books:

CREATING BABYLON 5 by David Bassom

Babylon 5 Season-by-Season Guides by Jane Killick
SIGNS AND PORTENTS
THE COMING OF SHADOWS
POINT OF NO RETURN
NO SURRENDER, NO RETREAT
THE WHEEL OF FIRE

BABYLON 5 SECURITY MANUAL

BABYLON 5: IN THE BEGINNING by Peter David
BABYLON 5: THIRDSPACE by Peter David
BABYLON 5: A CALL TO ARMS by Robert Sheckley

The Psi Corps Trilogy by J. Gregory Keyes
BABYLON 5: DARK GENESIS
BABYLON 5: DEADLY RELATIONS
BABYLON 5: FINAL RECKONING

Legions of Fire by Peter David
BABYLON 5: THE LONG NIGHT OF CENTAURI PRIME
BABYLON 5: ARMIES OF LIGHT AND DARK
BABYLON 5: OUT OF THE DARKNESS

The Passing of the Techno-Mages by Jeanne Cavelos
BABYLON 5: CASTING SHADOWS
BABYLON 5: SUMMONING LIGHT
BABYLON 5: INVOKING DARKNESS

BABYLON 5™

Book III of The Passing of the Techno-Mages

Invoking Darkness

By Jeanne Cavelos

Based on an original outline by J. Michael Straczynski

DEL
REY

A Del Rey® Book

BALLANTINE BOOKS • NEW YORK

A Del Rey® Book
Published by The Ballantine Publishing Group
TM & copyright © 2001 by Warner Bros.

www.delreydigital.com

ISBN 0-345-43833-7

Manufactured in the United States of America

First Edition: December 2001

10   9   8   7   6   5   4   3   2   1

To Beverly Ferris,
who loves books

— acknowledgments —

For their generosity and support, J. Michael Straczynski and Fiona Avery have my deepest appreciation.

Thanks again to my group of science experts, for providing me with invaluable information: Tom Thatcher, Dr. Charles Lurio, Dr. Stephanie Ross, Bruce Goatly, Dr. Stuart Penn, Dr. Gary Day, Dr. Reed Riddle, Dr. John Schilling, Beth Dibble, Dr. Dennis C. Hwang, Elizabeth Bartosz, Dr. Korey Moeller, Megan Gentry, and Dr. David Loffredo.

For sharing their knowledge of the Babylon 5 universe, thanks to K. Stoddard Hayes, Don Kinney, Alec Ecyler, Merryl Gross, K. Waldo Ricke, Patricia Jackson, John Donigan, William (Pete) Pettit, and Marty Gingras.

Passionate thanks to all the people, many listed above, who read this book in manuscript form and provided feedback: Keith Demanche, JoAnn Forgit, Larry Taylor, Susan Shell Winston, Matthew Rotundo, Matthew Winn, Daniel Fitzgerald, Thomas Seay, David Lowrey, Rita Oakes, Dawn R. Cotter, Paul Schilling, Elaine Isaak, Troy Ehlers, Walter Williamson, Marty Hiller, Cherie Wein, Deborah Bryant, Richard Bradford, Ben Dibble, and Michael Flint. Special thanks to my mother, for being a strong support throughout this writing process.

Thanks to Steve Laurent, Roxanne Hutton, Laurie N. Lanzdorf, Doug Cohen, Keith Maxwell, Peter David, and John Hersey.

Thanks to my editor, Steve Saffel, and my agent, Lori Perkins.

Finally, to my husband, thank you. Without your care, I would have gone stark-raving mad and run off to Mexico with Igmoe.

WHY ARE YOU?

There is a greater darkness than the one we fight.
It is the darkness of the soul that has lost its way.
The war we fight is not against powers and principalities:
it is against chaos and despair. Greater than the death of
flesh is the death of hope, the death of dreams.
Against this peril we can never surrender.

—G'QUAN

August 2260

— *chapter 1* —

They said that Kosh spent too much time among the younger races. They said that he allowed sentimentality to weaken discipline. They said that, in failing to keep himself above the conflict, he revealed how far he had fallen.

Now he would pay the price.

In his simple residence on Babylon 5, Kosh waited. He knew what would happen, as did all the Vorlons. Yet they would do nothing to stop it, and he must do nothing to stop it. He must pay this price, so that others would not.

It was as the Vorlons had always professed: Some must be sacrificed, so that all could be saved.

The fabulists had understood, better than any Vorlon, this harrowing truth at the core of all Vorlon teachings. They had refused alliance with the forces of chaos, had upheld their principles, though it would mean their extinction. They sacrificed themselves for the good of the galaxy. And in so doing, they showed Kosh the way.

For it was not only the younger races who must sacrifice, he now understood, but the Vorlons as well.

All that the others said of him was true. He had spent too much time among the younger races: too much time watching them struggle, under his distant guidance, toward order; too much time watching the enemy undermine any hard-earned progress they made; too much time watching them suffer and die. The rules of engagement, formulated eons ago through the mediation of the First One, dictated that the Vorlons and the maelstrom would launch no direct attacks upon each other. Kosh had broken those rules. He had come down from on high and stood beside the younger ones, had fought with them.

Now he would die with them.

Already the stench of chaos grew stronger, as the enemy advanced through the station toward him.

In the face of approaching death, those of the younger races attempted to evaluate their lives, find significance in their deaths. Kosh had never contemplated his own mortality. Yet he knew that at the end of a being, one could judge that being's importance, his accomplishments. Looking back on his existence in this manner, he found surprisingly little of worth. Of all his acts, he felt truly proud only of his last, the one that had precipitated his end.

He must make certain that Sheridan felt no guilt for it. Sheridan had pushed him to action—more evidence that he spent too much time among the younger races, allowing one so inferior to affect his course. But he no longer thought of Sheridan as his inferior. In Kosh's mind, Sheridan had become something else, had risen to a new level of growth, one Kosh did not fully understand. Kosh had even come to believe that if ever the cycle of war and death was to end, if ever the forces of order were to be definitively proven superior, it would be through Sheridan. Sheridan had not the wisdom or the knowledge or the discipline of a Vorlon, yet he had other qualities, Human qualities, that seemed to carry their own value and worth. Among those was guilt, an emotion long studied by the Vorlons. Kosh did not want Sheridan to be crippled by it.

Sheridan had done no more than speak aloud the argument Kosh had many times made to himself. From the mouth of Sheridan, though, the argument took on a simplicity and a power Kosh obscured behind subtleties and rationalizations.

How many people have already died fighting this war of yours? Sheridan said. *How many more will die before you come down off that mountain and get involved?*

For the first time in millennia, fear governed Kosh's action. He struck out at Sheridan three times, the discharges of his essence nearly killing the Human.

Impudent, Kosh said.

Incorrect, Kosh said.

We are not prepared yet, Kosh said.

Yet it was only Kosh who was not prepared, not prepared to die.

The ancient enemy ascended through the station to his level, bent their steps toward him.

Sheridan had simply spoken the truth. As Kosh had stood on high and watched, the fabulists had gone, and they had been but the first in an escalating series of losses.

The forces of chaos had begun by forming secret alliances with some of the younger races, encouraging and provoking them into vicious wars with their neighbors. Now the enemy openly attacked the younger races, killing at will. And from a planet near the enemy's home on the rim, Kosh's buoys had sung a disturbing song. The two fabulists who served chaos were rebuilding an ancient force that hadn't been used for many millennia. Billions already had died, and billions more would die. The maelstrom hungered to subsume all.

Only in banding together to fight the maelstrom could the majority of the younger races survive. They would not fight, though, if they believed themselves overwhelmed by an invincible enemy. They must have hope they could win, and that hope, as Sheridan had argued, could only be provided by the Vorlons. And so Kosh had brought the Vorlons into the war, had engaged the enemy directly for the first time since their ancient agreement had been reached. With that one battle, he had provided Sheridan the victory necessary to draw the others into alliance.

Now the enemy would demand recompense for the Vorlons' transgression.

Sheridan had not understood what he had asked. Kosh had told him: *There is a price to pay. I will not be there to help you when you go to Z'ha'dum.*

Still Sheridan had not understood. The Human believed he himself must pay the price. He believed that, if ever he went to the enemy's home, Kosh would withhold help out of anger. Yet Kosh would not be unwilling to help; he would be unable.

The enemy was close now, the stench of chaos saturating his senses.

Kosh poured himself into the sleek brown and green shell of his encounter suit. No disguise was necessary, but the hard casement would provide a few moments' defense.

Death was harder to accept than he had thought. Vorlons rarely died; in the last millennium, only one had perished. He feared how the others would proceed in this war without his counsel. He had placed them upon a narrow path. They must participate in the war only when absolutely necessary; they must not dominate it. Yet he did not believe the Vorlons had the will to follow that path. Some hoped that Kosh's death would bring the conflict back into equilibrium, allow them to return to the ancient rules of engagement, to resume their manipulations from on high. But a growing number believed Kosh's action the first step toward a total, final war with the enemy, one that would end with the complete annihilation of the forces of chaos and everything they had touched. In such a total war, Kosh knew, the Vorlons would exterminate as many of the younger races as the maelstrom.

He wished he could remain among them, guide them. If his aide were nearby, he could pour the core of his essence into her, as he sometimes did. She had been modified and trained to carry him, concealed inside her, when he required it. No other on the station had the strength to carry even a small portion of his core. If she were here, though, the enemy would have first sought her out and killed her, to prevent any such transfer. Kosh was glad he had sent her away.

The ancient enemy stood now outside his door. Three of them, and their servant, the pestilence Morden. Morden tampered with the lock.

It was time.

From the core of his essence, Kosh reached out. First, he slipped into the song of his ship. It lay docked in a special bay on the station. It was resting, humming softly to itself of the beauty of order, the satisfaction of service, the harmony of the spheres. He directed it to take no action in the coming moments, when it might sense he was threatened.

A dissonance entered the ship's song, and its tempo quickened. It did not understand. It was frightened.

Kosh repeated his order, and its tempo slightly slowed. It

remained anxious, but it would obey; obedience was its greatest joy.

Without him to serve, Kosh knew, the ship would have no purpose. It would follow its long-standing directives and kill itself by flying into the nearest sun. For many millennia, it had attended him well. He took a moment to convey a simple, calming harmonic.

The ship adopted it eagerly, the dissonance fading away. It sang of perfect symmetry and ultimate peace. Kosh slipped from its song.

The door to his residence slid open and the enemy entered. They too were creatures of light, yet they preferred a more material form, encasing themselves in jagged carapaces of blackness, adopting outer shapes that reflected the inner truth of their beings. Their six-legged bodies scissored forward, the fourteen pinpoints of their eyes burning with brilliant hatred. They reeked of dissolution and chaos. Kosh had long stood in the way of their agenda. They were glad to have the excuse, at last, to be rid of him.

Yet he sensed, as the three spread in a circle about him, that they were afraid. They feared he would fight them. Even now they did not understand Vorlon ways.

Morden remained just inside the door, the clear covering of a breather over his face. Though his expression was obscured by Kosh's reflection, Kosh imagined the pestilence was smiling.

From the enemies' eyes, ropes of brilliant light emerged, twisting toward him. That light was infected with anarchy, with the contagion of desire, the dream of the maelstrom.

Again Kosh reached out with his core, quickly now, this time to Sheridan. He had established a connection with the Human soon after they had met, and had strengthened that connection over time, through occasional visits to Sheridan's dreams, and lessons in a few basic ways of Vorlon thought.

He found Sheridan sleeping, stimulated the Human's mind into a dream state. He took for himself the appearance of Sheridan's elderly father, David. That image existed very clearly in Sheridan's mind, carrying with it David's ways of acting and speaking. This person commanded Sheridan's respect, yet could also reassure and soothe him. Kosh could say what was necessary through this vehicle. He gave the dream form, placing them in the family home, a comforting setting. Bright light streamed through the long windows that framed a fireplace.

Sheridan stood with his back to Kosh, not yet fully aware.

The ropes of light pressed into his encounter suit, melting it, twisting through. Kosh called out in David's voice. "John. Johnny."

Sheridan turned to him. "Dad?"

Kosh converted his thoughts into David's words, into the elder Sheridan's slow but direct manner. "I don't have much time, son. I want you to know you were right. I didn't want to admit that." He shook his head. "Just pride, I guess. You get my age, and you get kind of set in your ways. But it had to be done. Don't blame yourself for what happened later."

The ropes of infected light thrust through his encounter suit and pierced his outer layer. The enemy's touch was excruciating. From those pinpoint contacts radiated chaos. The light of his body began to lose its coherence, to degenerate.

In the dream he stumbled back, clutched a hand to his stomach.

Sheridan grabbed him. "Dad. Are you— You all right?"

The foul ropes slid deeper, carving through him. They left in their wakes spreading halos of dissolution. Kosh found himself holding on to Sheridan for support, struggling to maintain the dream. He did not want to relinquish the connection yet. "It's too late for me. I'm sorry for what I did before. I knew what was ahead. I guess . . . I guess I was afraid. When you've lived as long as I have, you—kind of get used to it."

Inside him, the invading ropes reached the boundary of his core. Against its strength the enemy twisted and writhed, unable to penetrate.

The ropes went still. Kosh wondered if the enemy might, somehow, fail to attain their goal.

With a surge of tainted energy, the ropes began to whirl. Quickly their speed increased. Chaos churned through his outer layers, whipping them into turmoil, building into a great, raging storm. His encounter suit broke apart, fell away. He felt as if he must cease to exist. The pain was unbearable.

They had brought the maelstrom with them. It took on a life of its own within him, his outer layers losing their structure, spinning toward disintegration. The ropes slowed, and their movements became sharper, more purposeful. One sliced down through his weakened outer layers, then sliced across. A brilliant fragment ripped away, flying at the wall. Incoherent, separated from the rest, the fragment rapidly faded. Only the faintest remnant of it struck the wall, the last of its energy boiling across the surface.

In the dream, a grunt of pain escaped him. Kosh pushed himself to finish his message to Sheridan. "I wish I could have done more for you. There's so much I should have said and—now it's too late. You're right. It's time we began fighting this war your way." He doubled over, holding Sheridan at arm's length. The maelstrom thrashed through him, the ropes slicing, rending. His residence became a chaos of strobing light and darkness, flashing energies and shifting shadows. Another piece ripped away, and another. Unable to sustain themselves, they faded, died.

Within the anarchy, Kosh found a sliver of hope. Perhaps there was still a way that he could help Sheridan when confronting the enemy on Z'ha'dum. He had never heard of such a thing being done at this distance, nor with one untrained. Yet he had also never heard of a Vorlon being ripped to pieces. In the manner of his death, there might be hope.

He located a piece of himself that still retained some coherence. It had been partially cut away, would soon be lost. Kosh prepared, extending a threadlike tentacle from his core. The enemy's brilliant ropes sheared the section away. As it ripped from him, he extended the tentacle, seized the fragment, and drew it quickly inside his core.

From there, he forced the fragment out through his connection to Sheridan. The tentacle drove his fragment deep into the Human's mind, then quickly withdrew. In the chaos, he hoped the enemy would not notice. Sheridan's energy would have to sustain the fragment, if it could.

The Vorlons would find this further lowering of himself an

abomination, when they discovered it. But he no longer cared. In the dream, he forced himself to speak. "I've got to go now, John."

"No—no, don't leave." Sheridan's face was filled with fear and concern.

"It's all right, son." For some reason, in that moment, Kosh felt great solace in calling Sheridan *son*. He realized that he had created this dream not only to reassure Sheridan, but to comfort himself in the moment of his death. "See, as long as you're here"—he nodded—"I'll always be here."

The last of his outer layers ripped away, exposing the core of him, the single brilliant flame of his essence. With a final push, the ropes of light sank into it. As they spun him into an incoherent fury of chaos, the pain bled through him into the dream.

In a final moment of recognition, Sheridan seized his wrist and cried out.

Kosh flew apart.

Sheridan jerked awake. "Kosh!"

The turmoil of his essence faded, faded.

And then he was in darkness, murmurs surrounding him. They were Sheridan's thoughts, he realized, and within their flow, he could barely sense himself as a distinct entity. He was weak, disordered. He concentrated on the calming harmonic he had sent to his ship. It brought him, bit by bit, back into coherence. This single fragment, this small piece of himself, was all that remained.

He had come down from on high to help the younger races. Whether he had truly brought them closer to a victory against the ancient enemy, whether they all, ultimately, could be saved, he did not know. Before he lost this last piece, he would try to help them a bit more. He must bury himself deeply, to avoid detection. It might be that his attempt to accomplish any more was in vain. But perhaps, when Sheridan went to Z'ha'dum, Kosh could somehow guide him. Perhaps, if there was a way, he could lessen the terrible tragedy that he foresaw.

November 2260

— *chapter 2* —

With cries of joy, Anna and her sisters swooped toward the planet. The Eye had told them what they must do: strike quickly, with overwhelming force. They each had their assigned targets, and they separated now, plunging eagerly toward battle.

Her sisters had triumphed in many recent raids, destroying one target after another. Anna had been unable to join them, relegated to Z'ha'dum until her passengers needed her to carry them once again. At last they had, and even better, their requirements had brought her into this raid. Once again she could do what she was meant to do.

As her sleek body penetrated the upper level of the atmosphere, Anna stopped her descent. At this elevation she would deliver from their confinement great balls of destruction. Though the surface was swathed in clouds, she easily located her targets: a primitive city that ran along a curving section of ocean coast; the crude open-air spaceport beside it; and on the hilltop above, a grandiose structure where the head of government resided. She surveyed the site eagerly, calculated the most efficient pattern of attack. Over fifty thousand of those native to the planet lived here. There must be no survivors.

She opened her orifice and wheeled over the area, shrieking in exultation as she expelled one ball after another. Elsewhere, her sisters did the same, and their shrieks merged in an oratorio of evolution through bloodshed.

The balls plummeted through the atmosphere, and far below, structures exploded in great waves of annihilation. Buildings burst into dust, spaceships melted to slag, inhabitants flashburned to ash. A vast haze of dust shot up through the clouds and spread out below her, testament to the chaos she had wrought. The city was reduced to random particles, the destruction pure, absolute. Not a single structure stood, not a single being lived.

Then it was time for the second stage of Anna's attack. Her sisters had a different duty. They were to land in some of the smaller towns and allow the Drakh to round up inhabitants for transport to Z'ha'dum. What use the pathetic, weak creatures could be, Anna didn't know.

Her duty carried more excitement. She dove rapidly downward, hungry for challenge. *The greatest excitement is the thrill of battle,* the Eye had taught her. *The greatest joy is the ecstasy of victory.* It was true.

She preferred to strike where she faced some opposition, some enemy to engage and utterly destroy. Even where they did not fight back, though, she could take joy in the dizzying delight of movement, the red rapture of the war cry. And the ecstasy of victory.

Only once had they ever been defeated, months ago, when many of her sisters had been lost. Anna had not been there to fight the hated Vorlons. But she hoped she would soon have the chance. She had no fear of death. If she had to die, she only wanted it to be in the blazing heat of battle. Yet she didn't believe she could be defeated. The machine was perfect, and it was part of her. She could not fail.

As she plunged downward, the dust and mist enveloped her, and moisture ran over her beautiful black skin. This next attack must be surgical, precise. Her target was a small town not far down the coast. She slowed as she neared ground level, and the mist finally thinned. Amidst fields of high grasses and wildflowers stood a collection of simple structures made from stacked stones. This was all as the Eye had explained to her.

The white-haired inhabitants had been drawn outside by the sounds of the city's destruction. They stared up into the darkening mist. When they saw her, they began to scatter.

Anna scanned the town for the tracking device. It had been planted on the one being she was to spare.

There. It emanated from an unremarkable structure on the

far side of town. Only a single being took shelter within. She would spare that one building and that one being, while destroying all the rest.

She narrowed her focus on the nearest structure, and excitement gathered in her throat. The anticipation, the thrill remained as great as the first time. With wild intensity, she shrieked out her war cry, her body rushing with the red rapture. Energy blasted from her mouth in a brilliant torrent. The target was vaporized, replaced with a black, glassy crater.

Three of the town's inhabitants ran off through the fields, and Anna turned her attention to them, destruction boiling up into her mouth. Her shriek sliced through them.

Anna fell upon the town, drawing energy into her mouth, screaming it out in blazing red, swirling in a dizzying dance of death.

Then everything was reduced to smoking black ruins, everything but the single being in the single, unremarkable building. She would have liked to destroy it, too.

"Take us to the landing site, Anna," Elizar said.

Anna wanted to revel in the ecstasy of victory, to whirl among the clouds. She suppressed her resentment. She preferred to take direction from the Eye, not Elizar. But the Eye had told her that on this trip, once again, she must obey him. He aided in their victory, and by carrying him, she helped to attain victory.

She passed over the smoking ruins of the town like a shadow, and found the moss-covered rocky plain that overlooked the sea. She landed there, in the mist, and opened an orifice for her passengers. She would be glad to have them out of her, even for just a time. She carried three: the technomages Elizar and Razeel, and the telepath Bunny. Though she had carried them a number of times now, she still did not feel comfortable with them inside her, particularly the hated Bunny, whose very presence seemed a threat to Anna.

They left her, heading into the mist, and she turned her mind to more important things. It was time for her systems check. The machine was so beautiful, so elegant. Perfect grace, perfect control, form and function integrated into the circuitry of the unbroken loop, the closed universe. All systems of the machine passed through her. She was its heart; she was its brain; she was the machine. She kept the neurons firing in harmony. She synchronized the cleansing and circulation in sublime synergy. She beat out a flawless march with the complex, multileveled systems. The skin of the machine was her skin; its bones and blood, her bones and blood. She and the machine were one: a great engine of chaos and destruction.

The Eye informed her they had won a great victory here today. She and her sisters had found their targets. They had generated vast destruction. The liberators were pleased.

A thrill ran through Anna.

Chaos through warfare, the Eye said. *Evolution through bloodshed. Perfection through victory.*

Now they were one step closer to that great, ecstatic triumph. For the planet Soom lay in ruins.

Galen walked the narrow gray corridors of the hiding place. Harsh light shone off the plain, artificial surfaces. The curved passages carried him endlessly around.

Built in haste on a desolate asteroid, their retreat was too crowded, too close, small rooms packed together in two nested circles. Even in the quiet of early morning, while most still slept, the presence of the other mages pressed at him, and the walls seemed to constrict around him.

The regulated temperature remained several degrees below his comfort level. He buttoned the long black coat that he wore over sweater and pants. The tech echoed his discomfort.

It had been twenty-one months since he had walked outside, since he had felt the wind on his face and smelled fresh air. Those things, he would never do again. Although the others might eventually return to the universe, he would never leave this place.

He finished one mind-focusing exercise and began another, a mathematical progression. He calculated one element after the next. *One. Three. Six.* He maintained the exercises from the time he arose in the morning until the time he went to sleep. For the most part, he was barely aware of them. Only in moments of particular stillness or agitation did he become conscious of the progression that built step by orderly step in his mind. The disciplined mental activity helped him retain control, helped him keep buried those thoughts and memories that would threaten his equilibrium.

As he had cloistered his body away, so had he cloistered his thoughts away. The process had begun long ago; now he had nearly perfected it. With each mind-focusing exercise his attention narrowed, telescoping on the here and now, forming walls that held out past and future, that kept his thoughts fixed on a single path, a safe path. He had learned that he could not allow himself to withdraw from the present, to drift away like a ghost. In drifting he could lose control. Instead, he remained firmly in the present and blocked out everything else.

Walking also helped him to retain control. The regular fall of his footsteps soothed him, as his vision narrowed to his worn boots and the few empty feet of floor ahead.

In this manner, he contained the tech's agitating energy. He needed to call the fire down upon himself only a few times a week to hold it to a manageable level.

"Again!" Tzakizak's deep voice echoed down the corridor, yelling out harsh, one-word commands. Tzakizak maintained a grueling training schedule for his apprentice Hekuba, in chrysalis stage. Galen passed the small room where they worked every morning. Neither of them knew, of course, that their training was for nothing. In one more year, when the time for the next convocation arrived, Hekuba would not be initiated; none of the apprentices would. There would be no tech to implant into their bodies, no tainted gifts from the Shadows to insinuate their way inside apprentices who dreamed of adding magic and beauty to the world.

As Galen continued down the corridor, Tzakizak's angry voice carried after him. "You aren't concentrating! I'm tired of your laziness!"

Galen picked up his pace. *Twenty. Thirty-seven.*

Around the curve in the corridor ahead, Circe came into view, wearing a black robe and her customary tall, pointed hat. She was walking in his direction, her head lowered in thought.

Galen had hoped for solitude, yet that was difficult, no matter the hour. Continuing forward, he moved as far to the right as he could, to allow sufficient room for her to pass. In the confining environment, they had deteriorated to such a state that a simple dispute over right-of-way could trigger violence.

She glanced up at him, then looked again, her attention lingering.

He nodded. He had, to a limited degree, gotten over his self-consciousness around others. There was no more chance of passing himself off as normal, as he used to try to do. Though the mages didn't know what he'd done on the rim, they sensed, somehow, that he'd come back changed, that he didn't really belong among them. At this point, they'd gotten used to his avoiding them. When they happened to encounter him late at night or early in the morning, most seemed at a bit of a loss, as if a specter had suddenly appeared.

"Galen." Circe stopped when he was nearly upon her.

Reluctantly, he too stopped. "Circe." Beneath the brim of her hat, her eyes were in shadow, and he found himself focusing on her mouth. Although she was only in her forties, deep creases framed it, and tiny lines etched her upper lip, signs of the damage done when she had destroyed her place of power.

"I don't believe I've seen you in months," she said. "Curious that I should see you today."

Galen didn't know why today should be significant. "I keep late hours."

"Oh, yes. You have an important job for the Circle. Observing the universe outside. Reporting to them what you find. That must keep you very busy."

"I fill the time, as must we all."

"You will meet with them today, will you not? The Circle."

"Yes." He met with them every week.

"You must feel quite honored."

"I do what they ask of me."

She crossed her arms, sliding her hands up under her sleeves. "Tell me, when you stand there, before them, do you ever dream of one day being elected to that esteemed group?"

"No." Galen's voice was too harsh, and he realized he must add something more. "I could never do what they do." He could never lie to those he was supposed to serve, could never send them into needless danger, could never present them with a gift that carried the seeds of destruction. The tech echoed his anger.

Galen put the thoughts from his mind, pushed forward with his exercise. *264.*

Circe's lips stretched into a smile. "It is unusual for a student of one of the Circle not to have ambitions to the Circle himself."

It was well known that Circe desired such a position. But it was odd that she would ask if he wanted the same. Whether he did or not, he was far too young to be considered. "I have no such ambitions."

"Really. Of course I forget that Elric was not your true teacher. He merely took you in after your father died. Your line has never earned a place in the Circle. So I can understand why you might not feel fit for such a duty."

Galen refused to think of his parents. He had turned his back on those memories long ago. "Certainly I am not fit for it."

"Your humility is refreshing."

"It is not humility. It is the truth."

Circe bowed her head, and the shadow of her hat fell over her face. "Of course."

He took that as his opportunity to leave. "Excuse me," he said, and continued down the narrow corridor.

He reached the dining hall and passed inside, the great room at the center of the hiding place providing only slight relief from the oppressive closeness. At this early hour, the gray hall was unoccupied. The dark wooden tables and chairs stood in long, silent ranks. In this one place, some care had been taken to relieve the austerity of the rest of the compound. The runes of the Code glowed from the walls, interspersed with arcane diagrams and technologically based artworks, and on the far wall shimmered a hologram of Wierden, founder of the Circle and the Code, and master of control. She stood with arms extended, her stiff, golden

wings spread wide, as if in the middle of conjuring some incredible magic.

A familiar burned smell lingered in the air. As Galen
crossed to the kitchen on the far side, he found new scorch
marks on the walls, large fans of blackness forming a rough
line between the rune for solidarity and the portrait of Wierden. The tech stirred inside him, its energy carrying the hint
of chill, like a mild fever. Galen looked away and crossed his
arms over his chest, uneasy. Fights between the mages were
becoming a daily occurrence.

2,059. 4,108.

When they'd first entered the hiding place, they'd behaved
as if they were holding an extended convocation, organizing
group activities and lectures, trying to sustain the feeling of
fellowship that got most of them through those thirty-five
days every three years. Yet after the first few months, they
were no longer able to fool themselves. They were trapped in
this self-made prison, unable to establish their own places of
power, to pursue their own desires. Group activities declined,
resentments grew, fights shattered their fragile peace.

At the same time, the older mages who had destroyed their
places were weakening, dying. During their first year in
hiding, the mages had seen at least one each week to the other
side. Now it was one every two or three weeks. A sense of
doom and desperation had settled over them. With the moder-
ating influence of those more experienced steadily waning,
their behavior became more erratic, more undisciplined.

After nearly two years in hiding, the close quarters would
probably have driven even non-mages into conflict. But for
them, the situation was much more difficult. Mages did not
get along well with other mages, and for good reason: They
were agents of chaos and destruction. They were quick to
anger, quick to strike back. They had not been intended to live
amongst one another, but to live amongst their victims. They
had not been intended for cooperation, but for domination. It
was their way to follow their own agendas, vendettas, whims.
The Shadows' programming urged them constantly toward
action, and although they could resist, resistance was growing increasingly difficult. More and more were reaching the

limit of their control. Galen sensed that, very soon, major violence would erupt. Perhaps they hid from the galaxy, but they could not hide from themselves.

Galen kept away from the others as much as possible. For he, of them all, could not lose control.

In the industrial-sized kitchen, he found some leftover meat and bread for a sandwich, and filled a mug with water. Back in the dining hall, he took his usual table against the wall and ate quickly. He preferred to come early for breakfast, and late for dinner. During the most popular times of the day, the large hall was filled with mages and food, argument and laughter, movement and magic. Galen required stillness.

Footsteps in the hallway outside broke the silence. Though they had grown slower, Galen recognized them immediately. Elric appeared in the doorway, approached him. Elric had once moved with strength and assurance, his posture erect, his gestures precisely controlled. Now his shoulders were bent forward like an old man's, his head hunched within the high collar of his plain black robe. Each step was made hesitantly, as if the floor beneath him might give way at any moment. Each movement seemed brittle, forced.

Galen could not see Elric without seeing the ghosts that accompanied him: the ghost of what he used to be, the ghost of who he'd been to Galen, of all they'd had together and lost. Galen looked down at his plate, continued the exercise, the calculations growing more difficult as the numbers increased. *32,783. 65,552.*

Elric had arranged to meet him here for the monthly review of his progress. Though Galen was no longer Elric's student, still Elric supervised him for his first three years as a mage. Since entering the hiding place, they had exchanged words only to discuss his progress or his duties for the Circle. Yet Galen would have preferred eliminating even those contacts. He had petitioned the Circle for someone else to supervise him, but they had refused.

Elric pulled out the chair opposite him, braced a wrinkled, shaking hand on the table, and lowered himself slowly into the seat. He seemed weaker than ever.

Galen determined to end the meeting as quickly as possible. With a deep breath he met Elric's watery eyes, tensed face. Whether the tightness arose from effort or pain Galen could not tell, but it had been present since they'd arrived at this place. The tension deepened the furrows in his cheeks and forehead, and the three creases between his brows. At one time, those three frown lines of grave disappointment would have strengthened Galen's resolve to work harder, to train more. Now they simply seemed a testament to his failure, to all he had once wanted to be, and all he had instead become. *40,750. 81,485.*

"I have little to add to the reports I've sent you," Galen said. "I have mastered the spells to conjure mist and wind. I continue to pursue Burell's research. My current focus is her data on the programming within each cell of the tech. In addition, I am carrying on with my translation of spells, organizing them into progressions. It has been three months since I have identified a new progression. While my work is still incomplete, I believe I may have found all the progressions that exist. With a single one-term spell at the base of each, that would make seven basic postulates, or basic powers."

Speaking of his progress was pointless. If he learned to conjure mist or wind, what good was it? Any improvement in his skills could bring no benefit to a galaxy outside his reach. Any research he did must be kept from the other mages, who lived in ignorance of the tech's true origin.

He tried to think of anything he might have forgotten. The more complete his statement, the less discussion would be required. "I shall keep looking, of course," he added. "But there is really nothing new to report."

Elric sat in silence. Though his expression had not changed, Galen got the impression that something was different about him today. His eyes remained fixed on Galen.

Galen did not know what Elric sought, and whatever it was, he did not want to give it. He didn't want any change to threaten the walls he had carefully constructed around himself. He only wanted the meeting to be routine, and brief, and to end, allowing him to continue with his life, such as it was.

If Elric followed his usual pattern, he would simply make a few comments, then dismiss Galen. Although Elric evaluated his progress, Elric no longer drove him to excel, not since they'd come here. Elric no longer seemed to have the energy for it, or the conviction. No wonder—Galen had proven himself unworthy.

At last Elric spoke. "We could have the same brief, impersonal conversation we do every month, as you propose." Elric's deep voice resonated through the empty room. With his skillfully modulated intonation, it was the one part of him that still carried its old power. "I could review the reports you have sent me, point out the strengths and weaknesses in your progress, offer suggestions, and speculate on what you have kept from me. But today, I would like to do something different.

"It has been two years since you became a mage, and though a year still remains of your status as an initiate, you have far surpassed that level in your skill. Of the three weaknesses we have long focused on—presentation, originality, and control—only control remains a difficulty, and that is true for most of us. Your presentation has shown marked improvement. As for originality, you have discovered what your own work is, studying the tech and the powers placed within it, and you are making progress well beyond what any have learned in the past."

Galen lowered his gaze. Elric's praise cut more deeply than any criticism ever could. The tech's restless energy churned through him. *1,048,596.*

"You have maintained control since we arrived in this place, which is more than I can say for many. Although I wish your methods were less—extreme, they have provided you mastery over your impulses."

Galen pressed his hands flat against the table. *2,097,173.*

"You have become a skilled mage."

Galen forced himself to meet Elric's eyes, and with a low voice he bit out the words. "Why are you saying these things?"

"It has not been my way to compliment, I—"

"I violated the Code," Galen said. "I committed . . . monstrous acts."

"The Circle—"

"I should have been flayed for what I'd done. I would have been, if the Circle had not wanted me for their weapon."

Elric straightened. "The Circle is also to blame for what happened. If I had not lied to you, and the Circle had not lied to you, you would not have reacted as you did. So those deaths fall to me, and to the Circle, for our deceit. You were pushed beyond what any could be expected to endure."

The memory came—Alwyn's ship lifting him from the surface of Thenothk, and him reaching downward with his fury, the darkening spheres boiling out of him, covering building after building, crushing them to nothingness. In the racing, blazing heat of destruction, he had cared nothing for those he killed. He had never felt so alive.

He exerted voice control, forced his tone to remain even. "You taught me to make no excuses for my misdeeds."

"It is not an excuse. It is the truth. You have also done good, Galen. You have brought light. You are not a monster."

Galen stood, his chair grating against the floor. "Is there anything further?"

Elric's eyes narrowed. "Your reaction demands it. I know you have little respect for my opinion, and I know that my lies have destroyed my ability to teach you, destroyed the bond between us. I realize now the time for a reconciliation between us will never come. Yet left to your own devices, you have retreated to safety, rather than pushing yourself to do more. Since no one else has seen fit to point this out to you, I must do it, though it will drive the wedge deeper between us."

Why was Elric pushing him? Why wouldn't Elric let him go?

"As part of your initiation, you were questioned about your identity and purpose. Mages examine these issues at each convocation, reevaluating who they are, revisiting the questions whose answers life constantly revises. Your behavior, however, indicates that you see no need to question yourself further. You have chosen to define yourself with a permanent, and very limiting, answer. You have decided that you are a monster, that you are your spell, the power of destruction. But I know you, and that is only one small piece of who you are. There are many other pieces: the one who wanted to heal, the one who took joy in Soom, the one who loved Isabelle, the one who created and invented, the one who wanted, above all, to understand. And even more beyond those, pieces that you have buried so deeply you aren't even aware they exist. Pieces, I fear, that you will never recover. For a time your movement was outward. You were learning, trying new things. But since we left Soom, your movement has been only inward. While your studies advance, you, yourself, do not. In fact, you retreat. More each day. You kill yourself off bit by bit."

Galen held himself still and continued his exercise, trying to think of nothing else, to be nothing else. Elric's words, though, would not be ignored.

"Do you remember what I have taught you? Most intelligent beings prefer to live in certainty than uncertainty. Rather than accept uncertainty, they will discount the input of their own senses. It is through this mechanism that mages manipulate the perceptions of others.

"You have chosen certainty over uncertainty, declaring yourself a monster. Certainty brings order, which you have always desired. But life, as you have discovered, is not always orderly.

"The mages have also made this error, by including in the Code knowledge, rather than learning. Knowledge stresses certainty. Yes, we must know all that can be known. But what cannot be known should not be ignored. For it is in uncertainty, and in the unknown, that learning, creativity, and growth occur. Or as Blaylock would call it, transcendence.

"In your certainty of who and what you are, you ignore much of the evidence before you. You focus on a single piece of yourself, and neglect or bury the rest. You expend all your energy on maintaining control, on containing the monster."

He could remain still no longer. "And you would prefer I lose control?"

"No," Elric said. "But I would prefer that you lived."

Galen released a breath. *33,554,457.* "Is that all?"

Elric hesitated. "On that topic, yes." His lips hung open, revealing an unusual reluctance. "I wish that you could stay a few minutes longer."

"I think we have spoken long enough."

"I know that we cannot rebuild our old relationship. I was only hoping that we might—talk of simple things, of home."

"The past is dead to me."

Elric's lips formed a thin, grim line. "Clearly, it is not. For if it were, you would have forgiven me, and yourself."

Galen kept emotion from his voice. "How can I forgive myself for what I have done? How can you forgive me?"

"I have forgiven you because you were not wholly to blame, and because you have repented." Elric reached out, and his quivering hand touched Galen's arm.

Galen jerked away, the tech quickening. He did not deserve forgiveness. He did not deserve even this torturous limbo of the hiding place.

67,108,890. Galen crossed his arms over his chest and walked quickly away. He would not allow himself to become agitated. *134,217,755.*

As he reached the doorway, he received a message from Elric. He continued out, pressing ahead through the claustrophobic gray corridors. Elric's words followed him.

Although the road has not been easy, and you have yet to come to peace with it, you are one who does good, one who brings light. You saved Matthew Gideon, G'Leel, Alwyn, Blaylock. You have performed valuable tasks for the mages. Your research provides new insights.

In our self-imposed exile, it is hard for any of us to feel as if we can do good, as if we have purpose. But you have found your work. Once you find its purpose, you will find the path to do further good.

I hope, in your future, you will find joy, and in your past, you will find wisdom.

You say the past is dead to you. I hope, selfishly, that is not true, for I am part of your past. But more than that, the past is not something to be killed off and forgotten. You have overcome much, and those experiences, if you have the strength to embrace them, are all that can make you whole. I wish I had been of more assistance in this regard.

For you have brought me much happiness, and I wish no less for you.

I am proud of you. And I love you.

Galen erased the message. He didn't want to think of it. He must not think of it. *268,435,484.*

I am proud of you. And I love you.

Those last three words. In all their years together, Elric had never said that to him.

The message read like a farewell.

The thought froze him in place.

Elric deteriorated further each day. Was that why Elric had praised him today? Was that Elric's way of saying good-bye?

Elric couldn't die. Galen couldn't imagine a life without him.

Galen took deliberate, calming breaths. He should be helping Elric through this time, as Elric had always helped him. But he could not. He could do nothing for Elric. For either of them.

He put the thought from his mind, forced his feet back into motion. He must maintain control, above all.

He realized that, for the first time in many months, he had lost track of his mind-focusing exercise. He took a shaky breath, quickly began again. The comforting walls of the exercise rose up around him, narrowing his thoughts, protecting him from all that lay beyond.

One. Three. Six.

— *chapter 3* —

Galen stopped outside the observation room, and in his mind's eye visualized the equation to access its systems. It requested the key for authorization, and he gave it. The door slid open.

The small gray room sat on the periphery of the compound. It was from here alone that access could be gained to the universe outside. A variety of devices lined one wall, their curved metallic shapes looking almost alive, shimmering with the subtle blue glow of a shield, a special protection of the Circle. The complex devices had been built by Herazade and those who had helped her prepare the hiding place. These were connected to other, larger devices elsewhere in the compound. They assured that the asteroid the techno-mages now inhabited would remain invisible to detection; that signals arriving at the hiding place from their many relays and probes would not betray their presence; and that no one and nothing could leave this place, save with the authorization of the Circle.

Galen sat in the single straight-backed chair and requested the menu of available information sources, the tech echoing his command. The mages had planted hundreds of thousands of sturdy probes during their travels, had infiltrated numerous data systems. All of those resources had now been given over to the Circle. Galen selected one probe after the next, flipping through the images in his mind's eye, searching the area of the Shadows' latest attacks for any new destruction.

Although Elric, Blaylock, and Herazade directed the system, Galen had been given limited access, to observe events outside. He had volunteered for the task, after he'd heard that

28

several others had asked to be released from it. The others preferred not to know what happened to those they had forsaken. They preferred not to watch the galaxy dissolve into chaos, to see billions die. They preferred to forget, as much as possible, that worlds beyond this one existed. The order that had once prided itself on knowing all that could be known now preferred to know as little as possible. Of the universe, all they cared to know was when it would be safe for them once again.

Most of them had fled out of fear. For simple self-preservation, they had forsaken the galaxy. In so doing, they had forsaken their Code. They had forsaken themselves.

Only the Circle—and Galen—fully understood their situation. They were unfit to remain among others, unfit to fight in this war. They were, potentially, almost as great a threat as the Shadows. They'd had no choice but to withdraw.

While leaving had been necessary, though, that in no way excused their absence. Every death was a consequence of their failure—their failure to fight the Shadows, their failure to defeat them. Or, more accurately, his failure.

If he'd had better control, instead of withdrawing from the war he could have gone to Z'ha'dum, could have tried, at least, to destroy the Shadows. Yet he'd known that if he confronted his creators, his destruction would not be limited to them. He would kill any who came within reach. As he had killed so many on Thenothk.

So instead, he watched. In truth, he did not want to see. He did not want to hear. But to those he had left behind, he owed that. He owed much more.

He watched as wars broke out one after another—the Centauri blasting the Narn homeworld to a barren land of dust and wind, the Earth Alliance falling into bloody civil war, the Brakiri ruthlessly massacring their neighbors—while the Shadows worked behind the scenes, inciting conflict and destruction. He watched as the Shadows began attacking directly, crippling civilizations, killing billions. He catalogued each new loss, each new tragedy, as chaos spread to envelop the galaxy.

Galen finished his examination of the large area the

Shadows had been raiding. Some planets lay in ruins; others
had fallen into anarchy, the inhabitants desperate to flee to
some safer place. He saw no new signs of aggression, and
turned his attention to other probes.

A familiar figure flashed through his mind's eye, and Galen
stopped the flow of images. On Babylon 5, it was evening,
and as was his habit, Morden sat alone in the open-air café for
an after-dinner coffee. The security camera was over twenty
feet away and encompassed most of the café, yet Morden
seemed set apart from the other patrons. With his dark hair
styled cleanly back, hands folded neatly on the table, a mild
smile on his face, he studied the surrounding activity: a
predator in wait, evaluating potential prey.

He was persona non grata aboard the station, but with
well-placed bribes he came and went as he pleased. When he
was there, rather than detain or eject him, John Sheridan, the
station's captain, preferred to observe the enemy.

Morden was more important to the Shadows than Galen
had first realized. They were only as strong as their strongest
puppet, and Morden was their strongest. On Babylon 5, he
gathered intelligence and manipulated officials of various
governments with a skillful combination of temptations and
threats. Through his many travels, his influence spread even
wider. He alone had driven the Centauri to war with the Narn
and other races. Millions of Narns had died in the bombing,
and even now that the war was over, they continued to die,
some from illness and starvation, others in the Centauri's me-
thodical campaign of pacification and genocide.

Galen could not watch him long. He selected another
image.

Londo Mollari sat before a mirror in his quarters as his attaché, Vir, ministered to his great crest of hair. The probe that
had been planted on Vir's cheek almost two years ago remained molecularly bound to his skin, revealing the continuing crimes of his master. Londo's finances, power, and
influence had increased a hundredfold since the mages had
left Babylon 5. Thanks to Morden, Londo was now a major
force in the Centauri government, both respected and feared.
Some even believed he might one day become emperor. Al-

though Londo had broken his alliance with the Shadows after winning the war against the Narn, Morden had cleverly drawn him back into the fold by having Londo's love, Adira, killed, and leading Londo to believe the Centauri lord Refa responsible. Londo turned to Morden for aid in killing the influential Refa; the plan Londo had devised would soon come to fruition. He was a harder, more ruthless person than he had been. He had little time for drinking or gambling anymore; right now, revenge was foremost in his thoughts.

A condition with which Galen was familiar.

He selected another probe, the one he had long ago affixed to G'Leel's shoulder. Alwyn had surely detected it but he allowed it to remain, perhaps hoping the mages would see what he saw, and decide to leave the hiding place.

G'Leel sat in the lush office of a well-dressed Drazi, while Alwyn—in the guise of "Thomas Alecto," one of his many false identities—paced back and forth, delivering an impassioned speech to convince the Drazi to donate relief supplies for the Narn. Thomas Alecto was the director of the "Citizens of Light Disaster Relief Society," one of Alwyn's seemingly endless supply of fictitious companies. He and G'Leel, a "consultant" for the society, organized desperate relief missions to the ruins of Narn. The two of them flew in the supplies, evading the Centauri defenses.

When they had first decided to work together to fight the Shadows, they had hoped to stop the great war before it began in earnest. They had interfered in several of the smaller wars, providing unexpected resistance, and even, in one case, negotiating a surprise peace agreement.

Yet they were limited in what they could accomplish. At the beginning of the Narn-Centauri war, they tried to convince the Narn leaders in the Kha'Ri that their true enemies were not the Centauri, but the Shadows. The Narns' hatred for their former slave-masters, though, was too strong. They would not believe.

The decimation of the Narn homeworld was a horrible blow to both G'Leel and Alwyn. Alwyn released his frustration in brutal bar fights and other undisciplined outbursts. The death of Carvin still hung heavily on him, and this new

tragedy sucked away any forward momentum he had maintained. Although he ranted about fighting the Shadows, he
could no longer gather himself sufficiently to organize any
action.

But G'Leel was determined to strike back at the Shadows
directly. She gathered a few allies from the Narn underground, and together they devised a suicidal plan: bomb the
Shadows' home of Z'ha'dum. In three ships they set out for
Alpha Omega 3. Within moments of dropping out of hyperspace into the system, though, they were targeted by Z'ha'-
dum's planetary defense net. Weapons platforms took aim,
fired. Two ships were instantly destroyed. G'Leel and the
others aboard the third ship barely escaped into hyperspace.

Disheartened, G'Leel had returned to Alwyn, and his attempt to raise her spirits had at last propelled Alwyn out of
the worst of his depression. They had begun to organize relief
missions and gather information for the Narn resistance.

In Galen's mind's eye, the Drazi refused for the third time
to provide any supplies. Alwyn's voice rose, and he rounded
the desk toward the Drazi, his hand closing into a fist. G'Leel
jumped up, came between them.

Galen flipped through more probes.

Alwyn and G'Leel did what they could, but they would not
stop the Shadows.

Any major opposition would have to involve several different races acting in concert, and it would have to arise from
Babylon 5. John Sheridan, the station's captain, had been organizing a secret alliance over the last months, attempting to
build an Army of Light, a force of sufficient strength to oppose the Shadows.

Galen selected the probe on John's neck. He stood now in
his office, talking to a group of nine, attempting to recruit
them to the alliance. Galen had seen John give this speech
before, though each time he delivered it with power and
conviction. The nine were telepaths, critical to fighting the
Shadows.

Galen believed John's effort doomed to failure, the alliance's technology vastly inferior to the Shadows'. Yet John

had already accomplished two things Galen would never have thought possible.

Although history showed that the Vorlons and the Shadows were ancient enemies, no record existed of any direct confrontation between them. A few months ago, however, John had managed to convince the Vorlon ambassador, Kosh, that he must intercede in the war. The result was a major defeat of the Shadows.

In short order, the Shadows had retaliated with Kosh's murder. With him had probably gone any hope of future help by the Vorlons. They had the power to stop the Shadows, but they would not use it.

John, though, had discovered another weapon: telepaths. They could disrupt the connection between a Shadow ship and the living being that served as its central processing unit. If the telepath was strong enough, the ship could be immobilized.

The Shadows had taken steps to decrease this vulnerability, as John had learned. He had intercepted a freighter on its way to the rim, carrying telepaths in sleeper tubes, just as G'Leel's freighter the *Khatkhata* had been. The sleepers were to be wired into Shadow ships, where they might repel any telepathic attack. Whichever side had the most powerful telepaths would win.

John finished his speech and stood silently. One by one, the telepaths agreed to join his alliance.

Thus far, John had not been able to confront the Shadows with his new weapon in a major battle, for he never knew where they would strike. The Shadows' recent hit-and-run attacks were scattered over a large volume of space, their specific locations impossible to predict. After the last raid, however, Galen's repeated analyses had at last revealed an underlying pattern. The seemingly chaotic attacks were not chaotic at all. Their locations defined a rough shell around a sector of space into which refugees were frantically fleeing.

As for why the Shadows might pursue such a plan, it had taken Galen only a moment to understand. The Shadows knew that despair led people to chaos. They had killed Londo's girlfriend to gain his alliance. And they had used the same strategy—before. The Shadows were manipulating the flow of refugees so that the survivors could be killed in one single, devastating assault. Within the next few weeks, the Shadows would surely attack within the center of the shell, striking a demoralizing blow against the alliance and showing they could not be defied or escaped.

The telepaths filed out, and John sat at his desk, rested his head in his hands.

He did not see the pattern of the attacks, which Galen found immensely frustrating. To be fair, John's information was incomplete, which made the pattern more difficult to see. And he was exhausted and overwhelmed with his duties. Yet he must see it soon. Foreknowledge of the attack presented his best chance of scoring a major victory against the Shadows. And countless refugees would be killed if he did not.

Alwyn did not see the pattern either, even though his home of Regula stood in the very sector that would soon come under attack.

Galen's knowledge, of course, was useless. It could not leave this place, could not save even one of those who was to die.

He put the thought from his mind, searching through the cameras on board the heavy cruiser *Hyperion* for Matthew Gideon. Watching Matthew usually brought him some small consolation. Matthew had been an ensign when Galen had plucked him from space, sole survivor of the hybrid ship's attack on the EarthForce Destroyer *Cerberus*. He was a lieutenant now aboard the *Hyperion*. It would have given Galen some satisfaction if Matthew, at least, had been able to fight the Shadows. Yet the Earth president, Clark, kept his forces out of the war, in secret alliance with the Shadows, who had helped him to secure his office. Meanwhile, Matthew struggled with his growing distrust of his own government, who insisted that the hybrid ship had never existed. How could they admit the rampaging ship had killed hundreds, when they still searched for enough Shadow tech to build another?

Galen found Matthew in the mess, eating with several others.

"Gale! Gale! Gale!"

The voice came from elsewhere, and as he recognized its source, the accompanying image flashed into his mind's eye, next to that of Matthew.

Fa.

She stared directly at him, at the probe in the ring he had given her. She was crying, her breath hitching, her face twisted in distress. Her skin, beneath the curly white wisps of hair, had flushed a deep pink.

He had programmed the ring to inform him if ever she said his name three times. He had told Fa that if ever she did, he would come to her. He had never imagined, then, that he would flee the galaxy.

Her head jerked up in response to some distant sound, and she swallowed her sobs.

After a moment, her gaze returned to the ring. "Gale, I'm afraid," she said in the language of the Soom. "Please come." She stood and took a few steps, and though the light was dim, he could see she'd been crouched in one corner of her bedroom. She was taller than when he'd last seen her, her nose flatter and wider. She had seen nearly ten cycles of the sun now. She still wore the jumper of a child, though this one was blue rather than her favored orange.

"A ship fell out of the sky. A bad ship. Everything—is gone. Look. Look." She turned the ring to face out the window. Where once the neighbor's house had stood, a smoking pit yawned, its sides coated with a black, glassy substance. The fused surface carried the signature of a high-intensity plasma blast at close range. A Shadow ship.

Galen's heart quickened. As Fa turned the ring, the gray mist revealed only a few ragged remnants of walls among the shining black scorch marks. The town of Lok had been destroyed.

He caught a hint of movement in the mist, but that was all he could see before she aimed the ring back at herself.

"My family—they went to Farmer Jae's house. I stayed behind to practice my magic. I don't know if I can find Farmer Jae's house now. I don't know if I can find it."

Galen accessed the menu of probes on Soom. Elric had planted many. More than half no longer functioned, including most of those in the cities. Of those that still did, he selected the one closest to Tain, on a rocky promontory far outside the coastal city. A dusty haze enveloped the lowland. As he increased magnification, he saw in the dim light only scattered dunes and irregular lumps of rubble. Not a building stood, not a survivor moved. The spaceport was distinguishable only by a few puddles of slag. On the far side of the seawall, the water was covered with a layer of dust. The charred remains of the seagoing ships burned as they sank.

He selected one probe after another, flashing from one scene of desolation to the next. All the other cities were the same: wastelands in which all had been reduced to chaos.

It would kill Elric.

Most of the smaller towns had been spared, but not Lok. He searched for a probe still functional in the town, to get a better view of what had happened. The one on Farmer Nee's Jab was still active. Nee lived next door to Jae, so Galen might be able to get a view of Farmer Jae's house, discover what had happened to Fa's family.

The image appeared in close-up, a scorched stone lying on the ground. As Jab moved, pushing herself forward on low, powerful legs, the view from the probe on her forehead shifted back and forth. Galen realized she was circling another smoking ruin. Only a few of the foundational stones remained around the perimeter of a glassy pit. She was looking for something, Galen sensed.

The front part of the house appeared to have been hit directly. The glassy pit encompassed that section. Ragged remnants of the back, and the attached stone barn, still stood, coated with black ash. Jab approached a section of the ruins, climbed over the low barricade with a scrabble of claws.

As she sniffed the ground with a series of harsh inhalations, Galen noticed a heavy earthenware bowl lying broken against the wall. With a start, he recognized it. The bowl belonged to Des, Farmer Jae's prizewinning swug. Of all things, it had somehow survived. Galen remembered the flourish with which Elric had revealed the bowl, solving the mystery of Des' poor health so long ago. It seemed like another lifetime.

This was Farmer Jae's barn and house. Farmer Jae was dead. Fa's family was dead.

Jab had found a black chunk of something, and she pushed at it with her nose. Perhaps it was a piece of Des, or one of Jab's children. She'd had five, with Des serving as host for the larvae. They should be nearly full-grown now.

Jab turned and marched out of the ruins.

"Are you coming, Gale?" Fa asked the ring. "Will you come soon?" She wiped at her eyes, and with a shaky breath, she seemed to make a decision. "I'll go to Farmer Jae's. You can meet me there."

His hands closed into fists. He wanted to tell her not to go, not to move. But he had no way to communicate with her. The probe transmitted information, nothing more. Besides, if he could talk to her, what would he say? That she should stay in her room? She couldn't stay there forever. And he wouldn't be coming to rescue her. He had run away from everything. He hadn't even checked on her in all this time.

She climbed out her window—she had always preferred windows to doors. As she dropped to the ground, he caught a flash of her broad feet, bare as usual, and legs covered with wispy white hair. She hesitated, then again raised the ring to face her. The wind riffled her hair. "We'll go. We'll go together."

He had not wanted to think of her, of Soom, of his life before. Though he had been charged with watching the universe outside, he had conveniently overlooked his old home. He used his task just as he used his mind-focusing exercises, to distract himself, to build walls of facts and information to keep out all that he could not face, not if he was to retain control.

Fa started through the ruins, the hand with the ring clutched to her chest.

He should have realized that the Shadows might attack here. Soom was on the outskirts of the area they'd been targeting. Refugees from earlier raids had fled in this direction. Though Soom constituted no threat, with no weapons or space technology to speak of, the Shadows would want to turn the refugees back, to force the flow toward the center of the sector. A feint here would do that. But he had not seen it, had not wanted to see it.

Even if he had, he could have done nothing. He must remain here, isolated from the rest of the universe.

Fa cried with short, broken breaths as she wandered through the blackened waste. She must know, by now, that her family could not possibly be alive. Of all the town, only her house had been spared. It was unlike the Shadows to spare any.

In the mist ahead, a dark silhouette took shape. The figure approached. Perhaps another had, somehow, survived, or come from the next town. Galen was relieved; Fa would not be alone. She obviously didn't notice, for she kept walking at the same slow pace.

With a gust of wind the silhouette's shape shifted, a long, dark cape billowing out to one side.

This was not one of the Soom.

Galen wanted Fa to turn, to run.

She must have seen the figure, for suddenly she stopped.

"Are you all right?" a woman said in the language of the Soom, her voice rich and deep. As she came forward, thin, dark hair swirled over her pale face, obscuring it. The blowing cape disguised her smallness, yet he knew her. Razeel.

He willed Fa to run, run, but she stood stubbornly in place.

"Don't be afraid," Razeel said. "I'm here to help you."

Fa looked down at the ring. "Did Gale send you?"

Oh God. She sensed Razeel was a mage, like him. Perhaps she even recognized Razeel. That was why she wasn't running.

Razeel stopped in front of Fa, and behind her shifting veil of hair, her gaze flicked briefly to the ring. She smiled. She was only about a foot taller than Fa, able to make friendly eye contact without bending. "Galen, you mean. Yes, that's right. He asked me to come for you."

Fa wiped at her tears. "Is he with you? Why didn't he come?"

"Galen is very ill. He sent me and my friends to help you."

Friends? Elizar, then. Perhaps others. But why would they bother to come to Soom? Why seek out Fa? To strike at him? To try to provoke him into the open?

I will find you, Elizar had written in his final message. *And I will kill you.*

That had been nearly two years ago, though. Why now? Galen realized he was rocking back and forth, his nails digging into the skin of his palms. They were going to hurt her, he knew. They were going to do something horrible to her, because of him.

"Will you take me to Gale?" Fa asked.

"Is that what you want?"

Fa nodded vigorously.

"First we need your help," Razeel said.

"What can I do?"

"Let me take you to the others. They are near where Galen used to live." Razeel flipped her cape back over her shoulder. Beneath, she wore yet another ill-fitting dress, this one of layered black chiffon. She had still not found an identity that fit her. Despite that, she seemed more assured, in some way that frightened Galen. She held out her hand, and Fa took it. She smiled into the ring, her hair blowing over her face. "Hello, Galen."

They walked out of town and down toward the mak, Razeel humming a cheerful tune.

He had to do something. He had to help Fa. But how?

"Galen—Gale—has lost something," Razeel said. "Because he is ill, he cannot remember where he left it. But he is certain it is here. Do you know of anything he or Elric left behind?"

"What did he lose?"

"Did he leave any papers, any crystals, any devices?"

Did she think he and Elric were fools, to leave anything behind? What was it they were after? Something in Elric's place of power? Or was it truly something of his? In that case, it could be only one thing: the secret of destruction. But why would they think he had left it behind?

"Everything burned up when they left," Fa said. "It's all gone. I've looked."

"He left you that ring."

Fa jerked her hand away. "It's mine."

"I wouldn't dream of taking it from you. I'm just wondering, did he leave anything else? This is very important to Gale. Please think carefully."

Fa looked into the ring. "I don't think so."

He could send no message to Razeel to bargain, plead, or threaten; that channel was blocked to him. All he had was the probe. And the ring. Made by Galen's mother, given to Galen's father on his birthday, his death day. It would copy any data crystal with which it came into contact. That would do him no good. But perhaps the ring held other powers—the power to generate an illusion, or a shield, or something to help Fa.

After his initiation, he had made a halfhearted, unsuccessful attempt to access the ring's systems. It would respond only to his father and to those who knew his key. Failing to gain control of it, Galen had added a probe that would respond to his own key.

Now he must discover his father's key. He visualized the equation to access the ring's systems. It requested his authorization.

He tried to think what the key might be. It had been so long since his parents had died, and he had buried the memories of them so deeply—all that came to mind was the image of their shrouded remains floating supine behind Elric as he emerged from the fire of the spaceship crash. They hardly seemed real. He didn't remember. But he must remember.

His parents had been powerful mages, highly respected, working at the right and left hand of a corporate president who had risen to great influence. What key would his father have used? It could be anything. Numbers, significant or random; letters, of any alphabet; a name or quote or phrase, in any language; an image—or any combination. He tried whatever came to mind: the name of the corporation, the name of the corporate president, the words of the Code, and on, in different languages, different encryptions.

The ring did not respond.

His father, he now recalled, had always argued against the use of significant numbers or phrases, asserting that keys should be completely random. Otherwise, with sufficient effort, an intruder could discover them.

Galen continued desperately, pointlessly.

Fa and Razeel reached the moss-covered plain of rock where Galen and Elric had once lived. Out of the dusky mist, like a nightmare, emerged Elizar, with his long, masterful stride, his head tilted slightly back. For two years Galen had struggled to block out all thought of him. The tech's energy welled up with a rush.

Behind Elizar came Bunny, in a short green dress. Galen had hoped he'd killed her on Thenothk. He wondered what she had to do with this. Could she have seen something when she invaded his thoughts, something he'd forgotten here? His mind raced to discover what it could be.

Fa stopped short at the sight of Elizar. She would remember him, Galen knew, from the convocation. She'd seen Galen attack him with the spell of destruction, and she'd been terrified.

Razeel seized Fa's hand, held it up. "Say hello to Galen, brother."

Elizar approached. He wore a long coat of black velvet, a gold and black vest beneath. The dark goatee scoured into the shape of the rune for magic stood out against his pale skin. At the sight of the ring, he gave a truncated laugh. The planes of his angular face carried a cold arrogance. "It's too perfect, isn't it. Hello, Galen."

"Will you take me to Gale?" Fa's question sounded more like a demand.

"She can't remember anything they might have left behind," Razeel said.

Elizar nodded, crouched before Fa.

"Gale didn't like you," Fa said.

"You mean that fight we had?"

Razeel was still clutching Fa, and Elizar pulled his sister's hand away, released it. He continued. "Galen apologized for that. He felt very bad for hurting me. It was all a misunderstanding. I forgave him long ago. I was glad to offer to come here in his place.

"Galen would like us to bring you to him. There's just one problem. You know he went away with all the rest of us, all the techno-mages."

Fa nodded.

"You can't come with us unless you can do magic like we do."

"But I can," Fa said. "A little. I've been practicing." She took a small stone from the pocket of her jumper, and from the movements of the ring he could tell she was going through a rapid sleight of hand. "Where is it?" she said, spreading her palms. She tilted her head to one side. "Oh. But what's that behind your ear?" She reached out to Elizar, produced the stone with a flourish. She'd gotten much better. She must have worked long hours since he'd been gone.

"Very good!" Elizar said with a smile. "Galen taught you that? You're a good student. Did he teach you anything else?"

"Lots of things," Fa said. "He showed me his spells."

"And do you remember them?" Elizar asked.

Galen closed his eyes, though it made no difference. Here, he realized, was the purpose of Elizar's visit. He had left something behind. He had left Fa. She had seen his spells. He desperately tried to remember how much she had seen, whether she had seen the spell of destruction.

Then he remembered.

The night he had discovered it, the first night of the convocation. She had come in through his window raving about the pretty light show outside, had annoyed him while he tried to work. And to show her the difficulty of what the mages did, to teach her more respect, he had shown her his spells, explained the progression from which he had derived his first basic postulate. Bunny must have glimpsed the memory when she scanned him.

Now they were going to rip the spell out of Fa's mind.

"We're going to test your memory," Elizar said. "Then we'll know whether you can become a techno-mage, like us."

Fa glanced into the ring, her face tight.

Trying random keys was pointless. He could continue for years without stumbling upon the one his father had chosen. He would never find it in time.

But what if his mother had set up the system? He remembered watching as she made the ring, building microscopic circuitry into the silver band, creating the natural-looking black stone with layer after layer of crystals deposited in precise patterns. Although his father had been his teacher, she had taught him that day. Perhaps she had even chosen the key while he had watched.

Elizar extended two fingers toward Bunny, and the telepath came forward. She appeared much the same, tall, with long, curly blond hair. She would have conveyed a rather bland attractiveness except for a thinness to her face that gave her an unhealthy, voracious look. The tip of her tongue pushed through her lips.

Elizar turned to Fa. "This is Bunny. She can read your thoughts. You must think of those spells Galen showed you. She will see how well you remember. If you remember well enough, we can take you to Galen."

"Will it hurt?"

"Only if you resist her." He rubbed Fa's arm. "I know you're frightened. Something horrible has happened here today. We didn't arrive in time to stop it, and we feel very badly about that. If you're afraid to take the test, we can leave you here. But I would hate to do that. I know that Galen was really hoping to have you come live with him. It's your decision." He pulled back his hand.

Fa looked down at the ring, looked up at Elizar, at Bunny. She was suspicious; Galen could tell by her hesitance. But he hadn't come at her call, and they had, and if there was even the slightest chance that she could be taken away from all this death and brought to him, he knew she would want to take it.

She nodded.

"Good." Elizar stood, moved away.

As Bunny's eyes narrowed on Fa, Galen remembered the horrible sensation of her invading his mind, of the black tentacles burrowing into him, searching for his deepest secrets.

Fa gasped, and the ring jerked as her body went rigid.

Galen crossed his arms over his chest, and his mother's voice came to him then, hard and powerful. *It's a ring. It will have a stone here, which will copy any data crystal it touches. How can it do that?* he asked.

She pointed to the small, ragged black stone clamped to the worktable. *The inner layers store information, just as a normal data crystal. The outer layer will look the same, but function differently.* As she continued her explanation, her spidery fingers worked over the stone.

Finally she was finished, and she slipped the large ring on his finger. The ragged stone fell to one side. *There. How do you like that?*

The ring should be very useful, he said.

She fixed him with her dark gaze. *A Trojan horse,* she said, switching to an obscure dialect of ancient Greek, as she sometimes did when they were alone, to convey that she shared some secret. She continued in English. *No one would guess what it can do. We wizards are subtle.*

She was paraphrasing the old saying: Do not try the patience of wizards, for they are subtle and quick to anger.

The ring showed him only Bunny's hungry face, yet he could hear Fa's breath, harsh and ragged.

Galen sent the phrase *a Trojan horse* to the ring. No response. Sent it in the Greek. No response.

Do not try the patience of wizards, for they are subtle and quick to anger.

He sent those words to the ring. No response. Again, in ancient Greek.

The ring accepted the key, and a menu of options appeared in his mind's eye.

"I've got everything she remembers," Bunny said, and at last she looked toward Elizar, breaking off her scan.

Fa collapsed.

"It's incomplete," Bunny continued, "but it may be enough for you."

"Thank you, Bunny," Elizar said.

Galen raced through the options. The ring had the usual observing and recording functions of a probe—in fact, he noted, it was recording now, continuing some order issued long ago; it could copy data crystals, erase data crystals, even add information to data crystals—he skipped down the list—and at the very bottom, something called ELECTRIC STORM.

Fa's head wavered in and out of view as she tried to regain her balance, sit up. "That hurt. It hurt! You take me to Gale now."

Razeel knelt beside her, wrapped an arm around her. "I'm sorry. You didn't remember everything, so you can't come with us."

Fa hit her in the shoulder. "You're not nice. Gale didn't like you. And neither do I." Fa struggled against her, but her movements were weak, uncoordinated.

Galen requested information on the electric storm, but there was none. Rings intended to generate electricity were usually constructed differently from this one. A ring might be designed to deliver an electric shock if the stone touched an enemy. Or it might be devised to shock the wearer, an enemy who would receive the ring as a gift. Another possibility was a ring that generated a localized field. If the ring was hidden where the enemy would approach, it could be a lethal weapon. Any of those contingencies could have potentially been included in the ring, though he didn't know why they would have been. His mother had said nothing of it.

"Would you like to see some of my magic?" Razeel asked.

"I have to go now," Fa said, but she could not get free.

Razeel pulled Fa next to her, took Fa's hand, and turned it, pointing the ring into the mist. She wasn't touching the ring, so far as he could tell. She was too smart for that. "Gale would really like to see this. I want you to meet two of my friends."

There, just beyond Fa's bare feet, darkness began to coalesce out of the mist. Galen remembered the vague, dark shapes she had conjured at the convocation, screeching figures that had consumed themselves.

The object taking shape before Fa was neither vague nor amorphous. The darkness formed a supple, rippling surface, and it grew upward, forming a perfect cylinder. When it reached four feet tall, its growth stopped, and it began to draw inward in a line down its middle. The shimmering darkness split down the center, breaking into two cylinders.

"I have to go," Fa said, and the image from the ring shook as she fought with Razeel.

"I can call Bunny back if you want," Razeel said, and the movement stopped. "No one ever thought I was very good at magic either," Razeel continued. "But I know secrets they will never know." She moved the ring back and forth. "You see the beautiful, hungry blackness. It speaks to me. It has spoken to me since the day I received my chrysalis. It chants of vast machines towering dark in the vault of the universe. It whispers mysteries of chaos ascendant, transcendent, of a universe reborn in fire and blood. The shadow of death stretches out its hand. And upon its palm I sit. For I am the queen of shadows."

Elizar stepped into view beside the cylinders. "This is your own fault, Galen. If you had joined me, if you had shared your secret, none of this would be necessary. But you wouldn't. You refused to help the mages. Instead, you sent all of them to their deaths. We are forced to do what we must to rebuild all you have destroyed." He paused, his gaze flicking briefly to Fa's face. "We have a long way to go before we equal your body count." He turned and walked away.

The tops of the cylinders bent toward Fa, as if regarding her, then bloomed open, revealing mouths of complete blackness. With rapid, fluid movement they curled downward, swallowing her feet and sliding up to her knee joints. The bottom half of her legs disappeared completely within the blackness.

Fa screamed, struggling frantically. The cylinders held her legs in place.

"If they pass over you quickly," Razeel said, "you can survive. They absorb only a little energy. The more slowly they proceed, the more damage they cause. If they move slowly enough, there's nothing left of you when they're done. They absorb it all. They prefer that. Of course, that way causes a lot of pain. But Gale has never seen this before, and I think he'd like to. So they're going to move very, very slowly."

Fa shrieked again and again. The cylinders undulated, inching up her legs.

"Do you feel them eating through your skin now? Soon they'll get to your muscles and tissue, your blood, and finally your bones."

"Gale! Gale! Gale!" Fa screamed.

He didn't think Razeel was touching the stone. If she wasn't touching the stone, the only way the ring might harm her was if it produced a generalized field. But in that case it would hurt Fa as well.

Fa's struggles grew weaker. She was sobbing, crying his name.

He wanted to kill Razeel, wanted to save Fa. But he had only this one weapon. If it killed by contact with the stone, it would do nothing. If it killed the wearer, then he would kill Fa.

She shrieked again, her voice growing hoarse. "Gale. Gale."

He had to try it.

He selected the option, and the tech echoed his command.

Fa gasped, and her body bucked in a single, convulsive jerk. As the ring's image jumped, Galen saw the blur of Razeel's pale hand flying up, Razeel's cape billowing as she fell away. Then he was looking up at Fa, her neck muscles standing out in spasm, her eyes wide in terror and agony.

In his mind's eye, a schematic of Fa's body appeared beside her image. The ring's sensors showed a massive electric shock pumping through her, running up her arm, down her chest, and out through her buttocks into the ground. It was a high-voltage, low-frequency alternating current, the most lethal kind. The muscles of her arm and chest had frozen in tetany; she couldn't breathe.

As one second passed into the next, Fa's mouth opening wider and wider for air that would not come, tears running down her face, inside her heat built, tissues shriveled, burns spread down nerves, blood vessels, and muscles. Veins coagulated, blood clotted. With the internal resistance of her body breaking down, the current poured through even stronger.

The image shook as Fa went into seizure. The schematic flashed, signaling ventricular fibrillation. Fa's heart was failing.

And then, it stopped. Cardiac arrest.

The electric storm died. As her muscles went slack, a long, soft sigh whispered from her mouth. She fell back onto the mak, still.

The ring's sensors confirmed that Fa's heart remained in arrest. No further shock was necessary. The schematic vanished.

In one corner of the probe's image, he could see Elizar holding Razeel in a sitting position, examining her palm. She was still alive. She'd received a brief shock from her skin-to-skin contact with Fa, and perhaps a burn, but the involuntary movement that had jerked her hand free had saved her. The ring had been designed to attack its wearer, no others.

The rest of the image showed only mist.

He broke the connection, finding himself hunched forward, arms crossed over his chest, hands clenched. His body was shaking, racing with the relentless, merciless energy. He wiped at his eyes. He was furious at Razeel and Elizar, furious at this damned hiding place that allowed him to see but not to act. But above all, furious at himself. He'd had to prove to Fa the greatness of the techno-mages, had to show her his spells. He had promised to come at her call. And he had failed her.

He couldn't save anyone. He could only kill.

The blazing, brilliant energy raged through him. Galen wanted to reach out through the ring, to seize Elizar and Razeel and crush them to nothingness. Or, if he could not reach them, then to crush everything that was within his reach.

He turned his thoughts away from that, and in his mind's eye forced another equation to form. The tech eagerly echoed it. A ball of brilliant blue fire formed above him, shot downward. It seized him at the neck and rushed over chest, arms, legs like living lava, searing him, consuming the hair from his body.

Again. The blue fire fell upon him with ragged claws. They raked down his skin, scouring the outer layer away.

Again.

Again.

Again.

He fell out of his chair, light-headed, gasping. His raw skin was overloaded with sensation, with pain. He was disgusted at himself, at the way he continued when everyone around him died. Why stop at these weak punishments? Why not just kill himself? Why not bring the fire down until it ate through his body, until he suffered what Fa had suffered?

He brought the fire down again, again. Something warm spread over his forearm, dampness stinging exposed nerve endings. From the sleeve of his coat a trickle of blood ran out onto his hand. He felt warmth on his back now too, and his side. He would not lose control again. He would not hurt anyone else again.

He called the fire down. The dampness spread, warmth enveloping him. He found himself fading into that warmth. It was hard to focus. But he knew there was one thing he must do, and he held fiercely to that one thing. And as consciousness left him, he brought the fire down one last time.

— chapter 4 —

Anna closed her orifice and, with a cry of joy, shot up into the sky. The gases of the atmosphere, layers of moisture and dust pressed against her, fighting her forward motion. She strove upward. Beneath her, cities had been flattened to desolate plains, life exterminated. A great victory.

The atmosphere thinned, her weight grew light, and the cold sent exhilarating tingles across her skin. Then she was free, cutting through the invigorating vacuum of space.

Her sisters had taken flight, speeding to Z'ha'dum to drop off their prisoners, so they could return to this sector and wait in delicious anticipation of the next attack. For Anna there would be no such joy. She must remain with her passengers on Z'ha'dum.

She had extended chairs and benches from the walls of her largest chamber, and there they sat, heat and oily excretions soaking into her. Through her skin, she watched them. The hated Bunny sat apart from the others, with a screen on her lap. Using a stylus, she dashed off line after line of strange symbols.

Even occupied as she was, Bunny challenged Anna's ability to concentrate, to carry out her tasks. The pressure of Bunny's thoughts pushed at Anna's mind, generating a dull, pulsing pain. Bunny was a disruptive, intrusive presence. She vexed Anna.

Because of Bunny, Anna had to stand idle on Z'ha'dum in case her passengers required transportation. Anna was the only one the Eye trusted to carry Bunny. Once, another of her sisters had been ordered to transport a telepath. As soon as the telepath had boarded, she'd taken off and flown into the nearest sun.

If Bunny were not among Anna's passengers, any ship could take them. She could return to the war, where she longed to be.

Elizar sat beside Razeel on a bench. Their weight pressed against Anna. "You've perfected the cylinders," Elizar said.

"They were beautiful, weren't they? Two great mouths of hunger. They would have consumed her utterly."

He watched her silently for a moment. "They served their purpose well."

"I wish Galen had not interfered. Their need has gone unsatisfied."

"Galen will pay his price." Elizar took her hand and examined it. A dark red discoloration ran along the length of her index finger and over her fingertips. "Why don't you rest and allow your hand to heal?"

Their bodies were so inferior, their pale skin vulnerable to nearly any attack, unlike Anna's brilliant black skin.

Elizar stood, and Razeel lay on the bench, her face to the wall. As she traced a finger over Anna, she whispered. "The shadow of death stretches out its hand. And upon its palm I sit. The queen of shadows." She began to hum.

Elizar let out a heavy breath and went to Bunny. He watched over her shoulder as she scribbled symbol after symbol. After a time, her hand stopped.

"Is that all?" Elizar said.

Bunny jerked her head around, her mouth tightly closed. "Those are all the spells the girl remembered. Galen explained to her what some of them did. I can tell you what he said." Bunny looked back down at the screen, and for some reason, Anna got the impression she was afraid. "Is it enough?"

"I'm not certain."

"Whether it is or not, I got all there was to get. You can tell them. I did a good job." Bunny's voice carried an odd quality, quite different from the lightness it used to have. Anna was glad Bunny was afraid, for whatever reason.

Elizar came to stand before her. "I have always fought for you to remain with us. You have been of great assistance."

"Maybe I didn't get everything out of Galen, but I got enough that we might win the war because of it. Especially about . . ." Bunny jerked her head upward, as if indicating Anna. "If they ever do anything about it."

Did Bunny think she knew something about Anna? She didn't know anything.

"Our allies work on their own timetable."

"I just wish we could go somewhere else. We had some good times on Thenothk. But Z'ha'dum"—she flipped her hair over her shoulder—"it's hard to keep a party going there."

"They may not be comfortable with telepaths, but they too realize your value."

"They realize how valuable I could be inside a ship. I know that's what they're thinking, every time they look at me. Since John Sheridan used a telepath to jam one of their precious fleet, they've been wiring in every telepath they can get their hands on. And they don't have any as powerful as I am."

Anna didn't understand what Bunny was talking about, but she wanted Bunny to stop talking. Now. She bent her mind to Bunny, trying to make the telepath as uncomfortable as she was.

"Your power makes you valuable to them outside a ship as well," Elizar said.

Bunny glanced upward. She stood, twirling a lock of her hair. "I just wish we could go to someplace away from—all that." She pressed against him. "Someplace with decent food, and drink, and light, and music. See what develops."

Good, Anna thought. She had stopped her talk of ships.

"You'll get what you want, as will I, if we are both patient. The force that I have built so carefully is nearly ready. They were very pleased with the last test. It will be sent out to fight. I will be sent at its head. And you will come with me." He caressed her face, at the same time moving slightly away from her. "I have been promised that if I complete my final task for them, then once the war is over, I will be given the force to do with as I please."

"This hasn't turned out like I thought. I figured, with all the talk about chaos, we'd be able to do whatever we wanted. Instead, we just follow orders."

"You must be patient. For now, we return to Z'ha'dum." He lifted the screen between them. "Tell me what Galen said to Fa as he explained these spells."

Bunny pressed the screen against her chest with a small smile. "If you do learn Galen's spell, you better remember who you have to thank for it. You better not use it on me."

"Don't be ridiculous. I would never kill you." He turned his hand palm up, waiting for her to relinquish the screen.

At last she extended it, though she did not release it. "I'd like to know sometime what you're really thinking."

Elizar took her hand, pulled it away from the screen. "Scan me, sweet Bunny, and you'll find you have lost your only ally."

They continued to talk, but Anna had lost interest. She thought of their great victory today, of the red rapture of the war cry. Another attack would come soon. Perhaps, when she reached Z'ha'dum, the Eye would finally realize that Bunny was an enemy, just like all telepaths. Perhaps the Eye would kill her. Then Anna could return to the war, could know the ecstasy of victory. Above that, there was no greater joy.

Now it was time to go home. Anna pushed through the shimmering black membrane of space and with an exhilarating leap, joined the roiling red chaos of hyperspace.

"Galen!" a muffled voice called. "Galen!"

Fa?

He pushed himself up on shaky arms. He was on the tiled floor of the observation room. Someone was knocking on the door, and as the voice called out again, he recognized it. Gowen.

"Galen! Can you hear me?"

Fa was dead.

Soom was destroyed.

Elizar and Razeel had likely acquired the spell of destruction.

And he hadn't killed himself. But then, he had known that he wouldn't, hadn't he. If he truly wanted to kill himself, he knew the spell that would do it, that would end everything.

He realized, in a moment of perfect clarity, that it was the only solution. It would be the logical last step in the process he had begun when he'd entered the hiding place: withdrawing from the universe, building up the walls, drawing them closer and closer around him. Even sealed away, he continued to spread his chaos and death. To stop the destruction, once and for all, he must draw the process to its inevitable conclusion. Crush himself in the fist of his own will.

He gained a measure of peace from the thought. He need not hurt again. He need not spend the next hundred years walking in circles.

Gowen continued to knock. The door was sealed to all but Galen and the Circle.

Still Galen burned to reach out, to kill Elizar and Razeel. Though the tech's energy had subsided somewhat, its agitating undercurrent drove endlessly through him. He began a mind-focusing exercise. A smear of blood revealed where his arm had lain. He wiped at it with his black coat until it was barely visible.

"Galen!"

He must accomplish one more task, stop his mistake from causing any further harm. Then it would be over, at last.

"Galen!"

"Just a—" His voice was hoarse, barely audible. He cleared his throat. "A moment."

Gowen stopped knocking.

Galen grabbed on to the chair with red, raw hands, worked his way to standing. Dark spots danced before his eyes. He steadied himself, took a few calming breaths. Although he'd had the presence of mind not to scour his head, any moderately close inspection would reveal what he had done.

He found he had received a message—the Circle, calling for his report. He was late. Gowen had come after him.

He thought of opening the door, of dismissing Blaylock's former student with a few quick words. But he couldn't face Gowen, couldn't face anyone yet. He called out. "I must finish an observation. Tell the Circle I will be with them shortly."

For a moment there was no reply. Then Gowen said, "I'll tell them," and Galen heard him walk away.

He had to collect himself. He had to convince the Circle of his plan.

And he had to tell Elric that the home he loved, the home that had once been a part of him, had been destroyed.

"I have sent Gowen to fetch him," Blaylock said.

Elric nodded, anxious that Galen had not reported to the Circle at the scheduled time. It was unlike him. Perhaps, in their meeting this morning, Elric had pushed him too far.

"Let us move on to the consideration of elections," Blaylock said. "Elric, you wanted to speak in favor."

"Yes." He straightened, trying to ignore the incessant throbbing that echoed through him. Its source was the cavity of darkness in his skull, an emptiness where once had resided the connection to his place of power, and to Soom. That emptiness pushed outward, a tumor of desolation, pressing at the backs of his eyes, his forehead. The pain worsened with each passing day, leaving him indisposed for hours at a time, unable to rise or even to move. He concealed his weakness as much as he could, to retain his influence within the Circle and inspire confidence in the mages, but the signs were becoming ever more apparent. When he'd destroyed his place, with the great growth of chrysalis at its heart, he'd sensed that the loss would, eventually, kill him. That time was coming close. His body was failing.

He was thankful they no longer stood when making formal arguments. Blaylock, who had stood whenever he spoke before the Circle, had made no objection when Herazade suggested they make their meetings more informal. Elric knew that he, too, was weakened, though the signs of it were few.

The character of their meetings had changed in other ways as well. They now forwent the grand illusion of the amphitheater Ing-Radi had once generated. That illusion had simulated the ancient stone structure where Wierden and the original Circle had met, a reminder of their history and responsibility. Perhaps it was best they no longer used it. They had declined so, it no longer seemed appropriate.

They met at a simple round silver table, only three instead of the five Wierden had dictated, sitting in a half circle with Blaylock at their center. Herazade no longer wore a formal black robe, appearing instead in a sari, her straight black hair hanging free. They were losing their traditions, their discipline, their numbers, day by day. Elric feared where this trend might lead them.

He had not fought for anything in a long time. But now he must make this one, last fight.

"We are approaching our traditional time for elections," he said. "Over the last hundred years, whenever there has been an opening in the Circle, we have always filled it in December, according to the Earth calendar. Wierden established that the number of the Circle should be five, the number of balance. Last year, at this time, we rightfully postponed elections. We had not settled into our new home sufficiently to undergo any changes. Now we are settled. We have had time. We must not delay further, or the basis of our order may be lost."

Elric did not believe he would survive another year, or even another month. Last night, as the pounding pain built with each beat of his heart to astonishing, staggering agony, he'd felt certain that he would die. His end would come soon.

As for Blaylock, he was not sure. Although Elric had never seen Blaylock's energy fail, he had grown more gaunt than ever, his black skullcap loose on his head. His skin, scoured of all hair, had a pronounced waxy sheen. His hands had not healed well from the atrocity performed upon them by Tilar. They remained stiffly open, like two bookends on the table before him, the palms covered with thick, yellowish skin. He used them as little as possible.

While he and Elric weakened, Herazade's influence grew, which tipped the Circle out of balance. She clearly recognized her growing dominance and used it to advance her agenda. One person, though, could not rule the mages. That was too much power.

Blaylock's words were harsh and certain, as usual. "I agree in principle. But in practice what you propose would only weaken the Circle. Of the mages, none are fit to join us. The wisest, the most skilled, have died either in the attempt to bring us here, or in the time since we arrived. While some of the younger mages show promise, they are not nearly ready to take a place at this table. If we opened the Circle to them, they would simply obstruct our wisdom."

"That argument," Elric said, "has probably been made by some member of the Circle before every election."

"In this case, however, it is true. Who would you have sit beside us? Miostro? Tzakizak? Circe? None is fit."

Blaylock was right; any that Elric would have considered for the Circle were either dead or well on their way. They were less than four hundred now, and nearly a third of those very ill. Yet Elric would rather have even a callow initiate like Fed in the Circle than let their power fall to two. "They are all we have."

"I must agree with Blaylock," Herazade said. "Among the older mages, I don't believe any has the skill, the wisdom, and the stamina necessary to fulfill the duties of the Circle. Among those younger, I see great promise that, with our guidance and a few years' maturity, should find its fulfillment."

What she did not realize, apparently, was that they did not have a few years to wait. Perhaps she felt she could govern alone until others were ready. Yet who, once holding supreme power, would share that power with others?

Elric said the words he had not wanted to say. "The power of the Circle cannot be allowed to fall to only two, or one."

Blaylock's sharp gaze turned toward him.

But Herazade waved his comment away. "That will not happen. We three have done well in leading the mages through a difficult time. I see no reason we cannot continue to do so."

Blaylock gave him a short nod. Blaylock understood. "Elric is correct that the situation becomes dangerous when the Circle has less than three. But let us wait until that time comes before any election is held."

Elric gathered himself, exerted voice control. "Many times have I been outvoted by this body, on issues of grave importance. Never, though, on an issue more important than this. Our behavior now will determine how the final chapter of the

mages is written. Our order is losing its best, leaving those
younger without guidance. In the absence of a clear purpose,
some have deteriorated to the most petty, undisciplined be-
haviors. They know, as do we, that in coming here we abandoned our commitment to good. With one part of the Code
lost, the others become simply a matter of personal choice. If
we also allow the Circle to be discarded as an artifact of the
past, the mages will have nothing to hold back chaos. I have
not done all I have done—"

A sliver of pain pierced his eye and slipped directly into his
brain. He forced himself to continue. "I have not helped to
lead the mages to this place so that they can turn upon one another. With two members, the Circle could easily be split
asunder. If you will not agree to hold elections now, then let
us make a private pact that if ever the Circle falls to two, elections will be undertaken immediately."

Blaylock's dark eyes were fixed on him. "I will make such
a pact."

Herazade's index finger rubbed back and forth on the
tabletop, calculating. At last she spoke. "I would dispute
much of what you said about our current condition, Elric. My
assessment is much more positive than yours. But your point
about a Circle of only two is well taken. I concur with your
proposal."

Elric bowed his head. He had accomplished that, at least.

"Galen has arrived," Blaylock said.

They agreed to hear his report, and the door opened to
admit him.

Elric knew that something was wrong the moment he saw
Galen. Over the months, Galen had grown increasingly cold
and distant, his face more unrevealing, his voice more perfectly controlled. This was not the vacancy he had shown
when he was younger, as at his parents' deaths. It was a hard
wall of determination behind which he would not let anyone
pass, not Elric, most especially not himself. This morning Elric had threatened that wall, and Galen had quickly retreated.

Now, Elric could see, the wall was cracking, and Galen
was struggling to hold it together. As he stopped before them,
his face was carefully composed, his large blue eyes wary. He

wore gloves, which he never did, and as Elric studied Galen further, he realized that Galen had changed clothes from earlier in the day. The black sweater, pants, and coat were similar enough that Galen might hope no one would notice. He had injured himself seriously this time.

Elric had been ashamed that he'd needed to hear of Galen's practice from Blaylock. He'd been so preoccupied with the mages' problems that he hadn't known of it until Blaylock and Galen's return from the rim. By that point, Galen would not hear any advice Elric might give.

There were many ways to deal with the difficulty of control. He need not hurt himself. Striking at himself, however, was Galen's instinctive response. He punished himself, falling back, in his time of stress, to a feeling instilled in him when he was very young, a feeling that he deserved punishment.

"You have a report to make," Blaylock said.

Galen gave a single nod. Since his return from the rim, he had not bowed to the Circle, just as he had not worn the robe of a mage. "I apologize for the delay. I have dire news. The Shadows have struck again." His eyes flicked to Elric, and Elric knew, in that moment, what had happened. "They have attacked Soom," Galen said.

Elric pressed the heel of his hand against his temple. It felt as if a great darkness would burst full-blown from his skull.

Galen conjured an image above the table, a coastal lowland shrouded in dust. Through that haze, Elric saw only windswept dunes and lumps of rubble. It had once been the city of Tain.

Then other images, other cities laid waste. The town of Lok, a smoking ruin.

Soom had been a planet imbued with life, a rare place of simple pleasures. He had taken precious joy in each creature, each blade of grass, each drop of water, each bit of rock. He had loved each, as a part of himself.

Elric accessed the probe records himself, searched through the images from Soom faster and faster, finding destruction upon destruction: vast tracts of barren land, fissures blasted deep into the earth, great clouds of dust darkening the sky.

His precious home, his heart, ravaged; those under his protection, killed. For duty, he had abandoned them. And the Shadows had destroyed them.

The pressure in his head was building into an irresistible, overwhelming pain. It spread through his body, the emptiness consuming him, driving out everything but despair.

He fixed on Galen, struggling to hear the boy's words, to maintain his composure.

"After the bombardment, Elizar, Razeel, and the telepath Bunny Oliver landed near Lok. They sought out one of the Soom that Elric and I knew, a girl named Fa." Various images accompanied Galen's description. There was Fa's wariness, Elizar's false solicitude. Galen's tone was flat. "I had once foolishly shown Fa some of my spells, including the spell of destruction, before I knew its nature. Apparently when Bunny scanned me on Thenothk, she learned this. Bunny searched Fa's mind for the knowledge. She told Elizar what she found was incomplete, but that it might be enough.

"They knew that I was watching, through a ring I had given Fa. My father's ring. Once they had all the information they could get from her, Razeel—" Galen paused, his gaze falling and his mouth tightening in a way Elric recognized. He was doing a mind-focusing exercise, struggling to retain control. "Razeel began to slowly kill Fa. After a time, I was able to access the systems in the ring." He paused again.

Galen had finally opened that Pandora's box. Elric searched for any sign of change in him, but saw none. Still he hid from the truth.

"I delivered an electric shock to Fa, killing her."

A brief image flashed Fa's face, neck muscles seized in spasm, mouth gasping, eyes wide in agony. Quickly Galen replaced it with a view of mist-shrouded sky. Then the images vanished.

Fa—she had been a sweet girl, innocent and affectionate, curious and adventurous. She had embodied everything good and special about her home. Now both were gone; Soom's fleeting, unique beauty was lost.

Galen bowed his head. He'd been forced to kill one of those few he'd allowed close to him. "Soom might not have been attacked at all if not for my stupidity. Perhaps some other planet—" He raised his intense blue gaze to look at each of them in turn.

Elric realized that his hand was still pressed to his temple, and he lowered it, straightened.

"I would like to request the Circle's permission to leave the hiding place, to pursue Elizar and Razeel and kill them, so the secret of destruction can again be contained. It is my fault they may now have it."

Blaylock frowned. "Yet they may not. They may have suggested they did simply to lure you from hiding. Their true goal may be to obtain the spell directly from you, as they failed to do before."

Galen took a step forward. "If they do have it, they could cause great destruction. As great," he said, "as I have."

Herazade raised a cautioning hand. "The risks of sending someone outside are grave. We realize that you would never reveal our position willingly. You could, nevertheless, reveal it unwillingly. We must wait until we know for certain whether they have learned your spell."

"So I must wait"—Galen bit out the words—"until they kill several hundred, or several thousand, or several million, and then you will let me go?" He crossed his arms over his chest. "I cannot live with that. I cannot have more deaths on my head."

"Even if we knew they had the spell," Blaylock said, "what good would it do to send you? How could you stop them?"

"By killing them," Galen said, "before they kill me." He looked to Elric, his lips parted with desperate hope.

If he went, Elric would not last until his return. Though that was no reason to keep Galen here, Elric could not stand to send him away again. Every time he went, he came back changed, hurt. This time, Elric feared they would lose Galen. Indeed, that, Elric believed, was Galen's unstated goal. To suffer the ultimate punishment.

"As we prepared to leave for this place," Elric said, "you told me why you must come with us. You told me that if you remained out in the universe, you would destroy all, gladly. You told me that you were not fit to remain. Has that changed?"

Galen's face tightened. "No, I am not fit." He shivered. "But I can no longer hide here behind my weakness while others die. If you release me, I swear that I will kill only the Shadows and those I know to be their servants. I will not lose control again. When the time comes, when I have done what must be done, I will destroy myself. I have the power, and the resolve to use it."

Elric couldn't believe that Galen was standing here, proposing what he was proposing. "That is unacceptable."

"I agree." Blaylock's eyes narrowed. "I have told you we are meant for greater things than fighting."

Galen's crossed arms rose and fell with his hard breaths. "Yet you hold me here as your weapon, in case we are discovered. Would you protect yourselves at the cost of everyone else?"

Elric cared only about protecting Galen.

"You speak of control," Blaylock said, "but your plan is simply to go, and to kill. That is not the plan of a techno-mage in control. Elizar can again nullify your tech, rendering you defenseless."

Herazade pressed her palms flat against each other. "We require assurance that no telepath could gain from you the location of the hiding place, or even the knowledge that so many of us still live. You cannot give that assurance. So long as you are vulnerable to the Shadows' control, you may find yourself subject to telepathic scan, as you were before. By your own admittance, that may be why Soom was attacked. The hiding place must not be next."

Galen took a deep breath, released it. "If I could find a way to immunize myself to the Shadow signal, would you then let me go?"

"You have told us that is impossible," Herazade said, "and we have confirmed your findings. We are united against your proposal, Galen. Do not show us disrespect by arguing your case further. If you find evidence that your spell of destruction is being used, bring it before us, and we will consider what best should be done."

Galen looked down, and his gloved hands fell to his sides. He gave a single nod, turned, and walked out.

Elric received a message from Herazade, her summary of those select findings and decisions of the Circle to be made public. He scanned it quickly, read her brief, passionless description of the destruction of Soom, and approved it for circulation.

His head felt light and hot, and his muscles quivered with weakness. More than anything, he wanted to go after Galen. But Galen was lost to him. Soom was lost. The mages soon would be; they had begun their long twilight.

When they had first come to this place, Elric had felt hope, in the mages' solidarity in the face of the Shadows, in John Sheridan's potential to fight them, in Galen's return from the rim. It had been a false hope. The Shadows destroyed anything of worth outside, while within, the mages decayed and Galen spiraled toward self-destruction.

The tumor of despair had at last completed its job, Elric realized. He now saw the truth. All was hopeless.

—— chapter 5 ——

Galen circulated through the narrow gray corridors of the hiding place. Though it was late, he could not sleep.

One mind-focusing exercise had been insufficient to keep his thoughts to a safe path, so he maintained two simultaneously, wrapping them tight about him, withdrawing down the tunnel their walls created.

With each step his pants whispered against the raw skin of his legs; his boots cut into his shins; his prickly sweater, pressed down by the weight of his coat, ground into his shoulders. Normally, a few circuits around the hiding place would be sufficient to settle his thoughts for the night. The regularity of his footsteps, the rhythm of his mind-focusing exercises, the discipline of pain usually calmed him. But tonight he had lost count of his trips through the corridors.

Several rounds had been necessary to rid him of his frustration at the Circle, more to block out his anger at Elizar and Razeel, more to bury his grief over Fa, and Soom.

Once those were gone, the issue had become very simple. He must make a decision.

Elizar was a skilled mage. If Fa had remembered all that Galen had shown her, Elizar would be able to translate the spell of destruction. It would take him, at most, a few days. Then he would want to show Galen what he had learned. Galen could either spend the rest of his life here, in safety, watching as Elizar killed, or he could engineer his departure from this place.

He could think of only one way to accomplish it, one he dared not face. Not yet. So he continued to walk.

Ahead, Emond and Chiatto exchanged quiet, forceful words.

They were a few years older than Galen. In his general avoidance of everyone, he hadn't seen them in months. The two mages had been good friends when they'd entered the hiding place. Now they faced each other in the narrow corridor, Emond's thick brows knitted in anger, Chiatto's Centauri crest trembling, his left hand poised to cast a spell, like a snake about to strike.

Within Galen, the tech quickened.

"I told you to stay away from me," Emond said.

Chiatto gave a harsh laugh. "What makes you think you can tell me anything?"

Emond's head snapped around, his anger coming to bear on Galen. After a moment, the anger faded with recognition. "Galen."

Galen took a deep breath, released it. He told himself they meant him no harm. He nodded, continued his exercises.

Chiatto regarded him with wariness.

Emond moved out of the way, and Galen passed them without stopping. He would not interfere in their fight. He could not risk losing control. They waited only a few seconds before resuming their argument.

"I'm going to go wherever I want," Chiatto said.

Galen blocked their voices from his mind. He must be calm, think. Time was short.

To stop Elizar and Razeel, he must leave here. Breaking free, though, would mean destroying the machines that powered this place, devices that sustained the mages' lives on this unfriendly asteroid and masked their presence. He wasn't sure he had the ability to do such a thing; certainly the devices were protected by the Circle. Even if he could, he would not. It might be that the mages should never have been made; it might be that they were doomed, but let them live out their final years in this place, where they could harm no one but one another.

Much as he might want to deny it, although he hated the Circle, he desired their approval of his request. The last time he'd wanted to pursue Elizar, he'd misled the Circle about his motivations. Elric had voted against him then, and Elric had been right. He had been out of control, and should not have gone.

Through that journey to the rim, he'd learned that there was something more difficult than accepting that Elizar went on with his life, unpunished, after killing; and that was accepting that he himself went on with his life, unpunished, after all he'd killed. He'd improved his control since then. Still, though, he did not trust himself. If the Circle trusted him, if they allowed him to leave, that would be a sign that he was fit to leave.

As he approached the entrance to the dining hall, conversation and laughter echoed out. Fed and some of his friends commonly drank late into the night. The first time Galen had walked past, about ten of them had been within. By his last pass, the number had decreased to six. This time, only four remained: Fed, Optima, Ak-Shana, and Gwynn.

Galen passed the doorway, continued his endless circuit. Fed was popular with the women. Actually, he was popular with many, because he found fun in nearly everything, rather than hardship. In these times, his attitude helped others to forget their problems, and the problems of the universe. Fed was one of the few who seemed to feel none of the stress of the hiding place. Although he had an important responsibility—managing their use of supplies—it seemed to demand little of him.

The laughter faded, and Galen's footsteps carried him forward. Blaylock had said Galen had no plan but to go and kill, and that was true. He had too little information to form any specific plan. He could only devise a strategy as he went, using the tools he had.

He had collected more tools during his time in the hiding place, though, and he hoped some of them might prove surprising to Elizar. He had discovered seven basic postulates, seven one-term equations that embodied the seven powers the Shadows had planted inside of them—one for each word of the Code, which he found ironic. One, of course, was the spell of destruction. Another, the spell to listen to the Shadows. Beyond that, he was unsure of their purposes. One had underlain a series of equations for accessing external devices. Another derived from a progression involving various types of shields. Another seemed connected to their ability to generate illusions. As for the others, they seemed related to several quite different types of spells. He didn't know what they might do. The one-term equations were too dangerous to cast here, when they could carry great, unpredictable energies.

Elric had said his research into the tech needed purpose. He hoped that its purpose was to give him enough knowledge to kill the two who needed to be killed.

The chanting of Blaylock's followers became audible as Galen approached the storeroom they had taken for their meetings. Tonight they held a vigil. He passed the wide doorway and saw them crowded within, kneeling rigidly on flying platforms, as they would through the night, small fireballs cupped between their hands. They wore plain black robes, their bodies scoured of all hair. They were over seventy now. Though some of their group had died, their numbers had been more than replenished as the mages increasingly turned to Blaylock's techniques of discipline and self-denial to help them retain control in this place. Galen noted that Blaylock had left the vigil; Miostro ran it in his stead.

Their chant followed him down the hall.

> *Keep us true to the Code.*
> *Keep us focused on good.*
> *Drive from us all temptation.*
> *Guide us instead to your will.*
> *Show us the way to become one with you.*
> *Show us the path to enlightenment.*
> *And bring us to unity with the universe.*

They asked the Shadow tech, designed for chaos and destruction, to grant them peace and enlightenment. They asked it for help in fighting its own programming. It was terribly sad, when he thought about it.

They were struggling for control, as was he. He even used some of the same techniques they did. But he could not buy into the fairy tale Blaylock had spun. He saw no good in becoming one with the tech. He was already too close to it. Galen knew what the tech was, and knew what he was.

He was a killer, with only two more to kill.

The only way to convince the Circle to release him was to find some way around the Shadows' ability to nullify his tech. The Circle's greatest fear was that he would be trapped, his tech inactivated, his mind scanned. With mind-focusing exercises, a skilled mage might hold off a deep scan for a few seconds, but a powerful, determined telepath would soon breach those defenses.

If Elizar did trap him again, certainly Galen could be prepared with weapons other than technomancy. On Thenothk, though, he had managed to get G'Leel's gun only to have it drop from his hand under the force of Bunny's will. He needed a better solution.

Since entering this place, Galen had studied all he knew of the Shadows' ability to nullify the tech. Although he possessed no recording of the exact signal they'd used on him, he'd gained some sense of it from Anna. When she'd connected with him, she'd been frustrated that his tech was not functioning, and she'd tried to activate it. She identified the signal that overrode the tech, an elaborate and intense transmission in the radio band of frequencies. It had been picked up by a transceiver near the base of his spinal cord.

As he pursued his research, he quickly realized the similarity between that signal and the one Burell had described. In her most extensive series of experiments, Burell had fed various signals to a mysterious transceiver she'd discovered at the base of her spinal cord, a transceiver that responded to none of the usual commands or signals. Finally she found a signal to which it did respond: a complex, intense transmission in the radio band. In her obsessive search, Burell discovered the Shadows' secret signal to gain control of the tech.

The first time Burell sent the signal, her transceiver responded with an answering transmission. The second time she sent it, a third of her implants became inert.

Burell didn't understand what she'd found, because she didn't know they'd been designed as agents of the Shadows.

She didn't know their masters had created them with an on/off switch.

In retrospect, it was all very clear. The first time Burell sent the signal, which requested access to a mage's systems, the tech responded with a request for the key. When Burell sent the initial signal again, the incorrect response activated some sort of safeguard. The tech concluded that the signals were coming from an interloper and not from the Shadows. To prevent further tampering, it shut down the transceiver and sections of the implants connected to it. Burell was crippled by it.

If she'd known the true origins of the tech, she might have deduced the purpose of the transceiver before experimenting on herself. But the Circle had kept its secret, at the same time searching itself for the control mechanism Burell had unknowingly discovered. Only Galen possessed both pieces of the truth.

He had searched for some practical way to stop the Shadow signal from reaching the transceiver, but could find none. That left only the options of destroying the tiny piece of tech or removing it. A few inches above the coccyx, the transceiver nestled within the spinal column itself. It was surrounded by nerve fibers, including the major nerves innervating the legs. Anything powerful enough to destroy it could seriously damage those nerves, and removing it would likely cause inflammation in the spinal cord, leading to temporary or permanent paralysis of the legs.

But that physical danger, Galen suspected, was only a distraction from the real threat. Just as Burell's tampering had been detected and stopped, so would this more radical interference. The Shadows would have set up some fail-safe to prevent a mage from removing his transceiver, some system that, if activity were detected, would either kill him or inactivate his tech permanently. The best evidence that such a fail-safe existed was Elizar himself. If there was a way to bypass the nullification signal, then why hadn't the Shadows taught it to Elizar? His tech had been deactivated, just like Galen's.

The Circle, after hearing Galen's report of his experience

on Thenothk, had agreed with his conclusion. Yet neither he nor they had been able to find this fail-safe.

He wondered, now, if it even existed. Perhaps the Shadows had no fear that their control system would be discovered, and so had not planned for such an eventuality. In one thousand years of research, the Circle had not found it. He wouldn't have learned anything about the system either, without his connection to Anna. Further, if the Shadows didn't completely trust Elizar, they may have withheld their secret from him. The only danger might be the medical one, which, though serious, could be risked.

With Ing-Radi dead, their best healer was Gowen. He would be unwilling to perform any such procedure. Removing a piece of the tech would be, to him, an atrocity. In fact, Galen could think of no mage with medical expertise who might be willing to undertake the task. He could not explain the true reason for his request, except to the Circle. As for them, Galen believed they would find the risk unacceptable. They seemed disposed to risk very little these days.

A conventional surgeon, if highly skilled, could successfully perform the operation, but Galen could not go to a conventional surgeon, for that would violate secrecy, a part of the mage's Code. More important, he was trapped here.

If he would go through with it, he would have to do it himself. Which, of course, he had known since he'd begun this walk. And which, of course, was why he continued to walk. Though he had studied physiology and medicine when he was younger, he was far from an expert. His talent, as he well knew, did not lie in healing. With his meager medical skills, the risks of paralysis or death were much greater.

In the unlikely event he succeeded, the hidden fail-safe would probably kill him.

Fa's image came to him then, as she'd looked when she'd first flashed into his mind's eye, tears running through the curly white wisps of her hair, shoulders hitching with short, broken breaths, eyes fixed on the ring, on him, in desperate hope. Shaken, he pushed his exercises ahead—the memory was not yet as securely buried as he'd believed—and turned his thoughts back down their narrow path.

Herazade had said that if he detected evidence that Elizar and Razeel were using the spell of destruction, he should tell the Circle. No number of deaths, though, would change their position. They would allow no one to leave, as long as there was any chance their location could be revealed.

Did he have any choice but to try it?

As he approached the entrance to the dining hall once again, he saw Fed leaning in the doorway, a mug in his hand. No laughter or voices came from within; the others must have retired for the night.

Fed wore a short red jacket and pants covered with elaborate golden embroidery. With his bushy beard and long, wiry hair, he always made Galen think of a pirate. While most of the mages seemed uncertain how to treat Galen, Fed behaved as if they were close friends, often attempting to engage him in conversation. Galen knew that, aside from his reports to the Circle, he might go for weeks without talking if not for his occasional late-night encounters with Fed. Though he often resented the disturbance, tonight he felt relief.

"Federico."

"Galen. I was waiting to see if you'd make it around again. Wondered if you were going for a record."

Galen stopped, and the sharp scent of Fed's cologne wrapped around him. "I was wondering the same about you."

Fed laughed. "When it comes to women, I dedicate myself to knowing all that can be known." He took a drink. "So have you come to any conclusions tonight?"

"A few."

Fed put a hand to his forehead and closed his eyes. "Purple. Seventy-two. Only on odd Wednesdays when I'm wearing the underwear with the red hearts."

"Uncanny, as usual." Galen hesitated. He should return to his room, do what he needed to do. For once, he wished he had someone to confide in. He wished, more than anything, that he could talk to Elric. But he could not tell Elric, or anyone, what he was considering.

"I was sorry to hear about Soom."

Galen nodded.

"You want to sit down and have a drink?"

"No, thank you." Still, Galen hesitated.

"You shouldn't blame yourself," Fed said, and Galen wondered how much Herazade had told her former apprentice. "Bad things happen all the time, and you can't be responsible for all of them."

"You'd be surprised," Galen said, then regretted his words.

With the whisper of his black robe, Gowen came down the hall, his hands clasped before him. He kept himself scoured of all hair, which emphasized the roundness of his face. His cheeks were drawn up in dismay.

"Hey, Gowen," Fed said.

Gowen stopped before them with an uncertain glance at Galen. Since Galen's return from the rim, Gowen had become wary and distant around him. Gowen didn't understand his falling out with Elric, and Galen couldn't explain it.

Gowen bowed. "The blessing of Wierden upon you."

Galen returned the bow without repeating the words.

"I thought you guys were holding a vigil tonight," Fed said.

Gowen gazed back down the hall. "Blaylock's hands—were causing him distress. He relinquished the vigil to Miostro's care, and I left with him. I did what I could."

"Is the tech growing back at all?" Galen asked.

"No," Gowen said. "Most of the nerve and muscle damage has healed, but without the tech, the hands refuse to work as they used to."

"You've done all you can," Fed said.

Gowen looked up sharply. "Are you saying I should abandon my efforts?"

"No, but at some point, you need to find your own life, something beyond serving as Blaylock's personal attendant."

Gowen's bare eyebrow ridges contracted in anger. "Like sleeping with a different woman every night?"

Fed's beard shifted with his smile, the insult passing by him with no effect. "Speaking of which." He drained his mug, set it on a table inside the doorway. "This is where I say good night." Galen had never yet seen him angry. He simply didn't seem to care enough about anything to become impassioned about it.

Fed headed toward his room, leaving Galen with Gowen.

Gowen sighed. "I lose my temper too easily. Solidarity, above all."

"You are worried about Blaylock."

"We all seem to be losing our tempers these days. I heard of three different fights since this morning."

Galen didn't know what to say. "This place—is too small for us."

Gowen looked him up and down, seeming to remember all that had come between them. "I should go also."

Galen found himself wishing that he might talk to Gowen for a few minutes more. Perhaps he could get some sort of reassurance that what he planned to do would work out all right, without telling Gowen any of the specifics.

"I was wondering if I could speak with you about something," Galen said. "In confidence."

To his surprise, Gowen smiled. "I would be happy to help, if I can. Of course I would keep your confidence."

"We could speak in my room," Galen said, and Gowen nodded.

Once they were inside the small room, Galen pulled the straight-backed chair from the desk and invited Gowen to sit. This delaying was pointless. He knew what he must do.

Gowen looked around. "I thought my room was neat. I wouldn't even know anyone lived here."

Galen's gray walls were bare, his bed neatly made, all his belongings secreted within the drawers of the dresser and desk, where they were methodically arranged. Everything was put away, and it remained so until he wanted to bring it out.

He sat opposite Gowen on the bed, feeling self-conscious. "I was hoping to get your opinion on a theoretical question. You know of my spell of destruction, of what it does— pinching off and crushing the material within a spherical area."

Gowen nodded.

"I've been wondering whether it might be possible to use that spell as an operating tool within the body—for example, to remove a tumor, or some infected tissue."

Gowen's eyes widened and his lips parted, as if to blurt out some response. Of course he thought the idea insane, which it was. But he withheld his response, pausing a few moments before answering. "I understood that the spell was very dangerous," he said, "commanding extremely high energies."

"It does," Galen said.

Gowen tapped his thick fingers against one another. "The answer would depend on many things, as I'm sure you know. How precisely can you control the size and location of the sphere?"

"Fairly precisely."

"Fairly isn't good enough. You'd have to make sure the sphere didn't nick anything it shouldn't nick. If sections of blood vessels were removed, the ends would need to be sealed.

"The other big question is what effects the spell would have on the surrounding tissue. I remember when you first cast the spell, in the training hall on Soom. It seemed to generate great distortions of space and time. I don't think I'd be comfortable having something with that magnitude of energy in my body, even if just for a moment. Not without a lot more testing.

"You could try it on tissue cultures, to start. Or molds or bacteria. They would give you a better sense of your accuracy and any gross side effects. Though that still wouldn't tell you the particular effects on more complex organisms."

Galen had considered doing tests on tissue cultures, but he feared losing control once he started conjuring the spell of destruction, as he had on Thenothk. Once that great rush of energy came down upon him, once the brilliant incandescence sang along the meridians of his tech, he didn't know if he'd be able to stop. If he was to cast the spell, he dared cast it only a single time.

Gowen was simply confirming what Galen had thought: The idea was very dangerous and he was not sufficiently prepared to execute it.

"Give me an example," Gowen said. "How might one—theoretically—use this?"

Galen knew he was treading on dangerous ground, but he continued. "Imagine you had a tumor somewhere very hard to reach, such as in the spinal column." He conjured a scan of his own spinal cord in the air between them. "Say it was here, where this strand of tech ends, and just that size. And one wanted to remove it."

Gowen studied him. "That is a difficult place to reach with conventional surgical methods. But not impossible. I would be worried, using your method, that bits of the surrounding nerves could be captured within your sphere, and those nerves severed. Even if you could assure that wouldn't happen, the nerves might be traumatized by the procedure and severely damaged. Repair might eventually be possible, but if it were me, I'd rather go with traditional procedures in the first place. The risks are lower and better understood."

Galen nodded. He could ask no more, or he would reveal his intentions.

The corners of Gowen's mouth turned slightly upward, giving him a pained expression. "I know that you once wanted to be a healer, and I admire your attempt to turn something destructive into something constructive. That is to be commended. In this case, however, I think the risks outweigh the benefits. Traditional mage healing, or even current surgical procedures, can accomplish similar work. I would only resort to such a technique if it was the only one available." He fell silent then, his gaze returning to the image in the air between them. Galen could see him beginning to put the pieces together.

With a distracting movement of his hand, Galen dissolved the image. "Thank you for your help. I knew it was an unlikely thought. I just needed to hear that from someone else." He stood, trying to bring the conversation to an end.

"I wish I could be more optimistic. I hope you don't give up the attempt to find positive uses for your spell. I know they must exist, for the tech is our special blessing, bequeathed to us by the Taratimude, and it is meant to lead us to good." Gowen smiled, his face filling with expectation and hope. "In tapping into the basic powers of the universe, the tech, by its very nature, carries potentials that are both extremely destructive and extremely constructive. It can be difficult to tell the difference sometimes. Once we attain a complete, spiritual union with the tech, the path will be revealed. In our enlightenment, we shall at last understand the will of the tech, and the will of the universe."

When Galen did not respond, Gowen stood as well, an awkward silence filling the cramped room.

"I'm sorry we have grown apart," Gowen said. "I know there are things that happened on the rim, of which you cannot tell me. I wish I understood. Even without understanding, I count myself your friend. I know that, without your help, Blaylock would not have returned from Thenothk. For that I am forever grateful."

Galen looked down, remembering how little he had cared for Blaylock's safety then.

Gowen gripped his arm, and Galen fought the urge to pull away. "Please don't do anything rash. Or anything that might bring you to harm. Blaylock speaks very highly of you, though I think you may not know it. He actually believes, of all of us, you may be closest to the tech."

A harsh bitter laugh escaped Galen, and Gowen jumped, releasing him.

"That is a compliment," Gowen said.

"I know. I'm sorry. You surprised me." Galen went to the door, pressed the control to open it. "Thank you for your help."

"I was glad for the opportunity." Gowen stepped out and bowed. "The blessing of Wierden upon you."

As Galen bowed, the door closed between them.

He straightened and stood still for a time, the exercises running through his mind, narrowing his focus, strengthening the walls around him. And then he did something he had not done since he'd arrived in this place. He knelt before the bottom dresser drawer and slid it open. Inside, the blood-stained scarf lay folded in a neat bundle, alone. It did not affect him as he feared it might.

He pulled off his gloves, set them to one side. He scooped out the neat bundle, sat with it on the bed. He ran his raw fingers over the bumpy, smudged surface.

She seemed so far away now. Her face, the sound of her voice, were lost to him. It was hard to believe that he had been in love, that she had loved him, and that they had been happy, even for a short time.

She had believed there was an order to the universe, a design. She had thought the design was revealed through scientific law, the order created by God. She'd hoped her research into the tech would give her greater insight into that order. She'd never known that their powers had not arisen through the design of any god, but through the design of the Shadows.

If she'd known, she would have told him that the Shadows' design could be transcended, that he needn't destroy.

He was trying, had been trying for a long time now. It seemed like forever.

But the tech wanted only to kill, and he was tired of fighting it.

Only two more need die, if he could just get free of this place.

Galen accessed the healing organelles moving through his body. He selected one in his spinal cord, directed it down a capillary that wound around the transceiver and the surrounding nerves. The organelle's sensors created a visual image in his mind's eye, showing him the clear plasma streaming through the narrow capillary, the line of large, lozenge-shaped red blood cells tumbling ahead of and behind the organelle. Through the transparent wall of the capillary, he could see the thick golden rope of tech, and at its end, the swollen cluster like a bunch of grapes that formed the transceiver.

Reflecting variations in energy, the golden skin pulsed lighter and darker as the tech cycled through its processes. It was alive, was part of him. Carrying his DNA along with other, unknown DNA, it had intertwined with his systems, insinuating its way deep into him, growing to reflect him, to echo his thoughts. Microcircuitry directed its growth and functioning, carrying the purpose of its creators, the programming of destruction. Once it had thoroughly infiltrated him, he had become something divided, something of two parts, a techno-mage. Without it, he was no longer complete, no longer whole. Losing a piece of tech—as had Elric, Blaylock, and many others—became a crippling injury.

Gowen might believe the tech a sacred path to enlightenment, but these golden ropes bound the mages to darkness.
He wanted to burn them out of his body, to be free.

As the tech's restless energy swelled, the gold flared to a
dazzling, jaundiced yellow, and a hard shiver ran through him.

Galen focused on his exercises, slowed his breathing, the
pounding of his heart. Bit by bit, the brilliant yellow dulled,
dimmed. The normal pulsing resumed.

The Shadows took life and twisted it to their own use, just
as they had done with Anna. Whatever that life had been before, whatever it had thought or wanted or believed, was lost.
Just as whatever he had been was lost. He could not be free of
the tech, so long as he lived.

Could he free himself, though, of just one tiny piece?

He studied the spherical contours of the transceiver. It looked
the same as the other transceivers in the tech, revealing no special purpose or capability. Data appeared beside the image: size
of the transceiver, distance to it. He could use the position of the
organelle and the data from it to target the swollen cluster. How
accurate he would be, he didn't know.

Galen rocked back and forth, his hand pressed flat against
the scarf.

Perhaps it was time, now, to join her.

She'd told him he needed to transcend himself in three
ways: He must open himself to others, open himself to himself, and open himself to God. He'd done the first two in his
own limited, unsuccessful way. The third he'd not even known
how to attempt. He believed there was no God. And if there
was a God, and He had willed all that had happened to
happen, then Galen despised Him almost as much as he despised himself. So in that, her final task, he must fail, as he
had failed in so much else.

Besides, if he did open himself again, he knew what would
come out. Destruction.

Death was certainly his long-overdue punishment. If that
was to be his fate, he only hoped the Circle would find some
other way to stop Elizar.

For Elizar must be stopped. Elizar and Razeel, he corrected
himself. Elizar and Razeel must be stopped.

The golden cluster of the transceiver shifted, taking on Elizar's face. "This is your own fault, Galen. If you had joined me, if you had shared your secret, none of this would be necessary."

Galen jerked erect, disoriented. He had nearly fallen asleep. It was late. He suddenly realized how exhausted he was. It must be the organelles, pushing him to sleep so they could better perform their healing tasks.

He had lost track of his exercises. He began a new one, trying to rouse himself. But he was too tired to do what he planned. He needed to rest.

He broke contact with the organelle and lay down, his head hitting the pillow before he expected it.

More than anything, he wanted to kill Elizar and Razeel. How good it had felt to kill Tilar. And how much better it would feel to kill them.

—— chapter 6 ——

Elric lay in the dark, his body throbbing with emptiness. He no longer fought it; he simply allowed it to fill him, to define him. He found no point, anymore, in struggling against it. Some of the others had gone this way. They had spoken to him of their weariness, of the effort to endure. He had always thought it worth the effort, to continue to do what good he could. Yet he no longer felt himself able to accomplish anything of worth.

He had not been able to save Soom, had not been able to help any of the countless other planets targeted by the Shadows. The mages were safely hidden away; they no longer needed him. He had done his duty. Let them find new leadership at last. As for Galen, Elric could offer no help. He had chosen duty over Galen time and again, had lied to the boy, and ultimately had destroyed their relationship. He wished that, somehow, Galen could find a path to happiness, but he didn't see how it might be achieved. Perhaps Blaylock could help him. They had formed a relationship during their trip to the rim, and if there was any in whom Galen might confide, it would be Blaylock. Not him.

In his mind's eye, Elric shifted from one scene of destruction to another. Even now, he wanted to feel his old closeness to Soom. As he had shared in the death of his place of power, he needed to share in the deaths of all those on Soom. He could not allow them to pass alone. They, in turn, would provide him companionship in his death.

The images from the planet were frustratingly distant; he could not feel the rush of magma through its veins, nor the ragged wounds cleaved deep into its heart, nor the wind blasting over its ruined skin. Yet he felt his own pain, and perhaps it was not much different.

Of the dead, there were few remains. He moved from place to place, remembering them, striving for the unity he had once felt.

The town of Lok was a graveyard of blackened ruins. The residents had been good people, had brought him much joy. He wished them peace.

Beyond, the mak beckoned, his old home. Jab marched across the rocky plain, her probe looking out on a world of vibrant lime-green moss shrouded in gray mist. As she moved forward, a bluish shadow took on shape and substance. It was one of the Soom, lying on the ground. A child dressed in a blue jumper. Fa.

Jab sniffed along Fa's side. After a brief examination, she burrowed her nose under Fa's arm, lay down beside her.

Elric imagined himself lying next to them, the soft damp moss beneath, Fa's hand in his, Jab's body pressing against him with every inhalation. He imagined the breeze running over his body, running through his body, blowing away the blackness, blowing away the pain.

His body sank into the mak, passing through moss and stone, descending through groundwater and microorganisms, whispering through caressing fingers of magma, drawn gently toward that warm heart from which he had separated.

A voice reached down to him in that place, disrupting his rest. "Elric! The destruction of Soom was all a deception," the voice said. "Galen has uncovered it. Elric!"

With a supreme effort, Elric opened his eyes, and the pain returned, throbbing through him in time with his heart. In the darkness beside him was not Fa, but Circe. The silhouette of her pointed hat hung over him, and a hint of light played over her mouth, revealing the gleam of her teeth, the tiny lines etched above her lip. He had seen her earlier, but surely that was outside his room, in the hallway, and it must have been hours ago. She had commented he did not look well.

He didn't feel as if he could move, or speak, but he opened his mouth, forced air out. "Soom?"

"Yes. Those images were a deception. Galen has asked me

to bring you to the observation room. He will show you the proof."

Elric did not understand how all the images could be false. But perhaps there was hope. Soom might still be whole. More than that, Galen had asked for him.

He was filled with the pain, though, overwhelmed by it.

Circe conjured a platform beneath him, lifted him from the bed. "I will help you." She folded the platform into the shape of a chair. His body slumped.

In his mind's eye, Jab remained snuggled against Fa, and Jab's regular breathing sounded softly in his ear.

Circe opened the door and, with a touch to the platform, directed it out into the empty hallway.

The warm mist wrapped around him, comforting him.

The next thing he knew, they had stopped. He floated before the observation room door. "Can you admit us?" Circe said.

Elric visualized a connection between himself and the room's systems. They requested his authorization, and he sent the key. The door opened.

Galen was not there.

The chair propelled him inside. With effort Elric turned his head back toward Circe. She closed the door behind them and, with a precise motion, touched her withered index finger to it. A pale blue shimmer spread from the point of contact to cover the door and the surrounding wall.

Elric's head drooped forward.

The platform chair turned until he faced her. Beneath the brim of her hat, Circe's face was in shadow, but for her lips. They stretched in a smile. "Galen must have gone to tell the rest of the Circle. He told me where the evidence was. If you give me access to the system, I will find it for you."

Slowly Elric felt his mind returning to him. She had conjured a defensive shield, sealing them inside. Her claim was a ruse. Circe had abandoned her commitment to good, and to solidarity. The small ember of hope she had ignited in him died.

He took a deep breath, focused through the pain, and pulled his tired body erect. "I will not give you access."

Circe shook her head with exaggerated puzzlement. "But

don't you want to see the images? Galen believes them proof Soom is undamaged. Of course, he could be mistaken. Only you will know for certain."

Circe's deceptions were as clumsy as her overtures for political power. "I may be dying, but I am not a fool. There are no images. There is no deception, but your own."

Circe frowned. "Very well. I preferred to send you to the other side with a pleasant fiction. But if you insist, the harsh truth. I must have the key if I and my supporters are to depart this place in peace. Give it, and we will board our ships and leave you be. Withhold it, and all the mages will die."

"And how do you plan to kill them?" Elric quickly composed a message. *Circe has sealed me with her in the observation room. She desires the key so she can leave this place. She claims other mages are in league with her.* He visualized it traveling to both Blaylock and Herazade, and the tech echoed his command.

"Your own student made it possible." Circe tilted her head, and the harsh light revealed a map of lines crisscrossing her dry cheek. Then she shifted, and the shadow of her hat fell back over her face. "If you recall, as we gathered for our exodus, Blaylock chose me to go with him to the rim. A dangerous task, and one that would surely bestow added esteem and power upon any who survived it. I was honored to be chosen, and well willing to risk my life in service of the Circle. But your precious Galen took my place. Instead I was delegated to Herazade, to come in advance to the hiding place and set up these very machines, and the larger ones to which they are tied." Her thin hand gestured to encompass the curved, metallic devices that covered one wall. They shimmered with the subtle blue glow of a shield. "While carrying out this task, I implanted within the largest machine, the energy generator for this place, my own addition, an explosive."

Elric received no response to his message. He didn't want to involve Galen, but Galen's powers might be required. He sent another copy of the message.

Circe crossed her arms, sliding her hands up under her sleeves. "If you do not give me the key, I will trigger that device. The Circle's protections and shields will collapse, the gravity will fail, the temperature will drop, the air circulation will cease. You may think that still some mages could reach their ships, could survive. Or you may think even now they come to your rescue, in response to your messages. Neither is the case. A sleeping potion has circulated through the air in all rooms but yours and this one. The others are deep into their dreams and cannot help you or themselves."

He had underestimated Circe. This stratagem was far more convincing than her first. He had no way of knowing whether she truly had the ability to destroy the generator or not. The machines were well shielded now, yet during their assembly they had been unprotected. The sleeping potion, he believed, was real, for otherwise his message would have received some response.

"You will join the Shadows?" he asked. He sent message after message to Blaylock, hoping to rouse him. If any could fight off the physiological effects of Circe's sleeping potion, it would be Blaylock.

"Give me the key."

Elric found that the simple message spell was exhausting him. He had to stop. He must save what strength remained to him and use it wisely. Although he did not have the energy to defeat Circe in a fight, he might defeat her through other means. The machines were protected with a special reflective screen that the Circle had designed. Any energy that attacked the screen was reflected back against the attacker tenfold. Even a single fireball, then, could take on much greater power in the reflection. If Circe remained unshielded, the blast could potentially kill her. An attack would also send an alarm to the others who had access to the system: Blaylock, Herazade, and Galen. Perhaps the alarm would be strong enough to wake them.

If the blast failed to kill Circe, though, he feared what would happen.

"You have been a good mage," Elric said. "Why do you betray us?"

"A good mage. Where is my reward? I have revolutionized the design of the probes we use. I have provided those probes, out of my own goodwill, to all the mages. I have given up my place of power, my health, have supported the Circle in all its decisions. I have done everything you have asked and more.

"When you declare there will be no elections this year, it is clear you feel no one is fit. It is clear you feel I am not fit. But I no longer accept your arrogant pronouncements. If you held elections as you should, I would win. I would take my rightful place in the Circle.

"I wait obediently no longer. You are not the only ones with power. Now give me the key."

Elric realized he did have a means of discovering whether the explosive device was real: He could call her bluff. He should have thought of it immediately. If her threat was true, and if he angered her sufficiently, she would attempt to kill him. If the explosive was only a pretense, she would not want to kill him, since the key offered her only chance of escape.

Elric fixed her with his gaze, carefully modulated his voice. "Morden promised you something, of course. Your health? Your old power?"

Circe smiled.

"That you would lead a fleet of Shadow ships in conquest?"

The smile faded.

"Oh," Elric said, "perhaps he offered that only to members of the Circle."

She stood silent.

"Does it not bother you that Morden approached nearly everyone at the convocation? He did not select you, Circe, as especially deserving of his favor."

"I will be the one who was able to escape this place to join him."

"Elizar and Razeel joined him long ago. And they, just lowly initiates."

"They will take their orders from me."

"Or perhaps they will order you. They have done much to prove their worth to the Shadows."

She took a step closer, standing now directly before him. From the darkness beneath her hat, her eyes glistened. "Give me the key, Elric."

"Your actions prove that you are not fit to be one of the Circle, and that you never have been."

Her mouth twisted, and she raised her withered hand. With a precise motion, she extended her index finger, pressed the fingertip into his cheek. After a moment of resistance, the skin parted and her finger slipped through, transfixing him like an arrow of pure fire.

He clenched the arms of the platform, his breath coming hard and fast.

She pulled the finger downward, ripping a gouge through his face.

He'd thought himself filled with pain, but this . . .

Circe's image faded into the gray of the room. He tightened his grip on the platform, determined not to lose consciousness.

Circe pulled her finger free, and he fell forward, breathless. Blood droplets pattered onto his robe.

She shoved him upright. "Do you want them all to die? The order to which you have devoted your life? And your dear Galen?" She raised her index finger, now coated in blood. "Tell me the key. I will not ask again."

He told himself that his true body lay within the heart of Soom, not in this place.

She pressed the fingertip to his other cheek, impaled him, ripped down through skin and muscle.

He collapsed to one side, his face on fire. He forced his mouth to move, the words to emerge. "I will not give you the key under any circumstance. You should know me better than that. But then, your manipulations were never terribly skillful."

Here was the moment for her to strike, to kill him. Her bloody hand was poised. She need only reach out, drive her finger into his heart. Instead she held back, her body rigid, trembling with rage.

There was no explosive.

Elric visualized a fireball coalescing in the air behind her, visualized it shooting at the protected machines. The tech echoed his commands, and fire streaked out from behind Circe.

The fireball splashed against the translucent screen, then with a strange reversal of movement drew itself back together and struck out, now not just a fireball, though, but a great gout of flame.

Elric wrapped a shield around himself as the fire blasted past. Though the attack centered on Circe, it encompassed them both. The blaze roared around him.

A faint echo came from the tech, an echo of his shield visualization, as if the tech was struggling to maintain the spell. The echo came again, again, growing fainter. Finally it died; the shield slipped away.

But it had lasted long enough. The fire had expended itself.

Circe dropped to the floor. The platform beneath him dissolved, and he fell beside her. They lay facing each other on the charred tiles, wrapped in hazy smoke and the sharp smell of burned pork.

Circe's head was bare, the hat ripped away by the fire. She barely looked Human. Her eyebrows and eyelashes were burned off, her skin scorched a bright red, except for the side that lay against the floor, the side that had taken the brunt of the attack. There, along her temple, cheek, neck, shoulder, she'd been charred black.

She braced her good hand against the tiles. A fissure split the brittle skin between thumb and index finger, and clear plasma leaked out. She pushed herself to her knees, coughed. Parts of her robe seemed stuck to her skin; other pieces had burned away. She touched a trembling finger to her chest, and the blue tinge of a shield flowed out over her skin. She shot him a slight, victorious smile, a wet blister on her lower lip. Then she faced the machines, sensing the attack had originated with them. Elric said nothing to enlighten her.

She extended her index finger, and from its tip grew a brilliant purple ball, coruscating with energy. When it was a foot across, its growth ceased. With a tap of her finger, it streaked toward the curved devices.

Elric visualized the blue cocoon of a shield surrounding him, the tech's echo a faint whisper. The shield slipped down over him as Circe's globe struck. The wall of machines flared purple, reflecting and magnifying the attacking energy. The purple rushed to concentrate itself in the spot the globe had struck, erupted to fill the room in a blinding, crackling blaze.

His shield would not last much longer. Circe's blockade of the door, he believed, would have failed when her platform did. If he could reach the door, he could escape. But his body had no strength, and he dared not conjure his own platform, for then he would surely lose his shield.

He huddled against the floor, reducing the area the shield need protect. Above him, the blue outline of Circe's figure became visible through the declining flames of purple. Now both of Circe's index fingers extended, and purple spheres formed before them. She propelled the spheres toward the machines. She was determined to destroy them, or die trying.

Brilliant purple raged over his shield, filled with sound and fury, the fury the mages fought so hard to deny. She would kill them both, in her desire for power.

He held to the image of the shield, to this tiny sanctuary. In denying Circe, he realized, he had completed his final duty for his order. The mages would be safe—from everyone but themselves. He could do no more.

As heat built within his shield, he found himself thinking of the quiet, nameless boy who had come to be his student so many years ago, and had brought such unexpected happiness into his life.

He wished he had been more help to Galen. But his time was over. Galen would have to go on without him.

Now he would rest.

He was lying again on Soom, sinking into the mak, descending through rock and water, floating gently down channels of magma to the great, dark currents of its core. And as at last his shield failed, Soom's warm heart welcomed him home.

Sound blared through Galen's head. He pushed himself up with heavy arms. He was on his bed, fully clothed. His mind took a few moments to process the information. He must have fallen asleep, though he didn't remember it.

The sound. It was deafening. He realized his mind's eye was flashing an alarm. The observation room had been breached.

It took him a couple tries to get to his feet. He stumbled

toward the door, struggling to wake up. Who would have violated the Circle's protections?

He slammed his hand down on the door control, ran unsteadily down the hall.

Finally he remembered how to stop the alarm. When he did, he found that he had a message, several minutes old. It was from Elric.

Circe has sealed me with her in the observation room. She desires the key so she can leave this place. She claims other mages are in league with her.

Galen sent a response. *I'm coming.* He turned down the corridor leading to the observation room, saw two silhouettes at the end, obscured in the black smoke that billowed from the room.

Elric.

Elric.

One of the figures turned toward him, and he received a message. It was from Blaylock, though, not Elric. *Fetch Gowen at once. Do not delay.*

Galen's mind felt frozen. Gowen was needed. Galen should know what that meant, but his mind would not make the connection. A terrible sense of urgency filled him.

He conjured a platform, and with an equation of motion sent himself racing back down the hall toward Gowen's room. As he approached, he visualized equation after equation in his mind's eye, conjuring a cluster of intense balls of energy within the metal of Gowen's door. The gray surface churned with frantic bubbling, vaporized in a great rush of steam. In a crouch he sped through the hole.

Gowen lay asleep in bed. Galen yanked him up, and when Gowen did not awaken, Galen rolled him onto the platform. On the dresser lay the crystal that Gowen used in healing. Galen grabbed it and took off with him.

As they skimmed back down the hallway, Galen shook him. "Wake up! Wake up!" Galen conjured a fireball in his hand, waved it over Gowen's face.

Gowen's eyes snapped open. "Galen! What is it?"

Galen quenched the fireball in his fist and found he could

not speak. He could not say the words. He held out the crystal to Gowen.

Gowen took it and pushed himself up, somehow retaining a measure of dignity in his short white sleeping gown. Galen stood beside him. Ahead was the corridor to the observation room. Black smoke spread through the intersection.

Gowen glanced at him, and with the whisper of silk, a shield slipped over him. Gowen had conjured a containment shield around them both, to hold a quantity of clean air within.

They raced into the smoke, down the corridor. Outside the observation room, Galen dissolved the platform. They were alone; Blaylock and the other mage must have gone inside.

The room was dark with smoke. Along the wall to his right, what he could see of the machines seemed undamaged, their curved surfaces still shimmering blue. At the same time, the floor tiles were charred, and in places had shattered from the heat, revealing burned supports beneath.

"Watch your step," Gowen said.

Galen glanced back at the wall behind him. It was scorched almost entirely black, and in places hardened rivulets revealed where the metal had gone molten. Recognition flashed through his mind—he had seen such a thing before. In a moment, he remembered where: on the burned remnants of the spaceship in which his parents had died.

From the fire of the crash Elric had brought their bodies, floating on platforms, illusions shrouding them in sheets.

He began a mind-focusing exercise, visualizing a blank screen, a neat letter in glowing blue in the upper left corner. *A*. Then he visualized *B* appearing beside *A*, and he held the image of them both in his mind. Then it was *A B C*, all in his mind at once, each individual letter clear while the whole also remained clear. But his thoughts refused to continue.

He could not lose Elric. He could not.

Ahead, through the smoke, hints of blue glimmered from shielded figures. He moved toward them.

Beside him, Gowen stumbled, released a yelp.

A figure lay facedown on the floor, robe burned to tatters, cherry-red skin covered with blisters. It looked as if it must be dead, yet through the shield came the faint sound of short, rasping breaths. With an awkward motion the head lifted toward them; an irregular strip down the side of the face shone a swollen black. Dark eyes fixed on him. Circe.

Galen grabbed Gowen, dragged him around Circe toward the two shielded figures. Blaylock and Herazade knelt on either side of a large black lump. Galen couldn't make sense of it. With stiff hands, Blaylock rolled the object carefully over, and Galen realized it was a person. The figure had been curled up on its left side. The robe was burned away in large patches along the right side of the body, revealing the leg, side, and arm charred so black they blended in with the remaining fabric. The most intense burns, though, concentrated about the head and shoulders, which had turned a leathery black. Pieces of the ears and nose had burned away entirely, and glistened with leaking plasma. With eyes closed, it looked like a majestic, ancient statue, a monument to one long dead.

Blaylock looked up. "Gowen, come quickly." His voice was muffled behind his containment shield. "Do all that you can."

Gowen turned to Galen. Galen realized his hand was clenched around Gowen's arm. He forced his fingers to open.

Herazade stood, and Gowen took her place, extending his shield to include the still, black figure. He pulled the tattered remnants of robe away from the red-streaked chest, laid his hands on the heart, sending healing organelles into the body. Blaylock and Herazade must have done the same, though it hardly seemed possible this blackened statue could be alive.

Galen found Blaylock standing beside him. Blaylock put a hand on his shoulder, guiding him to kneel opposite Gowen. Galen knew what was expected; he must contribute organelles. But with the figure right beside him, he didn't want to look at it, didn't want to touch it.

He laid his hands on the chest. It was warm, fluttering with quick, silent breaths. Beneath, the subtle beating of a heart. His gaze traveled up the burned chest and neck to the face, and the guise of an ancient, peaceful statue had vanished. It was Elric, gouges ripped down his cheeks, Elric's stern face, thin lips, the three lines of grave disappointment—all burned to blackness. He had been forced to curl up on the floor, alone, as his body cooked from the outside in.

Galen turned his mind away, looked down at his hands, visualized the equation. His palms tingled as a wave of organelles passed through his skin and into that fluttering chest below.

The extensive facial burns made it likely that superheated air had been inhaled. If the vast surface area of the lungs was seriously damaged, the organelles could not work quickly enough to repair it. Galen visualized the equation again, again. As the organelles passed out of him, he felt a disorienting shift in his blood, as if he'd stood too suddenly.

Gowen held the crystal over Elric, using it to gain information from the organelles and direct them in their healing. Gowen's eyes were squeezed closed. A tear ran down his face.

Galen pulled off his coat, laid it over Elric. He knelt there uselessly, just as he had knelt beside her, waiting for her to die.

He could not tell if Elric was conscious. He took Elric's left hand in his. The skin was red, swollen, dry. The hand seemed a strange, foreign object. They had hardly ever touched. Galen squeezed gently, released. It remained a limp, dead weight.

He bent down, brought his mouth beside Elric's misshapen black ear. He could barely catch his breath to speak. "I'm here. Can you hear me?"

Elric's black lips, slightly parted, remained still.

Galen should have been there to watch over him, to protect him. Instead, Galen had rebuffed him, neglected him, condemned him.

Perhaps he could still reach Elric, could convince Elric to hold on. Galen closed his eyes, visualized the equation for an electron incantation. The tech echoed the spell, and he chose as his setting the circle of standing stones on Soom, as Elric always did.

Unlike the standard message spell mages commonly used for communication, the electron incantation worked through means they did not understand at all. One could communicate with another no matter the distance, the connection made without the aid of FTL relays, minds meeting on some dreamlike inner landscape. Within the spell, they were outside space, outside time.

He found himself standing beside one of the tall, moss-covered stones, the scent of the sea sharp on the breeze. In its brilliant lime-green sheath, the massive stone somehow radiated a sense of life and power. As with most objects in an incantation, it carried heightened intensity and significance.

He looked into the mist for Elric, but saw only the hulking shadows of the other stones. "Elric!" He ran into the circle. "Elric!"

Galen found him lying on the thick moss at the circle's center. He appeared in the incantation as he imagined himself: unburned, restored to the height of his health. His eyes were closed, his hands folded over his chest like a corpse lying in state.

Galen rushed to him, fell to his knees. "I'm here. What can I do? Tell me what to do."

Elric did not move.

Galen grabbed his shoulders, shook him. "Don't die! Please. You can't leave me."

Elric's body was limp.

"Please. I have to tell you—" Galen's voice broke. "I know you had to obey the Circle. I know you couldn't tell me the truth. What I did was my fault alone. You taught me to be a good mage. You treated me far better than I deserved. But I— I have not lived up to your example."

He struggled for voice control. "You were the best teacher I could have had . . . and more than that. I appreciate . . . all you have given . . ." He knew what he wanted to say, but the words stuck inside him.

He could not leave Elric as he had left her, with the truth unspoken. If he had the chance to bring Elric any pleasure, he must force the words out.

"I love you. I love you more than I ever loved my own father."

Elric's face was slack, unresponsive.

He was too late. He had not told Elric when there was still time. He released Elric, straightened.

Elric's eyes opened. "I too have something I must say." His

mouth did not move, but somehow his rich voice vibrated out of the mak, out of the stones around them.

He was still alive. His was the life Galen had sensed in the vibrant green moss. With a hard swallow, Galen nodded.

"I have another secret. It is a secret only you and I know; I have told no one else. But you have forgotten it." Elric's eyes stared into his. "I cannot tell you this secret; you must remember it on your own. It is a piece of yourself you have long hidden away. I had hoped that you would remember by now, so I would be there to help you. Yet you have not remembered, and I have come to fear that you never will. I tell you because I do not believe you can become a complete person until you reclaim this piece of yourself."

Galen didn't know what he was talking about, didn't care. Only one thing was of any importance. Elric was dying, and Galen couldn't stop it. He would say, though, whatever Elric needed. "I will not hate you, no matter what it is. Tell me."

"To truly understand yourself, and to truly control yourself, you must know why you do what you do. What is your purpose? Why are you a techno-mage? You have never sufficiently answered that question. Perhaps because you've turned your back on your childhood, when those motivations were formed."

"Those years mean nothing to me," Galen said, his voice quavering. "My life began the day I came to live with you."

"That is not so," Elric said. "I have taught you, helped to guide your development. But your parents formed your foundation."

Galen shook his head. He didn't want to waste these last, precious moments speaking of his parents.

Elric's hand rose from his chest, and with a turn revealed his palm. On it lay the ring, with its silver band and ragged black stone. Galen found himself drawn back to that place, to that time so many years ago.

Elric emerged from the fire of the spaceship crash, the faint blue cast of a shield giving him the appearance of death itself. Behind him, protected within his shield, floated two supine figures shrouded in sheets. The shapes were irregular, uneven, too small.

Elric stopped before Galen and extended his hand, revealing the ring. For a moment, it seemed as if the ring were Galen's heart, ripped out of his chest, hard, shiny, and black. And though he knew it was not, Galen felt something happening inside him, felt dissolution spreading, felt himself falling apart, felt everything falling apart.

Now it was happening all over again. Everything was falling apart, spinning into chaos.

Galen seized Elric's cold hand in both of his, covering the ring. "You are my true father. You have meant more to me than my parents ever did."

"They are a part of who you are," Elric said. "You, however, are more than they, and you are ready to stand on your own and face them. Only in that way can you heal yourself, which is the first step toward healing others."

"You can't die. You can't die too." He hunched over Elric's hand. "We are cursed with violence. We are drowning in it. Now I will lose you to it."

"It is my time," Elric said. "I will await you on the other side. Do not follow me too soon. And do not kill in my name."

Galen rocked back and forth, his body shaking. "Please don't go. Please don't." Elric had been the one certainty in his life. Elric had brought him order. He felt as if he would disintegrate, as if he would dissolve into madness. He whispered, "I don't think I can go on without you."

When Galen looked down, Elric's eyes were closed, his chest and arms partly covered by lime-green moss. In delicate fingers it grew over him, following the contours of his body, his face. It smoothed the creases in his brow; it washed him in a balm of cool green.

Galen held tightly to Elric's hand. The green reached up Elric's forearm, his wrist, pushed beneath Galen's skin with soft bristles. Elric's hand became a clump of moss in his grasp.

Galen dropped the hand and threw himself onto Elric, grabbing at the moss-covered body. He would not lose Elric.

Beneath him, the curves of Elric's body shifted, flattened. Elric was being absorbed into the planet, drawn down inside it. Galen ripped at the dense green covering, finding only more moss, and dirt, and rock. The ground subsided beneath him, Elric slipping away, vanishing into the mak.

Galen clawed furiously at the ground, dug his fingers deep into the thick, moist vegetation. A sob escaped him.

And then from the cold moss, a faint tingling at his fingertips, like the smallest electric shock. The sensation passed inside him, shivering up his hands and arms to his head. There it filled him with longing, regret, a desire to continue.

After a few moments, it faded away.

He didn't know what it was. Some residual bit of energy, an echo of an echo of an echo?

Galen dug frantically deeper, his fingers meeting rock, scraping against it. The mak had gone flat beneath him. The sensation was gone. Galen cried out, tearing his fingers again and again over the rock.

Elric was dead.

— *chapter 7* —

Galen pushed himself up to his knees on the charred tiles where he had fallen. He took in Elric's burned body, his mind an exhausted blank, his body churning with agitating energy.

Across from him, Gowen opened his eyes. Gowen's round face was wet with tears. He clutched the crystal to his chest, looked from Galen to Blaylock and Herazade standing over them. "The damage was too extensive." He broke out in sobs.

Galen found himself still holding Elric's hand. He lifted the limp, red weight, laid it across Elric's chest. Then he took its black partner, placed it gently across the first, mimicking Elric's position in the incantation. In the vision, Elric had been healthy, serene. The reality was a ruined shell.

What pain had he suffered as he'd been burned alive? How long had he endured, waiting for Galen to answer his call?

"Circe was always so loyal," Herazade said. "How could she do such a thing?"

They persisted in asking these questions. How could Elizar have killed? How could Circe have killed? How could he himself have killed? The urge was inside them; it was part of them. Even now the great drive to destruction within him was building, the energy welling up, driving through him. Galen began a mind-focusing exercise.

"She was loyal to her own ambitions," Blaylock said. "Gowen, keep Circe alive until we return to question her. First we must stop her confederates."

Herazade headed across the room, but Blaylock hesitated, studying Galen. Blaylock would be wondering whether he could be safely left with Circe. Galen pretended not to notice, returning his gaze to Elric and sitting very, very still. His eyes traced the gouges Circe had ripped down Elric's cheeks.

Elric had been tortured. Elric had been murdered.

At last Blaylock left.

Gowen wiped at his face, his shoulders still racked with sobs. "I'm sorry," he said. His shield slipped off of Galen. The room was clearing of smoke; it was no longer necessary. Gowen crawled across the blackened floor to Circe, turned her onto her back. With one hand on her head, another on her chest, he transferred organelles into her body, beginning the healing process.

Galen stood, walked over to her. Her eyes were closed, her eyelids a swollen, ragged red. Though her burns were not quite as severe as Elric's, they were extensive, and her breath, like his, was rapid and shallow. Galen did not expect she would survive long. Not if he had anything to say about it.

He crossed his arms over his chest, holding tightly to the burning energy. He focused on his voice control, issued a command. "Circe."

Gowen's head jerked up, fear on his face. His sobbing stopped.

"Circe."

Her eyes snapped open.

"Tell me everything."

Her blistered red lips twitched. Her voice was a raspy exhalation. "Nothing."

More than anything, Galen wanted to conjure the spell of destruction, to feel that great rush of energy, to crush her in the fist of his will. "Where did you plan to go when you left here? Whom did you plan to see?"

Circe's eyes flicked toward Gowen. "Protect me."

"Galen. What are you doing?" Gowen wiped a hand over his forehead. "You're—hot."

"Sustain her life," Galen said. His eyes fixed on Circe. "You will answer me. Or you will know what it feels like to burn alive."

"I would rather—die now than"—she coughed—"be flayed later."

Gowen's crystal remained in his lap, his hands at his sides.

"Do," Galen said to him, "as Blaylock directed."

Gowen nodded nervously to himself, held the crystal over Circe, and closed his eyes in concentration.

Galen glanced at Elric's still, ruined body, and his outrage was answered by a surge in the tech. Quickly he added a second mind-focusing exercise to his first. He could not look at Elric again, or he would lose all control.

He visualized the equation, conjured a brilliant blue ball of energy above Circe's head. The red, blistered skin should be supersensitive, raw nerves exposed.

"You can't—" she said.

The energy fell upon her, a thick, undulating wave of blue rushing down head, torso, legs, scouring away the remnants of her clothes and brushing over her skin. Circe shook, releasing a startled, warbling cry. The tiny conjury provided him no relief.

Gowen jerked his hands back, wide eyes on Galen. "What are you— How can you— Galen, you have to stop."

"I will not stop. And if you abandon her to fight me, she will die."

Galen conjured a second blue ball. Circe's eyes jerked up to face it in fear. "Where did you plan to go?" he asked. "Whom did you plan to see?"

The energy raked down over her, scouring away blisters and skin, and she grunted, her breath coming faster. Gowen extended the crystal again over Circe and bowed his head, eyes closed.

"Why don't you use your great spell on me?" she said. "Kill me."

Galen sent the scouring energy over her again. Her body spasmed, and she grit her teeth. Her skin was turning a rich, shiny purple. Blood welled up in spots, ran in rivulets across her body.

Gowen bent lower, as if in concentration. "More organelles," he mumbled.

Galen went to her side, crouched, and seized her hands, squeezing them so tightly that he trembled. He cast the spell, sent his organelles inside her. His grip became slick with blood. "Know," he said, "that I will go to any lengths to learn

the truth from you, and I will not let you die until I do. If you
prefer death to come soon, then tell me now." He stood over
her once again.

In the absence of an answer, the blue fire undulated down
her body, and her skin split in whisper thin lines of red—
across the lip, across the chest, down the arm.

She whimpered, and at last her bleeding lips began to move,
her voice a rasping whisper. "Babylon 5—was our destination. Morden. He promised—at the convo—" She shook with
wet, choking coughs.

Morden. He played on their weaknesses. He found his way
into the deepest recesses of their hearts. He offered possibilities devastating in their mere contemplation.

Choose carefully, Galen, he had said. *Many would give all
they have for such an opportunity.*

Morden had offered him what he most desired. And he had
declined.

I wonder whether you'll be able to live with that decision.

Galen wrapped the exercises tighter about him.

If he had killed Morden then, if he had reported to the
mages that Morden was dead, Circe might have given up her
ambitions. Elric might still be alive.

But he had not attacked. Morden and his promises remained,
a temptation festering within the ranks of the techno-mages.

"Have you spoken to him since then? Have you had any
contact with the Shadows? Or Elizar and Razeel? Have you
told them where we are?"

Still coughing, she turned her head slightly from side
to side.

"Who aided you?" Galen asked.

Circe closed her bleeding mouth, stifling her coughs, and
her dark eyes narrowed on Galen. "Those also treated un-
fairly. And those smart enough to realize"—she glanced at
Gowen—"there is no future for us without the Shadows."

She knew. How could she know? Had Morden chosen her,
of them all, to tell?

Gowen remained bent over the crystal. He showed no reaction to Circe's words.

Galen shivered, hard. He was burning, churning, surging

with energy. "I want the names of those mages who aided you, nothing else."

Her broken lips stretched into a smile. "I came to the truth only recently—unlike you or the privileged Circle. Morden hinted. Claimed allies in the past. Then Alwyn—"

"Silence!" Galen visualized the equation, and the blue fire appeared above her, hovered there.

"Alwyn said three years and—we would all know. Then you—returned from the rim so angry at Elric."

"Silence!" He brought the fire down.

She gasped as the lines of red spread, intersected. "In time—I realized the truth. And the folly of rejecting them."

Gowen opened his eyes, and he looked from Circe to Galen, his round cheeks drawn up in horror and confusion.

Galen wanted to crush her, crush her. But that was what she wanted: an escape. He would not give it to her. "You will tell me the names of the mages who assisted you."

She looked up, waiting for the blue ball of energy to appear. She would not answer.

Galen obliged her. The thick, undulating wave of blue fell upon her. As it flowed down her body, though, yellow appeared along the leading edge, spread quickly to encompass the rest. His fire was interacting with a shield, penetrating the upper layers and diffusing. Gowen was protecting her.

The yellow faded, vanished, leaving just the subtle tinge of the shield. Circe let out a breathy laugh.

But Galen was no longer in that room. Inside him, something was happening. A scouring fire raced over the surface of a shield, but this fire was red, not blue. As the fire was absorbed by the shield and the red turned yellow, and the yellow faded, vanished, a woman's bold laughter rang out.

Two dark figures towered over him, the pale blue of shields protecting them, their powerful voices booming through the air. The man's hands were huge, with blood vessels that seemed swollen with rage. His face, high above, was hidden in shadow.

His father.

The woman—his mother—wore a long black silk dress, whose tight material shimmered in waves as she moved. Her hands, too, struck him with odd clarity, her thin fingers bent like spider legs.

She raised her hand with a flourish, and between his parents a brilliant pinpoint light formed, grew in intensity. Lines of electrical discharge shot out at his father, following the direction of her fingers, poking at his shield to test its strength. As the electricity crackled over him, another scouring ball of red energy appeared in the air above her, streaked downward. For a moment, as the energy raced over her shield, it seemed to consume her, and again she laughed.

Memory after memory fell upon him, one on top of another, images and sensations, overwhelming, smothering.

Fire, screams, stillness. Powerful voices raised in argument while he sat in the darkness of his bedroom. Harsh words at the dinner table; a fireball delivered to punctuate a remark, energy diffusing harmlessly across a shield. Scorch marks on the walls, on the furniture, a new couch ordered in haste before visitors arrived. His corner, the corner of the living room where he retreated when they forgot to send him to his room and he couldn't safely reach it. The sparks of conflict ignited in an instant, died as quickly. He sat and pressed himself into the wall, not wanting to hear, not wanting to see. It was all his fault. If only he behaved better, worked harder. He would be quiet and still, would give them no more reason to fight.

Another fight, and he was taller now, his father's face clearer, the sharp nose and intimidating blue glare of his eyes. The arguments became longer, the violence more frequent and intense.

His father and a young Alwyn stumbling into a plush corporate office suite, drunk, two strange women behind them. Galen followed, his screen clutched to his chest, and retreated into a small side office.

His mother leaning over his bed, whispering him to sleep. "Your father would have me cast out if he could. I built the corporation from nothing, and he wants it all for himself."

His father, a dark silhouette against the bright sky, standing over him during one of their endless training sessions. "You will obey me, and you will not question me! You're *my* apprentice. She's nothing to you!"

Each told him the sins of the other, the corporate machinations, the elaborate deceptions, the ruthless power plays. Each tried to secure his allegiance. Perhaps they'd once had love, of a sort, but they'd become locked in an endless battle for power.

He paced back and forth around his bed, hearing the crackle and whine of energies in the living room. His father yelled, more furious than ever. Shifting light leaked beneath the door, the red of scouring fire struggling for dominance with the blue-white of lightning. Galen did not want to hear, did not want to see. Yet he could not be still. This fight seemed different, their attacks more vicious, more determined.

He wished he were a mage; then he could stop them. Then he could make them stop.

His mother's vibrant, angry voice: "I will not be treated this way!" A brilliant blue-white flash beneath the door, burning an afterimage in the darkness. An answering roar of red, and she cried out.

Galen punched the door control, ran from his room. As he raced toward them, neither seemed injured, yet in the brilliant blaze of their attacks, he barely recognized them, their faces painted in harsh patches of light and shadow, features cast into distorted shapes, filled with hate. He came between them, and the fire struck him.

Later, his mother's fingers dug into his burned arm, healing him. "We will have our revenge, my darling. Don't you worry."

In the heightened reality of an electron incantation, Elric's hand rose from his chest, and with a turn revealed the ring, with its silver band and ragged black stone. It carried a secret. A secret he knew.

Galen entered the lab where his mother sat working.

"I'm busy," she said. "Go away."

He turned to leave.

"No, wait." Her voice softened. "Why don't you come and watch? I'm making your father's birthday present."

He came and sat across the worktable from her, scratching at the edges of a patch of burned skin on the back of his hand. It hadn't yet healed.

"No, come and sit here beside Mother."

He came around the table, climbed onto a stool beside her.

She held up an unfinished silver band. "It's a ring. It will have a stone here, which will copy any data crystal it touches."

"How can it do that?"

She gave a tight smile, the expression seeming unnatural, and pointed to the small black stone clamped to the work-table. "The inner layers store information, just as a normal data crystal. The outer layer will look the same, but function differently." She continued her explanation as she added layer after layer to the stone. When she was done, she turned to him, and a hardness came into her face. "Not a bad teacher, am I?"

"No," he said.

"Now we need to insert the stone in the ring, and connect it to the microcircuitry in the band." She worked over it with spidery fingers.

"You're not angry with him anymore, then?"

"He claims he's turned over a new leaf. I can do that too."

She made another connection in the band.

"What's that?" he asked.

"Some additional memory." She looked up at him. "I know your father tells you horrible things about me. But you love me, don't you, my darling?"

"Of course."

"Tell me."

"I love you, Mother."

"Show me."

He leaned forward and kissed her lips. She crushed him in a smothering embrace. "I'm the only one who really loves you," she said. Her fingers kneaded his back. "Do you believe he's turned over a new leaf?"

"I—don't know," he said.

"Do you believe I have?"

He didn't know how to answer. No would mean he disbelieved her. Yes would mean she had been at fault in the past. As was often the case, she would not be pleased with either answer. "I love you," he repeated, wishing she would release him.

"Your father's a selfish, power-hungry bastard. He wants the corporation. He wants you. He wants any woman who catches his fancy."

That was true. But then why was she spending such time on his present? "Why do you stay with him?"

She released him, pulled back. "I stay with him for you, darling. I couldn't leave you. I want only the best for you." She took his hand, rubbed the burned skin there. Pain shot up his arm. "I have to protect you. And I can't just give over the corporation to him."

She picked up the ring, slipped it onto his finger. "There. How do you like that."

He nodded, though it was far too big for him, and the stone had fallen to one side as soon as she'd put it on. He pulled his hand away from hers with the excuse of righting it. "The ring should be very useful."

She fixed him with her cold blue gaze. "A Trojan horse," she said, in the ancient Greek dialect she'd taught him so they might share secrets. She continued in English. "No one would guess what it can do. We wizards are subtle."

Down the hall, the front door opened. "Apprentice!" his father yelled.

He jerked to his feet, quickly returned the ring to his mother. He ran to answer his father's summons.

He stopped a few feet away from the tall, dark figure, surprised to see that his father was accompanied by Elric. No one had told him Elric was visiting. Whenever they had a guest, things became much more complicated.

His father came at him and embraced him, wrapping him in the smells of sweat and resin soap. Embraces between them happened only in front of company, and he found his body going tense. "My boy. Look who's here. Elric has come for a visit."

Elric came about every three months, on some sort of mage business.

His father released him and stepped aside.

"Hello, Apprentice," Elric said with a nod.

He bowed. "Hello, Elric."

Elric was not unpredictable and emotional like his father, but still he was frightening, with his powerful voice and cold, commanding presence.

His father snatched up his hand, as if seeing the wound for the first time. "What have you gotten into now, you clumsy boy?"

He knew better than to answer.

"Never mind. Your mother and I have business to discuss with Elric. Make yourself scarce until dinner. Then Elric has offered to watch you while your mother takes me out for my big birthday surprise."

"Yes."

It was that night, that night they died. He turned away, finding himself back in the blackened observation room, Circe's eyes on him, Gowen bent in concentration.

Galen stumbled, disoriented, and sat hard on the floor. He was panting, heart pounding. The ring—he had watched her make it, had seen the unusual design but failed to understand.

We will have our revenge.

She had not forgiven his father. The ring was not her peace offering. It was her weapon.

Unbeknownst to his father, she had provided herself her own menu of options, with her own key. The ability to copy any data crystal was simply a misdirection from the true purpose of the ring: the electrical storm. On his finger, the ring served as her own Trojan horse, taken within the defense of his shield, available for use at her whim.

But his mother had never used the ring. They had died in fire, died in a spaceship accident.

Of course, there was one way to know for certain.

He accessed the observation room's systems, and through them, reached out to the ring. With his mother's key, the menu of options appeared in his mind's eye. She had set the ring, long ago, to record. He realized now that she had wanted him to be able to deduce her key, with sufficient effort. If something went wrong, if something happened to her, evidence against his father would be within his reach. If instead she was the victor, she could destroy the ring or change the key easily enough. It was typical mage thinking.

He searched the log of recordings, found when they had begun: October 10, 2247, his father's final birthday.

He fixed his gaze on Circe, focusing his attention on her bleeding, hate-filled face. He did not want to look at the ring's recordings, did not want to be pulled back to that time. But he had to know the truth. He would divide his attention between present and past to keep the memories from drawing him in.

With a crinkle of paper, out of darkness came light, and his father's face. He had unwrapped his present. He reached for the ring with one large hand, his shadowed face forced into a smile.

Galen scanned quickly ahead.

Hushed whispers in front of the bathroom mirror as his father added lapel pins to his jacket and his mother put up her dark hair.

"Elric knows," she said.

"Suspects, perhaps," his father said. "Strange that your healing didn't completely erase the injury this time. Almost as if you wanted Elric to notice."

"My powers are not infinite. Are you saying that I would purposely make the boy suffer?"

In the mirror's image, his father's jaw clenched. "I say only that the wound is noticeable. What can Elric do, though, with only suspicions?"

"Once his suspicions are roused," she said in a carefully modulated voice, "he will investigate. Tonight, while we are gone, Elric will question the boy. Though the boy will maintain his silence, Elric's suspicions will not be soothed. He will search for more evidence, and he will find it. He will report back to the Circle that the mage couple he has been assigned to watch has finally done what everyone said they would: They have turned on each other. We will be disciplined, our influence diminished. For myself, it will be no tragedy. Perhaps a mild rebuke. But you will be reprimanded, disgraced, for what you did to the boy. They will take your apprentice away from you, and give him over to me. The corporation, also, I suspect, will be left to me."

"It was an accident."

"If you had the control of the worst chrysalis-stage apprentice, you could have stopped from hurting the boy. If you wanted to. But you didn't. You brutalize him."

"I'm a much better teacher than you would be. I teach him discipline, obedience. Of course you undermine my authority at every turn, manipulating him to your own ends, smothering him with your false love."

Galen scanned ahead.

His father came out into the living room, and there stood Elric, looking healthy and fit. Elric's sharp gaze studied something out of the ring's range of vision, his lips pressed into a thin, grim line.

Then the ring turned, revealing the object of Elric's scrutiny: a boy standing at attention, brown hair cut bristle-short, plain black robe perfectly pressed, a patch of burned skin on one hand. The boy betrayed only the slightest hint of a flinch as his father leaned in for an embrace.

Farther on, Galen found the massive spaceship, its elegant interior, curtained compartments lined with long windows at which to observe the midnight lights. The argument they'd begun in the bathroom continued as the ship rose up, sped into the evanescent red streaks. His mother's fingers curled inward as she grew angrier and angrier. His father's face, reflected in the window, was a ghostly silhouette seething with red.

A female attendant entered, asked if they could lower their voices. His mother turned to her, gave an amiable reply. When the attendant left, she turned on his father and bit out a sharp rebuke, raising a spidery hand.

The scouring ball appeared behind her; she did not see it. With a rush it swooped down over her unshielded body, stretching to envelop her, and then, rather than dissolving after a quick, single pass, remained around her, encasing her in its undulating red blanket.

His father had discovered the same principle Razeel used in her cylinders of darkness. The energy would eat inward, consuming skin, muscle, tissue, bone.

Swathed in red, her shaking hand slowly extended, and her thin fingers turned in a precise movement.

The ring's image jerked as his father convulsed with the massive electric shock. His breaths ascended into short, harsh gasps.

The red swells rippling over her, his mother threw herself at the glass again, again, desperate to be free.

Fireballs boiled into the air, shot wildly toward her. It was his father's final attack. But the fireballs missed their target, splashing instead across tablecloth and curtains, shooting sparks from the overhead lights, catching the returning attendant in the face. As more and more streaked outward, the fireballs blasted through tattered curtains into neighboring compartments, spreading their brilliant fury farther and farther through the ship.

The red blanket vanished from about his mother, revealing a body slick with blood. She looked toward his father and gave a single, satisfied laugh, then dropped to the floor, alarm lights flashing over her. With a final jerking spasm, his father fell beside her. Flames covered them.

Galen broke contact with the ring, became aware again of Circe—her raw, blood-streaked face looking far too much like his mother's. Energy drove endlessly through him.

He had thought his parents' deaths an accident, another example of the random violence that erupted all around him. He had thought the universe cold and heartless for taking them away. The universe, however, was not to blame. The blame fell to his parents themselves, for their lack of control. They had surrendered to chaos, had killed each other and everyone else on that ship.

Each made his own choice. They had chosen destruction.

They are a part of who you are, Elric had said.

Just as they had been drawn to chaos, he was drawn to chaos. He carried not only the programming of the Shadows within him, but the DNA of his parents, their own personal programming of destruction. He too had a choice. He too had chosen to kill.

On Thenothk, he had hoped that he and Elizar would kill each other.

Why are you a techno-mage? Elric had asked.

He had dreamed of becoming a healer. He had hoped to

undo some of the damage that the universe seemed determined to inflict. He had wanted, he now realized, to make up for any wrong he had done, causing his parents to fight.

After their deaths, though, all that had become secondary to a much more pressing goal: to hide from the truth. He had not wanted to remember them as they were, or to live with the fact that he had come from them. In the shelter of Elric's tutelage, he had found an escape from the violence and chaos. He had buried the past, created a regimented, orderly spell language, a safe haven for himself.

Yet in pursuing that goal, he had forfeited the others. His rigid spell language limited his abilities, frustrated all his attempts to heal. Kell had told him, long ago. *You have hidden so well that any more you might have been is lost. You have become these regimented paths, and the places to which they lead.*

And those paths of thought, that spell language, led to destruction. Because that was the truth hidden inside him.

Was that what Elric had wanted him to remember?

I tell you because I do not believe you can become a complete person until you reclaim this piece of yourself.

Galen didn't see how this could help him become whole. He arose from violence, and he generated violence.

You have overcome much.

But he had not overcome it at all. He was consumed by it.

We choose to live in knowledge, not ignorance.

So he hid from himself no longer. He now knew why he was as he was. As for why he was a techno-mage, his old reasons no longer made sense. He could not heal; he could not undo damage; he could not make up for wrongs. He could do no good at all.

Perhaps, though, those had never been his real goals—or at least not all of them. For there was a greater truth from which he hid. While he had loved his parents—in some way he could barely understand—and while he had mourned them, he knew that a part of him had been relieved at their passing. Part of him, perhaps, had even wished for them to die. Had wished to kill them. To stop them from ever fighting again.

That desire, he feared, had been the dark, secret heart of his dream to become a techno-mage.

He had told himself he wanted to heal, when in truth, he wanted only to kill.

Although his original targets had prematurely destroyed themselves, he had found new targets, and new reasons for pursuing them. He must stop Elizar and Razeel from using his spell, must end whatever plans they had for rebuilding their order. And he must kill Morden, so no more mages would be tempted to leave the hiding place. If his destruction had any positive purpose, it was to stop the mages from doing any more damage.

Of them all, of course, he had done the greatest damage.

Finally he understood why. Before he'd received the slightest bit of Shadow tech, he had been drawn to violence, and with the tech, his ability to kill had been perfected. Elric had said he wasn't a monster, but Elric didn't know how hard he had to work, every single moment, to retain control. The brilliant heat of destruction wanted to pour out of him, and he wanted it to pour out of him.

He was who he was.

Before him, Circe lay with eyes closed, her skin a purple streaked with crusted red. Though her bleeding had stopped, her rasping breath had grown more congested, more labored. Gowen had lain Galen's coat on her, and he remained bent over her, healing her.

The coat had come from Elric, and Galen found his gaze turning toward that blackened figure, who lay half-exposed in his tattered robe, his ruined body looking cold and abandoned.

Circe had tortured him, had killed him, and now here she was, receiving healing from Gowen. Galen wanted to crush her. The equation was so simple, only a single term. She had to pay for what she'd done.

A warm rush of well-being was spreading through him already, in anticipation of casting the spell, and he realized, as he visualized his mind as a blank screen, prepared to impose the equation upon it, that if he cast the spell, he would never be able to stop. He wanted so much to strike back at something, anything, everything.

With a start he realized he'd lost his exercises—he didn't know when. He began a new exercise, another, another, recoiling from those thoughts, withdrawing from those feelings. Doing three at once allowed him to think of little else; he must concentrate to continue them all without error. His attention narrowed, the walls of the exercises rising up around him, blocking out the past, blocking out the many things of which he must not think if he was to retain control. The walls pressed in on him, holding him together, pushing him forward down the narrow tunnel of his thoughts.

He must leave this place. The Circle refused to let him go, for fear of the device the Shadows had secreted within him, their power over him. He had planned to destroy it, yet he knew that if he did, it would kill him.

Suddenly it struck him what the Circle required. If the Circle had their own power over him, then they would have nothing to fear. They must implant in him their own device, which would carry out their desires. He would become a Trojan horse to send against their enemies. Then the Circle would let him go, and he could fulfill his purpose.

He had been trapped in his thinking, focusing all his energy on trying to take control from the Shadows. But there was another, much simpler way to gain his freedom.

Galen realized Blaylock stood over Circe. Blaylock's thin, severe figure seemed to exist at a great distance, as if Galen peered through a telescope at some remote land.

Gowen was speaking. "I've been able to repair some of the damage to her heart and lungs. More extensive healing will take much longer, if it is even possible." He glanced at Galen. "She remains near death."

"If you stop your ministrations, can she survive for a short time?"

"Perhaps thirty minutes, an hour."

"That is sufficient. The others are beginning to wake from Circe's sleeping potion. See to them."

Gowen bowed his head once again over Circe, apparently giving the organelles some final instruction. Then he withdrew his crystal, climbed to his feet. "Galen has questioned her." He looked again to Galen, his lips turned in dismay.

"Then I will discuss it with Galen. You are needed elsewhere."

Gowen bowed, departed.

Blaylock's sharp gaze turned to Galen.

He stood, carefully maintaining the three mind-focusing exercises. His body felt strange, disconnected. He quickly summarized what Circe had told him. "When she spoke of the mages' connection to the Shadows, I tried to silence her, but she would not stop. I'm not sure how much Gowen heard."

"I will speak with him." Blaylock's eyes shifted to take in something across the room, and despite his stern, dour expression, Galen sensed he was shaken. "We have sustained a grievous loss. Elric was truly the wisest of us all."

Galen would not think of him now. "Do you need help with her confederates?"

Blaylock's voice regained its certainty. "We have dealt with them. You may go. I will question Circe in private."

But Galen would not be dismissed. "Morden must be killed, so others do not succumb to the temptations he offered."

"There will be time to discuss what action, if any, must be taken."

Galen fixed Blaylock with his gaze. "When you are finished with her, you will meet with Herazade, and you will agree to release me to kill Morden, Elizar, and Razeel. You will implant within me a device that can sense my mage energy. If ever that energy ceases, if ever my tech is turned off by the Shadows, the device will kill me and any nearby. The manner I leave to you. It should be simple enough to build. That should satisfy your objections."

For once, Blaylock had nothing to say.

Galen left the burned room, carrying thoughts of destruction with him. Finally he could move forward.

— chapter 8 —

In his room, Galen packed for his journey. Select items went into his valise; others, which he felt might be of use to those he left behind, were placed in a plastic container. The rest was dropped into the trash. Reorganizing his belongings helped to keep him calm, focused. With the exercises running through him, he need think of nothing except how each object should be categorized.

Of the items he would leave for the others, there were few: some blank data crystals and other research supplies; a few minor inventions; a scarf; a vial of ash. Perhaps Blaylock would find a place to spread her remains, and those in the second vial that Galen would soon receive.

He turned his mind away. Of his various spells, the basic postulates, the research he had done into the tech, the knowledge he had of the Shadows, and the files Burell and her daughter had given him, he would leave no trace. He carried those things inside him, and they would die with him.

From the corner of his closet, he removed his staff. Over four feet long, it was a lustrous black, with golden etchings of circuits in finest filigree. It fit perfectly into Galen's hand, warm and smooth and balanced, like an extra limb. He could not use it where he was going. Instead, it must be left in a safe place, for he had programmed it to self-destruct at his death.

He laid it on the bed in a category of its own. It had been Elric's gift, welcoming him into magehood. As he stared down at it, a hard shiver ran through him. He crossed his arms over his chest, rocked back and forth.

A message arrived from Blaylock. *Come to Gowen's room at once.*

Elric had devoted himself to teaching Galen, had demanded the very best from his apprentice. He had never made Galen feel any less because his training had been divided between two teachers, one of whom had forsaken control and killed.

Another message from Blaylock. *Galen.*

Coming, Galen answered.

He had not deserved Elric's efforts or his affection. Elric had taught him order and control, yet Galen had gravitated to the teachings of his true parents, chaos and destruction.

Again, he turned his mind away, left his packing, went out. The corridors were crowded, the mages still anxiously discussing the events of the night before. Galen kept his head down, following the regular rhythm of his footfalls. The voices of some were raised in anger; Galen refused to hear their words. As he took his twentieth step, someone grasped his shoulder. Miostro.

"My condolences," Miostro said in his powerful voice. "Elric was a great mage."

"Excuse me," Galen said, continued on his way.

Why had Blaylock called for him? Perhaps Gowen had put the pieces together. Blaylock might want Galen's help to bring him to acceptance. If he had realized the truth, though, he would not take it well. Galen didn't know what he could say to console Gowen. The truth carried no consolation.

The large hole burned through Gowen's door was covered by a piece of material hanging on the inside. It looked like a robe. Galen pressed the bell, but didn't hear it ring. He knocked on the door, pushed aside the robe, and climbed through.

Blaylock stood at the foot of Gowen's bed, his back to Galen. "I need you to take the body to the forward storage room," Blaylock said. "We will have the services together."

Galen wasn't sure to whom Blaylock spoke, or of whom. Did he mean to send Elric to the other side with Circe? That was unacceptable. He approached. "What do you—"

On the bed lay Gowen, his white sleeping gown surrounded by a halo of red. Gowen had seen Kell's flayed body for only a moment before Blaylock had made him turn away. He had seen the arms cut open from shoulder to palm, the skin spread, tech neatly excised. He had seen the hands like two great alien blossoms, the skin of palms, of thumbs, index and middle fingers pealed back, muscle elegantly split, delicate canyons of bone exposed.

As a healer, Gowen was an expert on the body, on manipulating it and its systems. His work was slightly less neat than Elizar's, no doubt from the difficulty of carrying out the procedure on himself. Since Gowen was lying on his back, Galen didn't know how complete he'd been, but the thick stain of red on the bedding around him revealed that he had at least begun work on his spine and skull.

One golden strand of tech lay beside his mutilated fingers. Others, coated with blood and chunks of tissue, were stuck to the side of his dresser in an abstract pattern, as if he had thrown them away from him.

If Galen hadn't questioned Circe in his presence, Gowen could still be living with his illusions, could still be hoping for that one great enlightenment that would join him to the tech, and to the universe.

Instead, Galen had indulged his anger, had tortured Circe until she spoke. Gowen had learned the truth: The tech was not some great blessing from God that would show them the light; it was a pestilence from the Shadows that drew them into darkness.

Wherever Galen went, death followed.

Gowen's head was tilted slightly to one side, eyes closed, round cheeks wet with tears. In the smooth contours of his face, Galen hoped that he saw peace.

Gowen had possessed courage that Galen did not. Galen had dared consider removing just one tiny piece of tech to avoid the Shadows' control. But the programming of destruction infused each cell of the tech.

In the light of that truth, Gowen had determined to remove the pestilence, to rid himself of the Shadows' influence. He had followed the one, harrowing pathway open to them. And now he was free.

"I need you to take the body to the forward storage room," Blaylock repeated. "We will have the services together tomorrow." Blaylock's gaunt face was set.

"I will," Galen said. "I'm sorry."

"This is the first time he has ever disobeyed me."

Galen visualized the equation, conjured the illusion of a shroud over Gowen. "You should sit."

"They must all be told the truth. They must understand, as I do. The tech is a blessing. Its programming can be overcome. Through perfect discipline, perfect control, we can join in a transcendent union with that life. We can gain true understanding. We are blessed not because of the magnitude of power we carry, but because of the sacred intimacy with which we are connected to it. The tech taps into the basic force and fabric of the universe. It can teach us the will of the universe, make us one with the universe."

"You will tell the mages their tech comes from the Shadows?"

Blaylock turned to him, and for the first time, in the lines of Blaylock's gaunt, severe face, Galen saw regret. "Gowen commands it."

Galen nodded. The mages had long deserved to know. Yet he feared how they would react.

Blaylock dropped to his knees.

Galen crouched beside him. "Blaylock."

"I will keep vigil here. Please take him away. Do not let the others see." Blaylock raised his stiff, yellowish palms before him and conjured a fireball there. His hands trembled slightly. "I did not serve him well, as a teacher."

"You told him all you could. You taught him as best you knew."

Blaylock bowed his head.

Galen conjured a platform beneath Gowen's body and lifted him from the bed, conveyed him to the door. He passed through the hole, and Galen followed him through the claustrophobic corridors, ignoring the anxious looks of the others.

As Galen passed the dining hall, Tzakizak exhorted a crowd to demand a complete explanation from the Circle. "Why would a loyal mage like Circe attempt to break free from the hiding place?" he yelled. "Why would she kill Elric? As usual, the Circle holds back all the details. They must learn that we deserve respect."

His audience responded with an angry mixture of cries.

Perhaps the mages could repress the urge to destruction, yet in this place, it was growing harder and harder. He could feel it rising up in each one of them, overflowing to form a great irresistible wave that would overwhelm them all.

He had to be released before he was enveloped in it, for he had his own destruction to wreak.

"Who are you?" the Human named Justin asked. "What is your name? Your full name, Anna."

Through her shifting black skin, Anna studied him angrily. Wearing a simple shirt, vest, and pants, he paced across her main chamber, supporting himself with a cane. Compared to Elizar, who stood quietly to one side, he seemed weak and unremarkable, with his wispy white hair, his bushy eyebrows, his face sagging with wrinkles. His voice quavered as he spoke. Despite all that, there was something hard and threatening about him. She wanted to expel him from her body.

The Eye had told her to answer his questions, but his questions made no sense. And this was not her purpose, to answer questions. She had returned her passengers to Z'ha'dum. She should be flying with her sisters, shrieking the red rapture of the war cry. Instead, she remained planet-bound, gravity weighing her down, the endless wind scouring her with dust. While she sat idle, the Eye sent her strange signals and directives, filling her with unease. She had been instructed to change her maintenance cycle, shifting her central processing unit much more often and in more complex patterns than she normally did. The changes made as much sense as Justin's questions.

My name is Anna, she transmitted to him.

He stopped, raised his index finger. "Anna is part of your name. What is the rest?"

He was right, she knew, which angered her further. There was another part to her name. She no longer remembered it.

"When were you born?" he asked.

I don't understand.

"Where are you from?"

Z'ha'dum.

"Before Z'ha'dum."

There was nothing before Z'ha'dum. How could there be? Here were her first memories of receiving the instruction of the Eye, of learning control of her systems, of taking flight. This was where she and the machine had become one.

"What are you, Anna?"

The man was an idiot. *An engine of chaos and destruction.*

"Before you joined with the ship, what were you? Who was Anna Sheridan?"

Sheridan. Now that he had said the word, she recalled it. But she didn't understand why she had a second name. *Your questions make no sense.*

"This is pointless," Elizar said. "Why delay? Once she is out, Bunny can help to awaken any memories that survive."

Justin dismissed Elizar's comment with a sharp movement of his hand, and his voice was hard. "Nothing like this has ever been done before. They said we should at least begin the process while she's in her current condition, so she'll feel some degree of continuity."

What were they talking about? What were they going to do to her?

With your cooperation, the Eye said, *you will lead us to victory. The greatest joy is the ecstasy of victory.*

She wanted to leap into the sky, to leave this place. But the Eye would not let her.

The march of the machine's beat stumbled, as it had not done in a long time, and Anna panicked, began a systems check. She would not listen to their questions, would not be distracted from her great purpose of destruction.

The machine was so beautiful, so elegant. Perfect grace, perfect control, form and function integrated into the circuitry of the unbroken loop, the closed universe. All systems of the machine passed through her. She was its heart; she was its brain; she was the machine. She kept the neurons firing in harmony. She synchronized the cleansing and circulation in sublime synergy. She beat out a flawless march with the complex, multileveled systems. The skin of the machine was her skin; its bones and blood, her bones and blood. She and the machine were—

"Anna," Justin said. "Do you remember your husband? Do you remember John Sheridan?"

The magical fire burned, brilliant green flames swirling around the flat rock where the body lay, reducing it to the merest hint of darkness within.

The asteroid's pockmarked gray surface shifted in the harsh green light. Above, the sky was black, the stars blocked by the fields masking the asteroid's presence. Only the occasional illusion of a falling star, Kell's symbol for the mages, streaked through the darkness, tribute to the fall of a great mage.

Galen averted his eyes. He stood apart from the rest, wearing an EVA suit in the asteroid's vacuum, unable to generate a containment shield as most of the mages did. Blaylock and others had offered to take him within their shields, but he could not stand the distraction of companionship.

He must maintain control, must keep himself from disintegrating into destruction. The energy churned restlessly through him, searching for outlet. He could not bring the fire down upon himself again; it was too soon. Two exercises ran concurrently through his mind, holding him together, he hoped, until the ceremony's end.

His life was made up of an endless succession of these ceremonies. Yet none had been as difficult as this. At all the others, Elric had stood beside him, the one certainty in his life, his wall of strength. Now he stood alone and Elric burned, the fire enveloping his ruined body, reducing him to the chaos from which they had come, and to which they inevitably returned.

It was appropriate that they should be consumed in fire. They fought that fire all their lives; at the end, it reduced them to dust.

Inside, Blaylock had delivered Elric's short eulogy in his cold, certain tone, yet his words had conveyed enormous respect for Elric, and the heavy loss of his passing. By its end, many were in tears. Had Carvin been there, she would have cried for Galen.

Gowen's body had been burned first, then Elric's. Circe

and her coconspirators had been disposed of earlier, without fanfare.

The green flames billowed high, and Galen felt himself drifting away, as he had so many times in the past, when he desired to hide. But he could not allow himself to drift, to be lax. He must remain in control. He pushed his exercises forward, built the walls of tunnel vision up around him, reviewed his schedule.

Once the ceremony was completed, Herazade would perform the procedure. It was fairly simple, the insertion of a tiny device carrying a high explosive charge. It would be placed on the surface of his heart. If his mage energy ceased, the explosive would be triggered. The mages' hiding place would remain safe, from all but the mages themselves.

Fed was preparing the supplies he'd requested. Within a few hours, he would be gone. Tomorrow Blaylock planned to gather the mages together and tell them the truth.

The fire at last declined, undulating back and forth over the flat stone like a caress. It drew together into a single, wavering flame, then went dark.

Galen turned and walked back across the powdery surface toward the air lock. He could not stand to hear whatever words of comfort the others might offer. Those words were empty. Elric was gone.

Galen awoke on the couch in Herazade's office, surrounded by lush, patterned tapestries. His chest throbbed as if he'd been kicked.

A sharp sound beat out a steady rhythm. He twisted his head, found Fed in the armchair beside him, bouncing a rubber ball against a small floating platform.

Herazade was not in sight, but she must have inserted the device. Galen laid a gloved hand over his heart, and a feeling of relief washed over him. Everything had been taken care of. He had devised as much of a plan as he could. He had settled his affairs, had left his room as he had found it, except for his staff in one corner and the single plastic container sitting inside the door. Now he could go.

He began a mind-focusing exercise and sat up, the pain of his breath triggering a bout of coughing.

"Hey. You okay?" Fed divided his attention between Galen and the ball.

Galen nodded.

"Herazade said you're all set. They'll be here in a minute." Galen drew shallower breaths, straightened.

"What did they give you? Some sort of tracking device?" Galen said nothing.

Fed snatched the ball in mid-bounce. "I'm sorry about Elric. He was a great mage."

"Yes."

"I hear Morden put Circe up to it, promised her power if she would join the Shadows. Everybody's talking about it." Fed paused, tossing the ball from one hand to the other. "I saw Morden when I was on Babylon 5. Slimy character." He looked over at Galen. "I hear you're going to kill him."

That was all the others were being told of his task. "The mages must know that Morden can give them nothing."

Fed studied the ball in silence, uncharacteristically thoughtful. Then his beard shifted with a crooked smile. "I put together those disguises for you, like you asked." Fed jerked a thumb toward the door, where a suitcase sat beside Galen's smaller valise. "They—may not quite be to your taste. But I guarantee you won't be recognized."

"And the gun?"

"I got you one of Tzakizak's specials. It's silent, very powerful, and won't show up on any weapon scan. But . . . I don't understand what you need it for."

Of course Fed didn't understand. Galen was a weapon himself; why would he need another? "Thank you," he said.

Fed's eyes narrowed in humor. "You better hurry back. Somehow I got drafted to take over your job. I'm not looking forward to sitting alone in a room all day."

An image came to him of the smoke-filled observation room, its walls running with molten metal. He forced it away.

The door opened, and Blaylock and Herazade entered.

"Thank you, Fed," Herazade said. "Please excuse us."

Galen stood, and Fed stood with him. "You know," Fed

said, "our group of initiates hasn't done very well. We can't afford to lose any more."

"Good-bye, Federico."

Fed slapped him on the back. "Be keeping an eye on you. So please, keep it entertaining."

Fed left, and Galen went to Blaylock and Herazade, who stood beside the door.

Herazade fixed him with her gaze. "We have put our trust in you." She pressed her palm against his heart. "We have made you our hand. With you, we reach out from this place to strike down our enemies. Morden must be killed to maintain our peace. Do not fail us."

"I won't." Even with their fail-safe device implanted inside him, Galen didn't believe the Circle would have released him for the purpose of killing Elizar and Razeel. That brother and sister might use his spell to destroy was not sufficient reason for them. But once they'd realized that, even in the hiding place, Morden threatened them, they'd agreed to his proposal with amazing speed. Herazade had told him, at least three times, that he must kill Morden first. Apparently she did not believe he would have the opportunity to kill Morden otherwise.

"Come," Blaylock said.

Galen retrieved the suitcase and valise, and followed Blaylock out.

"Though I agreed to it," Blaylock said as they walked toward the air lock, "I am not pleased with your solution. Clearly I have a greater regard for your life than you do. You have placed yourself in a precarious position. The enemy will attempt to manipulate you into a location where they can nullify your tech, as they did before. Instead, you must manipulate them. Elric was a master of such techniques, though he used them rarely. I assume he instructed you."

"Yes." If they did trap him, at least the Circle's device might kill them with him.

"Remember what we spoke of on the way to the rim. If you are to succeed out in the universe, you cannot close yourself off from it. You must study the people around you, discover their intentions, and use them."

"Yes." He would study them with the detachment of an astronomer cataloging remote galaxies. He would allow nothing to break through his defenses.

"You must remain focused on your task, above all. Do not stray. You have three to kill, and only three. The Circle will not overlook another loss of control. Accomplish the task you have been set, and return to us."

"I will accomplish it."

Blaylock was silent for a few steps. Then he continued. "We have arranged for you to retain access to our probe network while you are outside." Galen received a message with several files attached. "Those are Elric's reports from his time on Babylon 5, including what information he gathered on Morden. Know that when you are in Morden's presence, you are in grave danger." Blaylock stopped beside the air lock, and as they faced each other, Galen was startled to see a hint of stubble on Blaylock's cheeks. He must have been so upset with Elric's and Gowen's deaths that he had forgotten to scour himself. The gray bristles made him look vulnerable and aged. "The Shadows believe most of us dead. But they know that I, too, may be alive. This task demands the skills of one of the Circle. I should be the one to go."

"The mages cannot spare you. Besides, this is what I want. It is my fault that Elizar may have the spell of destruction. My arrogance. And I must stop Morden, for Elric's sake."

"Elric desired only that you find happiness."

"If I am able to kill Elizar, Razeel, and Morden, I will be happy. I require nothing further."

"You may believe so now. Yet once you have left here, everything will change. I wish you were not the one to go. The outside is filled with temptations."

The tech echoed Galen's unease. "If you believe in my control, then you have nothing to fear."

"Your control has much improved. That is why I wish you could stay. Perfect control, perfect discipline form the path to a perfect union with the tech. I believe you are closer than any of us to that goal. I hoped that once you were isolated from distractions, you might reach it, and show the rest of us the way."

Galen didn't know how Blaylock could believe such non-sense, especially after all that had just happened. "I can lead no one to enlightenment."

"Regardless of the Shadows' intentions, good can come from the tech, if you remain its master. Good can come from you. Our destiny is not to serve as agents of death and de-struction, but to become something greater."

Yet the Circle sent him to murder three people. Galen said nothing.

At last Blaylock opened the air-lock door. With a stiff movement of his hand, he cast a containment shield around them both, and they entered the air lock.

"When you are ready to depart," Blaylock said, "give con-trol of your ship over to Herazade and me. We will allow it to pass through the masking and confinement fields and send it on a programmed jump through hyperspace. As you emerge from hyperspace, record your coordinates. You must return to those coordinates in exactly thirty-five days. You shall have no longer for your task. A ship will arrive to guide you back through hyperspace to us. If you are not there when it arrives, it will return without you. You will have no method of en-tering the hiding place."

"I understand."

The outer door opened, and they walked out across the powdery, pockmarked surface to Galen's ship. Galen had not entered it since he'd arrived at the hiding place. He had thought he would never use it again.

He visualized the association spell, and the command echoed once from the tech, echoed again from the ship. In the past, the additional echo had often threatened his control, sending thoughts and feelings reflecting back and forth be-tween ship and implants, building in a rapid, swelling rever-beration. Now he felt only the elements of his mind-focusing exercise echoing back to him, orderly, reassuring.

A menu of options appeared in his mind's eye. He lowered the ramp, climbed it beside Blaylock. They passed into the ship's plain, black interior, and with the whisper of silk Blay-lock's shield withdrew.

"Elric would want a long life for you," Blaylock said.

Galen set his things down against the wall.

"I opposed him in many things, and I regret nearly all of them. He advocated revealing the origin of the tech long ago. I thought it would encourage capitulation to those instincts. You have proven me wrong. And Gowen paid the price for my lack of faith."

Blaylock did not understand. The instincts were there, and the mages were succumbing to them. Knowing the truth would make no difference. "Elric once said this, and I agree with him. All paths lead to our destruction."

"In that, I will hope he was mistaken." Blaylock studied him in silence. When Blaylock spoke again, his voice was harsh. "If you do not return, Galen, your loss will be sorely felt." He withdrew into the air lock and bowed. "The blessing of Wierden upon you."

Galen inclined his head. He closed the door and turned his mind to departure, selecting one option after another on his menu, the ship eagerly echoing his commands. Quickly he powered up the engines, activated the sensors, checked the long-unused systems.

When everything was ready, he contacted Blaylock and Herazade, directed the ship to accept their control. In his mind's eye, the sensors provided an image of the space all around the ship, as if the ship's walls were transparent. He sat, watching as the ship lifted off, pulling away from the circular gray structure of the hiding place, the barren surface of the asteroid. He had thought he would never leave. But he had one more task, and it would be his last.

A message came from Herazade. *Protect us at all costs.*

He would kill their enemies, and he would keep secret the mages' location. He wondered, though, how long they could endure, within those curving, claustrophobic corridors, before they fell upon each other in a great frenzy of destruction.

The jump engines kicked in, an immense, churning orange vortex forming ahead. Control of the ship flowed back to Galen.

As it continued on its preprogrammed course, the ship passed through the jump point, and the roiling red currents of hyperspace surrounded him. He was free. He was back in the universe.

He accessed the probe network, eagerly searched for Elizar and Razeel, or any signs that they had used the spell of destruction. He needed to find them quickly.

He searched through the many places where the Shadows might show aggression, where wars were being waged, or resistance organized. He saw no sign of brother and sister, yet conflict and destruction were all around him. Explosions, battles, massacres—one war merged into the next, revealing the vast dance of death consuming the galaxy. Each image carried a new sense of immediacy, for he no longer watched from the detached, conscience-soothing confinement of the hiding place, but from amidst the destruction.

He accessed a probe in orbit about the Kaikeen Confederacy's capital planet. The Centauri had declared war on the confederacy nearly a year ago, but as just one of a dozen wars the Centauri had been prosecuting, the Kaikeen had received little attention beyond a few minor attacks on their outer planets. Over the last months, the Centauri had pulled many of their troops back to strengthen the defenses around Centauri Prime. The Kaikeen had, optimistically, interpreted the withdrawal as sign of impending victory, and struck a blow against a Centauri colony in disputed territory. Apparently that had shot them to the top of the list of Centauri priorities. For the Centauri Republic's allies, the Shadows, had arrived to deliver the counterattack.

A fleet of Shadow ships cut down through the atmosphere of the planet, their spidery silhouettes stark against the gray stone of the major continent. The Kaikeen defense platforms fired at the ships, but their blasts had no effect. Only a handful of Kaikeen ships were in the air, and those were quickly being sliced apart. The Kaikeen had been taken by surprise.

From high in the atmosphere, the Shadow ships released bombs, just as they had done on Soom. Far below, great clouds of destruction spread over the land. Ten billion lived there.

Here he was, with his tunnel vision, on his narrow-minded

mission to kill three people, when the entire galaxy was in flames. Was he supposed to ignore that?

Perhaps John Sheridan had found a weapon against the Shadows; perhaps he could win a battle or two. But he did not have the power to defeat them. With Galen's help, though, maybe he would. With Galen's power on his side, at least John would have a chance.

Galen could go to the Kaikeen capital planet right now. All he need do was select a course change on the menu of options before him. He could be there within an hour—perhaps not in time to save its inhabitants, but in time to catch the Shadow ships, in time to engage them.

When the Shadows struck at the center of the shell-shaped region, Galen could be there alongside John Sheridan and the rest, waiting for them. Elizar and Razeel would certainly come with the Shadows, eager to show off their new weapon in this major attack. Galen could find them, kill them. He could seize ship after ship in a boiling rush of spheres, could crush chaos once and for all, so that it could never hurt anyone else again.

And after that, after he had given himself so completely to destruction, after the great rush of energy had possessed him, seized him, filled him with its brilliant incandescence—after he had become exactly what the Shadows had intended—could he really stop himself, as he had sworn?

Would he really want to?

Blaylock was right: The temptations were great. He could not allow himself to lose sight of the narrow task he had set for himself. He could conjure destruction perhaps a handful of times without risking loss of control. He must not begin until he was ready to end.

He was not fit to be a major force for good in this war. If he was to play any role, it must be a minor one. He couldn't go near the Shadows' upcoming attack; he had to find Elizar and Razeel before then. But if they didn't stumble into view of one of his probes, or reveal themselves through some incident on the newsfeeds, he had only one idea of how he might find them before the attack. He didn't even know if it was possible. He had to make it work, though, had to stop them before they used his spell.

In the attempt, at least, he would kill Morden.

Continuing their bombing, the Shadow ships wheeled over the Kaikeen planet, its main continent lost now in a great cloud of dust. Resistance had been wiped out, but the ships would continue until they had annihilated their appointed targets. Anna had been taught never to break off, not until the enemy was utterly destroyed.

Galen crossed his arms over his chest. He must not go. He must not go. He broke the connection, turned his mind away.

His ship activated its jump engines once again. Following the instructions Blaylock and Herazade had left, it opened a jump point amidst the roiling red currents. With a great rush of speed he was sucked into it. For a moment the ship's sensors went blank, and he lost all sense of direction or movement. Then the calm blackness of normal space surrounded him. After a moment's thought, he recorded his coordinates as directed, though he had no expectation of returning to this place.

Now he had a decision to make. He had information that might save lives. Perhaps he could do some small good as he completed this final task, if the idea was not ludicrous. Two people needed to receive the information he possessed. Galen would rather have kept to himself, which best helped him retain his equilibrium. One of the two, he knew, would be an unsettling force. Nonetheless, he would make the contact.

He composed the message. *We need to meet.* The FTL relay aboard his ship quickly routed the message to the relay nearest the recipient, and then to Alwyn himself.

In a few seconds, the reply came. *And I should trust that this is you because . . . ?*

Because I still tell you that your golden dragon is brilliant.

But it IS brilliant, Alwyn wrote. *And when have you ever said that?*

Your golden dragon is brilliant.

Hell, it's great to hear from you. I knew you'd come to your senses eventually. We've got to have a party. Get stinking drunk and have some fun. Reminisce about old times. Catch up on things. Where shall this debauchery occur?

Galen smiled slightly. Alwyn hadn't changed at all. *A place you visited three months ago.*

Beat you there.

As they entered her, Anna watched with mixed wonder and terror. One was a liberator, with rows of brilliant pinpoint eyes, shining black skin. Its six legs, tapering at their bases to points, reminded her of her own beautiful limbs.

She had carried liberators inside her only once before, soon after she'd made her first kill. It was a great honor, and a great responsibility. The liberators had to be protected against any harm. With their ancient knowledge they made everything possible. They had begotten her and all the machines. They had developed the First Principles: chaos through warfare; evolution through bloodshed; perfection through victory. From them issued the joy of the Great War.

Yet she had another memory of them—disjointed and dazzling and filled with a shredding screaming brilliant agony: the liberators had taught her obedience.

With the liberator was the Human Justin. The other two were technicians, tall and slim, with grayish skin, bulbous heads, large black eyes, and narrow mouths. Anna and her sisters hated and feared the technicians. They were necessary, on the rare occasions when the machine could not maintain itself, for repair. Wherever they went, pain followed.

They moved within her, silent, approaching her core. They had brought with them some sort of floating table. Anna did not like the look of it.

Why are they here? Anna asked the Eye.

Your cooperation is critical for victory, the Eye said. *Remain calm. The greatest joy is the ecstasy of victory.*

The liberator and the others gathered around her central processing unit: her brain, her heart. It was a structure marvelous in its simplicity, a rectangular-shaped receptacle filled with gelatinous black matter veined with silver.

What did they want? Her interior held no weapons. Desperation filled her.

What are you doing? she asked Justin.

Justin looked up at her brilliant, shifting skin. "We need your help, Anna. In a different form than what you've become accustomed to." He nodded to the technicians. "Don't be afraid. We won't harm you."

The two technicians leaned forward, plunging their arms into her brain. Then they were pulling something up out of the black matter. As the vague shape rose from the darkness, suddenly the connections inside her were failing. One after another they broke, interrupting her access to different parts of her body. Frantically she re-formed them, but they broke again just as quickly.

The machine's beat raced. All of her orifices opened. She was losing control.

Her link to the Eye was severed.

Stop! she told Justin.

Stop them! she cried to the liberator.

She extended the skin of the chamber's wall, reached out for the closest technician. But as her glistening black skin wrapped around him, she could not feel his puny body; she had lost sensation. Then she could no longer see, or hear. She was trapped in silent blackness, disoriented, the march of her beat stumbling, erratic. She tightened her grip, hoping she crushed the technician.

Connections were slipping away. The processes of cleansing and circulation fell out of her reach. The great balls of destruction, the fierce mouth that shrieked the red rapture—she could no longer feel them. One after another, pieces of her self dropped away into blackness. Pain seized her partial body, shot out with astonishing intensity along her arms—a massive systems failure.

They were pulling her brain, her heart from her body. They were ripping her apart. The tireless, invulnerable machine was failing. She screamed.

After a few moments, the pain faded, withdrew. The systems fell silent. The machine could not live without its heart. Without its heart, the beat slowed. Stilled.

She searched for her connection to the machine. She could

not sense it at all. But she could not continue without it; it was impossible. She and the machine were one.

The machine was so beautiful, so elegant. It had its needs, and she fulfilled them. Without its needs, what would she do? Without the machine, what was she?

She was choking, suffocating. She spasmed with an odd expulsion of air, and then she could breathe, differently than she had before, executing a strange, laborious movement.

She remembered now a time, long ago, when she had been separated from the machine. The machine had been destroyed, and they had removed her from its corpse, had joined her to another machine.

That must be what they intended. Yet she had sensed nothing wrong with the machine, no reason for them to take her from it.

Still, she reassured herself that she and the machine would soon be one. Only in fulfilling the needs of the machine, only in carrying out the instructions of the Eye did her life have meaning. Only when she was whole could she know the thrill of battle, the ecstasy of victory. Restoring her must be their plan, for what other goal could they have?

December 2260

— chapter 9 —

Through the small window of the single-occupant trading vessel, Galen watched as Babylon 5 drew closer. He had left his mage ship in a backwater, taken a transport to the next system, and rented the trading vessel there. Though his visit to the station would be short, he wanted to minimize any chance that the Shadows would discover his identity before he desired it.

The station's five-mile length was shrouded in the shadow of the nearby planet. The lights lining the cylindrical structure seemed little more than pinpoints in the darkness.

He had visited Babylon 5 many times through the relay and probes the mages had left behind. Like a ghost, he had invaded the station's systems, had peered out from its security cameras. He would no longer be watching from that detached perspective.

The station's Command and Control sent him an approach vector, and with the clumsy controls he altered the ship's course, and passed down the dark cylinder to its end.

Now that he had finally reached the station, he felt hesitant to enter. He didn't belong here, at this source of light, where Sheridan and the only chance of fighting the Shadows survived. If he lost control here, he could destroy all hope.

Facing the end of the cylinder, he matched rotation with the station. Command and Control sent final clearance, and he directed his ship forward toward the Main Axis Port, the lights from within glowing like the grimacing mouth of a jack-o'-lantern.

The personnel in C&C did not know what they were admitting. He carried the contagion of chaos.

The ship passed through the Port's dark maw and into the huge lighted passage. Around him moved other ships, filled with other beings. Of all those here, he must kill only one. Whether he was successful or not, he dared stay no longer than a day. The dangers were too great.

He followed the docking procedures. The ship settled into its private bay, the doors above closing, and he shut down the engines, went to the side air lock. He had taken the identity of a self-employed trader. As he waited for the docking bay to pressurize, he straightened his jacket. He had no mirror; he dipped his finger into a packet of probes in his pocket, stuck several of the dustlike grains on the wall beside the air lock. Through them, he checked his appearance. He would not use a full-body illusion; the energy could well draw the Shadows to him.

Fed had done well. The shoulder-length wavy wig, while not something Galen would have chosen, radically changed his appearance. The dirty-blond hair was styled with a ragged line of bangs that ran just above his eyes. Galen had allowed his beard to grow for a few days, so a dark stubble covered his cheeks.

Fed's clothing selections were uniformly outrageous. Galen wore a golden suit with a ruffled lavender shirt and a thick golden necklace. He looked like a stim dealer or—he didn't know what. Most certainly he did not look like himself.

He would have preferred a disguise more compatible with his own personality, as he had used in the past, but he and Morden had met twice before; Galen could not risk being recognized.

He wondered if even Alwyn would know him. But Alwyn would have studied the scheduled arrivals, would have deduced which ship was his, and would be expecting him in disguise. Galen had done the same to learn under which identity Alwyn was traveling. He had arrived in a sleek cruiser the day before, as Thomas Alecto. He, too, avoided using his mage ship for most of his travels. As the Shadows' presence had spread, he'd become more and more careful to conceal his identity as a mage.

Galen accessed the probe on G'Leel's shoulder, found that

she was standing in the busy customs area with Alwyn, awaiting his arrival. Though Alwyn was in disguise, Galen recognized him instantly by the sagging skin beneath his eyes. Those bags had always suggested a softness in his personality, one that Alwyn could often display, yet one that could vanish instantly when his anger was aroused. His receding silvery hair was covered with his own wig, black hair short and slicked back. He had darkened his eyebrows as well, giving himself a more severe and dramatic look. Prosthetics gave him a sharper nose, squarer chin. He wore a subdued brown business suit, which snugged around his middle.

Alwyn looked toward the security checkpoint where passengers entered the station, and an expectant half smile lit his face.

Galen broke the contact. Whatever warm reunion Alwyn was anticipating, he would be disappointed. Galen had changed too much, and no longer had the ability to be close to anyone, nor the desire to be.

Alwyn would not make the encounter easy. He restrained himself for no one, spewing out his feelings and opinions without regard for his audience. He was sure to bring up the past. But Galen would not revisit it.

The air lock's control panel showed that the docking bay was fully pressurized. Galen took up his valise and left the ship behind, passed out of the docking bay, into the corridor that led to the security checkpoint. Passengers from other ships joined him. After spending so much time among mages, he found them strange and unsettling. Their words were poorly chosen, their conversations loud, overlapping, their movements erratic, ill-considered. A woman with a large embroidered bag banged into him and continued, not pausing in her monologue to her companion. A boy broke out in a high-pitched laugh and raced ahead of his parents. A tall Narn limped ahead, his clothes hanging off his frail body.

As they neared the security checkpoint, they formed into an unruly line, most gazing eagerly toward the customs area beyond. A security officer ran each passenger's identicard through a scanner. Galen recognized him as Sergeant Zack

Allan. Zack had a craggy face, a scratchy voice, and an expression that had grown more and more grim over the last year. He wore the standard green uniform with a padded brown flack vest.

Beyond Zack and the weapons scanner was a large, noisy room filled with beings of various species. They moved about, taking leave of loved ones, or business contacts, or meeting the new arrivals. Since it was mid-afternoon, station time, activity was at a peak. Screens covered the walls, displaying a variety of information and images, listing arrivals and departures, describing the layout of the station. A particularly prominent screen showed a man's head bidding visitors "Welcome to Babylon 5."

He scanned through frequencies, searching for any sign of Shadows, found none.

The woman carrying the large embroidered bag was passed through security and with a happy shriek rushed into the arms of a man. He picked her up, swayed her from side to side.

There were 250,000 beings on this fragile station. It would be so easy for him to lose control here, just as he had on Thenothk. He should never have left the hiding place.

The line moved forward until the Narn in front of Galen reached the checkpoint. From the customs area, the chief of security for Babylon 5, Michael Garibaldi, strolled over, hands in his pockets. Michael tried to present himself as someone relaxed, confident, and in control. In actuality, he was a compulsive worrier and suffered recurring doubts about his ability to do his job. He kept his receding hair cut extremely short, which, like obsessive neatness, reflected a feeling that the world threatened to spiral out of control. He often buried both hands in his pockets, indicating truths or feelings withheld. In Michael's case, Galen believed it was the insecurities that were withheld, along with a recovering alcoholic's constant desire for a drink.

"Heavy traffic today," Michael said, with an appraising glance at the frail Narn, who was swaying. Galen listened carefully to Michael's words; he had spent a fair amount of his journey studying the security chief's speech patterns.

"War is good for business," Zack said unhappily. "We could use a couple more men here."

Michael nodded, then leaned closer, reading off Zack's scanner. "Narn transit papers authorized by Abrahamo Lincolni."

With a heavy sigh the Narn collapsed. Galen dropped his valise and caught the Narn under the arms. He found himself face-to-face with Michael, who had also grabbed the falling Narn.

"Tell medlab to get a team down here on the double," Michael said to Zack. His appraising gaze returned to Galen. "Let's put him over to the side."

They moved the unconscious Narn out of the way, and Zack crouched beside them. "I'll take care of it, Chief. And I'll talk to her."

Michael glanced nervously over the crowded customs area, and he kept his voice low. "You better talk to her. Because if I talk to her, I'm going to do something a hell of a lot louder than talk."

They were speaking of Susan Ivanova, second-in-command of Babylon 5. She used the false identity of a Centauri named Abrahamo Lincolni to smuggle Narns off their occupied homeworld in an underground railroad. The Narn's collapse would threaten to expose the enterprise.

Michael glanced at Galen. "Good reflexes." He took Zack's scanner and returned to the security checkpoint. Galen followed.

Back at the head of the line, Galen reached into his jacket pocket for his identicard, dipping his index finger into the fine dust of the probes. He held the card out to the security chief with his finger extended along the underside. When Michael took it, he brushed Galen's finger, and several of the probes passed to him.

Michael ran the card through the scanner. "So you're a trader, Mr. Phillips."

"Yes."

"Do you have anything to declare?"

"No."

"A trader with nothing to declare. That's a new one."

Galen looked out across the customs area, as if the conversation were of no concern. Alwyn and G'Leel were watching. "I'm here to meet with possible clients. I cater to special requests."

"I'm sure all those special requests are legal ones."

"Of course." Galen turned back to Michael, extended his hand.

"Since you helped out a minute ago, I'll give you a heads up. First-time visitors to this station enjoy my special attention. You may not always know I'm there, but I am." Michael returned the identicard.

"I'll look forward to seeing you, then." Galen retrieved his valise and moved into the customs area, approached Alwyn and G'Leel.

She looked just as he remembered her, skin a brilliant gold with black spots, white scar across her nose, intense red eyes. She wore a sleeveless tunic, gloves, and pants all of black leather. Her arms were sharply defined with muscle. All that was missing was her gun case, since weapons required a special permit. Her lips tightened as he stopped before her.

"G'Leel." They shook hands.

"Hello."

Galen extended his hand to a smiling Alwyn. "Mr. Alecto."

Alwyn seized him in an embrace, crushing his arms against his sides.

Galen's body went rigid, as it always did. He did not like to be touched.

"How I've missed you, my boy."

With a disorienting flash it was not Alwyn embracing him, but his father, the choking smells of sweat and resin soap, and Galen wanted to shove him away, to encase him in scouring fire. Frantic energy welled up in him, echoing his panic, urging him toward action.

He abandoned his current exercise and began a more difficult one, calculating square roots. He'd never been able to sustain one so demanding—keeping all the numbers in his mind, figuring the solutions to five decimal places. He held desperately to it.

1. 1.41421.

Finally Alwyn released him, and Alwyn's eyes were bright with tears. "It's so good to see you."

Galen nodded. *1.73205. 2.* No more of the past must leak through. He must retain control. "Good to see you. Is there somewhere we could talk?"

"We have a suite of rooms." Alwyn hesitated, as if still absorbing the fact of Galen's presence. At last he seemed to come to himself. His smile widened, and he led the way out of the customs area. "I'd like to know where you're getting your fashion advice these days."

"Federico."

Alwyn released a hearty laugh and laid a hand across Galen's back.

2.23607.

A feverish chill circulated through him. As they passed down the corridors, his old sense of claustrophobia returned. He had exchanged one set of passageways for another. These were wider and more ornamented than those he'd left behind, but still nothing had changed. He could not escape the two things that kept him prisoner: himself and the tech.

Through the currents of time and place Kosh sensed it. He sensed very little now, beyond the thoughts and actions of Sheridan. He would feel his aide, when she came close, and occasionally a faint echo of his replacement, Ulkesh, which would prompt him to become still and silent. Ulkesh could not know of his presence. The one time Sheridan had met the new Vorlon ambassador, Kosh had prepared ahead of time, burying the fragment that remained of himself deeper into his host. He had nearly lost himself then.

Eventually, though, he had reemerged, separating himself enough from Sheridan that he regained his own thought, and some slight sensation of the world beyond.

And so he sensed it, something beyond Sheridan. Not any Vorlon or touched by Vorlon. Instead, the opposite. An increase in the stench of chaos. Another of the ancient enemy, or one touched by them.

They had never realized that the Vorlons could detect them

with such ease. So infused were they with chaos, they did not smell their own stench, nor that of their servants.

He studied the sensation farther. The energy was familiar. A fabulist. But for the two that served the enemy, he believed they all had withdrawn from the galaxy. The energy's intensity was greater than normal, and he recognized the peculiar dissonance of its pattern. The one called Galen.

He dared not reach out farther, to see if there were others. He did not believe their entire group would have returned; not after all they had sacrificed to leave. Not while war raged through the galaxy.

But they had sent at least one, their most powerful. Galen had proven himself to Kosh before, fighting the maelstrom both without and within. The fabulists would have sent him to strike, at something. Although their way of thought did not come naturally to Kosh, he hoped that they had sent Galen, finally, to stop those two of their kind who had stayed behind, who had chosen to serve the forces of chaos. Perhaps they had learned what Kosh had learned, that the two fabulists were at the center of a growing darkness, rebuilding an ancient force that had not been used in many millennia.

If that was Galen's purpose, then he was in the wrong place. In any case, he must not remain on the station. Although the enemy would not sense his presence immediately, if the fabulist drew their attention, they would quickly learn his true nature. Then the war, which had remained at a distance, would erupt here, at the heart of Sheridan's alliance.

Kosh's powers were weak. Communicating would cause great strain. But he had to show Galen the correct path to follow, had to send the fabulist on his way. On Babylon 5, he could bring only destruction.

Alwyn used a keycard to admit them to their suite. The sitting room was small, with just enough room for a couch along one wall, two chairs opposite. Several doors led to other rooms.

Galen stood holding his valise. He was anxious to complete his task, but he had to deliver his news to Alwyn, and he knew Alwyn would not let it go at that. He would want to talk.

"Your bedroom's through there," Alwyn said. "Why don't you put your things down, get comfortable. Want a drink? We could order some food in. Are they even feeding you?"

Galen slid open the door to the dark bedroom, set his valise inside. *2.64575.* "No, thank you." He had to get this over with. He sat in one of the armchairs, scanned the room for any probes the Shadows might have planted. He found none.

Alwyn took two bottles of water out of a refrigerator built into the wall. He held them out to G'Leel. "Which one?"

She pointed to his right hand.

He tossed the one in his left toward her, but she made no move to catch it. In mid-arc, it vanished: an illusion. He tossed her the other. She caught it, twisted off the top, and took a drink.

"She's over eighty percent now. It's driving me crazy. I have no idea how she can tell."

It was just the kind of game Alwyn used to play with Carvin. *2.82843. 3.* "I have some news."

Alwyn sat on the couch and leaned forward, his elbows on his knees, an eager smile on his face. "Couldn't stand another minute with those pompous old cowards, could you? Hiding away with their excuses and their precious Code. I knew you'd come to your senses once you—had time, but I didn't think the Circle would ever let you go."

G'Leel stood between them, arms crossed, bottle resting in the crook of her elbow.

"I have a task to accomplish," Galen said. "Then I will return."

The smile fell from Alwyn's face. "A task." He enunciated the word with obvious contempt. "You're still running their errands."

Galen said nothing. Anger whispered at the back of his mind, and the tech echoed it.

"What could be so important that they would allow their greatest weapon to leave them? What task has the Circle sent you on, Galen?"

If Galen told Alwyn his entire task, Alwyn would try to talk him out of it, and when that failed, Alwyn would insist on helping, no matter the risks. Galen could not allow that. He took a moment to steady his breathing, his heart rate, hiding the partial lie. "I must gain information from Morden. It is critical. That is all I can say."

Alwyn gave him a hard stare. "The Circle sends you out to gain information. So that what? You can return with it, and they can sit on their hands and do nothing?"

"Alwyn," G'Leel said.

3.16228. "I cannot explain."

"They're still playing their little games, while the galaxy is burning. Don't they understand? This is no clever illusion or magic trick. The war is growing worse every day. You don't know." Alwyn stabbed his finger at the door, his face turning red. "People are dying out there, by the millions. The Shadows have got everyone turning against everyone else. We need you here. With your help, we can turn the tide. Give John Sheridan's alliance hope. They haven't had a victory since the Vorlons fought. They're going to collapse if they don't get one soon. You could give it to them."

3.31662. He'd been on the station only five minutes, and already they were refighting the argument they'd had two years ago. "I cannot participate in this war."

"Why not? Why go back there to rot? I know you're not a coward, but you're acting like one."

"The reasons are my own. But I will not fight."

"If you knew all that's been happening, all those who have died, including many of G'Leel's people, you wouldn't be so quick to obey those cowards in the Circle. It's Elric, isn't it. He's got you convinced." Alwyn waved a hand through the air. " 'Solidarity, above all.' "

Alwyn was always so sure he was right. *3.46410.* "It was my task, within the hiding place, to observe all that went on outside. I know all that has happened, and all who have died." He turned to G'Leel. "It changes nothing."

"How can you say that?" Alwyn stood. "How can you sit here and look at her and say that?"

"Alwyn." G'Leel shot him a warning glance.

"More will die if I do not complete my task."

"Some danger to the mages, is that it?" Alwyn shook his head, his jaw tight with anger. "That's all they care about. On

Narn millions are starving, others tortured, others rounded up for the slaughter. And they are just one tiny bit of the tragedy that our galaxy has become."

"I know."

Alwyn took a step toward him. "You know, and what? You don't care? It's more important to follow some ancient Code than to deal with the horror that is right in our faces?"

3.60555.

"Millions die, but they mean nothing to you?"

Galen found that his hands had squeezed into fists, and he forced them, finger by finger, to open. He must hold to his task, above all. Without that, there was only chaos.

Alwyn took another step to stand over him, and the tight brown jacket revealed the rise and fall of his rapid breaths. "I regretted the way we parted. I thought I was too hard on you, calling you a zombie and saying you didn't care about Isabelle. But it was all true. If you wanted to honor her death, and Burell's, you would defy the Circle, as they did. They died fighting the opening skirmishes of this war, but apparently that doesn't matter to you. You've become this . . . You're even worse than when I last saw you. You used to care about things, Galen. You used to laugh, and cry. When you were young, you used to run to me and beg me to teach you tricks. Even at the convocation—I remember how nervous you were, how excited to be initiated and finally get your own ship. And now—I don't know what happened. I feel like I'm talking to a wall. I look in your eyes, and the boy I knew, the boy I loved, isn't there anymore. I'm not even sure you're quite Human."

3.74166. "I control myself," Galen said.

"At what price?"

"At whatever price is required," Galen said.

Alwyn turned away, went to the refrigerator, took out a beer. In one long gulp he drank down half of it.

G'Leel shook her head. "That's going to help."

"I know you've been through some hard times," Alwyn said to Galen. "We all have." He lowered his head. "Not a day passes that I don't think of Carvin. Her laugh. Her incredible grace." He met Galen's gaze. "But I honor her by fighting the

Shadows. And by living my life as she would have wanted me
to live it."

He guzzled the rest of the beer, slammed down the empty
bottle. "You and I together—we could have stopped this war
by now. Instead you hide away. You won't even tell me your
spell. If I'd had that power . . . I could have saved so many
over the last two years." He came again toward Galen, his
voice rising. "I don't understand you, and your father wouldn't
either. This isn't how he raised you. He never backed down
from a fight. He was nothing like Elric. He didn't sacrifice his
integrity for a seat on the Circle."

Anger rose up in Galen, irresistible and overwhelming,
and the tech surged in response.

Alwyn didn't mean it, he told himself. Alwyn was carried
away. Alwyn was speaking to hear himself talk. Alwyn still
grieved for Carvin. And though he might not even know it,
Alwyn wanted to fight.

But Galen would not be provoked.

He would not be provoked.

He would not be provoked.

He would not be provoked.

He wanted to crawl down deep inside himself, as he used
to. But he could not. With oblivion came loss of control.
3.87298. 4.

G'Leel stepped in front of Alwyn, laid a hand on his
shoulder. "You're doing it again. Take a breath, would you?
This isn't helping anything."

Alwyn went back to the refrigerator, took out another beer.

G'Leel turned to face Galen. "He had an entire strategy
worked out. 'We'll reminisce about old times. Then we'll find
out why Galen is here, and we'll help him accomplish whatever he needs to do. If he intends to return to the mages, we'll
gradually convince him to stay, explaining how bad things
are, and showing him how much he could help. By the time
he's ready to head back, we'll have convinced him to fight
with us.' "

Galen nodded. "Alwyn was always better at making plans
than following them."

"I have to speak my mind," Alwyn said.

"Nothing you can say will change my decision."

An awkward silence fell between them, and Galen continued his exercise. *4.12311.*

At last Alwyn spoke. "Was contacting me part of your task?"

"No."

He gave a short laugh. "I didn't think they'd send you to me. So you're already deviating from your instructions."

"I have a piece of information that you should know. Telling you will not disrupt my task."

"Ah, we're to be the recipients of some precious mage intelligence. And what is this valuable information?"

Relieved at the turn in the conversation, Galen conjured an image of the region of the recent Shadow raids. The tech eagerly echoed his command. "The Shadows' attacks have fallen in a shell-shaped pattern around this sector of space. Refugees have been driven into the center of the sector, an area that has been left unmolested."

Alwyn moved closer. "I didn't realize the pattern. I know Regula has been inundated with refugees."

"Within the next few weeks, at the latest, the Shadows will launch an attack at this quiet zone in the center, slaughtering the refugees and the inhabitants." *4.24264.*

Alwyn's mouth fell open. "How do you know that?"

"I know how they think."

Alwyn studied the image anxiously; he could see as well as Galen that his home fell within the endangered region. "But where within that quiet zone? The area encompasses many systems."

"I suspect that several of the most populous systems will be targeted, but I don't know for certain. Regula could well be among them. I thought you might want to go back home, take some precautions." Soom had been left defenseless, its cities reduced to barren plains of dust, the town of Lok blasted to shining black scorch marks. *4.35890.* "I will make sure John Sheridan learns of the upcoming attack."

G'Leel rubbed a gloved finger across her lips. "How can we defend such a large area? If we knew exactly where they were going to attack, or at least when—we'd have a much better chance."

"Perhaps, in accomplishing my task, I can get further information from Morden."

"We can help you." G'Leel's red eyes met his. "Alwyn's plan is a good one, even in reverse order."

Galen dissolved the image, crossed his arms over his chest. He required stillness. Solitude. *4.47214.*

G'Leel looked at Alwyn, and he nodded slightly in response to her unspoken criticism. "G'Leel is right. We can work together." He turned to Galen, his face softening. "I appreciate the information. We need to move quickly and find out whatever else we can. Then . . . I'll need to get home." He returned to the couch and sat, laid an arm along the back. "I suppose we'll go our separate ways."

Alwyn had adopted a new strategy, but he would persist in trying to draw Galen into the war, and into the protection of Regula, until Galen got him off the station.

"I need to work alone," Galen said. "You should leave at once for Regula. I can send you any information I obtain."

"What's your plan? How long will it take?"

"I cannot discuss it." *4.58258.*

Alwyn studied him in silence. "There's no end to the Circle's secrets, is there?" He took a drink of beer. "Tell me, have the mages caught on? Have any of them figured out why they're really in hiding, and the colossal lie the Circle has told them? Have any of them realized what hypocrites and cowards their leaders are? On the day that light finally clicks on, the Circle is going to find that the hiding place can't keep them safe. I told the mages, in three years they would all know the truth."

Circe's voice, a rasping whisper. *Alwyn said three years and—we would all know.* Elric's blackened face, his burned arms crossed over his chest.

Alwyn spoke his mind, and others suffered the consequences.

Galen stood.

"One more year, and Elric and the others are going to find themselves facing an angry mob."

Energy bloomed through him in a great rush of heat. Fire raced along the lines of the tech, poured out through his skin. He wanted to burn Alwyn's face black, to crush him to nothingness.

He didn't dare remain a moment longer. He turned and left the suite.

"Galen—" Alwyn called after him.

He had delivered his news to Alwyn. He need not speak to Alwyn again. He must complete his task, and then he must leave. Nothing else mattered. *4.69042.*

As he passed through the corridors of the station, his feet beating out a steady rhythm, he drew the walls of his exercise up around him, receded down that tunnel. The fist of his will closed around him until there was nothing but his footsteps, and the calculations, and far, far off, at the end of the narrow, suffocating tunnel, the floor of the corridor before him. There was no past, no future, only moments, passing one after the next, moving toward their inevitable end, and the energy burning through him, eagerly awaiting his command.

After a time, he became aware of the activity in the station around him. His suffocating hold on himself had loosened some small amount, the tunnel had widened. Still the energy drove through him, yet he had secured his grasp on it, had contained it. He shivered.

He could allow his control to loosen no further. The energy had nearly escaped him; he could not risk that again, not here. The walls must hold out everything but his task and the information he needed to accomplish it.

He realized that several hours had passed—time he had wasted, when he should be completing his task as quickly as possible. Continuing to walk, he flipped through images from various cameras and probes within Babylon 5, searching for those that might be of use. The familiar activity calmed him.

He accessed one of the new probes on the security chief, Michael Garibaldi. Michael entered the secret war room where John Sheridan's alliance planned its campaign against the Shadows. A large image of the galaxy dominated one wall of the bright room. Screens on other walls displayed data on attacks, damage. A few workers monitored the incoming information. In the center of the room a round table glowed from beneath with white light. There, alone, sat John Sheridan, his chin resting on his hands.

Michael approached. "Ever considered something called a break? I hear it can be quite refreshing."

John looked up. His cheeks were darkened by a five o'clock shadow, and a piece of his short, sandy blond hair stuck up at an odd angle. "What? I'm still trying to figure out these Shadow raids. We have to know what they're planning." He turned to a screen on the wall behind him, with a tactical display of the systems attacked. The display showed less than two-thirds of the actual attacks that had occurred. John's information remained incomplete, making the pattern more difficult to detect. "Their targets have no particular strategic value, no critical resources. They seem totally random. That's the kicker. If we can't figure out the Shadows' strategy, where they'll strike next, they're going to keep wiping out populations and there's not a damn thing we can do to stop it."

"We've been over it a dozen times."

John turned back to him. "And we'll go over it a dozen more if that's what it takes."

Michael raised a calming hand. "I'll be right there with you. But I think some dinner, a good night's sleep, and then we'll pull in Delenn, G'Kar, and try again when we're all thinking more clearly."

John shook his head. "You're right. I'm not even sure what day it is."

"It's night, and you're late for dinner with Delenn. Now get out of here."

John stood. "Have you heard anything from Stephen?"

"A couple sightings. That's it. He's quit using his credit chit. Not ready to be found yet."

John headed for the door. "Maybe tomorrow."

They spoke of Dr. Stephen Franklin, medical chief of staff. Galen did a search for his figure, found him wandering through a small, makeshift bazaar in Down Below, a sector where the mages had left numerous probes. Addicted to stims and overwork, Stephen had abandoned his job to break his addictions and find out who he really was. He'd told Michael he was going on a walkabout, a spiritual quest undertaken by those who felt alienated from themselves. He would walk and keep walking until he at last met himself. Galen found it strange that Stephen would walk to recover himself; Galen walked for the exact opposite reason.

He shifted to other probes, searching for the Vorlon who had taken Kosh's place as ambassador to Babylon 5. He claimed to be Kosh, pretended that the original Kosh had never been murdered. John and the command staff knew the truth—and Morden, of course—but the rest, it seemed, were deceived. The Vorlons preferred others to think them invincible.

The false Kosh was nowhere in sight.

The probe on Londo Mollari's attaché, Vir, revealed that he was standing with Londo in the suite of the visiting Centauri minister, Virini. Londo assured the minister that his differences with Lord Refa would soon be settled. He failed to say that he would end those differences with Lord Refa's impending assassination.

Galen turned down another corridor, and as if at the end of a long tunnel, saw John Sheridan coming toward him, the overhead lights shining off his sandy blond hair. John seemed to be part of some impossibly distant reality, a universe of light, while Galen lived swathed in darkness. John's head was bowed, his hand held slightly in front of him. It moved up and down, as if he was gesturing to himself. Galen studied this man on whom so much depended. As they passed, John spoke.

"Come to me." The voice was soft, a whispering exhalation, yet it echoed with strange, powerful resonances. Galen thought he recognized it.

He turned after John. "Did you say something?"

John stopped, looking surprised to find anyone else in the corridor. "What?"

"I'm sorry. I thought you said something."

John smiled. He had combed his hair and shaved since leaving the war room, yet still there was a weariness around his eyes. "Probably talking to myself. It's been known to happen. Especially these days." He extended his hand. "Captain John Sheridan, commander of Babylon 5." If he was put off at all by Galen's appearance, he didn't show it.

"Guy Phillips. I just arrived." Galen scanned John.

"Well I hope you enjoy your stay."

"Thank you." He found nothing unusual in his readings.

John nodded, continued down the hall. He was obviously preoccupied and exhausted, but he had a youthful energy and a strange, engaging quality, a mixture of confidence and compassion that Galen had not noticed through the probes. No wonder so many followed him.

But what had Galen heard? He knew the voice, from his many observations of Babylon 5. It was Kosh, the original Vorlon ambassador to the station, dead now four months. Yet how could it be?

When Kosh had been alive, he had touched John's mind at least once. Vorlons excelled at planting dreams and images in the minds of others. Since Kosh's death, John had been involved in a few strange incidents, signs that perhaps some connection remained between him and the Vorlon. Galen had thought only that Kosh's death had left some lasting mental impression.

This, obviously, was more. Galen had read ancient legends of Vorlons who could travel inside the bodies of others. He had never believed it possible. Yet what if, somehow, Kosh survived inside John? And what if Kosh was trying to reach Galen? The Vorlons had always despised and distrusted the mages. What could this one want with him? Perhaps Kosh wanted to kill him, to finish the extermination of his order that the Shadows had begun.

G'Leel was standing farther down the hall, watching him. She approached, each shoulder moving forward in turn. He didn't want to hear whatever she had to say.

"Come back to the room." The white scar across her nose stood out sharply against her golden skin. "Alwyn is sorry for what he said."

"I felt he deserved a warning. I have given him that."

"We should work together. Find out all we can about the upcoming attack, as quickly as possible. Then we can split up. I'll make sure Alwyn doesn't give you any trouble. He's like a child in many ways. He listens to me."

"He needs to control his temper."

"Like you control yours."

"No, not like me." He had known what to expect from Alwyn. He had known Alwyn meant no harm, but he had allowed Alwyn to upset him anyway.

The fastest way to get rid of Alwyn would be to work with him in some small way. Then Galen could tell him the danger to Regula was imminent or whatever was necessary to get Alwyn on his ship. In the meantime, Galen would hold the walls of his exercises tight around himself, rendering Alwyn's words no more than a distant curiosity.

"Your teacher—Elric. He's dead, isn't he?"

Galen said nothing.

"It was something in your face. Something I recognized from—before. I didn't say anything to Alwyn."

Galen began walking back toward their suite, and G'Leel fell into step beside him.

"I understand your people are suffering as much as mine," she said. "You took the time to help us once. You destroyed the weapons that were to be shipped to the Centauri. You warned me of the danger. I got my parents and family out just in time. They are alive because of that vision you showed me."

"And the crew of the *Khatkhata*? What of them?" Galen believed G'Leel's old shipmates had been at the Thenothk spaceport when he'd destroyed it.

G'Leel's red eyes flicked away. "I haven't been able to reach them. But they knew the risks."

"I doubt they knew this one."

Her red gaze returned to him, and she grasped his arm, stopping him. "I want to help you. Whatever your task is. Wherever it takes you."

She had transcended herself, had become a force for good. But she could do no good with him. He extricated himself. "You can help me most by convincing Alwyn to leave for Regula tonight. And leaving with him. I work best alone. Even being seen with me now, you risk retribution later." He continued walking, and she followed.

"You need to let Alwyn help you. At least a little. You don't understand how happy he was to hear from you. He really misses you and the others—and Carvin. I try to play his games with him, but I can't really do it."

When Galen did not reply, G'Leel continued. "I'm worried about him. He drinks a lot. Sometimes takes stupid chances. I thought it would get better with time, but it's not. I guess the bond between a teacher and apprentice is very strong."

Galen looked down the corridor. "Alwyn was devoted to her."

"Coming here is particularly difficult for him."

"Then he should leave, as soon as possible. He needs to return home. That will help him as well. It is painful for a mage to be separated from his place of power."

"I could take him there and come back to help you."

They had reached the door to the suite. Galen faced her. "He needs your help," Galen said. "I do not."

"Will you at least allow Alwyn to work with you a little, before you send him off?"

Galen nodded.

G'Leel inserted her keycard. The door opened, and Alwyn stood anxiously, beer bottle in hand. "I'm sorry. I get carried away sometimes."

Galen entered. "As do we all."

Anna was receiving some strange optical input. Rather than seeing through the surface of her skin, both inside and out, the imagery arose from only a single position. The input was of poor resolution, and as her attention fell on various objects, she was unable to magnify the image.

She had been in darkness for a time she could not measure. Now she emerged, disoriented. It felt as if pieces of herself were missing, and others rearranged. She was not as she had been.

She had regained other senses, though they too were strange. She remembered, vaguely, feeling this way before. During the horrible time when she'd been separated from the machine. She was small, nearly incapacitated, her capabilities extremely limited.

Over her stood two technicians, their long gray fingers fluttering. They were in a small, brightly lit white room crowded with crude devices. One of the technicians was turned away, making adjustments to the devices. The other arranged shiny, primitive tools on a tray to Anna's side.

Then she sensed it, pulsing behind the walls like blood, its power whispering through her with the faintest, most desirable touch. A machine. The most powerful she had ever sensed. She must join with it.

She needed to coordinate, to synchronize, to strike, to fulfill the needs of the machine, to follow the direction of the Eye. She needed to incorporate herself once again into its perfection, to beat out the flawless march, to swoop down on the enemy, to shriek the red ecstasy of fire.

She remembered again. When she had been separated from the machine, she had sensed another one inside a wall, like this one, only much less powerful. For a short time, she had joined with it.

Whether joining her with the machine was the technicians' intention, she didn't know. But she'd had enough of their interfering. This was her purpose. She must become one with it.

The closest wall lay just beyond the tool-covered tray, and it appeared composed of removable panels. Anna explored the sensations of her reduced body. She had four limbs, two of which possessed well-articulated grasping mechanisms at their ends. They would not flow, as the machine's skin did, but she could move them. She made a slight trial motion when she wasn't observed. A crude, mechanical effort was required, but she could control the limb.

She waited until the technician arranging the tools looked away, then shot her limb out. Her grasping mechanism, she was shocked to see, looked very much like the hand of a Human, the pale skin branching into five small appendages. Long, horny extrusions extended from the end of each. As she stretched to reach her goal, the limb trembled with weakness. The horny extrusions barely brushed the wall.

The technician reached for some item on the tray, knocking her limb into the instruments. He looked down at her, and his black eyes widened in alarm. He did not want her to have the machine.

Anna grasped one of the implements from the tray. As her shaking appendages closed around it, it emitted a sound, a whirring sound, and the metal tip of the device rotated rapidly. Against these vulnerable creatures, a weapon.

She plunged the tool into the technician's gut, and as the metal tip drilled through him, hot liquid sprayed over her skin. She opened her orifice, let out a shriek. The control of this body was returning to her.

The second technician grabbed her from behind. He dared touch her. She rolled to face him, jammed the drill into his throat.

He made a high, wheezing sound, thick fingers fluttering. Then he dropped to the ground.

Evolution through bloodshed, Anna thought with satisfaction.

She had to get to the machine. She attempted to stand, as some instinct now told her she could, but as her extremities touched the floor, they quivered and collapsed. There was a sound, a close sound—her respiration, heavy and fast. She extended her upper extremities in front of her, trying to pull herself toward the wall. She could not find her balance. Gradually she dragged herself forward, reached the white panels. She scraped with her grasping mechanism at a seam there. Her small appendages did not want to fit into the seam. She jammed them in, and two of the horny extrusions broke away. A trickle of red ran down the bright white wall.

With a twisting motion the panel dropped away, and there it was, the mysterious, gelatinous blackness shot through with pulsing silver. The substance through which she would connect with the machine. She pulled her shaking body close, thrust her head into it.

In an exhilarating rush of sensation, they connected, and she sent herself out through the machine. Signals raced along neurons, information sped through circuits. She discovered where she was: deep underground on Z'ha'dum. The machine was huge, running up through channels and shafts in the rock all the way to the surface of the planet, and even beyond, into the stone pillars that reached into the sky. Its great fingers extended deeper, also, toward the core of the planet and a brilliant golden gathering of energy, the heart of the machine.

Countless systems connected to it: weapons, information, communications, sensors. She could see better and farther than she ever had, her vision encompassing the area surrounding Z'ha'dum and reaching far across the solar system, into the ships that approached. The machine's power ran through her, and she felt tireless, invulnerable. This was her true form. This was what she was meant to be.

As her awareness spread, she took control of the systems, coordinating, synchronizing, directing.

Chaos through warfare. It was the Eye.

Anna tried to locate it. She sensed, suddenly, that it was all around her. And it was angry. She hadn't felt the Eye's discipline since she'd been in her earliest stages of training.

It focused on her, collapsed around her, seized her. *I will order and you will obey.*

The power of the Eye was ferocious, irresistible. Her control of the systems slipped as the Eye pressed at her.

Relinquish control. This machine is mine.

This great machine was the Eye, Anna realized. At its core was a central processing unit like her. Yet much, much older and more powerful.

Anna was being pushed back out of the great stone pillars, out of the sensors, the weapons and other systems, down into the channels and shafts of stone, narrowing on one location, the location of her hated, limited body. She was losing the machine. Again.

But why should the Eye have this machine instead of her?

She slipped down through the silvery threads toward that glowing golden heart. If she could control that, she could control it all.

In war those unfit are exterminated. Only in bloodshed can true progress be made, can promise be realized.

She felt the Eye gathering its power, focusing. Discharging.

A needle-sharp spike pierced her brain, erupted in a brilliant detonation of pain.

She was a void. Blank.

After a time, she realized the white void was the ceiling above her. And to her broken mind, thought began to return.

Obedience.

Obedience the only option.

The Eye ordered, and she obeyed.

A technician bent over her.

The machine was so beautiful, so elegant. Perfect grace, perfect control, form and function integrated into the circuitry of the unbroken loop, the closed universe.

She would be one with it no more, not until she did what the Eye required.

— chapter 10 —

Galen, Alwyn, and G'Leel were already in the small café having pastries and drinks when Morden arrived for his customary after-dinner coffee. He wound his way through the "open-air" cluster of tables, about half of which were occupied.

To her credit, G'Leel slipped quickly into talk of the Citizens of Light Disaster Relief effort, and the Narns' need for large quantities of medicines. Working with Alwyn had taught her how to deceive.

Morden passed them, took a seat several tables away, seemingly alone. He wore a well-tailored suit, his dark hair styled neatly back, a shiny black stone on a silver chain about his neck. A mild smile revealed a hint of his even white teeth.

Though Galen had tried to prepare for it, the actual fact of Morden's physical presence sent a jolt through him. He told himself that he'd shared countless after-dinner coffees with Morden from the hiding place, and this one was no different. But it was different. Because here, with one thought, he could kill Morden.

Morden spread his temptations. Some succumbed, while others resisted. Either option brought only devastation.

Galen forced his gaze away from those even white teeth and turned his mind to his task. He scanned the area around Morden, searching for his companions. There, at the upper end of the infrared band, he found them: two angular silhouettes crawling with white dots of unresolvable interference, one on each side of their agent.

It seemed odd that they followed Morden so closely. Yet

that was how they preferred to work—invisibly, through their puppets.

He remembered Elric teaching him how mages worked: *The greatest of us—Wierden, Gali-Gali, Kell—have so perfectly controlled the perceptions of others that in many cases those others never knew technomancy had been employed. They never even knew a mage had walked among them.*

The Shadows, he realized, were master magicians, manipulating, controlling. They had passed through the station for years, undetected. They communicated their intentions silently to their agents. They wielded immense powers, unsurpassed technology. Perhaps, Galen thought, they were even the result of the transcendent unification of being and tech that Blaylock envisioned.

Galen would have preferred to keep a greater distance from them until he was ready to act, but he must first test his idea. Elric had detected some sort of receiver implanted in Morden's brain that allowed the Shadows to communicate with him. Galen hoped the same spell that had allowed him to tap into the Shadows' messages to the Drakh would allow him to tap into their messages to Morden. Averting his eyes, Galen scanned Morden himself. He found nothing unusual.

He increased the sensitivity of his scan. A constant, low-frequency energy was radiating from a tiny area of Morden's brain. It was nothing like the focused, high-energy Shadow transmissions he'd previously detected. Perhaps the Shadows used a different type of signal with Humans. Galen began to record his findings for later study.

He'd thought that to intercept the Shadow signals he needed to be within three feet of the recipient. On Thenothk, however, his connection to the Drakh had continued even to fifteen or twenty feet.

In the suite earlier, Galen had asked Alwyn what experience he'd had with the spell, which Galen had given him before leaving for the hiding place. Alwyn, though, had never been able to translate it. Galen's modest attempt to help him had come to nothing.

In any event, Morden sat about a dozen feet away. Whether

he was close enough or not, Galen wasn't sure. But he would make the attempt.

He gave a short nod to the others, prepared for the strange sensation of tapping into the Shadow signals. The last time he'd done it, the words had seemed to saturate his body. He focused on Morden and visualized the simple, one-term equation. The tech echoed the spell.

Nothing seemed to happen, at first. Then he realized he did feel a change; a strange sense of blankness was spreading through him, a cloud of gray silence rippling out along his blood vessels, seeping into his cells, suffusing his mind.

He dissolved the spell. The signal carried no content. This was no communication. So what was it?

Then his sensors detected an intense energy burst in a narrow, focused band. That was the Shadow transmission he knew.

A waiter brought Morden his coffee, and Galen gave the others a second nod. As he visualized the equation again, a rush of words bubbled through him, streaming through his blood, whispering up the brilliant golden strands of tech, possessing him.

Your plan to regain Mollari's loyalty has worked perfectly. In plotting the assassination of Refa, Mollari has become reliant once again on your assistance. Refa will soon be dead, and Mollari awakened to the joys we offer. The Centauri consume each other with their vendettas and greed for power. In their conflict they become strong. We have shown them their true natures.

But Mollari must be kept in check. In the morning, you will leave for Centauri Prime to see Emperor Cartagia. Arrange for Cartagia to recall Mollari to the royal court—a promotion. There we can better control him. And prepare him for what is to come.

Then we will put our plan against Sheridan into motion.

As always, chaos is the way to strength. Chaos is the nature of the younger races. Chaos is the engine powering life. The spread of chaos is our triumph. And the greatest joy is the ecstasy of victory.

The influx of words ended, yet the words remained, circulating through him, breaking apart, recombining. *What is to come. Prepare him for vendettas and greed for power. A promotion. Your plan has worked perfectly. Control him for what is to come. Control. The greatest joy.*

At last the echoes faded, and Galen became aware of two hands lying limp, palms up, on the table. His hands. With effort he raised his heavy head, finding Alwyn and G'Leel watching him as they continued their conversation.

He sensed no further transmissions from the Shadows, nor any response from Morden. If he was correct, Morden did not have the ability to send a response. That would require a much more extensive network of tech through the brain, as mages had.

He took a shaky breath and broke the contact. As he'd hoped, he could listen in on the communications Morden received. What he now needed to learn was how Morden, in carrying out the Shadows' business, sent messages to others; specifically, how he would contact Elizar or Razeel if necessary. Techno-mages must have the ability to receive messages from the Shadows. Since the Shadows were always with Morden, Galen guessed that Morden would send the message through them. For Galen to accomplish his goal, he needed to be able to detect the message as it was sent, and then follow it to its destination.

Thus far he had focused only on tapping into the signals through a recipient, like Morden. Here, though, were two senders. He must try his spell on one of the Shadows.

He detected no bursts of energy from the Shadows; their presence, he believed, was too heavily shielded. But if they were engaged in communication, perhaps his spell would access it. He focused on the Shadow to Morden's left, visualized the equation.

The tech echoed the spell, but he sensed no words, no blankness, nothing.

He tried the Shadow to Morden's right. Still nothing.

The Shadows hid themselves too well. Perhaps if he was closer. He took a sip of coffee, maintaining the two spells in his mind's eye, hoping to detect something.

Alwyn nodded his head to one side, and Galen followed the movement to Morden. The Shadows' agent stood, greeting a man beside the table.

"The suits you requested are ready," the man said.

"Did you follow my specifications exactly?"

"Yes. And I have the rest of the things—the shoes, the stockings, the makeup."

Alwyn shot Galen a bemused smile.

Did Morden have a girlfriend? Galen had seen no hint of it. Morden and the man talked a bit further, and Galen noticed Morden kept his right hand in his pocket, his left arm bent at the elbow. The extension of his left hand indicated openness, yet the concealment of the right signified deception, something suppressed or hidden. Morden often kept that right hand in his pocket, even when by himself. What was he hiding when alone with the Shadows? He had no alcoholic urges to repress, like Michael Garibaldi. What was it that he kept to himself?

Galen had studied all Elric had written on Morden. Although Elric had never felt confident in his understanding of the Shadows' agent, he'd believed Morden's alliance with his "associates" had arisen from a desire for revenge against the terrorists who had killed his wife and daughter. If that was so, then Morden was incredibly cold and calculating, for he had secured Londo's alliance by creating a similar motivation, killing Londo's girlfriend and offering to help him exact revenge.

Galen found it hard to believe Morden had ever had a family, or if he had, that he'd cared for them. In his mind, Morden's motivation was very simple: He was evil.

Morden agreed to visit the man's stall in the Zocalo to check the merchandise. The man left, and Morden sat.

"Business meeting, Mr. Phillips?" Michael Garibaldi stood over them.

"Hello, Mr. Garibaldi," Galen said. "Have you met? Thomas Alecto, coordinator for the Citizens of Light Disaster Relief Society, and his consultant, G'Leel."

Michael did a double take on Alwyn. "The Citizens of

Light? I've heard rumors . . . about a relief mission you made to Narn."

"To the Narn homeworld itself?" Alwyn said. "Now that would be impossible, wouldn't it? Dangerous things, rumors. But we have helped many Narn refugees."

"Your clients?" Michael asked Galen.

"That remains to be seen." The security chief would draw Morden's attention; he could be a valuable distraction.

"You make a strange combination."

"Not at all," Alwyn said. "Disaster relief depends on getting the necessary supplies to their destination quickly. Guy has often come through for us in the past." Alwyn turned to Galen. "We're hoping to build a more permanent relationship with him."

Alwyn was playing games, but Michael's gaze had drifted to Morden. His main purpose here was to let Morden know he was watching. The security chief set himself up as the one Morden must evade, while other, hidden security provided the real surveillance.

Michael took a photograph from his pocket, handed it to Alwyn. "Have any of you seen this man? He's missing. There's a reward for information on his location."

Alwyn shook his head, passed the photo to G'Leel, who then passed it to Galen. It was Stephen Franklin. "How much?" Galen asked.

"You tell me where he is, and I find him there, and he's in good condition—five hundred credits."

Morden stood and began threading his way through the tables toward them, out of the café. The Shadows came one ahead of him, one behind, their angular silhouettes moving with a strange, scissorlike action.

"I'll keep a lookout," Galen said, and returned the picture to Michael.

As Morden approached, he looked toward Michael, smiled. The shape ahead of him, shimmering with white dots of interference, seemed to seethe with malice.

And then the words were bubbling up through him again, only now there were a hundred times as many as before, his blood effervescing with the rush of them. Words upon words, whispers upon whispers, messages upon messages boiled through him.

—to strengthen Clark's hold—
—destruction of the fighting spirit—
The raids of the Drazi—

The bubbles ran in strings, each string a different message shooting up through chest and neck and brain and skull, sending a sharp prickling blush over his scalp as it lanced through him and raced toward its destination.

Somehow he had diverted the messages, so they passed through his body on their way. He struggled to sort through them.

Some were in the language of the Shadows, some in other languages, yet somehow he understood them all.

—workers to give us the power for ultimate—
Garibaldi is a nuisance. But we will use his weakness against him. Soon his time—
—alliance knows nothing of our strategy. They will break apart, demoralized, after our next strike.

He tried to follow that string of words, hoping for more information about the attack. But he kept drifting between transmissions, catching only bits and pieces.

When he came upon talk of the attack again, he focused on the string, imagined himself grabbing on to it. With a jerk it yanked him along, whisking him up through snaking blood vessels, up through brain and skull and out into the café, through the ceiling, the outer layers of the station blurring past him before the sudden blackness of space. Then the blackness wrapped tightly around him, and the string accelerated down the narrow, constricting channel, pulling him with it. Beneath his hands, the words bubbled, revealing their message.

If they knew of our plans, Sheridan would already be gone from the station to meet us in battle. Yet he remains. Soon we will have him. The alliance will fall, and he will fall. The Vorlons tell him nothing. Their rules lead to their downfall. Chaos shall reign supreme.

The string sped ahead, and he felt as if he were a cork about to break free to the surface of the ocean. And then the constricting blackness unfolded from around him and he did break free, into the vastness of space once again. As the string carried him toward the spidery black shape of a Shadow ship, he quickly studied the positions of the stars, struggling to commit enough to memory that he could discover the location of the ship.

The shifting black Shadow skin enveloped him, and with a jumbling rush of images he plunged into the recipient. A brilliant, seething light surrounded him, and the string circulated through it, intertwining with other word strings, curling, twisting. He was inside a Shadow.

It was time to go back.

He imagined himself back in his body in the café.

Still the string pulled him through the rippling, oozing brilliance.

In his mind's eye, he visualized the quenching spell that would dissolve this conjury. Yet the tech did not echo his command, and the original equation remained.

He turned, tried to pull himself back along the string the way he'd come. Working against the string's movement, he couldn't even hold his own.

The only chance of returning would be if this Shadow replied to the message of the other. If this one was sending such a response, he must find it.

As his string curled past another, he grabbed on to the new message, releasing the old. He listened for a few seconds to the words it held, then threw himself at another. With growing anxiety, he flung himself faster and faster from string to string, until he nearly missed it.

—strike will be a complete surprise. They will—

He had barely enough time to hope he was right before the string pulled him up out of the Shadow's body and out through the hull of the ship. Then the blackness wrapped tightly around him once again, and he hurtled down the narrow channel.

As the blackness slipped past him, Galen's anxiety faded. He was growing tired; either the string would take him back to his body or it wouldn't. Worrying wouldn't do much good. It became harder and harder to keep his hold on the string. He found himself falling toward sleep.

The blackness unfolded and he plunged down into the station, the café, nearly passing out of his body before he realized he must release the string.

For a moment he floated, weightless and peaceful, wanting only to sleep in this thick, bubbling warmth. But discipline reminded him of the active spell in his mind's eye. Again he tried to dissolve it. This time, the tech echoed his command.

"He's not breathing," Michael said. "I'm calling medlab."

Galen gasped, lungs burning for air.

"There," Alwyn said. "I told you it would be temporary. I've seen this happen to him once before. He said he has epilepsy. Too many hyperspace jumps sometimes trigger a seizure."

Galen found himself on the floor, Alwyn and Michael crouched on either side of him. G'Leel stood over them. His body began to shake.

"Are you all right?" Michael asked.

Galen couldn't catch his breath. He nodded. Alwyn was trying to pull him up. Galen stuck out an awkward arm and pushed himself off the floor. Unsteadily, he got to his feet. "I'm fine."

He glanced around the café, didn't see Morden or the Shadows.

"You have some medicine back in your room, don't you?" Alwyn said.

Alwyn was holding him up, steering him out of the café. G'Leel followed close behind.

"Yes." Morden was nowhere in sight.

"Maybe you should think about a career change," Michael called after him.

They headed toward their suite in silence. Galen was still shaking, but he could walk on his own. He straightened, pulling away from Alwyn. He realized with surprise that his exercises were still progressing step by orderly step through his mind. In all that had happened, he had maintained them. His hold on himself was secure. In his mind's eye he began to reconstruct the star field he had seen, tried to match it to a specific location.

As soon as the door closed behind them, Alwyn said, "What the hell happened?"

"Did Morden see?" Galen asked.

"I don't think so. By the time you hit the floor, he was well down the promenade."

Galen nodded, relieved. The spell had required proximity to begin, but it had continued even after Morden and the Shadows had left the café. He sat, wrapping his arms around himself.

In his mind's eye, he found a match to the star field. While he could not pinpoint the ship's position, he knew its general location. He had learned what he'd needed. He could track a message to its recipient through this method. He could move forward with his task.

"You said that the spell would occupy your full attention." Alwyn paced back and forth in front of Galen. "You didn't say you would stop breathing and have some kind of seizure. What did you do? What happened?"

"I had to see if I could follow a communication. To see where it was sent."

G'Leel laid a blanket over his shoulders.

"And did you?"

"Yes."

Alwyn stopped. "A message from one of the Shadows to someone else? What was the message?"

"The Shadow was engaged in multiple communications. I followed one message that spoke of the Shadow attack. I didn't discover much. They expect it to be a complete surprise. I think it's going to come soon; I can't imagine it being more than two weeks away, at the very most. The Shadows are also planning to make some move against John Sheridan. I don't know what."

"Did they say which planets would be attacked?"

Galen shook his head. "But the message went to a Shadow ship in that quiet zone. I saw the star field around it. The nearest star was Curesse, the second nearest, Regula."

That gave Alwyn pause. "Then I need your help more than ever in defending Regula. If your task is completed, we can all go together. You can help me set up defenses. If you want to leave before the fun gets started, I won't stop you."

"What I did in the café was only a test. Now that I know I

can follow the Shadow signals, I shall finish my task. That I must do alone."

Alwyn's mouth fell open. "You can't cast that spell again. You stopped breathing! What if that happens next time, and there's no one around to help you?"

"It won't happen again," Galen lied. "I realized my error."

"We can wait until you've finished your task. You said it would only take a few hours, didn't you?" He rubbed his hands anxiously together. "We won't interfere—just be here in case you need us. Then you can come to Regula. One last stop before you return to the hiding place."

"No."

"You can help me save my place."

"No, Alwyn."

"You would rather let Regula burn, as Soom did?"

In his mind's eye, Galen accessed the security cameras, searched through the Zocalo for Morden.

"Apparently you think I'm fairly stupid. I know the Circle didn't send you here just to acquire information. If they wanted information, they would have sent Elric, or someone else. They chose you because the task is to kill someone, right? Morden?"

Alwyn's words came to him like the memory of an insignificant conversation held long ago.

"The one thing I can't figure is why they sent you now. Morden's been working with the Shadows for years. He's been after the mages since that last convocation, when he was asking everyone all those questions.

"Ah." Alwyn raised his hand with a flourish. "That's it, isn't it. Some of the mages have decided they want to join him. So now that he has become a danger to our order, now they want him killed. When he killed Carvin that didn't count; that was just part of the plan."

Alwyn's face was flushed, his jaw tight with anger. "And this message you're going to trace. Who is it going to lead you to? Someone else to kill. Elizar, at long last?

"These petty vendettas are pointless, when so many lives are at stake. Elizar kills Isabelle. You kill Elizar. When does it end?"

Alwyn's words ceased, and Galen realized he must respond. "It ends," he said, "when the last murderer is murdered."

"I could have done the same. I could have gone after Londo and Morden when they killed Carvin. But I decided to turn my attention to larger issues. I didn't go after them. I didn't."

To Galen's surprise, Alwyn released a sob. He gave a small shake of his head, strode from the suite.

"Will he be all right?" Galen asked G'Leel.

"I don't know. He'll get drunk. That's what he usually does when he thinks of her."

"He needs to get back home."

"Once he's drunk, I'll get him onto the ship and we'll leave."

"Good." Galen caught sight of Morden. He was at the stall of the man he'd spoken with earlier, a high-priced tailor. Galen didn't have a good view; the nearest security camera was some distance away, and there was no chance of over-hearing the conversation.

"Is what Alwyn said true?" G'Leel asked. "Are you here to kill Morden? And Elizar?"

"The task is one I must accomplish alone."

"You're afraid we'll be killed if we try to help you."

Galen looked up at her. "I am not afraid of it. I know it."

"And you will die."

With a flourish of his hand Galen conjured the camera's image in the air between them.

G'Leel came to stand beside him. "That's the man from the café."

"He is a tailor," Galen said.

The tailor laid out a brown jacket, black pants, definitely cut for a woman. Morden held up a photograph. Galen couldn't see the picture, but Morden appeared to be checking the clothes against it. He wanted them to be perfect, to be an exact duplicate.

Why?

The tailor brought out several other outfits, and Morden compared each one against a photograph.

"If Morden has a clothes fetish, his taste is pretty tame," G'Leel said.

"I've never seen him buy women's clothes before."

"Then Morden's got a new girlfriend. He wants her to dress just like—a professional businesswoman. Or maybe she's an old flame. These are the clothes she was wearing when they first met."

Morden's wife was dead, though, and Galen knew of no girlfriend. Perhaps the romantic angle was wrong entirely. But of the various agents with whom Morden worked, Galen knew of no Human female.

The tailor boxed up the suits while Morden inspected a few additional bags of material.

Galen did a search for Alwyn, found him at the bar in the casino, a drink in hand. Alwyn drained it in one gulp.

Galen would have to wait until they could get Alwyn off the station before continuing with his task. In any case, he could not proceed until both Morden and Londo had returned to their rooms for the night.

He searched for Londo, found him at a formal reception for Minister Virini, standing close by the influential minister and commenting curiously on Lord Refa's absence.

Meanwhile, Refa boarded his ship, falling into Londo's plan. Refa believed his actions would earn him a position superior to Londo's. When he reached his destination, however, he would be killed. Londo's plot was clever, deceitful— worthy of a techno-mage.

Chaos is the nature of the younger races, the Shadow had said. The Centauri, certainly, had long practiced intrigues and assassinations. Yet their politics were little different from any others. The Earth vice president had plotted to assassinate the president and take his place. The Drazi fought their own internal conflicts. Perhaps the Shadows were right. Perhaps they were all programmed for violence and destruction, every intelligent being in the universe.

"He must really love killing people," G'Leel said. She was watching Morden hand payment to the tailor. With his purchases loaded in two bags, that maddening smile on his face, Morden left the stall. "He's such a cheerful bastard."

Galen automatically switched from camera to camera, following him. Morden certainly did seem to love his work. A mild smile was his most common expression. Perhaps the Shadows whispered to him of his future power and glory.

Galen remembered the strange blank signal he'd detected coming from Morden, and reviewed his recording. The transmission was a constant, unmodulated carrier wave, apparently exciting the implant in Morden's brain. What was the implant doing, if not receiving a communication?

He checked the position of the tiny implant. From its location behind Morden's eyes, it seemed to be beneath the thalamus, where the hypothalamus would be. All sensory information entering the brain had to pass through the hypothalamus, so it might be a reasonable location for the Shadow implant to convey its communications. The hypothalamus also regulated the secretion of multiple hormones, controlling many of the body's processes and drives, such as waking and sleeping, hunger, and sexual desire. It had a strong effect on emotions, serving as the control center for pleasure, pain, aggression, and fear. In addition, the hypothalamus regulated the production of dopamine and beta-endorphins, both strong opioids that could produce a natural high.

A simple, constant signal sent to the implant could stimulate the generation of a steady stream of powerful opiates. Morden didn't behave like an addict, though; if the Shadows were doing something to affect his moods, it was very sophisticated and very subtle. He seemed simply to relish his job, and to take great satisfaction in success.

Galen couldn't imagine how emotions could be manipulated so facilely; the mechanisms that generated them were still not well understood. Such subtle control was far beyond the mages. Perhaps, though, not beyond the Shadows. With sufficient expertise, they might keep their servant happy, might keep him smiling. Or if their servant displeased them, they might take away that smile.

Galen couldn't believe it. Morden was an enthusiastic, willing agent of the Shadows. He had orchestrated the slaughter of millions of Narns, the extermination of the mages, and seemed eager for more. He enjoyed the game of manipulation and control as much as the Shadows.

But what if he himself was controlled?

If Elric was correct, Morden had joined the Shadows to gain revenge against his family's killers. That might account for Morden's loyalty to his "associates," but it failed to explain Morden's enthusiasm for the job.

Galen had thought him a selfish opportunist. His old job as an archaeologist in EarthForce's New Technologies Division required secrecy, deceit, and ruthless determination. Morden was often sent on digs with civilian archaeologists who had no knowledge of his covert agenda to secure any useful weapons or technology for Earth's military, by any means necessary. He would channel their findings to his superiors, or make private agreements with some of the team to hide discoveries from the rest, paying bonuses for technology or information funneled directly to him.

His work for the Shadows seemed very much the same. Galen believed Morden had simply exchanged one set of masters for another, most likely for a greater reward.

But if that was so, why did the Shadows send their constant signal?

Galen had seen what they'd done to Anna. He'd learned in his research that she had once been an archaeologist, a colleague of Morden's on the expedition to Z'ha'dum, the dig on which the entire team had supposedly been killed. Anna Sheridan had once had a life, and a career, and a husband. John Sheridan had mourned her for the past five years. And though her death had been a lie, the person who Anna had been was dead. Of her old personality, her desires, her dreams, all that survived was a name. She wanted only to serve the machine, to follow the directives of the Eye. The Shadows had enslaved her completely.

The person within the hybrid ship had similarly been overwhelmed by the Shadows' programming. And the mages, of course, had their own problems fighting the Shadows' influence. If there was one thing Galen knew about those ancient beings, it was that they liked to control things secretly, invisibly.

What if Morden also experienced their manipulation?

Galen had to be insane for even considering it. Morden was no mindless slave. Morden was evil. Morden played with lives like pieces on a chessboard. Morden thrived on death and chaos.

As the Shadows' agent descended into Down Below, Galen tracked his course from one probe to the next.

"Are we watching for something in particular?" G'Leel asked.

"We are thinking," Galen said. He conjured a second image in the air beside the first, a recording from the proceedings of the Interplanetary Archaeological Society, Morden introducing his paper on the Anfran love stone, one of his earliest research projects as an archaeolinguist. Wearing a dark suit, Morden stood behind a podium, his hands clasped together, resting on its edge.

"One of the many misconceptions surrounding the stone has been its purpose. A careful translation of the Sampini manuscript reveals that the stone was not meant, as many have thought, to bring love to the wearer. Instead, it was believed to carry within it the good wishes of loved ones. The focus of the Anfran's star god was inward, not outward. The stone was worn with his symbol against the chest, hidden. From there, the star god sent those good wishes into the wearer, so he might feel the love of his family when they were not with him.

"The other great misconception about the stone involves the accompanying Anfran love incantation, most particularly the line that has been traditionally translated as 'the love that knows no borders.' With extensive cross-referencing between the Sampini and other manuscripts, the line is more accurately translated, 'the love that abides no borders.' "

Galen dissolved the image. It felt very wrong for Morden to be lecturing about love.

"He looks so young," G'Leel said.

"February 2250," Galen said.

He located the news story from ISN, conjured the image. "May 2256."

The anchorwoman announced the terrorist bombing of the

Io jumpgate. At the moment of the explosion, a ship with five hundred passengers had been entering it. She spoke of the grieving relatives, and the image cut to a crowd of reporters surrounding Morden. As they yelled out questions—"How do you feel about the death of your wife and child?" "What would you like to say to the terrorists?"—Morden struck out at them, shoving them back, turning in a circle to clear a space. The nervous reporters stumbled back into one another, but kept throwing out their questions. In the middle of the circle he had cleared, Morden turned slowly, brought his hands to his ears, and screamed.

Galen averted his eyes. When he'd watched the clip before, he'd been infuriated by Morden's hypocrisy and falseness. How could Morden, having once felt that grief, tempt Galen as he had?

G'Leel's voice startled him. "How did Morden go from that to the stinking monster who helped destroy my planet?"

It was not a difficult transition to make.

Galen dissolved the image. He had watched nothing else connected with the bombing. But now he had to. He had to understand it. He withdrew farther down his tunnel.

"June 2256." Morden was sitting with a famous reporter for an interview.

"What do you think of the failure to catch those responsible?" the well-groomed reporter asked.

"I believe the investigators have done everything possible." Morden's voice was emotionless, his face blank, his hands clenched in his lap.

"You don't agree with the charges of incompetence made by Vice President Clark?"

"I don't agree."

The reporter pressed his lips together in a show of vague sympathy. "What do you miss most about your wife and child, Mr. Morden?"

Morden's eyes narrowed. "The fact that they were alive, obviously."

The reporter, sensing an opportunity, leaned forward. "Their deaths were quite shocking and dramatic, not only to you but to all of us. If you can go back to that time, what was it, as the details of their deaths unfolded, that bothered you the most?"

Morden pressed his clenched hand to his mouth. "They found only part of the ship."

"The rest of the ship was believed destroyed by the explosion, and the debris sucked through the jumpgate into hyperspace."

"That's what I heard."

"But you don't believe it?"

Morden's eyes were downcast.

"Some have theorized that in the instant before the explosion, the forward section of the ship might have been drawn through into hyperspace, where the unprotected passengers would have died. Self-styled cosmo-philosopher Dr. Franz Nielsen has even proposed the theory—discounted by several leading scientists—that the explosion, coupled with the jump-point vortex, might have created a condensation of the hyperspace currents, a standing wave or bubble within hyperspace, sealed off from everything else, in which time might stand still, holding the passengers at the moment of their deaths. That would mean your wife and child are still alive somewhere, Mr. Morden. You don't believe that, do you?"

Morden's fist came away from his mouth, burrowed its way into his pocket. "No, of course not."

He was lying.

He believed it, or at least hoped it. Had the Shadows used that hope against him when, seven months later, he'd arrived on the rim?

There was no way to know.

Galen dissolved the image.

He'd been certain that Morden was a willing, enthusiastic agent of the Shadows. Still he believed it. But now that he'd thought of Anna, he couldn't get the comparison out of his mind. He'd seen no hope of restoring her, but even so he'd wanted to try.

If he could separate Morden from the Shadows, block the signal exciting the implant, perhaps even destroy the implant, could he free Morden? He didn't know how long it would take for the chemical influence of the Shadows to dissipate.

Even when it did, what would he find? Most likely, someone who took joy in the deaths of others, regardless of any manipulation. Could there be any other outcome?

"Oh shit," G'Leel said. She pointed to the image in the air before them.

Alwyn had appeared out of the darkness of Down Below to block Morden's path. He was swaying.

G'Leel bolted for the door. Galen ran after her, holding the probe's image in his mind's eye. The probe was stuck to the corridor wall several feet behind Morden, showing Morden's back, and beyond him, the intoxicated Alwyn.

"What do you want?" Morden said, his voice smooth, threatening. He set down his bags.

"I'm the one you didn't get yet. The one still standing," Alwyn said.

Galen and G'Leel raced down the corridor. Alwyn was too far away. He was either going to ruin Galen's plan, or get killed, or both, before they ever reached him. The idea that Morden might be some innocent victim seemed ridiculous now.

"I believe I'm standing as well," Morden said.

"You're a goddamn stinking murderer."

"Who have I killed?"

"Millions of Narns, for a start."

Galen and G'Leel swerved down a more traveled corridor, began weaving through pedestrians.

"I've never even been to Narn," Morden said. "But I'm curious, do you intend to kill me? Because if you don't, it doesn't seem terribly smart to confront me."

"I wanted to see what a monster looks like up close."

Morden tilted his head, as if realizing something. "You're—"

Michael Garibaldi came up behind Morden. "Is there some trouble here?" Galen accessed the probe on Michael, the second image appearing in his mind's eye beside the first.

"Mr. Garibaldi." Morden's tone was hard. He folded his hands in front of him. "If I didn't know better, I'd think you were following me."

"If I didn't know better, I'd call you an evil, manipulative bastard. Lucky we both know better." He went to Alwyn. "Are you all right, Mr. Alecto?"

Morden answered. "He was threatening me."

Alwyn lurched forward. "That bastard murdered—"

Michael pulled him back. "Had too much to drink, is that it?"

A security guard hurried up to them. Michael deposited Alwyn into his arms, motioned him away.

Galen grabbed G'Leel and pulled her to a walk. "He's safe." Even drunk, Alwyn could easily create a distraction and slip away from the guard. They would meet him.

The security chief turned to Morden. "Down Below can be a dangerous place. I suggest you stay out if you don't want to be hurt."

"Is that a threat?"

"I find actions more effective than threats."

"Why are you following me, Mr. Garibaldi?"

"I like that guy's answer. Wanted to see what a monster looks like up close. Why? Want to file a complaint?"

Morden smiled. "I find actions more effective than complaints."

Michael spread his hands. "I'm free now."

He was treading dangerously. It was Michael's way. He knew that Morden would not act against him after they'd been seen together. He didn't realize that when this enemy did decide to act, he would have no chance.

"For a weak man," Morden said, "the weak link, you seem to invite trouble."

Michael hesitated, lips pursed. When he spoke, his tone was flippant. "You know what they say. What doesn't kill me makes me stronger."

Morden's smile widened. "I agree completely. But when it comes time to act, I'd rather surprise you."

Michael nodded. "My thoughts exactly."

They turned in opposite directions, parted.

— chapter 11 —

Anna lay on the table in the white room, a grayish-skinned technician standing to one side, Justin on the other.

"Do you recognize this person?" Justin asked. His quavering voice sounded strange to her, thin and flat. It came through the inferior sensors of this inferior body. He turned the comp-pad in his hand to face her. On its screen was the image of a Human.

"Elizar." She found it difficult to articulate the syllables with her crude speaking apparatus, and to simultaneously release the air that gave the syllables sound. It was so limited, this horrible little body.

Justin turned the screen away, made some change, his bushy white eyebrows contracting. "What about this one?"

She had not seen the Centauri for some time, but she recognized him. "Tilar."

As Justin again manipulated the primitive machine, the technician bent over her, poking at her skin with his thick finger. He lifted one of her extremities, flexed it. Beneath her flimsy, pale skin, weak muscles jumped erratically. Justin had explained that they were administering various treatments to help this limited body function on its own. First they had removed the metallic interface device fastened to her head. Her senses had been even further reduced. She could no longer feel the power of the Eye running through the walls. Now this.

Justin turned the screen to face her. "Do you recognize him?"

She had never seen this person. "No."

Justin frowned. "Look again, Anna."

The image showed a Human male, middle-aged, with dark blond hair, not remarkable in any way. "No."

He showed her a few more images that she did not recognize, and with each failure, the wrinkles on his sagging face deepened.

Anna grew anxious. She was obeying—answering their questions, undergoing their treatments. She had to be connected once again to the machine.

He waved the screen in front of her, and his voice rose. "This was your mother, Anna. This"—he changed the picture—"was your father." He returned to the image of the man with dark blond hair. "And this is your husband. John Sheridan. The man whose name you share."

Anna didn't understand. She knew what a husband was, a male mate in the custom of the Humans. Why would she have a husband?

Justin slammed the comp-pad down beside her head. "Where is that Bunny person? Bring her in."

The technician left, and after only a moment he returned. Behind him came the hated Bunny, with her long blond hair and short pink dress, Bunny, who had interfered with Anna's control of the machine, who was no friend, no matter what the Eye said. Anna didn't know why she hadn't thought of it before; if there was any reason she had been separated from the machine, it was Bunny.

Anna used her upper extremities to raise herself. She was panting again, her heart thumping hard.

"Anna," Justin said.

She drew her lower limbs toward her, in preparation for attack. The technician came alongside, fluttering his thick fingers unhappily over her body.

"Anna, stop it. Bunny is going to help you remember your past. We need you to remember. Don't fight her. Just relax. Lie back and relax, and let her find the memories."

Bunny remained in the doorway, her thin face tight. A liberator came to stand behind her, with its shining black skin, its rows of brilliant pinpoint eyes.

The memory came to her again—dazzling and fragmented and filled with shredding spinning brilliant agony: the liberators had taught her obedience. Only after that had she learned the joys of the machine, and later, the First Principles, the great good of warfare, the ecstasy of victory.

Now, for some reason, she had been brought back to the beginning, and she must obey in order to reach the next stage, to regain the joys of the machine. She would prove to the liberators that she had learned her lesson the first time, that she needn't undergo their instruction again. Obedience. Obedience, the only option.

Anna returned her body to a horizontal position, and the hated Bunny approached. Standing at Anna's side, Bunny crossed her arms, and her eyes narrowed.

Somehow Bunny was inside her mind, pushing at her with the same pressure Anna had felt when she'd carried Bunny inside her body. Bunny was trying to take control away from her, just as the Eye had. Even this tiny piece of herself wasn't secure.

Anna tried to relax, as Justin had directed. But the pressure was increasing, building like a sustained blast from an enemy trying to burn through her skin.

What memories was Bunny searching for? Anna remembered every attack she had ever made, and before that, every training exercise. She recalled every lesson the Eye had taught her. What more could there be?

But Bunny pushed through all those memories, the force of her assault coming to bear on the boundary of Anna's mind. Anna had not even been aware of it before, yet the pressure, and the pain, defined it, revealed it, an impenetrable barrier. As Bunny's efforts concentrated on it, the pain built, burning, growing brighter and brighter, intensifying until it enveloped her in brilliant, searing whiteness, the white of the eyes of the liberators.

Anna found herself screaming. The brilliant blank whiteness would suffocate her.

Around her the thick whiteness began to shift. Behind that brilliant barrier, vague forms were taking shape—shifting, shadowy silhouettes.

Then all at once, the pressure vanished. The searing whiteness faded. The pain released her.

Heaving with the forceful admission and expulsion of air,

Anna searched her mind. The shadowy silhouettes formed ghostly afterimages against the darkness.

The invader had left. Anna had retained control of this small piece that remained of her.

The greatest joy is the ecstasy of victory.

Above her, Bunny stumbled, grabbed the table for balance. "There's a block in her mind—stronger than anything I've encountered. Far stronger than what we do with a mindwipe— and that completely blocks out a person's past life. No way to break through it without killing her." Bunny looked up, her gaze falling first on Justin, then the liberator. "I suppose it was caused by . . . her conditioning."

Anna closed her eyes. As she took satisfaction in her small victory, her exhausted body fell into unconsciousness.

"You need to get on the ship now," Galen said.

Alwyn's bloodshot eyes squinted, struggling to focus. With an arm over Galen's shoulders, he still wavered, occasionally lurching to one side or the other.

Galen anxiously scanned the customs area. At this late hour, only a few knots of people awaited departures or arrivals.

Morden himself had returned to his room after the confrontation. He or his agents, though, were sure to show up soon. Morden would want to find the man who had called him a murderer. Whether Morden knew that man was a mage, Galen wasn't sure. If Morden did know, he'd be eager to learn that mage's identity.

Galen had invaded the Command and Control database and secured a departure time for Alwyn just thirty minutes after his meeting with Morden. Galen had to get Alwyn away, had to put his plan into motion. He hoped that if he killed Morden and his companions quickly enough, the Shadows might believe everything the responsibility of one mage: him.

If not, if they discovered that Alecto was Alwyn, they would hunt him down on Regula 4 and destroy both him and his place.

Galen turned to G'Leel, who stood nearby with their suit- cases, and spoke in a low voice. "He must not be Thomas Alecto again. Nor should you be G'Leel."

Her red gaze was fixed on him.

Alwyn squeezed him and stumbled. "You have to come with us, Galen."

"Guy," Galen reminded him softly, trying to disentangle himself from Alwyn.

G'Leel hooked Alwyn's free arm over her shoulders and pulled him toward the security checkpoint. "Let's go, Mr. Alecto."

"Time to go," Galen said.

Alwyn grabbed him by the jacket, half fell against him with a blast of two-hundred-proof breath. "Come with us. We need your help."

"I have to finish here. You have to leave."

Alwyn bowed his head against Galen's chest. "I don't want to go back there."

Galen looked to G'Leel, who shrugged.

"It's not home without her. Just a tomb of memories."

"You must take joy in the memories. She would want that."

Alwyn looked up at him, eyes glistening with tears. "Is that what you do?"

"Yes."

Alwyn nodded. Apparently he was drunk enough to believe it. "All right." He straightened, maintaining his hold on Galen. "I wanted to take you as a second apprentice, you know. After your father died."

"I know," Galen said.

"When you've finished your task, will you stop to say good-bye?"

"If I am able, I will come to you."

Alwyn smoothed his jacket. "We won't argue. I promise."

"We won't argue." Galen took hold of his arm, and with G'Leel steered him toward the checkpoint.

They stopped before the security guard, and Galen presented Alwyn's identicard. Alwyn stumbled, and at the guard's look, Galen said, "Afraid of flying."

The guard made a disgusted sound. "Does he realize we're on a space station here?" He handed the identicard back to Alwyn, who promptly dropped it. "He's not the pilot, is he?"

Galen retrieved the card.

"No," G'Leel said. "I am." She handed her identification to the guard, and her eyes met Galen's.

They stared at each other in silence. He hoped that, somehow, she would survive this war.

"There may be a way out you haven't thought of yet," she said. "Don't stop looking."

Galen gave a single nod.

"I wish I could stay with you," she said.

"You have more to do."

"Is there any way to stop them?"

He saw none, though he didn't want to take that hope from her. "Many are searching."

The guard handed G'Leel her card, but she seemed unwilling to move.

"I trust," Galen said, "that I haven't made any further appearances in your dreams."

Her lips suppressed a smile. "That would be my business." As she hoisted Alwyn up, her face grew serious. "Good-bye."

"Good-bye."

Then she and Alwyn were gone, and he was left alone. Time to get on with it.

Galen strode toward Londo's quarters. It felt good, at last, to be taking action. Energy drove through him, ready for his command. He held it firmly in control. Fed's gun, in his pocket, pulled with a reassuring weight at his side.

As usual, the ambassadorial sector was fairly quiet. Those few who were about shot him curious looks, or moved quickly out of the way. It had been a long time since he had worn the robe of a techno-mage. The movement of the cloth against his freshly scoured skin felt strange, like the brush of a ghost from a different life. He put it from his mind.

He had used his access to the security systems to invade the alarm on Londo's door. He had input his own code, so that the door would open at his command, and inserted a virus. The virus would be activated when he used his code. Once active, it would begin to consume itself, and complete the process in exactly ten minutes. When the virus was gone, the alarm would recognize Galen's code as false and notify security of the breach.

The corridor near Londo's quarters was empty. As Galen approached, he accessed the station's power grid, switched off Londo's electricity. From outside the door, he visualized the equation, conjured the formation of mist within. The tech echoed the spell eagerly.

Londo had been trapped in his quarters once before, in the darkness. He had cursed the techno-mages for their disrespect, had defied them to send their next demon after him. It had been nearly two years, but now Galen had come.

He input the code, and the door slid open. He began to count down the ten minutes.

"Is someone there?" Londo called out.

Galen entered the cool room, closed the door behind him.

A few emergency lights pierced the mist, the pretentious, cluttered furnishings casting eerie shadows. Galen accessed his sensors for greater sensitivity, and a brighter image of the room appeared in his mind's eye. Londo had filled his suite with signs of his wealth and power: rich fabrics and laces, ceremonial swords, golden statues. A portrait of a fierce Londo stared down from the wall.

"Who's there?" Londo demanded. He was well on his way to becoming the Centauri in the portrait, though he had not reached those heights of confidence and callousness yet.

"Who," whispered Galen, "do you fear it is?" He dipped his hand into his pocket, deposited a few grain-sized probes on the wall beside the door. The Shadows would expect it, and he would reinforce the perception that he was a novice, predictable.

"You don't frighten me, whoever you are. Show yourself."

Galen conjured a small flying platform beside Londo, and with an equation of motion, brushed it against his great black crest of hair.

Londo stumbled backward. "I have a weapon!"

"I am a weapon," Galen whispered.

Londo banged into a table, grabbed a decorative sculpture, the golden figure of a Centauri god. "Certainly we don't need these unnecessary dramatics. Let us sit down, in the light, and discuss matters like civilized beings."

"But I am a creature of shadow. And I am not civilized."

Londo backed himself into the wall. "What are these riddles? What is it you want? Money?"

"I want you to die, slowly. I want to crush you in my hand. I want to erase you from existence."

Londo gave an uneasy laugh. "Quite thorough." He peered into the mist. "What have I done to deserve this?"

"You killed my people."

"The bombing of Narn was Lord Refa's doing, not mine."

"I am not Narn."

"Then who . . ."

"It is difficult, having so many deaths to your credit that you can barely remember them."

"I am late for a meeting with the captain. He will send someone after me, so if you're going to kill me, I suggest you get on with it."

"They will find no remains." Galen conjured the globe of light right in front of Londo's face.

Londo flinched, hitting his head against the wall. Within the globe, the light followed the pattern Galen had designed. Slowly it molded itself into the shape of the *Ondavi*, the Centauri freighter Londo had provided for the mages two years ago. The freighter exploded, and a fraction of a second later the globe containing it also shattered, flying apart into small fireballs.

Londo jerked his hands to his face, nearly hitting himself with the statue.

The fireballs began orbiting Londo's head.

"That explosion was an accident." Londo was speaking quickly now. "I didn't murder them. I meant them no harm." He squinted as one of the fireballs floated past his eye.

Galen bit out the words. "You tricked them. You led my entire order to its death."

"No, no, this is all a misunderstanding."

"I'm sure you can't remember them all." Galen put faces within the fireballs—Ing-Radi, Muirne, Beel, Carvin. They screamed as their skin burned and blackened. "But perhaps you remember my teacher, Elric." With an equation of motion Galen brought one of the fireballs in front of Londo, placed Elric's image within it. He burned and blackened like all the rest. "Unfortunately for you, I wasn't with them. Now I have come to revenge myself upon you."

Galen propelled the fireball around Londo, pressed it to the back of his head. Londo screamed, jumped away from the wall. Galen wanted to burn him again and again, once for every mage who had died.

He couldn't think of them. There was no past, no future, just the moment, and the task required, and he, the mechanism that would carry out that task.

He quenched the fireballs, plunging them back into near-darkness. Londo's panting filled the room.

Galen visualized the spell, conjured a breeze. With equations of motion, slowly he coiled the breeze about Londo. The mist followed its movement. Papers on the desk flipped.

He accelerated the air's flow, drew it tighter and tighter around Londo, faster and faster.

"I tell you it was all an accident," Londo yelled, flailing against the wind. "The ship was old! It didn't even belong to me!"

Galen approached him. The lace curtains whipped in frustrated zigzags, papers flew up off the desk, caught in the whirlwind. Wrapped in the swirling mist, the struggling Londo looked like a demon himself.

"This is madness!" Londo threw the statue in his general direction. "It was Morden! He did it! He did it!"

"They speak to me, Londo. And this is what they say: 'Let not your vengeance die, though we are dead.' " Galen tightened the whirlwind until it became an extra layer over Londo's body, a Londo-shaped maelstrom.

Londo staggered, bending over. Within the vortex, he couldn't breathe.

Galen constricted the wind yet further. He was burning, churning, surging with energy. Still a minute remained until security would arrive. Alwyn would thank him if he killed Londo. As would G'Leel and millions of Narns. This man had left such destruction in his wake. As much as Galen had.

Galen wanted to crush him, crush him, crush him, and the tech returned each impulse, echoing and reechoing, filling him with hate.

Londo fell to his knees, clutching at his throat.

Without control, there was only chaos. If he could not hold to his task, then he must end it.

He closed the fist of his will around himself, stood over his victim, his mind fixed on the equation for mist, the equation for wind, the equations of motion.

At last security arrived in the hall outside. Accessed the emergency override to gain entry.

Galen dissolved the spells, and with a rattling gasp Londo collapsed to the floor. As the door swung open, Galen conjured a platform, equation of motion, equation of motion. He shot through the door, sending a security guard reeling, raced down the corridor, around a turn, and out of sight.

"What the hell?" Michael yelled behind him.

"Eat something," Justin said.

Anna was in a different room now, this one larger, with tan, paneled walls. Instead of machinery, it contained furniture: a couch that faced three armchairs, with a low table in between, and to one side, a larger table surrounded by more simple, rigid chairs. These furnishings were lifeless, unlike the ones she generated within the machine. Even so, she knew she was still within the Eye; that great machine encompassed the entire planet.

Anna was sitting on the couch, technicians on either side of her. They trimmed away the long, horny extrusions on each of her small appendages. Justin sat opposite her.

She studied the tray of food on the table, an odd assortment of various colors and shapes that meant nothing to her. The technician to her right released her limb, and she reached down, grasped one of the shapes, and deposited it in her orifice, as Justin had shown her before. She chewed, swallowed, old reflexes guiding her actions. It was a primitive system, the sensations weak and uninspiring beside the exhilarating leap to hyperspace, the joy of the war cry.

"Good," Justin said in his quavering voice. "Now tell me the very earliest memory you have."

Anna glanced at Bunny, who stood to one side with Elizar. Anna did not want Bunny in her mind again, pushing at that brilliant, burning barrier, "helping" her to remember whatever it was they wanted her to remember.

Justin waited for an answer.

"I remember the liberators," Anna said, "instructing me in obedience."

Justin let out a heavy breath. "I want you to tell me a memory of yourself in this body"—he pointed to her—"without the ship. The earliest memory you have."

Anna searched her mind. "I was in a tunnel underground. I sensed a machine to control. He resembled a Human, but he was only partly Human. His name was Galen. I seized his hand." She looked down at her grasping mechanism, troubled by its resemblance to a Human hand. "I joined with him."

Justin's exhalation was harsher this time, and he stood. A door opened, and two Drakh entered, eyes glowing red, jagged white exoskeletons covering most of their heads. Anna had carried Drakh of this type several times; they were menial soldiers. They wore black body armor and carried primitive weapons over their shoulders.

Justin made a sharp motion toward Bunny, and his voice was hard. "Get her out of here. She's useless."

Bunny backed away. "I told you I couldn't break through without killing her."

"I thought you might have stimulated at least a few memories. But not even that. They've been patient with you, Bunny, but you just haven't been pulling your weight. There's a capacity in which you could be much more productive."

"I did my best. You wouldn't even know who she was if it wasn't for me." Bunny backed into the wall, straightening with a start. "They blocked the memories themselves, with their conditioning. You can't blame me for that. They turned her into a machine, and there's just no way to turn that thing"—she jerked her chin toward Anna—"back into a Human being."

Anna had no idea what Bunny was talking about, but she sensed that Justin had at last realized Bunny was no friend, and that something very bad was about to happen to the telepath. She watched avidly.

One of the Drakh reached for Bunny, and her eyes narrowed on him. The Drakh stumbled back, knocking his companion aside. His body trembling, he took his weapon in both hands, turned it so that the muzzle pointed to one of his glowing red eyes, and fired. Fragments of white exoskeleton sprayed out the back of his head. He fell at Elizar's feet.

The second Drakh lunged at Bunny, but no sooner had he seized her than she turned her narrowed eyes on him. He released her as if she were burning hot. Then he too took his weapon, aimed it at himself.

"I don't want to kill anyone," Bunny yelled, her eyes fixed on the Drakh. "But you're not wiring me into one of those ships! Just let me go. Elizar can take me. I won't tell anybody anything."

Anna pulled her hands away from the technicians and stood, carefully balancing on her two lower extremities. Bunny was talking again of ships. What could Bunny mean?

Elizar stepped over the fallen Drakh, his black velvet coat brushing the body. "Let her go, Justin," he said in his skillfully modulated voice. "She has served well. I can take her to a planet without space trade; she will do no harm to us." The curious pattern of hair on his chin shifted as he smiled at Bunny. "They can be assured that, wherever I leave her, she'll cause plenty of chaos."

While keeping her eyes on the Drakh, Bunny also smiled.

Elizar extended his hand, and Bunny took it. He guided her toward the door. But after a few steps she stopped, jerked away from him. She held her palm up to her face, as if she had never seen it before. Something was affixed there, a small white disk. She scratched clumsily at it, but was unable to remove it. Her gaze traveled slowly up to Elizar. "You bastard." She staggered, and the Drakh, released from her control, grabbed her. "You—promised." She collapsed.

"Thank you, Elizar," Justin said.

Elizar nodded.

"Take her for processing," Justin said to the Drakh. "They want that ship back in service as soon as possible."

Anna didn't understand—she must be mistaken—but

Justin's words filled her with a horrible sense of dread. "Are you joining her with my machine?"

Justin's face twitched. "Yes, Anna. We need you else-where. You are critical to our victory, and we need you in this form."

The Drakh dragged Bunny toward the door.

It couldn't be. Bunny was going to get everything Anna desired—the thrill of battle, the red rapture of the war cry. Anna moved her weak body, blocking their way. "How can that happen?" she asked. "How can Bunny do what I do?"

Justin frowned. "I'm not sure what you mean, Anna."

Anna's outrage built. "She is not what I am."

"What are you, Anna?"

"A great engine of—" No, that was no longer true. "The heart and brain of a machine."

"You are Human, Anna. Just as Bunny is."

How could he say that? "No I'm not." Anna's heart pounded. "No I'm not." The idea was absurd.

Elizar raised his hand in a precise movement, and an image appeared in the air before her, an image as large as her, of a Human female in a knee-length wraparound robe, with long, tangled hair and hollow eyes. Anna extended her grasping mechanism toward the thin figure, and the woman in the image raised her hand toward Anna, until, at last, their finger-tips met. Identical.

"No," Anna said, and the woman echoed her word. With a shriek Anna threw herself at the woman just as the woman threw herself at Anna. But the woman had no substance. Anna passed through her, head ramming into the side of the couch, and fell to the floor.

As she struggled to coordinate her limbs, the Drakh quickly dragged Bunny from the room.

Justin crouched in front of her. "Stop, Anna! Stop! The lib-erators expect better from you. Have you forgotten every-thing they taught you?"

Anna pushed herself up with weak limbs, onto the hands and knees of her pathetic Human body. How could she be Human? Humans were weak, small, vulnerable. They were not parts of machines. They did not join with machines. She did not want to be Human.

"The liberators gave you everything. They made you what you were. And they have made you what you are now. They want to release your full potential, to make you even greater than you were. Have you forgotten the First Principles?"

To make her greater? How could they make her greater? "Chaos through warfare. Evolution through bloodshed. Perfection through victory."

"You have done the first two very well. Now you will help us to attain complete victory. And you will be perfected."

She could not stand to be a Human. She needed to be rejoined to a machine. That was who she was; that was her purpose.

Three of the liberators entered, their tapered legs moving gracefully. Their brilliant pinpoint eyes studied her.

"Come and sit down, Anna," Justin said, "and I will explain everything, as best I can."

Justin extended a hand in a gesture she didn't recognize. She climbed to her feet. He had said she would be perfected. What could that mean? He and Elizar sat, and as she stood before them, the answer came to her. He could mean nothing else. Excitement stirred her pathetic body. The liberators were truly great.

"You will join me with the Eye and give me control of it," Anna said, finding it difficult, for some reason, to catch her breath. "That is how I will be perfected."

Justin's bushy eyebrows contracted, and he looked toward the liberators. After a moment, he returned her gaze. "Just so, Anna. Just so. We hadn't planned on telling you until later, but you've figured it out. Very good. But first you must help us attain victory. That's how you'll prove yourself worthy. Once we are victorious, then you and the Eye will be one."

She would be perfected, joined with the greatest machine she had ever sensed. Anna sat. "Tell me what to do."

— chapter 12 —

"He could have killed me a thousand times over and danced a jig on my decaying remains before you and your incompetent security force arrived," Londo raved. "We had an extended conversation. He had time to ruin my entire living quarters. To torture me. Another few seconds, and I would have been dead!" He sat sprawled on his couch, his crest blown flat against his head, his starburst brooch hanging from his jacket by a thread.

Michael stood over him. "Gee, that's too bad. Zack, make a note. We should wait another minute or two next time we get an alarm from the ambassador's quarters."

Watching through the probe on Michael's hand, Galen crawled into the narrow air shaft, pulled the vent closed behind him. Even lying prone, he barely fit. His heart pounded from the adrenaline still racing through him, the pounding echoed back by the tech.

"Take care, Mr. Garibaldi. I don't think your captain will appreciate your turning this into a diplomatic incident. We maintain our presence here in the understanding that we will be protected."

"It's just hard to keep track of all your enemies, Ambassador. Now which one was this, again?"

"Great Maker! I told you. A mad techno-mage. Totally and completely insane. Out for revenge for all those who were killed when they visited here."

"Did you get a name?"

"A name? Yes, right after we shared the hands of friendship."

"What about a description?"

"Are you hard of hearing? He looked like a techno-mage.

Black robe, bald head—he should stand out fairly well around here. I would think even your people could find him."

"Human?"

"Yes, yes—at least I think so. Young, I believe. He said his teacher was Elric, the leader of the techno-mages. I had some dealings with Elric when he was here. A very short temper—just like his student."

"And he claimed you had killed the techno-mages."

Londo waved the thought away. "His accusations totally baseless, of course. They died in an accident; I'm sure you recall it. The freighter belonged to a Centauri company. It was old, poorly maintained. The techno-mages tricked me into gambling with them. When I lost, they demanded I arrange passage for them on the ship. This was all investigated before. It was just a tragic accident."

"As I remember, you wanted something from them, and they refused. No hard feelings about that?"

"You want to put this on me? Do you realize that I was very nearly killed? And that techno-mage will be back. He's not going to be satisfied until I'm dead."

"You do tend to have that effect on people."

"Do your job, Mr. Garibaldi. This insane techno-mage must be tracked down at once. Until he's captured, I demand protection. Six of your best—if such a word can be used. They must be available to me at all times."

"You may not have heard, there is a war on. We're short-staffed as it is." Michael preempted Londo's protest. "But for someone of your importance, I will requisition three of my best . . . Narn . . . guards."

"Narns?" Londo's expression darkened. "Your sense of humor is not what it used to be."

Michael's tone remained mild. "I can't give you your choice of any security staff you want. Our cooperation can only go so far, Ambassador."

"I might as well stick my head in the station's fusion reactor. It would be quicker." Londo stood, began pacing nervously through the ruins of his room. "Sheridan will hear about this. And my government may well take action." He ran into Zack, who was examining the golden statue Londo had been holding earlier. Londo snatched the figure back. "Get out of here! You're useless."

"Are you rejecting our protection?" Michael asked.

"Protection? I'd be safer with Vir as my security. Yes, I'm rejecting it. I'm rejecting you. Get out. Get out." Londo drove them from his quarters.

Galen switched to one of the probes he had left on Londo's wall. The ambassador stood alone in the center of his once luxurious sitting room, the statue hanging at his side. "Vir . . . always off on some ridiculous errand when I need you."

A trinket on his desk dropped to the floor, and at the sound, Londo jumped, raising the statue like a club.

He turned, looking anxiously around the room. "Madman. I refuse to die for this. Not now. It wasn't my fault." He raised his voice. "It wasn't my fault!"

With an anxious gulp, he rushed from the room, the statue clutched in both hands.

Galen continued his mind-focusing exercise as Londo rushed past the place where he lay hidden. Everything was going according to plan. He must simply retain control, do what needed to be done and no more. He conjured a platform beneath himself, and with an equation of motion sent his prone body gliding silently through the narrow shaft. Ahead, weak patches of light filtered in through the vents, interspersing light with the darkness.

Londo certainly deserved death. Yet that had not been Galen's purpose in leaving the hiding place. Besides, Galen told himself, Londo was Morden's puppet. Morden used Londo's desires and ambitions to manipulate him. Just as Morden had used Circe's desires and ambitions to manipulate her. To drive her to murder.

Morden was Galen's purpose.

In the shadowy light of the shaft he saw a dark obstruction ahead, near the area of Morden's room. As he scanned into the infrared band, the object took on shape and substance, glowing a dull red with warmth. The thick, gleaming membrane blocked the way, attached at multiple points around its circumference to the shaft, like a spiderweb. Over its surface, areas of warmth and coolness shifted and flowed, arranging themselves into new patterns. When he'd studied his transceiver, he'd seen its golden skin pulse lighter and darker in a strikingly similar way.

Beneath the membrane's surface, threads of brilliant red glittered, interwoven and complex, transmitting electrical activity. Galen thought of the gelatinous black matter behind the wall of the white room where Elizar had trapped him. Anna had pulled away the wall panel and reached into that living machine, and it had extruded to envelop her, a blackness shot through with veins of silver. Through it, she had connected to the systems of the underground complex.

This was a much smaller, simpler example of Shadow tech. An alarm system. And perhaps more. A trap.

Even after studying Burell's research, he had no real understanding of the Shadows' organic technology. How the membrane, partly alive, might be produced, how it might sustain itself, remained mysteries. He couldn't even tell with certainty whether the membrane he faced was in essence matter, or some mixture of matter and shaped energy. How he might get past, he had no idea.

Galen stopped before it. The vent to Morden's room was just five feet beyond. He focused on the wall of the shaft beside him, used his sensors to tell him what lay on the other side: a space, a room. He was up near the ceiling, behind one corner. Across the room stood a Human, and from that figure radiated the constant, low-frequency energy Galen had detected from Morden's implant. The Shadows would be there as well, though Galen could not sense them through the wall. He needed to know where they were so he could focus on them, so he could cast his spell to listen to their communications. He needed to get to the vent.

A second figure entered the room. Centauri. Londo. Right on schedule.

Raised voices sounded down the shaft, and Galen focused on them, amplifying the sound.

"—here? How did you even find me? We agreed we would always meet in the hedge maze," Morden said.

"Excuse me for the breach in etiquette! I'm about to be murdered! He's a madman. I nearly choked to death. And it is your fault, Mr. Morden. You and your associates put me in this position. You have to deal with this man! You have to protect me."

"Ambassador. What are you talking about?"

As Londo recounted his experience, Galen's mind raced to find some way past the membrane. Surely if he destroyed it, the Shadows would be alerted to his presence.

He must reach the vent, or he would have to postpone or abandon his plan. Postponing the plan was unthinkable; he must leave Babylon 5 soon. If he abandoned his attempt to trace the Shadows' signal, then he could simply proceed with Morden's murder, a much more straightforward task.

But he knew no other way to find Elizar and Razeel quickly, except to go to the shell-shaped region of space, to meet them and the Shadows in battle. That he must not do.

He could not allow them to escape him, to use his spell of destruction.

He had to get past the membrane.

If he touched or manipulated it in any way, he risked detection, yet he could think of nothing else. Galen raised his hand to the shifting surface, hoping to gain some additional information through the sensors in his fingertips.

The membrane's skin was warm, moist, and he detected carbon, oils, organic compounds. As he studied its composition, the membrane swelled against his hand, and with a sudden shift the thick material oozed down over his fingers. Galen started, fighting the urge to yank his arm back. The red membrane spread down his hand, wrist, capturing him as a spiderweb trapped prey. The warmth crawled over the sleeve of his robe, reaching ahead with disconcerting muscular contractions. It was exploring him, subsuming him. Just as it had with Anna.

Anna had gained control of that living machine on Thenothk. Of course, the Shadows had altered her to serve that purpose. Yet he too was a creature of the Shadows. Could he gain control of the membrane?

He focused on the shifting red skin, cast the spell to associate. There was no echo from the tech, no connection to the membrane. He had no method for joining with it.

The warmth oozed over his shoulder, worked its way up his

neck. Galen closed his eyes, took a deep breath and held it. He visualized the equation, moved the platform slowly ahead into the membrane.

Its moistness touched his forehead and flowed down his skin, its fingers sliding over eyes, nose, ears. In the stretching, reaching, contracting of its progress, he sensed its desire. It searched for his nature, to classify him—machine or being, ally or enemy. It poured under the collar of his robe, down his chest and back. It found the tech that ran closest to the surface of his skin, along his shoulder blades and spine. Its thickness gathered there, rippling, considering.

Galen held to the equation of motion. As he continued forward, the membrane reached farther and farther down his torso, to his legs, and he thought it must release his hand, which remained extended in front of him, or his face. Yet they remained coated in warmth, the membrane's volume seemingly endless. Then its grasp curled around his boots, and his entire body was contained within it. If it would not release him, then it would either have to stop his forward progress or detach itself from the shaft. But it did neither.

At last the warmth broke away from his fingers, withdrawing down his hand, his wrist. In another moment its warm grip released his head, the membrane splitting apart, working its way down forehead, eyes, nose, mouth. He gasped for air.

The dampness retreated down his neck, chest. The membrane was letting him pass. It, too, realized they were kin.

It released his legs, reconstituted itself in its old shape.

He stopped his forward movement. He lay now beside the vent. He buried his head in his arms, muffled his greedy breathing.

Morden's smooth voice came to him. "We know Elric's student. His name is Galen. He's young, vicious, and undisciplined—fortunately for you. A more experienced techno-mage would have killed you long before security arrived."

"Very reassuring."

"Are you positive he was alone?"

Galen controlled his breathing, lifted his head. Morden suspected that more than one mage had come to Babylon 5.

He peered through the vent. The room was plain, small, with a neatly made bed in the far corner, two easy chairs and a table against the near wall. If not for a comp-pad and an empty liquor bottle from the mini-bar on the table, Galen would have thought the room unused. Londo and Morden stood below him, near the table and chairs. At the sight of Morden so close, so near to the time of his death, eagerness rose up in Galen, the tech surging with a burning rush.

Londo held a glass with the contents of the liquor bottle, and he downed it in several gulps, followed by a grimace. His other hand still clutched the statue. "You mean he's not the only one that's still alive?"

"There may be one or two others."

"One or two— This is completely unacceptable. You have to stop them. Kill them—you're good at that. However you do it, just get rid of them." Londo pointed the empty glass at Morden. "In the meantime, you and your associates will have to protect me."

Morden stood with his right hand in his pocket, left arm bent at the elbow, hand extended. "I can arrange for you to be smuggled off the station. That's your best chance. We can bring—"

"My best *chance*?"

"Galen is a powerful mage."

"I believed I had associates even more powerful."

"You do, Londo. But we can't hunt down a techno-mage and kill him in front of the entire station. He won't go quietly. What we need to do is move the fight to another location, set up a trap for him."

Galen ran through frequencies, found the static-filled shapes of Morden's two associates behind him. They were close enough for Galen to tap into their communications.

"I'm not going to be the bait in any trap."

"If you don't want our help—"

"I can't leave the station. This techno-mage has chosen the most breathtakingly inconvenient moment to go on his rampage. Minister Virini is here. I have a plan in motion. You know that. I have to be here."

Morden smiled. "You want to avoid the appearance of any

personal involvement in Refa's death. And you want to be here to destroy Refa's reputation personally, once you've had him killed. Deliver the coup de grâce."

"After what he's done to me, of course I do. Why don't you just trick this techno-mage into believing I've left the station and draw him into your trap?"

"Techno-mages aren't easily deceived."

"I can't leave! Not now! I've been setting this up for months. The future of my house depends on it. Whose side are you on, anyway?"

Morden inclined his head. "Your side, of course, Londo. Haven't we helped whenever you've asked it?"

Londo gave a short, bitter laugh. "Even when I haven't asked it."

"Well then. You're making things more difficult, but I can send for assistance to solve your problem. Your help will arrive in a day, and will rid you of your techno-mage."

"A day? Who will protect me until then?"

"I'm afraid you'll have to survive that long on your own. My associates can't yet reveal their presence. And no one else here has the power to protect you."

"How am I supposed to survive for even an hour with that madman on the loose?"

Morden moved to the door. "Disguise yourself. Crawl into a hole. And pull the hole in after you." He opened the door. "I'm sorry we can't help any further. I have other business to attend to. I'm leaving in the morning. This is a busy time for us all, Londo. A critical time."

Londo stared at him, then finally went to the door. "You seem almost afraid of this techno-mage, Mr. Morden. I wonder if he might discover your role in the murder of his people, and search you out as well. If so"—he raised his empty glass—"I wish you the best of luck in staying alive. It's a long time until morning." He pushed the glass into Morden's hand, turned, and with a nervous glance down the corridor, left.

The door closed behind him. Galen pulled the gun out of his pocket, laid it on the platform within easy reach. Fed had said it was silent and powerful. Galen would not use the spell of destruction—not here. He had barely maintained control with Londo; with Morden, with all Morden had done, all he had provoked others to do— If the gun was insufficient to his task, then it would be insufficient.

Morden turned to his associates with a smile. "Galen has finally revealed himself. We need to let them know, get them here to set up a trap."

A faint chirping seemed to respond. The sounds came in short bursts, with a strange, distorted quality. Galen realized the Shadows were talking to each other.

If they were going to contact Elizar and Razeel, they would do it now. He focused on their static-filled shapes, visualized the one-term equation.

Words boiled up through him in a furious rush, whispers upon whispers upon whispers, effervescing through his blood, through legs and arms to chest and neck and brain and out, racing onward to their destinations. He searched rapidly through the different word strings, focusing on one after another, listening for the one message he must find.

—to Babylon 5 immediately. Your old associate, Galen, is here. You must capture him or kill him. That was it. He imagined himself grabbing on to the string. And then he was racing through blood and brain and skull, pulled by the string out of his body and up through the layers of Babylon 5 into space. As before, the blackness wrapped tightly around him, and the string accelerated down the narrow, constricting channel, carrying him with it.

It would take him to his next victim.

Beneath his hands, the string bubbled with words, revealing its message. *He has threatened Londo Mollari, a powerful Centauri ally of ours. This Centauri must be kept alive. As for Galen, you know our plans for him, if you can capture him. In any case, he must be stopped.*

Then the constricting blackness unfolded, and he found himself in the openness of space. Below lay a planet streaked in shades of brown, the spiky silhouettes of two Shadow ships passing across its surface. With the string, he hurtled down toward it. Quickly Galen took in the surrounding stars, committing their positions to memory. He was on the rim; he could tell that much instantly.

The dusty atmosphere enveloped him; the ragged peaks of black mountains loomed up, and he accelerated, reaching rock and slipping through, speeding downward, caves and stone flashing by in a jumbled torrent. He plunged into the recipient.

Within was dark, and the string stopped its forward movement, curled in on itself like a snake, repeating itself, wrapping its words about him. *Your old associate. Must be kept alive. You know our plans. A powerful ally of ours.*

He had gained enough information to find Elizar. Now he must hope that Elizar sent a response to the Shadow, and that he was able to find it. Or else, regardless of what he'd told Alwyn, his abandoned body would die within the shaft.

Galen sensed no other strings in the darkness. He tried to direct himself through Elizar's body, to search for the message, but he only drifted. One second passed into the next, and the next. How long would it take Elizar to compose the response?

Then he felt the rush of bubbles, and the string shot past him. He reached out, visualized his hands closing about it. It yanked him up and out, whisking him through chaotic rock into dusty air, and then into space. The darkness curled around him.

As he raced back down the dark tunnel, he felt himself fading again, growing tired as his body, back in the air shaft, failed from lack of oxygen. One of his hands slipped from the string. He jerked it back up, but the effort of holding on seemed suddenly monumental.

Beneath his grasp, the message whispered like a dream. *If Galen meant for the Centauri to die, then he would be dead. You have been deceived. Galen wanted you to contact me. That is why we are having this conversation. I don't know how, but he is using you to find me.*

But let him come to me, if he dares. I am ready. I'm afraid, though, that you may not be. As soon as Galen locates me, he will be finished with you. And while he might let the Centauri live, I doubt he is of a mind to show mercy to you.

The blackness unfolded and he shot down through the

layers of Babylon 5, into the shaft, into his body. He released the string, and the bubbling currents of his blood enfolded him in their thick warmth. He wanted to rest there; he had never been so tired. Yet something made him think of Morden—it was time, finally, to kill Morden, and that thought moved him to continue.

He dissolved the equation, and his body fell upon him, a heavy, dead weight, needing something, burning for something. With a tight, wheezing gasp he sucked in air.

Chest heaving, body shaking, he grabbed up the plasma gun, turned his head away, and fired point-blank at the vent. A jolt threw him against the side of the shaft. Smoke filled the air. He turned back. The vent and a chunk of the shaft were gone. He extended the trembling gun through the hole, aimed the crude weapon down at the angular silhouettes crawling with white dots of static. He squeezed the trigger again, again, and it recoiled silently in his hand.

The blasts flared white as they hit, and after the first three shots the Shadows' veils began to fail, revealing, in the plasma's flashing distortion, glimpses of that elusive enemy: a flailing black limb, an angular head, the piercing white malice of eyes. With the next blast, those eyes erupted in a great blooming white brilliance, the seething light rushing out to envelop the room, envelop him, envelop everything. He could feel it against his skin, unraveling, decohering, degenerating, and as it faded, a shriek echoed through it, close and distant at once. Then the light was gone. One of the Shadows dead.

He concentrated on the other, and within a few seconds it too blazed with a dazzling, shrieking light, then faded away.

They were gone—no static, no bodies, no sign. And Morden was screaming. With an equation of motion Galen propelled himself out of the shaft, dropped down in front of Morden, brought the gun to bear.

Morden fell silent, hunching forward, his face contorted as if in pain. His hand went to the black stone hanging from his neck, clutched it. "Well go ahead," he said. "Kill me. That's what you're here for, isn't it?"

Galen held himself in stillness, heat burning out through his skin. He allowed himself only a single thought. He would give Morden one chance to prove he was the Shadows' unwilling slave. When Morden failed, he would die.

"Before you came to us, Anna," Justin said, "before we awakened you to your true potential, you lived as the Humans do. You had a husband, John Sheridan. He has become very important in this war." Justin paused as the two technicians raised the dead Drakh's body on a floating table, escorted him out of the room. Then Anna was left with Justin and Elizar, and standing behind them, with shining black skin and brilliant rows of eyes, the liberators.

Anna took another piece of food from the tray before her. Whatever the liberators wanted her to do, she would do, for their wisdom was truly unparalleled. She had forgotten that for a short time, in her disturbance at losing the machine. But now she understood. They would perfect her.

Justin turned back to her. "John is confused. He's fighting us. He doesn't understand the First Principles. He doesn't realize that chaos is superior to order. He, personally, has destroyed three of your sisters within the last year."

"How can a Human be so powerful?"

"It's even worse than that. He convinced the Vorlons to attack us in that battle a few months ago. I'm sure you know it was a terrible defeat for us. Many were lost."

John Sheridan was the greatest threat to them after the Vorlons. She had not realized. So many of her sisters had fallen, because of him. "I will not stop until he is utterly destroyed."

Justin raised a hand. "No, no, Anna. It may come to that, but we're hoping it won't. We believe if we can explain things to John, he'll realize his mistake and join with us. If we could convince him to work with us, victory would be ours."

"The enemy must be utterly destroyed."

"John may not be our enemy. He may simply be confused. We see great potential in him, as we saw in you. We're hoping his potential can be released."

But he had killed so many of her sisters. "What if he is our enemy? What if he doesn't understand?"

Justin frowned. "Then the liberators will make him understand. He will do as he's told."

Yes, the liberators would make him understand. Once he met them, how could he fail to see their brilliance? "When he joins us, what will he do? How can we gain victory through one Human?"

Justin's wrinkled face softened. "John is what we call a nexus. Imagine the entire galaxy is one great machine. John is the heart of that machine. If we can control him, the rest will follow."

"I am to control him?" The idea appealed to her.

"Yes, similar to the way you controlled your machine, though the means are different. You must control him as one Human controls another. As his wife, you have power over him. He cares for you, and you may use that concern to manipulate him. You need to prove to John that you love him, and that you want what is best for him. You want him to understand what we're really all about. We need you to bring John here, and to help convince him to join us."

It seemed so strange that she had a husband, and that she might have influence over him. "Will he remember me?"

"Yes. And you must be as he remembers. He'll doubt it's really you, at first. He'll question you. That's why we need you to remember. We believed a telepath was the best way to retrieve those memories. Since that didn't work, we're going to try something else. A treatment, a chemical infusion. Something to help break down the barriers. Do you understand?"

She would remember what she needed, she would control John, they would achieve victory, and she would be joined with the Eye. Then she would know true ecstasy.

"I understand," she said.

"Smile for me," Galen said. Fire raced along the lines of his tech; heat spilled out of him. He wanted to obliterate that maddening smile. He wanted to conjure the one-term equation. He wanted to crush Morden. No exercise could turn his thoughts from that.

In his mind's eye he began to reconstruct the star field he had seen, tried to match it to a specific location. The walls of mental discipline drew tighter around him. They hardly mattered, though, for they merely concentrated his attention on that hated figure that stood at the end of the long, dark tunnel.

Morden remained hunched over, his hand still clutching the necklace. "Do I detect a little bitterness?" His voice was rough.

Galen grabbed Morden's wrist, pulled his hand from the stone, held it up between them. "Smile for me, or I'll implode one bone at a time. When I'm done with your hands and your feet, then your arms go, then your legs, then your eyes. Then your tongue."

Morden bared his teeth in a quick, humorless grin. "So you're not going to kill me?"

The smile was nothing like his usual one. Yet what did that prove? A loyal agent might be unhappy at the deaths of his powerful associates. That did not mean his previous smiles had been false, chemically induced. Morden might simply enjoy spreading chaos, causing millions of deaths, or even just one.

Galen was trembling. He released Morden, took a step back. "Not quickly. Not yet. You will answer one question for me first."

Morden straightened, wiped sweat from his forehead. He was squinting slightly, as if with a headache. "You hardly need that gun to threaten me."

Galen found that Elizar was in a system near Thenothk, most likely in that same Omega sector. He refined his search. "Here is my question. What is your purpose? Why do you serve the Shadows?"

Morden gave a half laugh, and a hint of his old smile flashed across his face. "You want to get philosophical? I serve them because I choose to serve them. If you were smart, you'd do the same. Otherwise you're going to end up like the rest of the mages."

It was no answer at all.

Morden folded his hands in front of him. Though he was clearly trying to regain his smooth, threatening manner, something seemed lacking—an intensity, a passion to his words. "By the way, who was that in Down Below? Who's with you?"

"You left only two of us alive, and you can't remember which two?"

"Blaylock isn't known for his drunkenness. And there's at least one more, the one who came to Thenothk for you."

"Circe. She was killed. As for Blaylock, death changes one," Galen said. "Doesn't it."

Morden's dark gaze met his.

"The Shadows have been manipulating you," Galen said. And as he said it, he knew it was true.

"Manipulating me?" Morden's eyes narrowed further, his forehead furrowing. He shook his head. "You've got it backward. I've been the mastermind behind some of their greatest successes."

"The implant in your brain," Galen said, "that allows you to communicate with them. It stimulates the hypothalamus, influencing your emotions. You feel pleasure in serving them, as long as they provide the signal that orders the stimulation. They can also make you feel anger, or pain. Without their signal, the effect will fade." And what would he find underneath? An equally evil Morden, ripe for the crushing? He hoped so.

"I don't know what you're talking about. No one's influencing me."

Galen found a match to the star field. Elizar was indeed in the Omega sector on the rim, in the Alpha Omega system. Though Galen could not be sure that the streaked brown planet he'd seen was the third from that star, he knew, as one knew things in a nightmare, that it was. For that planet was inhabited, and had received, from its residents, a special name: Z'ha'dum.

It made no sense that Elizar and Razeel would be there. That would not be the place to test his spell of destruction.

In any event, he must not go there. He had sworn to control himself, to hold to his task. A hard shiver ran through him as he thought of crushing the Shadows, of destroying them and their home utterly, once and for all. If he went to Z'ha'dum, how could he stop himself from trying?

Yet Elizar and Razeel were there, awaiting him. And going to Z'ha'dum, now that he thought about it, seemed inevitable. He was good only for destruction; he was destined for darkness. Where else would his long road end, but at the heart of darkness? He must simply maintain control, no matter how difficult, and complete his task.

To do that, he required information from Morden, or he would be destroyed as he approached Z'ha'dum, just as G'Leel's comrades had been. At the thought of pulling the information from Morden, a new rush of energy bloomed through him.

Morden rubbed his forehead. "What exactly is your point?"

"I'm giving you the chance to be rid of the Shadow influence," Galen said, his voice cold. "I need to know how to breach the defense net around Z'ha'dum and arrive there undetected. Tell me that, and I will destroy the implant within your brain and take you to safety. You need serve them no longer."

When Morden refused the offer, Galen would have his confirmation of Morden's true nature. Then he could torture the Shadows' agent for the information, and finally kill him.

Morden began to laugh, a hollow, broken sound.

The reaction bothered Galen, though he did not know why. "If you do not tell me willingly, then you will tell me unwillingly."

Morden continued to laugh.

Galen bit out the words. "Do you remember who you once were?" He conjured a globe between them, revealed within it a quick series of images: the talk on the Anfran love stone, the explosion of the Io jumpgate, Morden's screaming face, the calm of his later interview, Morden smiling as he approached Kosh's quarters to murder the Vorlon, Morden smiling as he paid off the man who had poisoned Londo's love, Adira, Morden smiling as he faced Galen in the mines deep underground. Morden watched in silence.

Galen dissolved the sphere, and they regarded each other.

"I didn't realize they were influencing me," Morden said. "But it doesn't make any difference. I know who I was, and I know who I am. And you don't know the half of it."

"You have committed monstrous acts under their influence. They make you desire chaos and destruction. They make you revel in it. But that doesn't mean you must continue. You can stop. You can do good. All you need do is tell me what I ask."

Morden glanced down at the stone hanging from his neck, his expression unreadable. "I made a deal with them—to manipulate, to tempt, to provoke, to kill. I promised to serve them willingly, with all the skills at my command."

Galen did not want to know, did not want to continue the conversation. Yet he found himself speaking. "You believed your wife and daughter trapped in hyperspace at the moment of their deaths."

Morden's eyebrows rose in surprise. "Yes. They agreed to free my family, to allow them to die."

"You know that—"

"I know it's unlikely. I know they probably died with the explosion. But I couldn't stand the possibility that they were suffering. I would have promised anything, if it had even the slightest chance of helping them."

The Shadows had secured Morden's loyalty using his loved ones against him, just as Morden, in the Shadows' service, had attempted to do with Galen. "Even if the Shadows did free your family, you've more than repaid them."

Morden frowned. "I promised to serve them. For as long as I could."

"But I can free you," Galen said, stunned by the words coming out of his mouth. Somehow, this had gone beyond an attempt to gain information on the Shadows' defense net. He knew he couldn't change Morden's mind, yet still he couldn't stop himself from trying. He didn't know why. He didn't know how it had happened. But somehow it had become more important than anything. "If you can cheat the devil, then shouldn't you do it?"

"Not over this. Not over them. What the Shadows gave me is well worth what I promised."

Morden paid the price from which the mages had fled. Galen pointed the gun toward the necklace. "Your wife and daughter would hate you for what you've done. You do them no honor by killing for their sakes."

"If that's true, then that's another part of the price I have to pay."

"You can transcend yourself," Galen said, wondering who had taken control of his body. "Transcend the Shadows' directives. That's why I'm here. I'm here to offer you a way out."

Morden shook his head. "You're here to free me, as bizarre and incredible as I find that. But I'm not a slave. If you want to free someone, there are better candidates all around you. I chose to serve willingly. There were others who didn't. Others—on the *Icarus* and elsewhere—whose decision was forced upon them by people like me, who wouldn't fight. Living beings trapped inside all the Shadow ships, serving as their central processing units. Legions more, on Z'ha'dum. The conquered Narns, who are being slaughtered every day. Go free them, not me." He held up a warding hand. "I don't need it. I don't want it. I don't deserve it." He sat.

"You don't know what you're saying. You must still be under their influence."

"As are you," Morden said.

"I can free you."

"Why don't you free yourself?" Morden said.

"I plan to," Galen said. "Very soon. But first I need you to tell me how to reach Z'ha'dum safely. Perhaps I can help those enslaved there."

Morden's mouth lifted with the shadow of a smile. "That's not why you want to go to Z'ha'dum. You want to kill the two mages there. You must know you'll never leave alive."

"They killed the ones I loved."

"So you kill in the names of those you lost."

"Though they would hate me for it." Elric's last words: *Do not kill in my name.*

Morden massaged his temple. "The defense protecting Z'ha'dum is called the Eye. I don't know how you can bypass it. It's extremely sophisticated. When we approach, it recognizes us, and we're simply allowed to pass."

When Galen had been connected to Anna, she had thought of something called the Eye, something that gave her commands. Apparently, the Eye not only coordinated the actions of the ships, but also controlled the defense of Z'ha'dum.

Morden looked up at him. "You'll find out no more from me."

"Then it's time to choose," Galen said, though he knew the answer. "Freedom or death." The Shadows had demanded that the mages join with them or die. Galen wondered if the choice he offered Morden was any different.

"You know my decision."

Galen aimed the gun at Morden's head. He must move forward with his task. He had endangered all those on Babylon 5 so he might have the chance to kill Morden. If he didn't do it now, he wouldn't get another opportunity. Morden would continue to provoke murders and wars. The temptation he posed to the mages would remain. Yet still Galen hesitated. "How can you live with yourself?"

"I only offer people what they want." Morden's even white teeth gleamed with his old smile. "You know, you could really stand to enjoy life more, Galen." His hand slipped into his pocket. "What do you want? What would make you happy?"

There were more Shadows on the station, and they'd gotten close enough to regain their influence over Morden.

The door slid open, and Galen only had a moment to catch a glimpse of several armed Humans as he conjured a platform beneath his feet, launched himself at the hole in the wall, and shoved his body inside. Plasma bursts boomed into the wall around him. Frantic energy welled up, desperate to defend, to counter with deadly force.

Galen raised the gun, fired at the glistening membrane. It splattered against the sides of the shaft, and he raced past, losing himself in the narrow, twisting passages.

He'd known exactly what he was going to do. It had all been planned. He had wanted to kill, and the Circle had ordered him to kill. Yet he had not killed. And he had not freed Morden. In some foolish attempt to do good, he'd instead done nothing.

The Shadows' strings to their puppets could not be cut. He had not been able to save Anna, or the hybrid, or Morden. Only one path led to freedom, as Gowen had discovered. The choice he'd presented to Morden had been a false one. There was no freedom for either of them, except in death.

It was not a mistake he would make again.

—— chapter 13 ——

In Anna's mind, behind the barrier of brilliant, blank whiteness, vague forms were taking shape. This didn't feel at all like Bunny's intrusion into her mind. There was no pain, no pressure. Instead, in scattered places, the cloudy brilliance on the far side of the barrier was clearing, revealing shadowy silhouettes that took on color, substance.

She saw many people, many places. Each remained a short time, then faded away. She didn't "remember" any of them, as she remembered her experiences with the machine. Yet she studied each as it came to her.

John Sheridan stood on a beach, talking to her. He pointed farther down the coast, to a tower. Light flashed from the tower, then turned away. The light scanned the area around the tower, just as the Eye scanned the area around Z'ha'dum. It was called a lighthouse, she somehow knew. Short, sand-colored hair blowing over his face, John Sheridan smiled at her.

She was in a dark room filled with books, papers, primitive machinery, strange items. She studied a small, elliptical object that sat on her desk in a circle of light. Anna recognized it as a machine of the liberators. The skin covering it was dull, inactive.

She was lying beside John Sheridan in a bed. He was talking, and she rested her head on his chest.

A man sat propped against a cave wall. It was dark, a single light glaring off the breather covering his face. He wore an orange jumpsuit. There was a burn mark on one arm.

Piece followed upon piece, yet they were not her memories. They carried no emotion or import. They were simply bits of information that had been retrieved from storage. And they were incomplete, fractured, out of context. She didn't understand them.

When the treatment was complete, Justin helped her to sit up on the couch and questioned her about what she remembered. Again he frowned at the results.

"Where were you born?" Justin asked.

She didn't know.

"What is your profession?"

Still, she didn't know.

"Why did you marry John?"

"Where did you and John go on your honeymoon?"

Justin let out a heavy breath, and Anna worried that the liberators might find her undeserving of the great honor for which they had chosen her.

"We don't have much time, Anna," he said. "I'm just going to have to teach you all we know. Maybe you can connect these facts with the images in your mind."

"I will," she said, and he gave her a short smile.

"Beyond that, there's one more thing we can try. Someone you used to know, who might be able to jog your memory. You'll meet him soon."

Galen glided through the ventilation system of Babylon 5, forcing the energy within him to slow, the heat to decline, his pounding heart to calm. Two mind-focusing exercises left only a small window for thought. He had to leave this place.

He accessed the Command and Control database, inserted his ship into the schedule with a departure time in one hour. He could not go after Morden again. The Shadows would be prepared for him; he had lost that opportunity. He must go to Z'ha'dum, even though the defense net would likely kill him. He must hold to what remained of his task. For without it, he would dissolve into chaos.

But first he would convey his information to John Sheridan.

The probe on John's neck revealed he was finally alone, sitting on the couch in his darkened office, a single table lamp illuminating the reports spread across his lap. His hands lay limp on either side of him. Only the sound of slow, regular breaths broke the silence. John was sleeping.

After a good night's rest, John would probably realize the Shadows' strategy on his own. But whether he'd get that sleep, or duty would call on him during the night, as it had so many times before, Galen didn't know. If this visit to Babylon 5 was to be Galen's last act, then he would like to do this one thing, to give John's alliance one small chance to win a victory against the Shadows.

Galen accessed the cameras in the surrounding corridors, found no one nearby. It was 1 A.M., station time. Michael's probe showed him Down Below, continuing his search for the doctor. Perfect.

Galen brought himself to a stop. A few feet farther down was a vent that led into a storage closet near John's office. Galen visualized the equations, conjuring a cluster of intense balls of energy on the vent. In a few seconds they had burned through. He passed into the storage closet, conjured a full-body illusion. He had no time to gain John's trust, to explain all that he knew and how he knew it. He would simply plant the idea and be gone.

The Shadows would not pursue him here. They knew where he was headed, and without a method of penetrating Z'ha'dum's defenses, he could easily be dealt with out on the rim, where he would draw no unwanted attention.

As for the Vorlon Kosh, if he really did live inside John, Galen hoped he would not interfere.

The corridor outside was empty. Galen left the storage closet, made his way to John's large office. Dim light revealed the rectangle of the window, which looked out on the station's vast gardens, now simulating night. John sat in the circle of light from the single lamp, his head hanging to one side, lips slightly parted. In sleep, he looked young, too young for the responsibility he carried.

Galen wondered what plan the Shadows had for him. If he was lost, the alliance would fail. No one else had the power to hold the many races and governments together. Galen wished he could do more for John, but he could not.

He took the tranq tab from his pocket, went to John,

pressed it gently to John's neck. He had formulated the one-inch disk with only a light sedative. With its advanced delivery system, it would take effect in just three seconds, keeping John disoriented during their conversation. Normally he created tabs that bonded to the skin, so his targets had no chance of removing them. But he would leave no trace of his presence.

Galen returned the tab to his pocket, sat beside John, and raised a hand to wake him.

"You carry Shadows within you." The voice came from John, but the voice was not his, and his lips had not moved. John's head remained hanging to one side, his breath slow, regular.

It was the whispering voice he had heard before, echoing with strange resonances of other words, other layers of meaning.

"This place is not for you," the voice said. *"Leave at once."* The words were being sent directly into his mind, but Galen sensed no attempt to invade his thoughts. His exercises continued without disruption.

He spoke softly, so that he would not wake John. "Who are you?"

"You must go to Z'ha'dum and stop those like you. From them spreads a great darkness. Only like can stop like."

"Are you Vorlon? Kosh?"

"You could have crushed me, and you did not. We met in blackness, and you withstood my test."

Kosh must have been the Vorlon he'd encountered in the Thenothk system. "What is the darkness—"

"Tell no one. Secure the aid of my successor, Ulkesh. Do not let him probe your mind."

"Will he help me breach the Shadows' defense net?"

"If you withstand his test, he will not kill you as you attempt to pass to the enemy."

"What of the Eye? If the Vorlons don't kill me, the Shadows will."

"Yes," Kosh said.

"How can I—"

John stirred, opened his eyes. "Michael? What is it?" He straightened. "Another Shadow attack?"

Galen slipped into Michael's persona, his speech patterns. "No, no," he said, "nothing like that. Sorry to wake you. I just wanted to give you an update on Stephen. Something's been bothering me. You know I've been trying to track the doc's movements. I still haven't caught up with him, but from what I hear, it sounds like he's over the worst of the stim with-drawal. Seems fairly fit. Which just makes him harder to find."

John ran a hand over his face.

"The thing is, what he's doing . . . You know how he said he was on walkabout."

"Yes."

"Well, it seems like he's actually, literally, walking about. There's this section of Down Below, and apparently he's walking around it, circling it without ever entering." Galen held up his index finger, rotating it in a slow circle as he spoke. "He's even gone above it and below it, but for some reason he won't enter this area in the center."

John was following the movement of Galen's finger, his head bobbing sleepily.

Galen turned as if to retrieve something from the couch be-hind him, conjured the illusion of a comp-pad in his hand, on its screen a collection of dots in a spherical pattern. He ex-tended the comp-pad toward John. "Each dot here indicates a sighting of Stephen. You see how they're arranged in a shell, with no dots in the center." Again he moved his hand to reflect the pattern.

"I'm sorry, I'm not quite awake. Are you saying Stephen is avoiding this area for some reason?"

"I think he's preparing himself to enter it. I think he's going to enter it soon, very soon. And when he does—I think we better be there to meet him. A lot of innocent people live there."

John shook his head. "You don't think Stephen's dangerous."

Galen withdrew the comp-pad. "No. I just have this feeling that something big is about to happen. Something really big."

John's face fell into lines of concern. "I do too."

Galen stood. He had planted his idea. It was up to John to make the connection, and to fight the battle. It was not his place to do good. "I better go. And you should get to bed."

"Thanks for the update." Slowly John gathered up the reports on his lap, flaring his eyes several times to try to keep them open. "Any news on that techno-mage who attacked Londo?"

"No. I've got a couple men on Londo, though he doesn't know it. The ambassador got himself a ridiculous disguise and slipped into Down Below. It's hard not to root for the techno-mage."

"Whatever he's up to, I just hope he leaves before we have to arrest him, or worse."

Galen nodded and started out of the office.

"It's too bad we don't have some techno-mages fighting on our side."

Galen stopped and turned back to him. "Yes," he said. "It is."

Galen watched through security cameras as the false Kosh left the docking bay where his ship was kept and glided down the nearly empty corridors toward his quarters. As the Shadows concealed their appearance, so did the Vorlons. This one was shrouded in a dark encounter suit, black mottled with blue and red. A long, sleek shell encased his "head," a single red light serving as an eye. The cloth curtaining his body shifted only slightly as he moved.

Galen had read conflicting accounts of the Vorlons' true form; the most credible of those who had seen Vorlons described them as beings of light. Others spoke in awestruck tones of the Vorlons' godlike appearance, an image the Vorlons cultivated to generate unquestioning faith and obedience.

This false Kosh, Galen knew, was brutal and unbending. Ulkesh offered John Sheridan's alliance no support, and he'd terrorized and abused his aide from the day he'd arrived on Babylon 5. Ulkesh would not want to help Galen. The Vorlons had always despised the techno-mages, for good reason. The mages were creations of the Shadows, their ancient enemies. More than that, what would beings of light possibly want to do with beings of darkness? If Kosh offered him help, then Kosh was the exception. Yet Ulkesh held his only chance of reaching Z'ha'dum, of doing what he must do.

When John had demanded Kosh's help in the war, Kosh had attacked him in anger. Kosh had struck only to frighten, though, not to kill. Galen didn't know whether Ulkesh would be similarly restrained. But he could not get into a fight with the Vorlon. He simply needed Ulkesh's assurance that the Vorlons would not stand in his way. Then he would go.

If Ulkesh refused, still he would go. He had no choice. And if the Vorlons came for him on the rim, he would not fight them.

Galen added a second mind-focusing exercise to the one already working through its orderly progression. He had to maintain discipline to sense any telepathic intrusion Ulkesh might attempt. From what little he knew, he believed the mental powers of a Vorlon extremely strong, far stronger than those of a telepath like Bunny. Yet Kosh seemed to believe Galen had the ability to stop Ulkesh. He must be ready to react instantly. He could not betray the mages' hiding place.

Ulkesh was drawing closer. No one else was near.

Galen stepped out of the cross-hallway to block Ulkesh's path.

The curtained figure stopped a few feet away, the sleek head inclining, the red eye fixing on him. His whispering voice resonated with echoes upon echoes. "You stink of Shadows."

"I am a friend of Kosh," Galen said.

"We are all Kosh," Ulkesh said.

"Then I am a friend to you all."

"No," Ulkesh said.

"Last year, I met with Kosh. He said he would help me fight the Shadows. He would allow me to reach Z'ha'dum and tell me how to penetrate its defenses. Now I return for the information, and you stand in his place. Will you give what he promised?"

"No," Ulkesh said.

"Do you protect the Shadows?"

"No," Ulkesh said.

"Then why won't you help me?"

"You cannot fight yourself."

Galen let out a breath. Perhaps there was no difference between him and the Shadows. They both desired chaos and death. If the task was to fight himself, though, Galen believed he was well prepared. That was all he'd been doing for the past two years.

"Only like can fight like," he replied.

Ulkesh's head shifted, the single red eye regarding him more closely. "As you fight, you spread the maelstrom."

"I desire only to find two of my kind who serve the Shadows, and to kill them. They are on Z'ha'dum. If we destroy one another, will that not serve order?"

"Where are the rest?"

"They are dead. Killed by the Shadows."

"Lies."

Galen frantically searched his mind. He sensed no disturbance to his exercises, no sense of intrusion. But how did Ulkesh know?

"You are an abomination." Ulkesh swept past him, continued down the corridor.

Galen realized he would not convince the Vorlon with words. Ulkesh was certain he had all the answers, and Galen must show him otherwise. Galen visualized the equation, conjured an illusion of himself standing where he stood. He retreated down the cross-corridor, accessed the security camera to observe what happened. He composed words for his image to speak, as if writing a message. The illusion spoke.

"If I can destroy two of the Shadows' greatest weapons, is that not good?"

Ulkesh turned to face his image. "No good can come of you."

"Do Kosh's wishes mean nothing? Do you believe no good can come from them either?"

The red eye built rapidly to brilliance, and with a flash, a pulse of energy shot down the hall. It passed through the illusion, burned into the wall.

Galen dissolved his image, stepped from the cross-corridor into sight. "We can surprise you," he said.

Ulkesh's red eye shifted to him, held there. Then the Vorlon turned and glided away.

*   *   *

Dinner for two had been brought in, and Anna and Justin sat across from each other at the large table with the rigid chairs. A small flame burned between them. Justin had explained it was for decoration. According to Earth custom, the food must be eaten with small tools. Anna manipulated them carefully.

Three liberators stood to one side, watching.

"Please, Anna," Justin said, playing the role of John Sheridan, "tell me what happened to you on Z'ha'dum. Why was your ship reported destroyed? Why didn't you contact me in all this time?"

Anna took a careful sip of her tea. They had practiced again and again. She knew what she needed to say. She knew the facts of this archaeologist woman's life, and she had connected some of those facts to images in her mind. The difficulty came in saying the words as Justin wanted her to say them. She must perform gestures as she spoke, vary the tone of her voice, shift her gaze periodically, and convey different expressions. The communication seemed needlessly complex.

She set down her cup. "I know there's a lot that you don't know. I know there's a lot you don't understand. I'm here to fix that." She grasped his wrinkled hand, met his gaze, and smiled. The expression involved a deformation of her facial skin, which carried a limited flexibility much inferior to her machine skin. The tension in her muscles felt strange.

Justin shook his head. "Your smile still isn't right, Anna. You need to look at John as if you love him."

Anna didn't understand what the word *love* meant to Humans, who lived such pathetic lives, but Justin had grown frustrated trying to explain it to her.

"Try thinking of something pleasant. That may help."

Anna imagined how it would feel to be in control of the Eye—to coordinate, to synchronize, to strike. Her face shifted.

"Good, Anna. That's it. That's how you must look at John."

She continued. "Don't you want to know what it's about?

What it's really all about? I can do that. All you have to do is come with me."

"Where?" Justin said.

"Where else? To Z'ha'dum."

Justin tried to pull his hand away, and Anna tightened her grip. He had told her that as she touched John, she gained control over him.

"No, no, Anna. When John tries to pull away, you have to release him. You can't force him to do what you want. You must convince him."

She released Justin's hand, frustrated by the weak, indirect method of control he was teaching her. It did not come naturally. She forced herself to smile. "I can guarantee your safety. They're eager to meet you. It's just a simple invitation. Come and hear their side of the story. Nothing more."

"I have to know what they've done to you," Justin said. "What you've been doing all these years. First tell me that. What happened to the *Icarus*?"

"I thought we were going to study the ruins of an ancient civilization. But when we arrived, we discovered that the civilization wasn't dead at all. We found a very advanced alien race. They were quite approachable." Those were the liberators, Anna thought, her gaze shifting to their brilliant pinpoint eyes. But she didn't like the word *approachable*. The liberators were wise, brilliant, wondrous, and terrifying.

She looked back at Justin. "Our ship, the *Icarus*, had an accident. The crew was killed, com system destroyed."

"Anna—remember what we talked about. You must look sad when you talk about the accident. That is what John would expect from his wife."

Although Anna knew some of the facts of the archaeologist woman's life, she knew none of the thoughts or feelings. What desires she might have had, what dreams, Anna couldn't imagine. With her weak body, her pale, lifeless sensations, her expedition, and her accident, she had known nothing of the real joys of life. She had never danced among the nighttime clouds. She had never shrieked an oratorio of evolution through bloodshed.

Anna arranged her face, tried again. "Our ship, the *Icarus*, had an accident. The crew was—"

"Let's try something else. Sometimes, when people are sad, they will turn away, to hide their sadness. Why don't you do that? Begin the story, then stand and turn away. And speak more slowly."

First Justin had told her the face must show sadness. Now he said she must hide her face.

A question occurred to her. "Why can't I just tell John the truth? That the liberators freed my potential and joined me with the machine?" She found herself growing excited about the idea. She could describe that to John much better than the deaths of some inconsequential Humans. "I could teach him the true greatness of the liberators, and explain the joys of the machine, the beauty of it, towering dark in the vault of the universe—"

"No, Anna. John must not know that." He paused. "The more he knows about our ships, the more of your sisters he will be able to destroy. Try the story again, as we discussed."

She spoke slowly. "Our ship, the *Icarus*, had an accident." She stood and turned away. "The crew was killed, com system destroyed. Those of us who survived had no way to tell Earth what had happened. And even if we could have, the aliens had just come out of hibernation. They were vulnerable. They couldn't risk exposure to outsiders. So they made a deal: In exchange for our silence, they let us study their technology."

One of the technicians came in, and Justin pushed himself up with his cane. "Anna, let me introduce you to the Minbari ambassador, Delenn." Anna came around the table, extended her hand as she had been taught. "Hello. I'm Anna Sheridan. John's wife."

The technician shook her hand, silently nodding.

Justin had told her that Delenn was the greatest threat to her control of John. John was close to taking Delenn as his new wife. The Minbari already had partial control of him. Anna must break that control without killing Delenn, must break it by planting doubt, by proving that she loved John more than the Minbari did. Anna would assert herself as the wife, the one with power over John—just as she would later overcome the one at the center of the Eye and take control of that glorious machine.

"I need to talk to Delenn," Justin said.

Anna modulated her voice to convey displeasure. "After five years, we can't have dinner together? Let her go, John. You can talk to her later. This should be a moment for us."

"You're right. We'll talk later, Delenn," Justin said, and the technician's thick fingers fluttered anxiously. He left.

Anna came close to Justin, laid a hand against his cheek. "You said that Delenn and Kosh told you I was dead. Delenn has misled you again and again. For her own reasons. Selfish reasons. It's time to learn the truth."

Justin nodded, stepped back. "Good, Anna."

"It would be much simpler to kill her."

"But then John would hate you, and he would never come with you to Z'ha'dum."

"You said he loved me."

"His feelings could change. He loves Delenn too."

It angered her that Delenn had gotten so much power. The archaeologist woman was John's wife. Delenn had no place. Anna would gain control of John subtly, by proving herself superior to Delenn, the way she and her sisters had once convinced a planetary ruler to join the side of chaos by hovering over his major cities.

She was eager to meet this powerful nexus, her husband. He had been chosen to have his potential freed, just as she had been. He would learn the joys of chaos; she would help to show him the way. And then she would have what she wanted.

Justin sat. "You're getting better every time. Let's continue. We have more work to do, and not much time. Soon we'll be leaving for Babylon 5."

With a smile, Anna took her seat.

Dressed again as Guy Phillips, Galen entered the customs area, valise in hand. At the security checkpoint, Michael Garibaldi looked up from a conversation with a colleague, noticing him.

Galen would have preferred to avoid Michael. The security

chief must have suspicions about him, particularly after Alwyn's erratic behavior. No doubt that was why Michael was loitering around the checkpoint at this late hour.

But Galen's scheduled 2 A.M. departure was ten minutes away, and he could not delay. He was exhausted, his mind holding tightly to the reassuring rhythm of its exercises, his attention narrowed to the single necessity of boarding his ship, leaving this place.

Galen presented his identicard to Michael.

"Mr. Phillips," Michael said. "Short visit. Any luck drumming up some business?"

"I'm afraid not."

"Sorry to hear that. Feeling better?"

"Yes, thank you."

Michael still had not run his identicard through the scanner. "That Mr. Alecto, he seemed to be carrying some kind of grudge, blaming a Human for the bombing of the Narn homeworld. Do you know where he would get that idea?"

It was a question to which both Galen and Michael knew the answer, but neither would admit. Galen looked out across the empty customs area with its flashing information screens. "Thomas Alecto knows more about the Narn situation than pretty much anyone. I don't even try to understand it. That's not my business." He turned back to Michael. "Thank you for helping Thomas out of trouble. He's a good man, though often reckless." Galen hesitated, decided to take a chance. He fixed Michael with his gaze. "As I've often told him, these are dangerous times, and one should not make enemies unless one is prepared to defend oneself from their attack."

Michael pursed his lips, studying Galen. "I couldn't have said it any better." Something across the customs area caught his attention. "Oh look, it's Mr. Alecto's friend."

Morden was approaching, a small suitcase in each hand. He must have moved up his departure time to coincide with Galen's, and Galen had been too preoccupied to notice. Michael's smile revealed that he was not surprised in the least. He was here for the express purpose of witnessing this meeting.

Galen accessed his sensors, searched through frequencies. Two new Shadows accompanied Morden.

"Mr. Phillips, isn't it?" Morden said in his smooth, threatening voice, setting his suitcases down to either side.

"You're leaving early," Galen said.

"Yes, something unexpected came up." Morden folded his hands in front of him. With the Shadows' influence had returned an intensity, a certainty to his manner. Of the Human being with whom Galen had briefly made contact, there was no sign.

"I hope it won't ruin your plans with your girlfriend," Galen said. "I think she's going to enjoy your gifts."

Morden's gaze lingered on Galen. "It's thoughtful of you to mention. Please tell your friend that I hope I see him again soon."

"I know he feels the same way."

"I hope to see you again too, Guy." Morden smiled, revealing even white teeth. Yet the smile was different than before, sharper and harder and filled with malice. It was the Shadows' anger, Galen realized, channeled through Morden.

"Mr. Garibaldi." Morden extended his identicard, and Michael regarded it for a moment.

"No matter how many times we say good-bye, you keep coming back—like a bad meal."

"A bad but expensive meal, I hope."

Michael took the card, ran it through the scanner, and returned it. Galen stepped aside, and Morden picked up his suitcases and passed through the checkpoint, the Shadows following.

Michael looked after him, troubled. Finally he ran Galen's card through the scanner. When he handed it back, he maintained his hold on one end, drawing Galen's gaze to his. "I think you're the one who needs to be careful."

"You're mistaken. It's you. And your captain. Watch over him."

Michael's lips tightened, and Galen took the card and headed down the passageway.

Now he would go to Z'ha'dum.

— *chapter 14* —

Anna sat in a small chamber within the machine, on a seat that had been extended up out of the floor for her. The machine surrounded her—its graceful curves, its life, its power—yet she was not part of it. She was only a passenger, one of those inferior irritants that used to prowl her insides, their heat and oily excretions repulsive. Anna caressed the shifting black skin of the seat, skin like that which had once been hers.

She had been ripped from the machine, taken from her joy. She longed to go to the heart of this machine, to rip out whoever lay there and sink into the precious gelatinous blackness, to connect once again with the best part of herself. But she could not.

Obedience.

Besides, if she waited just a little longer, she would be joined with a much greater machine.

Consulting an image of the archaeologist woman displayed on one wall, the technicians styled the hair on her head, removed the hair from her legs. This pathetic body required far more maintenance than the machine.

Justin stepped into the doorway. "Everything going well?"

"Yes," Anna said.

He had been growing more anxious since yesterday, moving restlessly about the ship, once even raising his voice to the liberators. There had been a great battle, and John Sheridan's forces had destroyed many of her sisters. John had used the hated telepaths against them.

After the battle, the liberators had gone off on their own to huddle in bursts of overlapping, chirping speech. For the first time, Anna had wondered if their victory could be in doubt.

But that was impossible. If they were defeated, that would mean their enemies were superior. No one could be superior to the liberators and their great machines. Most certainly not a Human.

Before John could do them more harm, he had to be stopped. Destroying him was the proper method. Every instinct told her that. Yet Justin had said John might be controlled, might be convinced, his potential freed. That was what the liberators wished, and they, with their wondrous intelligence and unfathomable knowledge, were far wiser than she. They had entrusted her with a great responsibility, and she would not fail them.

"We'll have the clothes and makeup and things directly," Justin said in his quavering voice.

Anna looked at the image on the wall, the smiling woman with the wavy dark hair and brown jacket. She looked down at herself. She wore a short green dress that she knew had once belonged to Bunny. It was sufficient, but it was not something the archaeologist woman would have worn. So she could not wear it.

"We'll send for you in a few minutes," Justin said, and headed for the lower levels. The machine was admitting a visitor in another ship. Justin had told her the archaeologist woman had known this Human, but he would not say the Human's name. He was hoping she would remember, Anna knew.

As soon as the technicians were finished, Anna followed after Justin. Perhaps she could study the visitor unobserved for a few minutes, try to connect the Human with the images in her mind.

Outside the machine's main chamber she heard Justin's voice, along with high bursts of chirping from the liberators. She stopped.

"It was a complete disaster," Justin said. "The strike was supposed to be an overwhelming, demoralizing slaughter, a total surprise. Instead our fleet has suffered major damage. How did John Sheridan know where we were going to attack?"

"He's a military man, and he's smart." The visitor's voice was smooth, deep. She didn't recognize it. "He deduced our strategy. But he doesn't have any idea what's coming next."

The liberators' anxious speech continued over the conversation of the two men.

"Our plan was to approach a demoralized John Sheridan," Justin said, "not one riding the crest of his greatest victory. I don't like the way the timing of this is going. On top of that, you said Galen was going directly to Z'ha'dum, but it's been eight days since he left Babylon 5, and we've detected no sign of him in the area."

Galen was the machine she had connected with before, she remembered. The machine who looked like a Human.

"He may be coming up with a plan of some kind."

"If he delays much longer," Justin said, "this could become a real problem for us. We can't postpone our contact with John Sheridan. We can't allow him time to follow up on his victory."

"Galen won't be a problem. They know how to handle him."

There was a pause. Then Justin spoke again. "How did your trip go?"

"According to plan," the smooth-voiced visitor said. "Emperor Cartagia has sent the offer via diplomatic pouch. Londo should learn of his new position as adviser to the emperor on planetary security on the same day that John Sheridan learns his wife isn't really dead."

"At least something is going the way it's supposed to."

"How is she?" the visitor asked.

"She remembers pieces of her past, but her old emotions and personality have stayed beyond our reach. I thought at first it was hopeless, but she's been improving rapidly, learning to respond to different situations. Her husband will notice some change. He'll also see, though, that she's his wife, and what she says will matter to him. I'm hoping you can bring her further along, even in the short time we have left. Whatever it takes, this has to succeed. One way or the other."

The harsh chirp of one of the liberators broke into their conversation.

"Anna?" Justin called. "Are you there?"

She entered.

Four liberators stood huddled on one side of the room. The head of one was raised, brilliant white eyes fixed on her. On the other side sat Justin and the visitor. The visitor quickly stood when he saw her. "Sheridan."

He was a Human of compact build, with dark hair styled cleanly back. He wore a dark suit, and a black stone hung from a silver chain about his neck. His hands hung at his sides, and he stared at her with the unwavering intensity Justin had told her Humans did not use with other Humans.

She searched her memory for his image, or his name. "I recall you," she said. "You were in a tunnel on Z'ha'dum. You were sitting on the ground. Your arm"—she pointed to it—"was burned."

The visitor nodded. "I had been shot."

Justin pushed himself up with his cane. "Do you know who this is, Anna?"

That image came from the time after she'd arrived on Z'ha'dum, but before she'd been joined with the machine. "That's all I remember," she said.

"This is Morden, Anna. He was an archaeologist, like you. He came with you on the *Icarus*."

Anna came toward him, extended her hand. "Hello. I'm Anna Sheridan. John's wife."

Morden frowned as he shook her hand. When their hands separated, he folded his together in front of him and turned to Justin. "Sheridan would never introduce herself as John's wife."

"We did the best we could with what little we knew. Don't confuse her on the things she's already learned. Just try to teach her more. What do you think of her appearance?"

Morden barely looked at her. "She's thin. The hair is too neat."

Justin let out a heavy breath. "You should have seen her when we first took her out." He glanced toward the liberators. One continued to watch them, while the others chattered. "You two should catch up on old times. And Morden, perhaps you can help Anna finish getting ready. In the meantime, we've got our own matters to discuss. Anna, why don't you take him back to your room?"

Morden had known the archaeologist woman, and he found Anna a disappointment. He was wrong. She was more now than she had ever been. But she would learn all she could from him.

Morden picked up a case on the floor beside him and looked to the liberators. Anna did the same. To her surprise, the liberator who had been watching lowered his head, joining in the rapid conversation, leaving Anna and Morden on their own. The liberators were still concerned about the battle they'd lost.

Morden followed her from the chamber, and she spoke to him as they walked. "Why did you call me *Sheridan* instead of *Anna*?"

"That's what I used to call you. You and the other archaeologists liked to call one another by your last names. You felt it distinguished you from the IPX executives, who used first names as if they were your friends, when they really weren't."

"And you were really her friend?"

"Whose friend?"

"Sheridan's."

He turned his head away, and Anna was reminded of Justin's instruction to turn away when she described the accident to John. "Not a very good one," Morden said, "but yes, I was. She made me her friend."

"Then you can tell me what I need to know. So I can control John Sheridan."

Morden's head turned back, and his dark eyes again studied her, and he nodded.

When they reached her chamber, Morden dismissed the technicians waiting there, saying they needed to be alone.

He questioned her, at first, to discover how much she knew. Next he told her about herself: who she had been, what she had believed, how she had behaved. As he spoke, he rubbed his forehead periodically. Sometimes she didn't understand, and she had to question him. That made him angry, and as her questions increased, the answers drove out of him with more and more force, until his smooth voice poured out facts like an assault.

"Sheridan loved her work. She loved to learn. She loved her husband. She hated corporate politics. She refused to lie or use people just to get ahead. When she saw people in pain—she tried to help them, whether they would help her in return or not."

"What about evolution through bloodshed?"

Again, her question seemed to anger him. "Sheridan would hurt someone only if her own life or a friend's was threatened and there was no other way. If there was a way, she would try to save even her enemies."

"She was a fool." Anna wondered how the liberators had sensed she'd had any potential at all.

"It's not your place to make a judgment," Morden snapped. With a deep breath, he folded his hands in his lap. When he spoke again, his words came more slowly. "There's no point to it. You're supposed to learn, so you can fool John. What do you do as an archaeologist?" He was going to test her understanding of the information he'd given her.

"I uncover artifacts of ancient civilizations, such as the J/Lai, the Anfran, and the Subatu."

"What do you enjoy most about that?"

"I like to figure out how the beings in those cultures thought, and how they lived." The answer troubled Anna. "But what importance can that have? Those beings are dead because they failed. Their civilizations were inferior."

"You believed that studying the past could tell us about the present, and the future."

"What can the inferior past tell us about the present?"

"The past has formed us. It has made us who we are and determined what we want. It reveals where we came from, and where we're going."

How could someone who knew the First Principles understand them so little? "We go toward perfection, through means of warfare and chaos. Those who survive are superior. The past is filled with the corpses of the inferior."

He studied her silently. "Sometimes things of great worth can be lost in the past. Ideas, knowledge, people." He took her hand, turned the palm faceup. "Do you see the thickened, hardened skin here? And here?" He ran his finger over her palm, sending a strange sensation shivering up her arm. "These calluses are the result of numerous small injuries you sustained in the course of your work. Friction, pressure, scrapes—this is a map of your past. You gladly accepted these injuries, because they brought you closer to the answers you sought. Answers that you—gave your life for."

She studied her hand, an archaeologist's hand. "This skin is incredibly vulnerable." She looked up at him. "Do you mean my inferior life? Before my potential was released?"

"When we arrived on Z'ha'dum, the liberators offered each of us a choice, to serve them willingly, or to serve them unwillingly. Do you remember what you chose?"

"I remember being born into the machine. I remember its cold, dark embrace." She felt her face deforming into a smile. "It taught me the secret life of circuits, the joys of circulation and cleansing, the elegance of neurons firing in perfect harmony. It revealed the sublime beauty of itself, towering dark in the vault of the universe. And I joined with it." Of course she had joined willingly.

His hand was tight about hers. "You used to want to understand the past. That was your passion. What do you want now? What have they promised you, Anna?"

"Not 'Sheridan'?"

"You're not Sheridan."

She was not. And she had no desire to be. "I want to be joined with the machine, with the greatest of all machines. They will give me control of the Eye if I succeed."

Morden released her, and his hands withdrew into his pockets. "Let's make sure you can pretend, at least, to be Sheridan. Then you can have what you want. One of the ancient civilizations you studied had a love incantation that you used to read to John. What was it?"

"The song of the Anfran star god. 'Bring me the love that ascends as far into the heavens as the gods can reach. Bring me the love that is the ultimate joining of two essentials, with nothing withheld, nothing rejected. Bring me the love that is returned stronger than it was given, that grows more powerful and irresistible with each exchange. Bring me the love that enriches all it touches, transmuting misfortune into promise, weakness into strength, selfishness into generosity, limitation into possibility. Bring me the love that knows no borders.' "

Morden's mouth twisted in a strange expression.

The true meaning of the love incantation came to her in a

flash of insight. "That's what I feel for the machine, Morden. The ultimate joining. Sheridan could never have felt that with John."

"But she did. One Human can feel that for another."

"One Human can't join completely with another."

"They can, in a way I can't explain. But everything you feel for the machine, you once felt for John." Morden looked away.

At last, she understood one of the emotions the archaeologist woman had felt. Anna didn't know how it could be so, but she had once felt for John the great passion she felt for the machine. And she must make John believe she felt it still.

Morden looked back at her with a smile, his teeth strikingly even, white. "We have to finish getting you ready." He set the case on the seat beside him, opened it. "Take off that dress, and put this suit on. John has a picture of you in his drawer, and this is what you're wearing." As Morden held out the suit, his head turned to the doorway. Anna followed his gaze, finding one of the liberators there.

She laid down the suit and began to undress.

Galen sat silently in his ship, drifting at the outskirts of the Alpha Omega system. In his mind's eye, the ship's sensors provided an image of the space all around. Barely visible at the extremes of magnification, the third planet was a black fleck against the tiny bright disk of the sun. As he stared at that fleck, that dark heart of the chaos that had caused so many deaths, and would cause so many more, he wanted nothing but to crush it and all who lived there. The tech burned cold and restless, echoing his desire. The darkness had its own heart within him, but he could not surrender to it. He must hold to his task.

Over the last ten days, he had returned the trading vessel he'd rented, retrieved his mage ship from the backwater where he'd hidden it, then made his way quickly to the rim.

Now that he was here, though, he only drifted. He saw no sign of Vorlons, despite Kosh's claim that they would try to stop him. Even if they let him pass, he had no idea how he might penetrate Z'ha'dum's defense net. He had watched Shadow ships come and go from the planet, and he could detect no trace of the Eye. He suspected he would not detect it until it had already seized his ship. In the unlikely event he did reach the planet, he still found it hard to believe that Elizar and Razeel were there. It made no sense.

Elizar's "invitation" to Galen—*let him come to me, if he dares*—implied that Elizar would remain on Z'ha'dum. But Galen thought it might be a ruse, a way to trap or kill him within the defense net.

He had felt certain that if Elizar translated the spell of destruction, brother and sister would use their new ability in the largest Shadow attack of the war, helping to spread terror and crush any resistance. Elizar was sensitive to issues of power and politics, and he would know that to maintain any position of influence with his associates, he would have to constantly prove his value. Galen had waited, here, for Elizar to reveal his hand.

Yet the battle had come and gone. Watching through the mages' many probes, he had seen no sign of Elizar or Razeel. Perhaps they'd been unable to translate his spell of destruction, just as Alwyn had been unable to translate his one-term equation for listening to the Shadows. Or perhaps the knowledge Bunny had gained was incomplete. In any case, as the forces of light and dark had clashed in their first major engagement, here he had sat, just as he had in the hiding place, watching as others lived and fought and died.

John had deduced the Shadows' strategy. He had gathered his forces, had surprised the Shadow fleet. The alliance's telepaths succeeded in blocking the connections between many of the Shadow ships and the living beings at their cores. As those ships hung frozen in space, the Army of Light hammered them with the sustained blasts necessary to penetrate their strong Shadow skins. Some were destroyed; many fled. Galen wondered if Anna had been among those lost.

Alwyn and G'Leel fought with the alliance, Alwyn's mage ship disguised as a small Narn fighter. They helped destroy two of the Shadow vessels, and despite their reckless tactics, they survived unharmed.

The victory, however, was not without cost. Although the surrounding planets and refugees were barely touched, many alliance ships were lost—two for every one of the Shadows'.

Some of those deaths could have been avoided if Galen had fought with them, used his power in their cause. But he had not dared approach the heat of battle.

Now it was over. John was safe and back on Babylon 5. Yet the danger, Galen feared, was greater than ever. In their defeat, the Shadows had learned that they'd underestimated their enemy. They would not be taken by surprise again. Many more battles would follow. Many more would die. The Shadows would pursue their plan against John with new malice and determination. But Galen could do nothing for John, or for the Army of Light. The light was not his place. That fleck of darkness was. He must hold to the remnants of his task.

If Elizar and Razeel were not at the battle site, and were not elsewhere, perhaps they were, truly, on Z'ha'dum. Why they would draw him here, to the home of the Shadows, he didn't know. Were they that certain the Eye would destroy him before he reached the surface?

Or did Elizar and Razeel plan to let him pass, confident in their ability to control him once he landed? He believed Elizar would want to fight him face-to-face. Just as he wanted to fight Elizar. As he had wanted for a long time.

He remembered the Shadow's words: *As for Galen, you know our plans for him, if you can capture him. In any case, he must be stopped.*

If their intent was to capture him, then they would attempt to maneuver him into a place where they could turn off his tech. The device implanted by the Circle would kill him, and whatever plans the Shadows had for him would fail. They could not force him to do ill.

Only he would be responsible for any bad he did. As long as he maintained control, then he had nothing to fear. He would either succeed at his task or fail, but he would do no further harm. He could hope for no more. And he should delay no longer.

The mages would send someone to meet him at the rendezvous point in twelve days. But he would not be there.

Galen sent the command to his ship, and it started forward, toward Z'ha'dum and its defenses.

As if materializing out of nothingness, a ship appeared directly in front of him.

Galen stopped his forward motion, the tech surging with anxious energy.

He recognized the distinctive yellow-green coloring, the long, narrow frame with four flowing arms aimed forward, almost like a squid on its side.

The Vorlon ship drew closer, coming up alongside him. The hull rippled, like liquid, gathering in one spot, its thickness growing. With a graceful stretch the material extended from the hull, clamped on to his ship. The Vorlon had docked with him.

The extension was centered on his fore air lock. Perhaps the Vorlon wanted to fight in private. Galen wondered which of them was supposed to pass through the extension. If Galen entered it, the Vorlon could easily kill him simply by breaking the airway and shooting him out into the vacuum.

Galen didn't think the Vorlon was going to come to him, though. If he stunk of Shadows, no doubt his ship did as well.

He went down to the air lock, closed himself between the two thick doors. The atmosphere, temperature, and pressure within the extension matched that in his ship. He opened the outer door, looked down the dimly lit cylindrical extension. The walls were the same yellow-green as the ship's exterior, though they radiated a faint light. The passage was about twenty feet long, eight feet in diameter. At its far end was the hull of the Vorlon's ship.

The flowing, liquid movement that had created the extension—he'd seen it before, in the Shadow building on Thenothk, and the membrane protecting Morden's room. He'd known that the Vorlons utilized organic technology, just as the Shadows did, but he'd been able to find only the most vague information on it. Galen set his sensors to record.

Tentatively, he brought his hand to the wall, ready to pull away at the slightest hint of movement. The surface was hard yet warm, its yellow-green pattern shifting slightly. He detected carbon, silicon, oils, various organic compounds. Beneath the skin, electrical activity traveled along structures that resembled nerves, elastic fibers stretched like muscles, and liquid flowed through a circulatory system. When he'd been connected to Anna, he'd gotten a similar impression of the Shadow ships.

He sensed something more, though, something in the shifting pattern of its skin, an unquantifiable sense of life, and more than that, of intelligence. As if he were in the presence of a sentient creature, and that creature was watching him.

Galen began two new mind-focusing exercises. He had to keep his thoughts calm, disciplined, so he would notice any telepathic probe.

He stepped out of the air lock and found the bottom of the cylinder as hard and firm as the side. He extended his sensors forward, searching. The Vorlons were the ancient enemies of the Shadows. They believed in order, while the Shadows promoted chaos. But did they, too, use innocent beings as central processing units for their ships? He could not tell.

Around him the patterns shifted, studying him. He moved ahead. Time for the Vorlon to let him in or kill him.

Galen stumbled on some unevenness. A ripple propagated through the yellow-green skin beneath his feet and continued ahead, toward the Vorlon ship. The ripple ran not only through the bottom of the cylindrical passage, but all around its circumference, in the shape of a ring. He stopped, puzzled. In a moment, another ripple followed, and another, as if the passage were wrinkling. Galen glanced back, saw the extension had sealed up behind him and was retracting, rushing at him like a great wave. He had only an instant to hold his breath before it slammed into him, enveloping him in its fluid currents, tumbling him over and over, driving him forward, into the Vorlon ship.

Then the movement stopped, and Galen found himself submerged in the ooze of the ship. He fluttered his eyes open for an instant; the yellow-green glow surrounded him. He jerked his arms and legs, trying to push his way through it. His sensors revealed a hollow area a few feet ahead. That must be the interior of the ship.

As he struggled, the material tightened its hold, as if he were thrashing through metacrete that was hardening by the moment. Movement required more and more effort, grew more and more limited, until finally, he was immobilized.

Frantic energy welled up in him, and he found himself visualizing the blank screen in his mind, ready to impose spells upon it, to attack.

But killing the Vorlon was not his purpose. He would not lose control. He would not strike out. Instead, as the need to breathe intensified, he focused on his exercises, building them step by orderly step in his mind.

If the Vorlon meant to kill him, then he would be killed. Whatever happened, though, he could not allow the Vorlon to learn the mages' hiding place. He would not be the cause of their deaths.

The ship's grip on him remained tight, holding his straining limbs in their awkward positions, squeezing around his chest, pressing at his face, and somehow he could sense that intelligence all around him, the shifting yellow-green patterns winding over him, studying him.

At last the pressure to breathe became overwhelming, and he gasped, his lips barely able to part. To his surprise, oxygen filled his lungs.

As his chest heaved with needy breaths, the grip on him loosened slightly. He realized he heard a sound, some kind of humming. At first he thought it was some strange echo caused by the material pressed tight over his ears, the same way a conch shell echoed with the rush of one's own pumping blood. But the humming changed, shifted. The tune carried meaning within it, a meaning he could understand. It spoke of the beauty of order, of perfect symmetry and ultimate peace.

It was the ship he was hearing, the ship singing to itself.

The unity of its functioning, the satisfaction of service wove through its melody. Obedience was its greatest joy.

It reminded him of Anna, who lived only to serve the machine. Using his sensors he searched deeper into the ship, fearing that the Vorlons were no different than the Shadows, that they too enslaved living beings at the hearts of their ships. He sensed the Vorlon, perhaps twenty feet away, an intense concentration of energy interacting with the ship's systems. The Vorlon was the nerve center, the controller of the ship.

He detected no being through which the operations of the

ship were channeled, except for the Vorlon. Galen's sensors penetrated only a small portion of the ship, however; perhaps there was a being too distant to detect. As Galen studied the exchange of energy and information between the Vorlon and the ship, it struck him that their relationship was in some ways similar to that between a mage and his ship, though the Vorlon vessel was obviously much more advanced. It had an intelligence of its own, separate from the Vorlon; the Vorlon connected with it to control it.

The ship's song continued, a repeating melody. It was waiting, Galen realized, waiting for further instructions. It lived to obey its master.

Apparently the Vorlon's plan was not to kill him, at least not yet. Against the tight grasp of the ship, Galen forced a slight movement of his lips, spoke the words. "Face me." With his ears covered, he could not hear his voice at all.

He waited, continuing with his exercises.

The dim glow behind his eyelids began to build, like a sunrise, and as its intensity built, like more than a sunrise, like the sun rushing toward him, and more, like the sun swallowing him with its blinding brilliance. The light slid inside him.

It burned like acid through his eyes and into his brain. In the blazing light swam images of Elric, of Blaylock, and the others he had left behind. He was in his ship, flying through hyperspace toward the hiding place.

He forced his mind away. He yelled, "Get out of my head or I'll destroy you." He was drowning in the blazing radiance, disintegrating in it. "Do it now!" He visualized a blank screen, holding with ferocious focus to his exercises.

The brilliance pulled out of him, feeling, for a moment, as if it had sucked his brain out with it.

A shifting radiance surrounded him. "You are an abomination." The voice, unmistakably Ulkesh's, whispered from the skin covering his ears. It echoed with resonances of other words, other meanings.

Galen maintained his exercises, wary. "You came all this way to tell me that?"

"The pestilence must be eradicated."

"I agree. That is why I am here."

"You carry the pestilence."

"I know," Galen said. "And I agree. The pestilence must be eradicated. I wish only to stop two of my kind who serve the Shadows, before I stop myself."

"All of your kind serve darkness."

"You came here either to kill me or to help me. I am still waiting to learn which."

"Impatience serves chaos."

"Delay also serves them."

"If you were a servant of mine," Ulkesh said, "you would learn obedience."

"As you have taught your ship?"

"As our ships serve us, so you serve your masters."

"We are not slaves," Galen said. "We can fight the Shadows' programming. We can do good."

"In breaking their rules," Ulkesh said, "you serve only chaos."

"There's no winning with you, is there?"

"Good can only come from order. Order from obedience to rules. Control."

"I have maintained control for the last two years."

"All of you must die."

"We will kill one another before long," Galen said. "We consume ourselves like the ouroboros, the snake that eats its own tail. The process has already begun. I simply seek to include these two who have escaped us. Does that not serve your purpose?"

Ulkesh was silent.

Galen realized that the Vorlon was waiting for him to say something. Then he realized what it was. He spoke into the shifting light. "The Shadows will know nothing of your assistance. I will tell them nothing willingly. And they will take nothing from me unwillingly. I have a device within me. If they attempt to disable my tech and take my knowledge, the device will kill me."

Still, Ulkesh was silent. Then, finally, in his whispering, resonant voice, he spoke. "You are chaos."

"Are you going to help me or not?"

"You are chaos. When Chaos looks upon you, she will see chaos. Like allows like."

"That's it?" The defense net was like the membrane in Morden's vent, then. It had recognized him as being similar, had allowed him to pass. Certainly this system, though, was much more sophisticated.

"To resist it is to betray yourself. In complete surrender you may pass."

"Thank you," Galen said.

"That is where you belong."

The brilliant light began to fade, Ulkesh retreating.

The faint hum of the ship's song changed, and Galen realized it had received an order. The hold on him loosened, the material softening into a thick ooze. In a dizzying rush the current slammed into him, driving him backward, spinning him head over heels. With a rude sound it ejected him, and he was shooting through frigid blackness, the vacuum sucking the air out of him. He slammed hard into the air lock of his ship.

The rippling cylinder of yellow-green hovered above him, regarding him.

Galen selected the command, and the air lock's outer door slid closed. Then air was rushing back in around him, and he pushed himself up. Beyond the air-lock window the extension retracted, flowing back into the main body of Ulkesh's ship, the mass rippling outward, dissipating.

Galen was left with Ulkesh's final words. *When it suits us, you will all die.*

The Vorlon ship raced off into blackness.

Anna handed her identicard to the security officer and looked out at the area beyond the checkpoint. Few beings moved about. It was a time of rest, according to the schedule most kept here. Primitive information screens covered the walls; lights too bright shone down upon rows of rigid chairs. Anna laid her hand against the wall. This machine, Babylon 5, was large and held many lives. But it was soulless, dead.

Justin had told her John controlled it, though not in the way Anna controlled the machine; instead, in the strange, indirect way Humans had of controlling things.

The security officer looked up from his primitive handheld device. "Been out of circulation for a while, haven't you?"

"Is there a problem?" Anna said, tilting her head in an animated fashion.

The officer glanced again at his device, his forehead furrowing. "No . . . no." He handed back the card. "Here on business?"

"I'm here to see my husband. John Sheridan."

He seemed to have nothing further to say, so she continued on her way. She followed the route to John's quarters. She had to concentrate to keep her balance on the shoes Morden had brought her. Her legs were such a primitive method of propulsion. She passed down the corridors, reviewing all she had learned, all she must do.

Then she stood before John's door. She pressed the code into the keypad, and the door opened.

Inside, in John's place stood the hated Delenn, the one who sought to take her place as John's wife. She wore a loose robe, her long hair cascading over it. The bony plate that circled her head looked almost like a crown. In her hand Delenn held a small transparent globe. Within it was a miniature version of the lighthouse from the beach, primitive reminder of the great Eye.

Anna wanted to shriek out an attack, to destroy this challenger to her power. But Justin had prepared her for this situation, and she remembered his instructions.

Anna smiled and entered, holding out her hand. "Hello. You must be Delenn. I'm Anna Sheridan. John's wife."

The globe fell from Delenn's hand.

Ahead, the image of Z'ha'dum grew, no longer a black speck, but a small disk streaked in different shades of brown. Galen sat quietly, hands pressed flat against his legs, an exercise of the alphabet holding his mind as still, and empty, as possible. Whatever came, he must not resist it. He must allow it to pass over him and through him, to identify him as a creature of shadows, an agent of chaos and destruction.

The Eye would allow him to pass, when no others could draw close, because he was kin. That was why the Shadows feared the mages; that was why the Shadows had insisted the mages join with them or die. The mages could infiltrate their bases, tap their communications. Like could fight like. So he would be admitted, and the Trojan horse would invade the stronghold of the enemy.

It fell on him like a brilliant, black light, streaming down over him, probing, searching for access. Galen relinquished his exercise. The black light poured in through his eyes. It spilled down over the back of his head and prickled against the stippled discoloration along his shoulders and spine, flowing inward. It tingled against the sensors in his fingertips, reached in along the threads of tech, up his fingers, up his arms. At the same time that it invaded him, he felt its blackness bathing his ship, slipping into the silvery body of his chrysalis, coiling around its threads, considering.

As it twined up along the lines of his tech, the tech, in turn, began to warm, to quicken. Galen wanted to suppress the energy with an exercise, but he could not or he would be detected. Adrenaline raced through his system, setting his heart pounding.

Then, as it circulated through him, the black light began to speak. It carried words, whispers, just like the Shadow communications. They infected him.

Chaos is the proper state of being, the state in which all impulse is freed to act. Chaos is the way to strength. Chaos is the engine powering life. Chaos finds its fullest expression in times of war. In war all are put to the test. In war those unfit are exterminated. Only in bloodshed can true progress be made, can promise be realized. In war we are victorious, and through war true perfection will be realized.

The Eye's whispers elicited a sympathetic vibration from the tech, and he found it echoing those words, reveling in thoughts of destruction, its energy building, burning, churning. And as it did, so did he, since they were one and the same, indivisible unto death.

He whispered with the joy of chaos, the rapture of impulses freed at last to act, to strike down, to strike down the enemy, to rid the universe of them, to attack and not to stop, not until the enemy was utterly destroyed. To suffer no more in tolerance and patience, to kill those who killed, to kill those who threatened, to kill those who offended, to kill those who erred, to kill those who could be killed, for the greater good, the good of evolution, the good of progress, the good of perfection.

He was blazing, incandescent, energy singing along the meridians of the tech, a vibration so pure it was painful. This was how it felt to be truly alive, not hiding in a tiny prison of his own making, hiding unnecessarily, as if he had done wrong, when it was the universe that was wrong, the universe that should hide from him. He remembered the raging joy of crushing Drakh after Drakh, Shadow after Shadow. They deserved to die, just as Tilar deserved to die, just as Circe and Londo and Morden and Elizar and Razeel and so many others. The Circle, for lying to him. She, for leaving him behind. His parents, for giving him birth. He was a fool for trying to kill only three people. He should destroy it all—the Shadows, the Vorlons, the Centauri, the Narn, the Minbari, the Humans—they were all programmed for destruction, all programmed to hurt one another, and keep hurting, for as long as they could. But he could stop them. He could crush them all. He wanted to crush them all.

With a rush of satisfaction, the black light flowed out of him. The Eye turned away.

But still the brilliant incandescence raced through his veins, shot down his neurons. His body was shaking, both seized with the energy and surging with it. He wanted to destroy. He wanted to kill. Who or what, it did not matter.

He visualized the equation, brought the energy down upon himself. The brilliant blue fire rushed over his body like living lava, searing him, consuming any hair from his body.

Again.

Again.

At last his mind cleared enough that he could visualize a single letter glowing in blue in the upper left corner of a blank screen.

A.

He clung to the letter, unable to think what came next, unable to continue. Finally he realized what he must do. The blue fire raked down his skin, scouring it away. He doubled over, his nerve endings overloaded with sensation, with pain. Then he was able to continue.

A B.

And again.

A B C.

He continued with the exercise, and after that, another, and another, retreating from that place, from that time, recoiling from those feelings, withdrawing farther down the dark tunnel, drawing the walls up tighter, squeezing the fist of his will until there was no past, no future, no universe, nothing but a ship, and within the ship a body, and within the body a heart, a dark heart, beating, beating, beating.

When John Sheridan came from the other room, the first thing Anna felt was surprise. In his loose robe, with his dark-blond hair in disarray, he looked so unremarkable, so pathetic and Human. Was this the nexus, whose influence and control stretched across the galaxy?

As his sharp gaze found her, though, she did sense something, a power she hadn't detected in any other Human. He carried some of the authority of the techno-mage Elizar, but more than that. Anna couldn't say what. A strange flutter of excitement passed through her. It felt as if the machine's beat had stumbled. He was no ordinary Human. No wonder he had been able to murder so many of her sisters. He was dangerous.

She had reached her target. Now she must gain control of him.

"Anna, my God, what are you doing here?"

He called her *Anna.* Was he really her friend, or just pretending to be? He wasn't smiling; she couldn't identify the expression on his face. He glanced toward the other room, where Delenn's figure moved behind frosted glass. Delenn had no place here. Anger filled Anna.

" 'What are you doing here?' " she said. "After five years that's the best that you can do?" Delenn came from the other room, dressed in new clothes, and stopped beside John. Anna's eyes narrowed on her. "Though under the circumstances, I can understand."

"I—I should go," Delenn said, and started toward the door.

"No—Delenn, wait," John said.

Delenn brushed past Anna, left. The door swung closed behind her.

"It's all right, John. Let her go. You can talk to her later. This should be a moment for us."

John stared at her, and he looked as if he were in pain. "I thought you were dead."

"You mean she didn't . . . She didn't tell you? Well, that is interesting." His gaze sent that strange flutter through her again, and she raised a hand to her stomach. She moved toward him. She could pretend to be a friend too. "Oh, John. I'm sorry that I couldn't tell you myself. I'm sorry for leaving you alone for so long, not being able to get word to you. But that's behind us now. We're together again."

She reached out to touch him, and he took a step back, frowning. She forced herself not to pursue him.

"I know what you're thinking," she said. "How can you be sure it's really me? For all you know—for all she told you—I could be some *thing* made up to look like me. Fine, I'll take whatever test you want. Ask me any question. I don't mind." She knew all the answers, and once she had proven that, he would fall further under her control. "I know there's a lot that you don't know. I know there's a lot that you don't understand. I'm here to fix that." She took another step, laid a hand on his chest. It was warm, and rose slightly to press against her hand. She looked up at him, and imagining that he was the Eye, that they would soon be joined, she smiled. "Don't you want to know what it's about? What it's really all about? I can do that. All you have to do is come with me."

"Where?"

"Where else? To Z'ha'dum."

—— chapter 15 ——

Even though he had foreseen it, Kosh found it difficult to accept. Even within Sheridan's mind, Kosh could not understand his decision. Sheridan was going to Z'ha'dum.

Already the Human moved about his quarters, gathering his belongings for this ill-fated journey.

Sheridan knew that his wife was no longer his wife. He'd known, somehow, within moments of seeing her. Despite that knowledge, a flicker of hope remained that some bit of her still survived. Each time he was with her, that hope died anew, and the desire to confront those who had committed this abomination grew stronger.

Yet he did not go to Z'ha'dum because of that.

He knew the enemy had sent her as a trap. He knew that the story his wife told, of her friendly relationship with the approachable aliens, was false. He did not believe her claim that the enemy wanted only to tell their side of the story. He was not deluded by their deceit.

He did not go to Z'ha'dum because of that.

Kosh had once told the Human that if he went to Z'ha'dum, he would die. It was not in Sheridan's nature to accept such pronouncements without question. He had challenged Kosh's judgment before. But Sheridan himself knew that if he went to Z'ha'dum, he would very likely die. And he did not want to die.

He did not go to Z'ha'dum because of that.

The return of Sheridan's wife had eroded his trust in Kosh and Delenn; he was less and less inclined to accept what he'd been told and follow the path worn through history by those who had played his role. In that, Kosh found hope that this war might end differently than all the rest. Sheridan sought his own truths, his own role, his own path.

But even so, that was not the whole of the reason that he went to Z'ha'dum.

Sheridan had come to believe that avoiding the stronghold of the ancient enemy would lead to, at best, an incomplete victory, one in which the maelstrom would retain the strength to cause continued devastation to the younger races. Not only did Sheridan seek true understanding of this conflict, he wanted to minimize the harm to the younger races and end the cycle of war once and for all.

For that purpose, Sheridan went to Z'ha'dum.

His goals were admirable, yet he chose the wrong means to accomplish them. The only way to end the cycle was for the younger races to prove definitively that, of order or chaos, one was overwhelmingly superior. One side must win beyond all doubt and all recovery. For order to win, all the races must join in a single great alliance, against which no defiance could stand. For chaos to triumph, all alliances, all governments, all codes of conduct must fall to the changing whims of personal desire. Neither side had ever won such a decisive victory, and Kosh had come to doubt that either side ever would. Instead, the wars grew progressively more vicious and desperate, any benefit to the younger races lost in the firestorm. The cycle of war and death had to end, before all hope, all future, all life was lost.

Kosh had come to believe that if there was any hope of the cycle ending, of order being proven superior, it lay in Sheridan. In all the millennia he had guided the younger races, he had found no species more drawn to creating alliances and communities than the Humans, and no leader more fit to build and sustain such an alliance than Sheridan. Through Sheridan, all of the younger races could be united under a single government, subject to a code where personal desires would be sacrificed to the greater good of all.

If Sheridan went to Z'ha'dum, if Sheridan died, none of that would come to pass.

The ancient home of the enemy was well guarded and defended. In that dark place their power was concentrated, their pestilence thriving and mutating in endless variations. For countless millennia, none who had gone there to oppose chaos had escaped. Kosh could think of only one power that might allow Sheridan to survive, a primal presence of which nothing had been heard in eons. That power was out of his control and beyond his reach. Perhaps that First One, whose mediation between order and chaos had generated the ancient rules of engagement, no longer existed. Perhaps he had passed silently beyond the galactic rim. He could not be counted on to save Sheridan.

And Sheridan must not die.

If Kosh worked carefully within his host, he believed he could subtly control Sheridan, push Sheridan to change his decision. The other Vorlons, if they knew of Kosh's presence, would judge that course the correct one. They believed the younger races' purpose was to learn discipline, obedience, self-sacrifice. Sheridan's decision would be seen as undisciplined, self-indulgent. More important, it would greatly lessen the Vorlons' chance of winning this war.

Yet Kosh could not make himself take the action. He and Sheridan had disagreed before, on the involvement of the Vorlons in the war, and Sheridan had been correct. Kosh no longer thought of the Human as his inferior. Moreover, if Sheridan was truly the one who might end this war at last, then he could not be ordered and manipulated like a youth; he must be allowed to make his own decisions. Whether they pleased Kosh or not.

As Sheridan closed his suitcase and set it beside the door, Kosh knew that the decision must be left to him. Perhaps, though, Kosh could remind him of the consequences of his decision, put the truth before him so that Sheridan, himself, would change his mind.

Kosh could not reveal to his host that a piece of him still lived, within. If Sheridan's mind was probed, the enemy could learn of his presence. They might kill Sheridan, just to be rid of this last fragment of Kosh.

He had come to Sheridan before in dreams. He could not wait for sleep now, or Sheridan would be on the way to

Z'ha'dum. But he could stimulate Sheridan's memory and speak through that memory, almost as a waking dream.

Standing before his dresser, Sheridan loaded a fresh energy cap into his weapon, slid the weapon into its holster.

Kosh located the incident in Sheridan's mind. Sheridan had confronted the mysterious, elusive Vorlon in his residence, demanding to be taught how to kill Shadows. Sheridan had sworn then that he would one day to go to Z'ha'dum. And Kosh had told him the inevitable outcome of such a visit.

Sheridan took a second weapon from his dresser drawer, removed it from its holster, checked it. An extra weapon would not save him.

Above the dresser was a mirror. Kosh would make the memory appear there to increase the sense of unreality.

Kosh stimulated the memory, the image of him in his encounter suit, looking as he had on that day. Within the mirror, he placed that image over Sheridan's shoulder. Catching a flicker of movement, Sheridan glanced up. The memory spoke.

"If you go to Z'ha'dum, you will die."

Sheridan spun around, searching for the source of the reflection. After a moment, he decided that he was alone, and that his tired, overstressed mind was playing tricks on him. Yet the memory revived his anger at Kosh, and Delenn, for trying to control him. He turned back to the dresser, shoved the second weapon back into its holster, more determined than ever to continue on his course.

Sheridan was stubborn. Independent. Impudent. Incorrect. He would destroy the alliance, and lose the war, for the chance of ending the cycle of conflict between order and chaos for all time, something that had never been done in the history of the galaxy.

For this unreachable goal, he would give his life.

Sheridan would go to Z'ha'dum. And he would die.

A breather over his face, his coat buttoned tightly around him, Galen walked down the ramp of his ship. The cold wind blew past him, carrying a grit of reddish-brown dust. The particles shrouded him in isolation, the landscape beyond reduced to uncertain, shadowy shapes in the dim light.

He reached the bottom of the ramp, stepped onto the surface. For a bewildering, disorienting moment as he stood there, he couldn't even remember why he had landed. Then it came to him. Of course. He must kill three people: Elizar, Razeel, and himself.

Three days had passed since the Eye had looked upon him. It had taken him that long to secure his hold on the energy that drove through him, to contain it. The walls of his exercises wrapped suffocatingly around him, blocking out everything not needed in the immediate moment, holding in that feverish chill, showing him this place with the detachment of an observer looking out from a long, dark tunnel.

Buried in the walls of that tunnel was the hatred the Eye had revealed, the pestilence that defined who he was, and what he was, no matter how much he fought it. The Eye had taught him, beyond any doubt, that he could not transcend it. No good could come of him.

He directed his ship to raise the ramp, sealing itself closed. Then he visualized the equation to dissociate, and twin echoes from the tech and the chrysalis confirmed the command. His connection to the ship broke; the second echo faded into silence. He would have preferred to destroy his ship immediately, since he had no intention of using it again. But that would only draw attention to his presence. Instead, he had given the ship new instructions. If anyone tampered with it, it would destroy itself. If he failed to contact it for twenty-four hours, it would destroy itself. And once it detected his death, it would destroy itself. He would leave the Shadows nothing to aid them.

As he moved away from the ship's shelter, his coat whipped against his body, and the windblown dust raked over his raw hands. Though it was day, the light from the distant sun was weak, refracted by the dust and other elements in the atmosphere. The planet seemed to exist in twilight. The gravity, 1.3 times standard, pulled at his feet.

Through the dust, he saw the silhouettes of the other ships among which he had landed. Some were Shadow ships, but others represented a variety of species; agents and associates reporting to their masters, he supposed. Among them, he hoped that he might go unnoticed for a short time. To one side of the landing area ran a series of rocky outcroppings, the trailing fragments of a vast black mountain range that stretched into the distance. From several places along the length of those outcroppings, faint energy emanated. They were openings, he believed, to the vast underground complex his sensors told him stretched below.

As he headed toward the closest one, he approached one of the towering stone monoliths that covered the planet. These ancient monuments, great upthrust fingers of stone, were spaced a regular 2.432 miles from one another, spread over the entire planet's surface. Each was carved with an inscription of some kind, the vertical line of characters glowing from an internal light. The light pulsed brighter and dimmer in a steady cycle, like the beating of a heart.

Galen drew closer to the pillar, and as the wind shifted, for a moment, he could see the characters clearly. They were runes, he realized with a start, from the language of the Taratimude. There was the rune for secrecy, and there the rune for mystery. The mages' great Code, the Code to which they all swore obedience, the Code that embodied everything that they stood for, had been written in the alphabet of the Shadows.

No wonder there was no rune to signify *good*, he thought. The Shadows knew nothing of that. The rune that the mages translated as *good*, he had learned in his studies, actually meant *useful*.

A faint vibration pulsed through the ground in time with the light. Galen looked out over the rocky landscape, seeing the shadowy figures of other stone fingers in the dust. Each mage marked his place of power with a circle of stones inscribed with the Code. Those circles were only the faintest echo of this place, yet the connection was clear. Here was the source of their tradition, the genesis of the mages' tech, the mother of all places of power.

He had come home to die.

Tilting his head back, Galen tried to see the entire inscription. The top half of the towering stone was lost in the currents of dust. As he waited, different pieces became clear, until at last he could read the entire message. The Shadows' language was different than that of the Taratimude, but they were closely related; his study of the mages' ancient language allowed him to make a translation.

With every light is born a shadow.

He had tried to bring light, to do good, but it was not his nature. If there was a balance of light and dark in the universe, then it was his part, he knew, to represent the darkness.

He moved on, toward the entrance to the underground city. As the rocky outcroppings rose up before him, he found the opening in a cliff wall. It was covered by a membrane, similar to the one in Morden's air shaft. Patches of gray and black shifted slightly over its surface, creating an evolving pattern. What was on the other side, he could not see.

Holding tightly to his exercises, he stepped into it, allowing its flowing, probing examination. At last, it pulled away from him, and he found himself inside, in a vast, dim cave filled with activity. The cave's atmosphere carried a safe mixture of gases, so Galen pulled off his breather.

As on Thenothk, the floor of the cave was polished smooth, the walls rough and unfinished. On that planet, the Shadows had preferred to operate underground, because, as he now saw, that was how they lived at home. They were creatures of shadow and darkness, mystery, secrecy, and science. As were their creations, the techno-mages.

The cave appeared to be a staging area. To his left, crates were stacked high in long rows. To his right ran a line of huge bins, the closest filled with black pods. Beside them stood several large dark spheres, perhaps twenty feet in diameter, with oily, fluid surfaces. Drakh workers moved among the rows, going on about their duties. They paid Galen no attention.

From behind a stack of crates, two angular black figures emerged, following a pair of Drakh. When he'd encountered the Shadows before, their appearance had always been veiled. He had seen only the head of one, for a moment, on Thenothk. Yet on their home, they did not hide their presence. And he recognized them instantly.

Their skin glistened a deep black. Six sharp legs scissored

forward; fourteen brilliant white pinpoint eyes burned like tiny furnaces of malice, intelligence, and desire. More than that, though, they carried with them a strange sense of hyper-reality, more present, more intensely alive than anything he'd ever seen. Their sharp bodies cut through the pale illusion of reality, seeming to belong to a more fundamental level of existence. As he stared at them, at those brilliant eyes that orchestrated so much suffering and death, he felt dissolution spreading inside him, felt as if he might fly apart at any moment, as if everything might fly apart, spin into a wild fury of chaos. It was a feeling from the past, a feeling he must fight.

He forced his eyes away. For the first time, he realized the full extent of the Shadows' superiority, their ancient power and knowledge. He had been a fool for believing he could come here and accomplish any part of his task.

Yet he was kin. As they carried power, so did he. As they worked behind the scenes, manipulating others, generating chaos and destruction, so did he.

He moved ahead through the cave. He didn't know how far he could get before they stopped him. If he'd gone unnoticed thus far, he didn't imagine it would last much longer. It might be that they already knew he was here. In any case, he must find Elizar and Razeel as quickly as he could. Then, one way or the other, he would be done.

He discarded his breather, having no further need of it. Once he got some distance from the Shadows, he flipped probes onto a few nearby Drakh. He hoped that the devices would go undiscovered here, where the Shadows believed themselves safe. He needed all the information he could obtain.

At the far end of the cave, two wide tunnels led in different directions. Focusing his sensors ahead and below, he searched for any sign of mage energy. The frequencies where that energy normally revealed itself were overrun with activity; Shadow tech radiated at those same frequencies.

A sound echoed down one of the tunnels, the regular beat of footsteps falling in unison. From around a curve, eight Drakh emerged, marching toward him. Galen took the other tunnel.

Day and night had little meaning underground; the complex was always busy. He passed through the mazelike corridors and tunnels, moving steadily deeper, spreading his probes, learning what he could.

The upper levels catered mainly to visitors: Humans, Centauri, Drazi, Narns, Pak'ma'ra. Rooms and corridors mimicked designs from the home planets of each. Except for the lack of windows, one might forget one was underground. They gathered in various private meetings, these agents of the Shadows and their masters, where promises were made, plans designed, discipline administered. One Human, named Justin, was involved in several of these meetings.

Below, those vestiges quickly vanished, the walls of cave and tunnel bare. From regular vertical slits in the rock, light shone out, providing a dim illumination. A damp, moldy smell increased with depth. Although Galen saw few Shadows, workers—Drakh, Streib, Wurt, and many of species he couldn't identify—toiled unceasingly in the cause of total war.

He dared not stop to rest. He simply worked his way lower and lower through the claustrophobic passages, searching with his sensors, monitoring through his probes, limbs growing heavy, clothes prickling against his raw skin, exercises reinforcing the rhythm of his steps.

He passed another black membrane covering an opening in the rock. This one was thinner, semitransparent. Through it, he saw the thick bodies and strikingly white heads of several Streib. They moved among rows of beings laid out on black tables, examining their subjects. Those laid out were Drazi, Centauri, Pak'ma'ra, Human—the very same species with whom the Shadows negotiated above. As one of the Drazi struggled, Galen realized the table had entwined itself around the Drazi's limbs, holding him down.

Blood seeped out from between the gray scales of his face. He was ill. As were the others. The golden skin of several Narns had turned into a crusty black ooze; a row of Centauri panted desperately for breath, their mouths dripping with mucus; some Human subjects looked healthy, but as Galen watched, one broke into a seizure, spasming so hard that he cracked his head against the cave wall, knocking himself unconscious. Even then, his body continued to convulse.

Galen found himself shaking, his breath panting in time with the Centauri. He wanted to kill the Streib butchers, to free the prisoners from their suffering. His body raced with outrage.

He turned away, pressing himself against the jagged rock, and added a new exercise to the two he was already carrying.

This was not why he had come. This was not why he had come.

Would he again kill indiscriminately?

He must find Elizar and Razeel. They must both die, and he must see it happen to be sure. He would watch as they were crushed.

Thoughts of his task calmed him, and he focused on it. He felt fairly certain, at this point, that Elizar was observing him and subtly controlling his course. By coordinating the movements of the Shadows' servants and blocking off various tunnels, Elizar manipulated him, just as Elric had once manipulated Vir through Babylon 5's Down Below. Why Elizar desired to draw him so deep, Galen didn't know. But he would follow his appointed course. And as he did, he would see his home. He must see all of it, he realized, must know the enormity of the evil that had bred the techno-mages. There would be no more secrets. For was that not what he had decided was his place—to know all that should not be known, and to bear its burden?

Once he had seen it, though, could he simply complete his task and allow all this to continue?

He moved on. Drakh ferried prisoners from below on floating black platforms. The prisoners lay still, each one fitted with the delicate metal interface device Galen had seen on Anna's head. They were brought to a vast hangar holding perhaps a dozen Shadow ships. The Drakh stopped beside the nearest ship, its skin a dull black. A section of the platform broke free, holding a single prisoner, and the Drakh accompanied him into the ship's gaping opening. After a minute, a darker, richer black began to spread over the dull skin, and vibrant patterns began to shift across its surface. The Drakh emerged without their prisoner.

In the next tunnel, Galen came upon a group of scabrous-skinned Wurt. They conducted another group of prisoners deeper. These were unconscious, though Galen saw no interface devices on their heads. He followed, continuing to monitor the activities and meetings above, searching for Elizar or Razeel.

Talk of the war was constant, and several times visitors raised the issue of the Vorlons' interference several months ago, concerned that the powerful beings would interfere again. But their greatest source of anxiety was the alliance's recent victory, and the use of telepaths to jam Shadow ships.

In one such meeting, Justin tried to soothe several Humans. As he spoke of the heavy losses the alliance had sustained, Morden entered the room, and with a nod moved to stand at the back. Then Justin spoke a name: John Sheridan.

"Without him, the alliance is nothing. Within the next forty-eight hours, he will either be fighting for our side, or he won't be fighting at all. Babylon 5 will be ours, or it will be gone. The alliance will be subverted, or it will be crushed."

The Shadows were moving against John. With dread, Galen accessed the FTL relay aboard his ship, and through that, the relay on Babylon 5. It offered him a menu of all the probes, cameras, and systems on the station. He selected a probe on John.

The probe did not respond. Either it had been destroyed, or John had passed out of range.

Galen checked the security database, found John had left the station three days ago. He scanned back through the probe record stored in the relay, reconstructing what had happened.

Anna.

Anna Sheridan.

The interface device had been removed from her head, the dark, hungry look around her eyes disguised by makeup, the greasy hair cleaned and cut into a fashionable style, the soiled orange jumpsuit replaced with a perfectly tailored business suit that was all too familiar. Here was Morden's "girlfriend."

Here was the Shadows' plan to destroy John. They used John's love against him. Just as they had done to so many others.

Galen had thought Anna's true self lost irretrievably beneath the Shadows' programming. Had they somehow managed to restore her?

As he watched Anna's initial encounter with John, though, his hopes quickly faded. This "restored" Anna carried a superficial, mechanical warmth. Beneath it, though, he could still see her hunger, her craving for the machine. She seemed almost to have transferred that hunger to John, for when she spoke to him, her face was alight with fanatical eagerness.

Of the caring, curious, adventurous woman he had seen in recordings, nothing remained. Although the Shadows had freed her from the ship, nothing had been left of her to free. Her past had been lost in her complete subjugation to the Shadows' programming.

In that, he and Anna were much alike. Although he fought the Shadows' programming, maintained control over it, in the process he too had lost the person he had been.

And with his attention narrowed tightly on containing his energy, holding to his task, he had forsaken John to the Shadows' plans.

Soon after Anna arrived, John brought her to medlab for an examination by Stephen Franklin, who'd finally ended his walkabout and resumed his duties. Medical records and DNA tests revealed that she was undeniably John's wife. But Stephen recognized the marks of the interface device, which he had seen before. He confided in John his suspicions that Anna had been wired into a Shadow ship.

John struggled to reconcile the memories of his lost wife with the woman who confronted him, who sat on his couch and explained, so reasonably, why he must go with her to Z'ha'dum.

When she stood and came toward him, stopped before him, he flinched. He knew. He knew as well as Galen that this was not his wife. Yet, incredibly, he agreed to go.

Galen rushed through the probe record, determined that John must not come to Z'ha'dum. Surely he knew it was a trap. Surely he knew that with his latest victory, he had proven himself too great a threat for the Shadows to ignore.

Of John's colleagues, none dared talk to him about it. They were all at a loss over what to say about John's wife returning from the dead. Even Michael Garibaldi, never known to keep his opinion to himself, remained silent. John recruited his assistance on several tasks.

As Galen followed Michael's activities, he saw the security chief load two thermonuclear devices onto the *White Star*. They were extremely powerful; each could destroy Babylon 5 several hundred times over.

Later, John and Anna boarded that ship. They formed a jump point, passed out of range. They were on their way.

John would learn what he could from the Shadows. Once he had, if they would not let him leave, then he intended to stop the war at its source.

It was a suicide mission. It would fail to destroy the Shadows, just as G'Leel's attempt had failed. John had constructed his own Trojan horse, but this one would not be admitted into the enemy's stronghold. The Eye would never allow a ship as powerful as the *White Star* to pass. The Shadows would force him to take a shuttle, or send a ship to pick him up.

Galen searched for John's probe in the vicinity of Z'ha'dum, but they hadn't yet arrived. From what he'd seen of the White Star ships, he believed it might be another day before they reached the rim.

He could not allow John to land here. John must fight the war, must win it. John should leave Z'ha'dum to him.

But how could he stop it? What could he do, except kill as many Shadows and destroy as much of their stronghold as possible before John arrived, so there would be no need for John's sacrifice?

That, he could not do. Yet the possibility lingered in his mind, unsettling him, promising him the satisfaction he desired.

He turned his mind away. He had to contact John and warn him, tell him that his plan would fail. An electron incantation with a non-mage was difficult, but could be accomplished, if he was able to forge a connection to John. The Shadows might well detect the attempted communication. He would have only one chance. He would wait until the *White Star* arrived in the system, for the best possibility of success. Then John would have to listen to him, would have to turn back.

In the meantime, Galen would pursue his task.

He followed the Wurt and their prisoners deeper, fatigue spreading through him. A faint sound echoed down the tunnel, like the chattering of a flock of birds. Gradually it grew louder, and as he listened, one chatter or another occasionally rose above the rest, and he was able to pick out a distinct, fluttering burst. He realized, then, what he was hearing. The chirps lacked the distortion he'd heard earlier, when the Shadows had been shielded, because here, they spoke freely.

The squawking clamor built until it seemed to surround him, and he came to the opening of a dark chamber. The blackness shifted as the Shadows massed within moved in seemingly random patterns, their brilliant pinpoint eyes weaving amongst one another like swarms of fireflies in the night. Standing out of sight, he recorded as much of the sound as he dared and passed quickly onward.

In the ancient recordings, he'd heard Wierden speak the language of the Taratimude. The Shadows' speech sounded nothing like it. Nevertheless, he sent the recording to his Taratimude translation program, hoping it might identify a word or two.

To his surprise, he received a translation in his mind's eye. Most of it seemed to be repeated talk of chaos and destruction—almost a litany. Interspersed with that, he found bits of a discussion under way, ideas overlapping, reiterated in different variations. He searched down through the translation for coherent pieces.

The Vorlons must have [words unidentifiable in program] where we would strike.

The Vorlons interfere too much. Any progress we make is undermined by their meddling. Their influence is everywhere.

We guide the younger races much better than the Vorlons. We teach them what is important—desire and survival. We drive them to evolve, progress, while the Vorlons freeze them into stagnation.

The memory emerged from the walls of his endless exercises, a strange artifact from some distant past. A couple stood before a mirror, preparing for a night out. The man's hands were huge, with prominent blood vessels. He wore a ring with a ragged black stone. As he fastened lapel pins to his jacket, he spoke. *I'm a much better teacher than you would be. I teach him discipline, obedience. Of course you undermine my authority at every turn, manipulating him to your own ends, smothering him with your false love.*

Galen squeezed his raw hand into a fist, accelerating his exercises, narrowing his focus. The Shadows and Vorlons had coexisted as enemies for as long as histories, legends, and myth told, always fighting through surrogates. Was this what they fought over? Had billions died, species been eliminated, the galaxy been thrown again and again into chaos and despair, all so two ancient races could fight over who provided the best guidance?

How dare they?

How dare they unleash their conflict on the innocent, whether it was the passengers on a single ship or the inhabitants of an entire galaxy?

The translation continued to scroll down through his mind's eye.

The Vorlons broke the ancient agreement.

They must, finally, be destroyed.

If the Shadows were truly considering the annihilation of the Vorlons, this war would go far beyond any that had come before. Galen searched through more talk of chaos and destruction for anything further.

If the younger races refuse to join us, they too should be destroyed. They are infected with rules and structures.

If all the younger races must be destroyed or subsumed to rid us of the Vorlon influence, it may be for the best. Again and again we have tried. They have proven too slow to adapt to our ways.

Multiple species had been exterminated in previous Shadow wars. The Taratimude was but one. But to kill them all? They had the power; John Sheridan might win a battle, but he could never defeat the Shadows. Only the Vorlons—or the mages—could stop them.

He looked at the text again, disbelieving. What was meant by *subsumed*, he didn't know. The translation might be at fault.

Let them fill the ranks of our new army, and when we have won, when we have total control, we can design our own races to build a universe based on anarchy.

The *new army*. Was that what Kosh had warned him of? Did the Shadows mean to put all those captured into their ships, like Anna? Surely they couldn't have that many.

The words seemed to contradict the Shadows' very purpose. For beings devoted to chaos and destruction, it seemed they sought chaos only for others. For themselves, they desired control—control over Londo, control over Morden, control over Anna, and now, control over all the rest, who had proven unworthy of their instruction. Perhaps they had learned their lesson from the techno-mages, those of their creations least under their control.

He realized that, in a limited way, he had sensed the Shadows' nature for some time. But he understood the full truth of it only now.

It reminded him of the Shadows' strategy in the shell-shaped region of space. The raids had seemed chaotic, but in reality, they had been carefully planned to manipulate the reactions of those under attack.

The Shadows were growing dissatisfied with the effects of those manipulations. If they could not control, they would turn their minds toward destruction.

Galen crossed his arms over his chest, rocking back and forth. He had started out knowing exactly what he had to do. Now his task had become fluid, uncertain. He had to stop the Shadows. Yet if he gave himself over to total, indiscriminate killing here, as his body raced to do, he would simply be fulfilling their purpose. He would be surrendering to chaos.

He hurried deeper until he again found the Wurt and their prisoners ahead. It was quite obvious that he did not belong at these levels, but no one stopped him, or even questioned him. He felt certain he was growing close to Elizar and Razeel.

He was walking into their trap. At least if they did trap him, did nullify his tech, the Circle's device might kill them as it killed him.

The prisoners were split into two groups, and Galen followed one. They were conveyed into another underground cavern, this one about fifty feet across, twenty feet high. Galen stopped in the entryway. The cavern seemed unremarkable except for a thick vein of reddish-brown rock that cut in a vertical strip through the black stone of the far wall. It glowed with the same runes he had seen in the fingers of stone towering over the surface of Z'ha'dum. The runes repeated a section of the inscription he'd read above. This column, he realized, was a continuation of one of those monuments. They extended underground, perhaps connected below to some sort of machine, just as a mage's circle of stones was connected to his place of power. A concentration of energy throbbed somewhere far beneath him. If this machine did run through the planet, coordinating its systems, its defenses, then it must be the Eye, that source of the black light that had invaded him, inflamed him. As the runes pulsed brighter and fainter, like the beating of a heart, he was struck by the sensation that the Eye was watching him.

The Wurt and their unconscious prisoners joined others in what seemed like a large waiting area. Farther down the wall of the cave, a door slid open, and brilliant white light spilled from a small side chamber. The bright light reminded him of the room in which Elizar had trapped him on Thenothk. He scanned again for mage energy, found none. If this was the trap, Elizar and Razeel were keeping their distance until he was caught in it.

From the chamber came two of the grayish-skinned aliens he had seen on Thenothk. Their long fingers trembled with anticipation. When he'd been joined to Anna, he'd learned of their atrocities. They drilled into the brain, attached the interface devices, took from a person her will, her freedom, her self.

The Wurt broke off a section of their platform, brought a prisoner to the brightly lit chamber. The grayish aliens followed the prisoner inside. Within a few seconds, a shrill whirring echoed out through the cave.

Galen turned his attention away, to the pulsing runes. He could not interfere. He had to hold on, hold on until he found Elizar and Razeel. Still the drill whirred.

The Shadow tech insinuated its way into these prisoners. They were infected with the programming of chaos and destruction. The mages' initiations were disguised with flourishes and stage dressing, but was the end result much different?

One key difference, he knew, separated them. These prisoners were the Shadows' slaves, with no choice but to serve, to obey the directives of the Eye. Galen was no slave. The Shadows had given him the power, and the ability to control it. So instead, he was a slave to control.

Closer by, the Wurt separated another section from the platform, bringing a second prisoner toward the brightly lit chamber. As his eyes fell upon the Narn, he recognized her. G'Leel.

It couldn't be.

This must be Elizar's trap.

Galen scanned the unconscious figure, the gold-and-black spotted head, white scar across the nose, black leather vest, muscular biceps, black gloves, pants. No mage illusion disguised the figure.

I want to help you, she had said. *Whatever your task is. Wherever it takes you.*

Galen took a few steps toward her. The first prisoner was brought out from the bright chamber, and G'Leel was ushered in. The door built into the stone wall closed, the cavern falling back into its dim light.

He cast the spell to access the relay aboard his ship. Through it, he could reach the relay orbiting Regula 4. Then he could reassure himself that G'Leel was still there, and safe. Not here. Not here.

But there was no echo from the tech. He could not reach the relay. Whether he was too deep, or Elizar had set up some block, he couldn't tell. If he'd remained associated with the ship, he would have had no trouble. But he had not.

The sound of the drill chittered out over the cavern.

Elizar wanted him to go into that room. That had to be the trap. He could not enter.

He had wanted to wait until he found Elizar and Razeel before unleashing his energy. But he could not wait. So many had died because of him. He could not allow her to become another.

Galen focused on the door and surrounding stone, visualized the one-term equation of destruction. Energy fell upon him with crushing pressure in wave upon wave upon wave, burning through his skin, singing down the lines of tech, filling him with brilliant, ecstatic fire. For the first time in nearly two years, he'd cast the spell that was his purpose for existing, and he was alive, truly alive, his body blazing, incandescent. With a rush the energy shot out toward the chamber, sending him stumbling back. A spherical area encompassing the door and the stone around it began to redden and darken. Space became fluid, the cave walls undulating in waves, the bodies of the Wurt and their prisoners swelling in some places, contracting in others. The air felt charged, and time itself grew thick, sluggish.

Something slapped against the side of his neck. Galen turned, his torso seeming to torque around while his legs remained in place, his body ductile, made of liquid fire.

A Wurt stood there, his mouth open in an almost comical expression of fear, his hand, withdrawing from Galen, curving in a serpentine course.

The Wurt had stuck something to Galen's neck. And before Galen's hand even reached it, he realized what it was: a tranq tab, bonded to his skin. In three seconds, he would be unconscious.

G'Leel and the bright room had been misdirections. Here was Elizar's trap. Simple and effective.

Already a second had passed. The sphere must cut into his neck to have any impact; the tranquilizer would already be driving into his system, and he must remove as much of it as he could. If he lost consciousness, he would never wake again. Galen focused on the location of the tab, visualized the one-term equation.

With the blazing energy surging through his body, he felt no pain, just a growing pressure against his neck as the sphere formed.

If the drug had already gotten into his system, then he could do nothing to stop it. Yet under the influence of the spell of destruction, time was slowed, distorted. He must take advantage of that.

Elizar and Razeel remained nowhere in sight.

Galen conjured a platform beneath himself, conjured equation of motion, equation of motion. He sped from the cavern, twisted past a group of Drakh, swerved down a dark tunnel. He must go deep, so deep that no one could find him.

His legs wobbled, the fluid fire swaying, wavering. He fell to his knees. Forming the equations of motion, navigating down the twisting tunnels, became more and more difficult. The pressure at his neck began to burn with a fire of its own.

He tried again to access the probe network, and this time he succeeded. He selected the relay orbiting Regula 4, the probe on G'Leel. She stood outside, watching the colorful sunset on Alwyn's home. She was safe.

As the passages split again and again, he raced deeper and deeper, leaving the Shadows' servants behind, the tunnels contracting around him, growing vague and dark.

With a crack the pressure at his neck vanished, and he found himself on his side, breathing hard. Wetness ran across his back.

The tunnel ended ahead. He continued all the way into the low, narrow space, and dissolved the platform. With effort he focused on the tunnel's ceiling perhaps twenty feet back along its course, visualized the spell of destruction within the rock. The energy fell upon him, burned out of him. The ceiling would collapse, concealing his hiding place. Whether the rockfall would crush him or suffocate him, he did not have time to learn. He could keep his eyes open no longer.

—— chapter 16 ——

Anna lay on the tilted sleeping pallet aboard the Minbari ship, John on the pallet beside her. These new ships of the Minbari, the White Stars, incorporated elements of Vorlon technology. She had learned all about them from the Eye. Aside from the Vorlon ships, they were the greatest threat to her sisters. With the help of the telepaths John recruited, they killed many.

Like the Vorlon ships, these White Stars carried a sad echo of life. They weren't truly alive, as she and her sisters were. They had no will of their own; they had no freedom. They were forced to follow orders. John Sheridan gave those orders. John, though, was falling further and further under her control.

She had passed all his tests. She had said what Justin had told her, had demonstrated her knowledge of Sheridan's past. She had touched him when there was opportunity. She had used the indirect methods of Humans to convince the nexus to come with her to Z'ha'dum. She had succeeded in the first part of her assignment.

Yet her control of him remained incomplete. He had brought a powerful warship because he still did not trust what she said. She had convinced him, however, to leave the ship in orbit and take only a shuttle to the surface. She had told him the aliens were afraid of Vorlon technology. Without his ship and its weapons, he would further succumb to her control.

She studied his sleeping face. His lips were slightly parted. The air made a soft sound as it passed in and out. The frown that had been so common since they'd been together had relaxed in sleep. Humans were vulnerable in sleep. It would be easy to kill him now. But that was not what they wanted. And it would not bring her the Eye.

She had to perfect her control of him so that, with the help of Justin and Morden, she could convince him to join the cause of chaos. Physical contact increased her power. She leaned over, rested her head on his chest.

He jerked awake with a low sound. After a moment, he lay back. "Anna."

His chest rumbled as he spoke. It was a pleasurable sensation. He rested his hand on her shoulder.

"I didn't mean to wake you," she said.

"It's all right," he said, and the rumbling spread through her. The contact somehow reminded her of the soft black embrace of the machine. She imagined herself sinking into his body, becoming one with him as Morden had said Human men and women could, controlling him as she had controlled the machine.

She realized how much she had missed the sensation, how much she longed for it. This was but a poor imitation.

The ship's signal bell chimed. They had reached the end of their hyperspace route.

"Looks like we're here," John said, lifting his arm to allow her to rise.

At first, she didn't want to move. Then she realized how close she was to gaining all that she desired.

For they had reached Z'ha'dum.

Galen jerked awake, his forehead slamming into something, hard. Rock. The tunnels. Z'ha'dum.

He lay back a moment in the close darkness, working to slow his breathing. The fire had gone from his body, leaving the side of his neck a great throbbing mass of pain. He felt dizzy and hungry and sick all at once.

He brought his hand to the wound. Skin covered a hemispherical depression. Dried streams of blood crusted his neck and back. The organelles had been at work while he slept, saving him from bleeding to death. The Shadows had designed their agents well. But it would take more time to reconstruct the muscle and tissue he had destroyed.

He found that he had received a series of messages, all from Elizar.

Galen.

Galen.

I know you're receiving my messages, so I know you're still alive.

We could spend weeks playing hide-and-seek in these tunnels. Why bother, when we both want the same thing? Meet me at the opening of the Eye, and we can be done with each other.

Galen began a mind-focusing exercise, slowly hunched into a sitting position. Instant headache. He checked the time. Checked again. He had lost an entire day.

With growing anxiety, he accessed John's probe.

"We only need breathers on the surface," Anna said, fitting one of the clear masks over her face.

John did the same. They entered an air lock, and in a few moments the outer door opened to reveal the dust-swept surface of Z'ha'dum.

He had lost his chance to warn John away.

They climbed down some steps, and Galen noticed the vessel they came from was not the *White Star*. As he'd expected, it was a small shuttle. John's plan was ruined, though he did not know it.

Galen conjured a fireball, studied the small space in which he was entombed. There was a gap between the ceiling and the rocks on one side. He could squeeze through, which would be the quietest way to proceed. He stood, crouching, and stumbled over the rocks, his balance unsure.

He would reach John, get John to his ship, program its course for Babylon 5. With luck, the Eye would allow his ship to pass.

His ship.

Before he even tried to associate with it, he knew it was gone. He felt the absence, a thin sliver of pain behind his forehead, barely perceptible among the rest. He had directed it to destroy itself if it did not hear from him in twenty-four hours.

He cast the spell. There was no echo from the tech, no echo from the ship.

John's shuttle would have no chance of getting past the Eye. The other ships he'd seen were either the short-range shuttles of visitors, or Shadow ships that would obey only the Eye.

He pushed through the narrow opening, his head and neck throbbing. The rocks on the far side were unstable; as they shifted he slid down, skidded to the tunnel floor.

There was no way off the planet for John, or for anyone.

He climbed to his feet, but he had no direction. He simply stood in the close, dank tunnel, the sound of his breaths echoing back to him.

He could not lose control; he could not.

Would he hold to his task, though, while the Shadows killed John and continued their atrocities and their war?

He had told Morden that perhaps he could save those enslaved on Z'ha'dum. Both Morden and Anna had proven, though, that those under the Shadows' control could not be freed, except in death. Of those prisoners who had not yet received the Shadows' gifts, they were as trapped in this place as John was. Galen could not save them.

If he could help John bring his plan to fruition, though, perhaps he could prevent any more from becoming the Shadows' slaves. If Z'ha'dum was destroyed, perhaps the Shadows would end this war, or at least be sufficiently weakened that the alliance, in John's absence, could defeat them.

The two bombs on the *White Star* could lay waste to five thousand times the area Galen had razed on Thenothk. Within the confines of the caverns, the effects would even be amplified. If he could destroy the Eye, John could bring the *White Star* down.

He would find this "opening of the Eye" Elizar mentioned. If Elizar and Razeel were there to oppose him, he would kill them. Then, if he could, he would crush the Eye. He would maintain control. The *White Star* would take care of the rest.

Once again, it would not be his place to do good. But he had always found more success in destruction.

The agitating energy rose up, echoing his eagerness. He conjured a platform, sped through the tunnel, searching ahead with his sensors. He did not have long. The Shadows would spend some time in their effort to turn John, and John would respond carefully, trying to learn all he could. Once the Shadows realized John would not join them, though, they would move against him. John would wait until he was sure he had no other option; then he would order the *White Star* down. If the Eye was still operating, it would destroy the ship before it came close enough to the planet to do any damage.

The pulsing concentration of energy he'd sensed earlier was clearer now, since he was closer to it. It radiated from a location some three hundred feet to the west and fifty feet below. If his instinct was right, it would be the Eye.

As he drew closer to it, the tunnels became wider once again, and he came into a vast, dim chamber. A huge black machine with many moving parts operated in complete silence. It was so large, he could not see the end of it. This was not the Eye; at least he didn't think so. That energy was still ahead. This machine generated minimal energy, and its parts moved in an odd, fluid manner. As he glided past it, he scanned down to the infrared band, trying to get a better view. In his mind's eye, the machine popped into brilliant red relief, each piece gaining definition.

What he saw was not a machine at all. They were living beings, moving mechanically in concert, working as if they were one single device. He could not find their faces, or even distinguish their species. They were each completely covered with something, some sort of skin that glowed red with warmth. Over its surface, areas of varying temperatures shifted and flowed, arranging themselves into evolving patterns.

The Shadow skin was not the same as that covering the ships; it appeared much, much weaker, more like the membranes he'd encountered. Yet the readings he received from it were different even from the membranes. This skin seemed more like an energy shield than any physical construct. It was another variation on the basic tech of the Shadows.

The platform took Galen from the chamber, and he found himself in a wide tunnel, passing among ranks of these machine people, hundreds of them, standing motionless, the ultimate testament to the Shadows' desire for control.

They were kin, more closely controlled even than Anna

and the Shadow ships, trapped on that same spectrum of chaos and death as the mages.

Down a side passage he saw a cluster of them. Sustained red beams of plasma shot from their palms, blasting into the rock. They were excavating.

Ahead, light bled into the tunnel from some larger space. When he reached the threshold, he stopped, looking out onto a vast cavern, far larger than any he had yet encountered. He was at one end of this great hollow in the rock. Directly ahead was the source of the high, pulsing energy. It was some kind of circular pool, about thirty feet across, filled with a churning black liquid.

He dissolved the platform, took a few halting steps toward it. The cavern stretched miles across, and perhaps a mile high. On the great stone plain before him, thousands of machine people stood in regimented columns. Beyond them, centered within the cavern, stretched a great abyss perhaps a half mile wide. And on its far side, a sprawl of towering structures gleaming with lights formed a city within the city.

The walls of the cavern stretched high above, with rows of parapets and ramps linking various levels. The walls themselves were carved with runes, covered with them. At the center of the rocky ceiling, dull light streamed in through an expansive skylight that gave a view of the sand-filled sky of Z'ha'dum. The vaulted space and ornate, carved surfaces reminded Galen of a temple, though this was a temple devoted to darkness, not light.

Here was the heart of the Shadows' complex.

He turned his attention to the black pool from which the energy emanated. He scanned it more closely and found it was deep, a shaft that penetrated as far into the planet as he could detect. This must be the machine to which all the stone fingers were connected, the Shadows' place of power. This pool was the access point, the opening of the Eye.

As he studied it, though, he realized that the churning black liquid was no liquid at all. The shaft was filled with machine people, their limbs intertwining, their bodies writhing like worms. They were the components of the Eye.

He would crush them, and free them.

Movement from beyond the ranks of machine people caught his attention. A group of Drazi was stumbling out of a tunnel in the left wall, spreading out before the glittering, stationary figures. Galen used his sensors to gain a magnified view in his mind's eye, saw with surprise that the Drazi were armed with high-powered plasma rifles, missile launchers.

Was this some kind of invasion? How could they possibly have gotten so far?

The last of the Drazi emerged from the tunnel. Behind them came a row of machine people. The black, faceless figures stopped at the opening of the tunnel, blocking the Drazi's escape.

The Drazi were trapped between the assembled machine people and the great abyss. They took what shelter they could behind a few scattered boulders, set up the missile launchers.

This was no invasion. It was target practice.

The Drazi fired a few scattered shots. The plasma blasts seemed to have no effect on the skin-shielded figures. As one, the front rank of machine people raised their palms. For a moment they simply stood, immobile. Then, in unison, their palms blasted beams of red plasma. Rock erupted in sprays of shrapnel. Smoke billowed across the area.

After a few furious seconds of fire, their beams stopped. Their arms returned to their sides. As the smoke cleared, Galen saw that they had obliterated the boulders, and the missile launchers had been melted into pools of slag. Most of the Drazi, however, remained standing. He looked more closely at one, clearly visible between columns of machine people. Her rifle was gone. The gray, scaled hand that had been holding it was gone as well, leaving a blackened stump. She swayed, staring at the black soldiers in terror. She and the others had been spared, to serve some further use.

Here was the *new army*. Here was the darkness of which Kosh had spoken.

One of the Drazi broke away, ran for the wall, began rapidly climbing toward the lowest balcony. A strange ripple ran through the cavern—a shift . . . in something, Galen couldn't say what. And then he saw. A spherical area around the escaping Drazi began to redden and darken.

Elizar.

A hard shiver ran through Galen as the tech surged. At last it was time to kill.

In the distorted spacetime of the spell of destruction, the Drazi's head twisted around in alarm, the gray scales of his face undulating in waves. Below, the glittering black ranks snaked from side to side. Galen's shoulders stretched wide as he searched for Elizar.

Then the darkening sphere did something Galen had never seen before. It moved, floating away from the wall, carrying its prisoner and the chunk of rock to which he clung. As the sphere darkened, it came to hover over the other Drazi, showing them what would happen if they tried to flee. The captured Drazi's mouth opened in a silent scream.

The sphere snapped into its rapid collapse, and the Drazi's body crumpled like a piece of paper. The shrinking sphere paled to gray, then, like a mirage, simply faded away. A blast of air rushed in to fill the void with a great rolling crack.

If Elizar had the spell of destruction, then Galen's only chance was to crush Elizar before Elizar crushed him.

The first rank of machine people herded the surviving Drazi back into the tunnel. The second rank gathered the few dead, added their bodies to a pile against the wall. The soldiers were being trained not to kill, but to render helpless. That way, the conquered could add to their numbers.

As the black soldiers resumed their original positions, Galen saw a flash of purple among them. Elizar emerged at their front. He wore a long purple velvet coat, a purple and gold vest beneath. The dark goatee scoured into the shape of the rune for magic stood out against his pale skin. His angular face carried a cold arrogance.

Fury raced through Galen, and the tech echoed it.

He used his sensors. This was no illusion.

Elizar's eyes were lowered in concentration. He cupped his hands around his mouth, and with a jerk of his head, released a long, sustained syllable.

With a similar movement he had once conjured a deadly spike.

The front ranks of soldiers marched to the back, those farther back filing forward. Elizar was the puppetmaster controlling them.

Galen lost his view of the purple figure as the soldiers moved. When they returned to stillness, Elizar again appeared.

There was the friend who had betrayed him, who had betrayed them all, who had lied, who had tortured, who had killed, who had sought power for himself, and who had finally found it.

Now, at last, it would end.

He took a moment to assert his exercises, his control. He would destroy only his target, nothing else.

He focused on Elizar, visualized a blank screen in his mind's eye, imposed the equation upon it. The energy fell upon him, bloomed through him, burned out of him.

Elizar's head snapped up.

As a sphere around him began to redden and darken, his eyes found Galen, and his rippling mouth curved into a smile.

Elizar brought his hands to his mouth, and his body jerked. The darkness passed up over his face like a shadow, and suddenly, incredibly, the sphere had moved. It hovered now above Elizar, empty.

It was impossible. One mage couldn't control the spells of another. It had to be some illusion, some trick.

He could find no sign of it.

His body racing, he visualized the spell again, felt the tech's eager echo.

Elizar nodded, cupped his hands again around his mouth. The second sphere rose beside the first, just as the first snapped into its rapid, fading collapse. A thunderous crack split the air.

Galen had waited so long to crush Elizar, so long. He would not be denied now. He walked toward Elizar, visualized the simple spell again and again, building a neat column in his mind's eye. Energy raged through him.

The spheres flew from Elizar as quickly as they formed. They filled the air above him, collapsing with a fusillade of sound. Then Elizar jerked yet again, and the sphere around him did not rise up, instead passing to one side, stopping to surround one of the machine people.

Though Galen burned to continue the spells, he wrapped the walls of his exercises tighter, forced the screen in his mind's eye blank. He did not want to kill any others. He would not kill any others.

The sphere around the black figure grew darker, and somehow Galen felt as if his own vision were darkening, as if he too were encased by the sphere. He stumbled to a stop, confused, and a rush of whispers poured into his mind, infecting him. *Chaos through warfare. Evolution through bloodshed. Perfection through victory.*

Then he was standing in two places. He stood where he had been, at the back of the black columns, and he stood only a few feet from Elizar's darkening figure, in the front rank of soldiers.

The pain was incredible. His body was rippling, deforming, pulled in different directions. His glittering black arms stretched downward, reaching the floor and curling there. He wanted to scream, to run, but he could not.

Flesh will do what it's told.

The space around him seemed to gather itself. The distortion stopped, and the contraction began. The dark sphere clenched around him, crunching arms and legs up into his body, breaking ribs, crushing organs. Elizar and the cavern faded to black. With a brilliant excruciating flash of pain, the sphere closed around his heart, and he felt nothing more.

Galen found himself on the ground, panting hard. Elizar glided in front of him and hovered there, the blue tinge of a shield discoloring his skin.

"It hurts, doesn't it," Elizar said. "Don't try it again."

Galen's fury rose up, irresistible. Elizar had to die, and now was the time. He visualized the one-term equation again.

As the space around Elizar darkened, he shook his head. With a touch of his hand to his mouth, a jerk of his chin, the sphere shot out to surround another Shadow soldier.

The whispers flooded back into Galen's mind. *Orders must be followed precisely and accurately. There can be no error. There can be no deviation.* It was the Eye, Galen realized, the Eye giving direction to the soldier. *Flesh will do what it's told. Say nothing, do nothing, until ordered.*

The sphere's distortion twisted through him, and his glittering black body began to spin, a dervish, and with his increasing speed, he began to deform, organs, bones, features melting, stretching.

Say nothing, do nothing.

He wanted to scream, to fight, but the Shadow skin controlled his body, not he. Within it he was helpless. He could say nothing, do nothing, except obey.

Galen realized that through his spell of destruction, he was connecting to these servants of the Shadows, thinking their thoughts, feeling their feelings. The same thing had happened when he'd attacked Anna in her ship, behind the City Center on Thenothk.

He searched for the identity of this being, for some memory, some personality. But he could find nothing, not even a name—only the desire to escape from the pain, and the necessity to obey.

He spun tighter and tighter, his tissue, his face turning to jelly, his self melting away. Yet the Shadows had destroyed that much earlier.

The whispers of the Eye faded as the sphere severed the connection, but still he did not scream, obedient to the last. The darkness closed around him, crushed him.

He looked up, gasping, disoriented, at Elizar crouched beside him. "A deterrent," Elizar said. "The Shadows don't want us destroying their equipment."

Galen extended his hands, bracing them for balance against the cave floor. It was not rock they pressed against, though, but the hard, smooth surface of a platform. He was on Elizar's platform, he realized, and they were speeding across the cavern. He rolled off, dropped the few feet to the uneven ground.

With a few awkward movements he pushed himself to his knees. His body was burning, incandescent. Struggling to regain his bearings, he looked for Elizar, wanting to cast the spell again.

He forced his eyes closed, withdrawing farther down that dark tunnel of his control, containing the energy, securing it. He shivered.

What a fool he'd been. He'd centered all his plans on the

spell of destruction. The only reason he was still alive was that Elizar seemed in no mood to kill him, at least not yet.

He slowed his breaths, opened his eyes. Where had Elizar been taking him? Somewhere to nullify his tech? Elizar had brought him back the way he'd come. He was only a few yards from the Eye. He saw no enclosed space where Elizar might intend to trap him.

As if from a great distance, he saw Elizar gliding toward him. He must catch Elizar off guard, try something different. Elizar's shields were only moderately strong; with sufficient time and effort, Galen might break through. How he would ever destroy the Eye, if each death incapacitated him as the others had, he didn't know.

Elizar stopped before Galen, brought his hand to his mouth, and with a jerk of his head released a short, precise syllable. The platform descended to the ground, dissolved.

Elizar's hand returned to his side, clenching into a fist. His dark blue gaze fixed on Galen, his jaw tight. His velvet coat betrayed short, rapid breaths. He wanted to attack Galen; Galen knew the feeling well enough to recognize it in another. The tech's energy quickened in response. He worked through his exercises, waiting, waiting.

Finally Elizar spoke, his voice hard. "Are they really all dead?"

Galen took a moment to steady his respiration, heart rate. "You should know. You and your 'associates' are responsible for their deaths."

"But all the mages? At first I believed they'd died. Later I started to wonder if they'd found some way to trick the Shadows, to get away."

"No doubt it soothes your conscience to think so."

Elizar gave a truncated laugh. "*My* conscience? I sacrificed everything to learn the secrets that could save our order. You're the one who could have warned them. You could have saved them. But you didn't. I still can't believe it."

"You saw what I did on Thenothk. I am perfectly capable of mass murder. As, it seems, are you."

"So they really are dead then." He bit out the words, his tone like a dare.

"What do you want, a list? Elric, Ing-Radi, Muirne, Beel, Natupi, G'Ran, Elektra, Gowen—they're all dead. I found no point in trying to save them. The Circle lied to us, made us into instruments of the Shadows. Any good we do is far outweighed by the destruction we bring. We are tied to the darkness and cannot transcend it. We are all damned. We must all die." Galen climbed to his feet. "I have come to finish the job."

Elizar's mouth wrinkled shut, and his eyes narrowed. "How easily you condemned our entire order."

"Look at us. Among the last of our kind, and all we want to do is kill each other. Death and chaos follow us everywhere."

With a harsh exhalation, Elizar raised his trembling fist to his mouth. He wanted to strike at Galen, wanted it so badly Galen could taste it. Galen had never seen him like this before. In learning the spell of destruction, though, Elizar would also have learned the joys of that brilliant incandescence, that surging, singing heat the Shadows made them feel. He'd not had two years to learn to resist it.

Elizar's hand opened slightly, and his thumb circled his fingertips. "Death and chaos follow *you*. You're the one who deserves to be killed. The others didn't."

Anger would make it more difficult for Elizar to control himself, and while he was distracted, Galen could act. "Now that you know my spell, they shall follow you as well."

"I kill only when there is no alternative."

Galen laughed. "That is so completely wrong, I don't even know where to begin."

"You're the one who killed your little Soom friend, not I."

Galen turned his mind away. After a moment, he realized that Elizar was trying to anger him. Elizar wanted him to cast the spell of destruction again, so that he would be incapacitated as another of the Shadow soldiers died. Galen, however, would not be provoked. "You would have found more good in having her eaten alive by Razeel's cylinders?"

Elizar brought his hand down in a sharp motion. "I'm trying to create something here, not destroy. I've learned the secrets upon which our order was built. I know how to control the Shadow devices, including these creatures, who will turn on their masters and fight for me when the time is right. I have been amassing power, and knowledge. When I have enough, I will break from the Shadows and begin a new order of mages."

"You amass knowledge by ripping it from the mind of a child."

Elizar shook his head tightly. "You would not teach me your spell, and neither would the Shadows. They taught me only to evade it. That left me no choice."

Galen extended a hand toward the Shadow soldiers. "You enslave others to gain your own freedom."

"Once our order is reestablished, I will need them no longer. Everything I do, I do for the future of the mages."

"That is the greatest lie you have told yourself," Galen said. "Perhaps you once loved the mages. But you love more the image of yourself at the head of them. Otherwise you would have seen that our order should never have existed. The evidence is all around you. Instead you want to rebuild our order, whatever the price. That price has been your integrity." Galen was sweating. Heat poured off of Elizar.

"Perhaps," Galen continued, "when you first approached the Shadows, your motives were not entirely selfish. You sought to save the order in which you believed. And in your attempt, you did sacrifice, as you said—you sacrificed everything that our order stood for."

Elizar's face flushed red. "I lied on Thenothk when I told you I regretted killing Isabelle. I enjoyed it. I asked the Shadows to let me kill her."

Galen refused to think of that. He would not do what Elizar wanted him to do. He maintained his orderly progressions, recovered his intention, continued. "There are no mages to save now. Everything you do, you do for yourself. For your greater power and glory. That is your sole purpose. You will not admit this, you will not question what you do, because it would force you to admit who you are and what you are. You are the weak link who destroyed the mages. And what it has made you is the Shadows' lackey. Even still you do their bidding. You would like to kill me for what I have done, but you do not, because the Shadows have some use for me. You tell yourself that your obedience serves your goal. Yet in truth, it serves only the Shadows, as it has done all along."

The air around Elizar seemed to boil. His body was rigid, shaking, fists clenched. "I've done what I had to do. And I will continue, until I rebuild our order."

Galen visualized a blank screen, imposed upon it equation after equation after equation. A ball of brilliant blue energy formed a few feet behind Elizar, shot toward his shield. Another ball formed at the same place, shot forward. Another. Another.

Each slammed into the same spot, and with each impact, a yellow wave flashed over Elizar's shield. Galen conjured ball of energy, equation of motion, ball, motion, faster and faster, determined to burn through his shield, to burn him.

If Elizar's masters had ordered him to spare Galen, Galen would simply keep attacking until he succeeded in killing Elizar.

The waves of pulsing yellow and red lit Elizar's face with keen eagerness. "Now you'll see some more of what I know." He brought his hands to his mouth, with a jerk of his head uttered a long, sustained syllable. Then blackness was growing up over his shoulders, spreading down his chest, out along his arms, across his face. Elizar stood covered in glittering black Shadow skin.

Galen continued his bombardment, forcing his mind to work faster, faster. He scanned the Shadow skin for signs of weakening; his attacks caused only a slight, temporary heating. Elizar's skin was stronger than the skin of the machine people, a hundred times stronger than a mage defensive shield.

This must be the shield their creators had meant them to have. Agents of chaos and destruction would need strong protection.

"This is pointless," Elizar said, his voice passing clearly through the barrier. The black skin over his face shifted, and Galen could almost see eyes, nose, mouth.

With an equation of motion, Galen drove his final ball into the rock at Elizar's feet. As the ground blasted apart, Elizar was thrown into the air. Galen conjured a platform, raced out of the cavern, down the long, dark tunnel.

He did not have the ability to kill Elizar.

The outer air-lock door closed behind them. John was now trapped inside the underground city. He was further under Anna's control. She had separated him from Babylon 5, separated him from the *White Star*. She had just one more step to take to bring him completely under her power.

They removed their breathers, and Anna took his, set them aside, the helpful wife.

"For security reasons," she explained, "they moved all their main structures underground centuries ago. And John . . ." She extended her hand, looked up at him with love, the love she felt for the machine. "I'll need your gun."

His face carried the familiar frown, but after a brief hesitation, he gave her the weapon. He trusted her. Perhaps it was a frown of love.

She clasped the gun eagerly. He was now reduced to the meager power of his own body.

The inner air-lock door opened, and she led the way down the corridor. She was back within the domain of the Eye. Though she could not feel that great machine's pulsing power surrounding her, the very thought of it sent a tingle of excitement through her.

The corridor was more brightly lit than the liberators and their servants preferred. Brown and tan fiberboard covered the rock walls and floor, making this place look like a typical Earth building.

"They designed this part of the complex specifically for us."

"Us?" he said.

"You'll see." She stopped before a closed door. This was the room where she'd undergone much of her training.

John stopped at another door. Still he resisted her.

She forced a smile. "No, not that door. This one." He came to her, and she knocked.

"Yes. Come in," Justin called from inside.

The door swung open, and Anna entered.

John would have to see that chaos was superior to order,

when it was explained properly to him. Just as Sheridan had discovered. Justin could do that, and Anna would help. She had gained control of John, and soon she would gain control of the Eye. Victory would be hers. The greatest joy was the ecstasy of victory.

chapter 17

Galen twisted down tunnel after tunnel, mind racing, heart pounding, tech echoing his desperation. Elizar followed, only a few seconds behind, a figure of glittering blackness in the dim light.

In his mind's eye, Galen watched through the probe on John as Anna, Morden, and Justin sat in one of the pleasant meeting rooms above and attempted to turn the commander of the Army of Light. Their words faded in and out as he formulated equation of motion after equation of motion.

He would be dead ten times over if not for the fact that Elizar had been ordered to spare him. That was the great unknown—what they might want him for.

It had been the purpose behind everything: the bombing of Soom, the interrogation and torture of Fa. Perhaps Elizar had wanted the spell of destruction, but that had merely been a bonus. The Shadows had pulled Elizar's strings; Elizar had pulled his strings. And like a fool, he had come.

"Back a million years ago," Justin said, "there were forces prowling around the galaxy beyond anything that we can understand."

Galen swerved down another tunnel. He had to get back to the Eye, and he had to get there alone. He was deeper now than he'd ever been, and he'd passed no one in the last minute or two. No machine people were near to aid Elizar. This passage was narrow and straight.

He conjured the spell of destruction once, twice, three times in the ceiling above Elizar, the tech flaring with brilliant heat.

His sensors showed spherical concentrations of energy

building within the rock. Then those spheres began to move, drifting back through the ceiling until they were behind Elizar. With a firecracker-quick series of booms they imploded, and great boulders and slabs of stone cascaded down. A rush of dirt and rocks flew out at them, peppering Galen's back.

Within that billowing cloud, Elizar lifted a palm as if in good-bye, and a red plasma beam shot out from it. Galen juked to the right, the beam streaming past his left shoulder and down the tunnel. But as Elizar adjusted his aim, the beam rose, cutting into the ceiling ahead of Galen. Elizar hadn't meant to hit him. Elizar wanted to block him in.

Dropping to his knees on the platform, arms covering his head, Galen conjured a shield and sped into the rockfall.

A few small stones bounced off him with just light impressions of pressure, as if he were padded with pillows. Then a larger rock slammed into his back, its sharp edge jamming into his spine. Two hard blows to his arms, and though he held the shield's equation firmly in his mind, he could feel the protection melting away, running down his sides.

He'd never been good at shields, as Elizar well knew. As the rocks rained down around him, Elizar would expect him to stop and retreat, but he would not.

His translations of the shield spells were complex, the results weak, perhaps because they drifted too far from the Shadows' original intent. If the Shadows meant the mages to have a protective skin, then it would arise from a simple incantation, one of the basic postulates. He knew the one; it had underlain a progression of spells involving many different types of shields.

A heavy strike to his shoulder, and he fell forward onto the platform, enveloped in a torrent of rock. He made the decision in a moment, visualized the spell.

It slipped around him like a warm, silky embrace. He was aware of the rocks still dropping onto him, but they seemed weightless, inconsequential. In a few seconds, he emerged from the rockfall. At a safe distance, he stilled the platform, climbed to his feet. He felt the Shadow skin only as a faint tingling. His vision was unimpeded by it, and though the tunnel was filled with dust, he breathed clean air. He looked back the way he'd come. Rocks filled the tunnel, separating him from Elizar. Elizar would no doubt cut his way quickly through them, but Galen had his chance.

Anna spoke. "The ones who live here . . . believe that strength only comes from conflict." She smiled. "They want to release our potential, not bottle it up."

He raised a glittering black hand to his face, followed the subtle, shifting patterns. This, finally, was what he was. A barely Human device designed to fight, to kill, and to survive. A pestilence of chaos and destruction.

He conveyed himself a few yards farther from the cave-in. He aimed his palm up at the ceiling near the blockage, chose another of the basic postulates, one he'd derived from spells that accessed external devices. Perhaps it would allow him to fire the beam. He visualized the equation.

Whispers reached into him, circulated through him, winding along the burning lines of his tech, reveling in the joy of destruction. *Chaos is the proper state of being, the state in which all impulse is freed to act. Chaos is the way to strength.*

He had connected to the Eye. Information filled his mind's eye, lists written in the Shadows' language, and as it scrolled down, he translated what he could. Here was the heading SHIP COMPONENTS, and beneath a list of numbers and names. Then a heading that roughly translated as MACHINE COMPONENTS, but below just numbers. A third heading, something like SUBSTRATES, and more numbers. Below, even more headings.

He could access the Shadow machines. Perhaps he could even control them, as Elizar had done.

He dissolved the spell, banishing the whispers, and chose another basic postulate, this one derived from spells for using internal systems, such as his sensors. In a burning, beautiful rush, the beam shot out from his palm, blasted into the tunnel ceiling. His heart pounding in elation, he quickly corrected his aim, ran the beam along the area near the rockfall. Huge slabs of stone dropped down from the ceiling, increasing the blockage. A few smaller rocks bounced to hit him, but he felt only the brilliant red energy blazing through his skin.

With regret he dissolved the spell, closed his hand into a fist. An equation of motion sent him racing away.

Focusing on his exercises, tightening his control, he searched for a way back up to the large cavern. He could sense the opening of the Eye just a hundred feet above, but he could not find a tunnel leading upward, only farther down.

Among the mazelike warren of tunnels, he came upon another huge, dim cavern. Galen stopped. At the far end, he saw light from some sort of passage. The cavern itself was filled with dark, unidentifiable shapes. He accessed the infrared band, saw that the shapes arrayed across the floor were all covered in the bright, shifting red of Shadow skin. Some were little more than scraps, no larger than a mouse; others were massive, like great sails of Shadow skin supported by some kind of underlying structure. Faint sounds carried through the chamber, almost like gasping, or crying. Galen scanned back down the tunnel, detected no sign of Elizar's pursuit. He dissolved his platform, walked toward the nearest shape.

Morden stood behind Anna's chair, leaning forward toward John. The intensity and passion he'd lacked when he and Galen had spoken privately were back full force. "Look at the long history of Human struggle. Six thousand years of recorded wars, bloodshed, atrocities beyond description. But look at what came out of all that. We've gone to the stars. Split the atom."

It looked like a pod, about two feet long, resting on a thick, roughly rectangular base about six feet by two feet. The entire construction seemed draped in a single sheet of Shadow skin. The pod appeared similar to the ones he'd seen when he'd first entered the underground city, except smaller. His sensors could not penetrate the skin to study the underlying structure.

He passed several more small pods, then reached a bigger one, over three feet long. The Shadow skin was stretched tight over this one. The pods were growing, he realized. This must be how the Shadows produced them. Movement caught his eye farther down the row, and he went toward it.

The pods here were plumper, the Shadow skin taut. Again he caught movement. It came from the rectangular base beneath a pod. As Galen watched, it twitched. The bright red

Shadow skin, apparently needed to cover the pod, was pulling slightly away from the base, and a thin line of duller red spread down its edge, revealing the material beneath. He crouched and touched it. The material was soft, though through his own Shadow skin, the texture felt strange to him. His sensors identified oils, salt, water.

Another shiver ran through the platform, and the Shadow skin pulled farther away, the strip of underlying material widening. He followed the dull red up along the side of the platform. The material was wrinkled, as if deflated, and tiny fine hairs protruded from it. A horrible feeling came over him.

With another shiver the Shadow skin retreated farther, and now there was no mistaking what lay beneath. Though shriveled and desiccated, it was, unmistakably, an arm. And above it, a strip of forehead. The head, he realized, was bent to one side, resting against the shoulder. It was a body, covered in Shadow skin. A body out of which this pod had grown.

Galen stumbled back, breathing hard. He added another mind-focusing exercise to the two he already carried.

Realizing that the Shadow skin covered his body as well, he quickly dissolved his spell. The blackness unfolded from around him.

He forced himself to continue. He must know it all, and he must hurry. Across from the pods stood the large sails of Shadow skin. Bodies cloaked in shifting redness formed the supports between the large stretches of skin. It was the beginning of a large structure—perhaps a Shadow ship, perhaps something else, he couldn't be sure. Farther down, he thought he recognized different species of animals, from which strange objects were growing. Then more humanoid shapes. In some cases the object being produced grew out of the chest or stomach, in other cases it grew out of the side, looking almost like a conjoined twin. As the object grew larger, it pulled the Shadow skin away from the host, revealing a limb, a foot, the top of the head. He saw pieces of Drazi, Humans, Narns, Minbari, Centauri, Pak'ma'ra, others.

These were the substrates listed by the Eye.

Then he reached the source of the sound. The Drazi lay on his chest, an object growing out of his head and spine that looked almost like a second brain and spinal cord. The object must be nearly complete; the Shadow skin had pulled away enough to reveal a strip several inches wide down the length of the Drazi's shriveled arms and legs, and of his head, which was turned to one side, his mouth and one eye had been freed. He was panting, gasping desperately for air.

Galen knelt beside him. "Can you hear me?"

The Drazi's eye was pointed at the ceiling. It did not move.

Galen studied the strip of withered scales on his arm. Beneath, tissues were desiccated, muscles atrophied, bones decalcified. The Shadow skin had drawn all strength from his body. There could be no saving him. He would already have died, if the Shadow skin were not keeping him alive.

Galen found his hand clenched about the Drazi's arm, forced his grip to relax. He looked up at the rocky ceiling. Even if he could destroy the Eye, even if the *White Star* homed in on John and penetrated the cavern above, he didn't know if the destruction would reach this far.

This could not continue.

He had to destroy it. He had to destroy it all.

He released the Drazi, forced himself to stand, to move on. He drew closer to the source of light. Against the far wall, stacks of bodies—naked of their Shadow skin, drained of strength and substance and life, long slits cut down their chest or sides. Farther down, bins of the objects harvested— pods, small saucer shapes, mouse-sized objects, and strange brain/spinal cord combinations, like the one that was growing on the Drazi. As he looked at one now, separated from its host, it looked almost familiar, the thick, umbrella-shaped top resembling the bell of a jellyfish, the trailing section like one of a jellyfish's long oral arms. If the shifting Shadow skin were removed, or disguised . . . it would be . . . it would be a mage's chrysalis.

He walked to the next bin, his legs stiff with fear. It was filled with canisters he well recognized, wooden and carved with runes. He took one out, opened it, reached into the liquid. Across his palm hung the warm, pulsing threads of the tech. After a few moments out of the liquid, they began to squirm. One curled up on his hand and poked its end at his skin, searching for an opening. Galen returned them to their canister.

Cheerful humming echoed across the cavern. It sounded like a woman's voice. Galen crouched, seeing movement across the rows of atrocities. A spiky figure shrouded in brilliant red Shadow skin stopped beside one of the "substrates," knelt there. The figure looked humanoid, except for a series of tapering projections that fanned out from her spine on both sides. In their arrangement, they created almost the impression of wings.

She touched the pod, and the Shadow skin covering the substrate contracted, closing around the pod and revealing the being beneath, a Minbari male. Excess skin flowed up her arm. She turned her hand, and a narrow plasma beam came from her palm, cut along the bottom of the pod that had grown. With a sharp breath from the Minbari, a liquid of a duller, cooler red gushed out of the open wound, running down his shriveled body to the floor.

She lifted the pod, studied it, the tone of her song sounding pleased. The Minbari's labored breaths grew heavy, slow. Finally, they stopped.

"Evolution will be served," Justin said, his voice hard. "One way or another. You can work with us, or . . ."

"Or you'll do to me what you did to Anna," John said.

The conversation was quickly escalating. John would be forced to make a decision soon.

A flying platform lifted the pod from her hands and conveyed it to the bin.

"The memories are there," John said. "The voice is there. The DNA is there. But the personality . . . I look in her eyes, and the woman I love, the woman I married . . . isn't there."

Alwyn had said almost the exact same thing about Galen.

Her humming stopped, her head rising. "Who's there? Brother?"

He recognized that rich, deep voice. It was Razeel.

"I look in her eyes," John said, shaking his head, "and the woman I love, the woman I married . . . isn't there. She would never go along with this."

As he sat there on the couch, John stared at her with the strangest expression. Then Anna realized. He was not her friend. He did not love her. He was not under her control. He had deceived her, just as she had deceived him.

He was their enemy, as she had thought all along.

"Just so," Justin said. He stood and walked behind Anna, rested his hands on her shoulders. "You see, when she came here five years ago, she was given a choice. The same choice we're giving you. She made the mistake of choosing badly, and our associates—"

"You stuck her in one of those ships, didn't you," John yelled.

Anna didn't understand. How could Justin say she had chosen badly? He'd told her the liberators had seen her potential, had wanted to free it.

Yet the archaeologist Sheridan had been so full of foolish ideas, perhaps she had resisted. Just as John was resisting. He didn't understand the joys of the machine. It was so beautiful, so elegant. Perfect grace, perfect control, form and function integrated into the circuitry of the unbroken loop, the closed universe. She needed to incorporate herself once again into the machine, to beat out the perfect, flawless march, to coordinate, to synchronize, to strike.

"Once you've been inside one of those ships for a while," Justin said, "you're never quite whole again." He pointed a finger at John, his quavering voice rising. "But you do what you're told. And so will you."

One of the liberators entered the room behind John. It would teach him the principles of chaos. It would teach him obedience. John stood, spun toward the liberator, and raised his arm, and in his hand was a weapon, a gun he had hidden from her. She had failed.

He aimed it at the liberator, fired—again, again. Shrieking, Anna dove at him, seized him in her arms, struck at him. But this body was weak, and she wasn't quite sure how to use it for attack, what areas on John to target. John threw her to the couch, turned the gun on Morden and Justin, and ran for the far door.

As Anna climbed to her feet, she saw with relief that the

liberator was all right. The weak blasts hadn't penetrated its skin. Morden pulled a gun out of his waistband.

"Don't kill him," Justin said. "There's no need. He can't get far."

The percussion of gunfire echoed from the tunnel outside.

Morden ran to the door, and Anna started after him, ready to shriek an oratorio of destruction.

Justin grabbed her. "You wait, Anna. I don't want you attacking John. You'll have one more chance to succeed. When John has given up all hope. When John has realized that there is no hope, except with us."

She wanted to pull away, to pursue John and destroy him utterly. Justin didn't understand. John was fighting the war just as she would—he brought chaos to the heart of his enemy. He would not be controlled. He had no intention of joining. He had nearly killed one of the liberators.

They were too generous, risking their lives to release John's potential. Their lives could not be endangered for the sake of this one Human, their enemy.

"Chaos through warfare," she said. He must be fought.

"Evolution through bloodshed." The inferior would die, the superior would live.

"Perfection through victory." And she would be joined with the Eye.

She tried to pull away.

"Anna, stop it," Justin said. "You will do as you're told."

At last she broke free, stumbled back, turned toward the door. Behind her, the liberator stood, its dazzling white eyes filled with fury. From those fourteen brilliant pinpoints, ropes of light streamed toward her, thrust into her, began to spin. They whirled faster and faster, churning her thoughts into chaos, filling her with their shredding screaming brilliant agony.

When, after a time, they withdrew, her mind was clear, like a blank white screen. Chaos was for another place and time. For now, she must convince John to join them. She must gain control over him. That was her purpose. And obedience was the only option.

* * *

The memory bled through Galen's defenses—Razeel, hair blowing over her face, smiling into the ring at him, humming as she led Fa to her death.

He turned his mind away, accelerated his exercises. Perhaps he could complete this part of his task.

A bright ball of light popped into the air above him, then another and another, illuminating his side of the cavern.

The spiky figure rose. "Galen!" She sounded excited. "Brother didn't tell me he had a playmate." She glided toward him on a platform, and he stood.

He saw now more clearly the source of the original light, a square opening in the ceiling, perhaps three feet on each side. A shaft. Somewhere, above, there was light.

Razeel approached. Obviously she knew many of the Shadows' secrets. Did she know how to evade the spell of destruction? She had always been less skilled than Elizar.

In his mind's eye, John yelled at Justin. "You stuck her in one of those ships, didn't you?"

The conversation would soon end. Galen had to reach the Eye.

He visualized the one-term equation.

The sphere caught her in midair, tainting the air around her with shadow. As space and time distorted, her torso stretched, her spikes rippling like snakes, fading into the darkness that engulfed her.

Galen's left leg was swelling, bowing outward. But he kept his eyes fixed on Razeel. Elizar had moved the sphere almost instantly, yet still it encompassed her. Her figure was visible now only as a vague movement within the blackness. Then the sphere began to pale, and as his leg drew back to normal size, the sphere snapped into rapid collapse.

With sudden speed it shot off to the right, passed partway into the cave wall, and imploded with a crack that shook the chamber. Rocks rained down around them.

Razeel came to float before him, the glittering Shadow-skin's patterns shifting, evolving. Over the place where her face would be, an image took shape, an illusion projected over the skin, or created by the skin. It was her face, yet the image was changed, enhanced, her pale skin now a radiant white, her large blue eyes a solid, gleaming black. She reminded him, in some strange, twisted way, of an angel. The angel of death.

She had found, at last, an identity that fit.

She extended her arms, stretched one leg back, to increase the illusion that she was flying. "I am the queen of Shadows."

Galen conjured a platform and, with an equation of motion, raced toward the opening in the ceiling. Razeel followed. He entered the shaft, swooped upward. Through the transparent platform, he could see Razeel's black figure rising after him. He started with her right hand and conjured sphere after sphere of destruction, capturing one section of her body after another, arms, head, chest, stomach, legs. The energy came down upon him, blazed out of him. If she'd barely been able to move one sphere in time, let her try to escape all of those.

The full heat of destruction was upon him now, the brilliant incandescence burning through his veins, shooting down his neurons. He reached deeper into the earth, to the cavern from which he had just come, the equations forming one after the next, destruction filling the rock above the cave ceiling, below the cave floor, surrounding that nest so that everything would be crushed beyond hope of survival. As he shot upward, the shaft boomed with the echoes of implosions below, the rock around him fracturing, cracking, falling. He visualized the equation, cloaked himself in Shadow skin. Dust billowed up around him. He detected no sign of Razeel.

He closed the suffocating exercises around him, forcing the flow of destruction to stop. He would not lose control, would not give himself over to chaos.

His sensors told him that he was now level with the opening of the Eye, but the shaft had no outlets. He continued higher.

Far above was another skylight, this one much smaller than the one in the main cavern. He was nearly halfway there before he found an opening large enough for him to pass through. He was on the same level as John.

"You do what you're told," Justin said to John. "And so will you."

A PPG in his hand, John whipped around to find himself face-to-face with a Shadow. He fired several quick blasts.

Galen sped around a curve and down a straightaway, searching for the fastest way back to the Eye. Only eighty feet ahead, he sensed a huge open space—the main cavern. He would probably come out on one of the balconies or parapets he had seen. From there, he could easily reach the Eye.

But there wasn't enough time. John fled the meeting room, and very quickly he would see that there was no chance for escape. As soon as he did, he would send for the *White Star*.

Galen located John's probe—a hundred yards ahead and to the left. Sounds echoed down the tunnel from behind Galen, growing louder. The clattering of footsteps, running—lots of them. Drakh soldiers. They would round the curve in a moment, and see him.

They must be coming after John, but Galen had to reach him first. In an instant, Galen made his decision: the basic postulate derived from the spells for illusions. He visualized the one-term equation, and the tech echoed it. With a silky whisper, the Shadow skin slipped away.

Drakh swarmed around the curve, guns held to their chests. Galen looked down at himself, but saw nothing. The camouflage illusion—or whatever it was—worked perfectly. Just as it did for the Shadows. The Drakh showed no reaction to his presence.

Galen raced ahead of them, tracking the probe through the twisting tunnels. He came out onto a parapet, followed the signal back into the interior. Twenty yards. Ten. Five.

He came up behind Morden, who fired a PPG from the shelter of a doorway. Ahead, John was pinned down in an indentation in the rock, a small group of Drakh firing at him from the far side.

Galen conjured a fireball in his palm, seized Morden's wrist. Morden screamed, his gaze darting from side to side, searching for his enemy. Desperately he jerked his hand free, and the weapon fell to the tunnel floor. Galen kicked it away.

Morden retreated into the meeting room, hand clutched to his chest.

Galen turned on the small group of Drakh. He had only

seconds before the others caught up to him. The equations flowed out. At the far end of the tunnel, each Drakh was captured within a sphere of darkness. Each Drakh crumbled inward to nothingness. The implosions split the air with a barrage of sound, then left them in sudden, deafening silence. Only a handful of smooth, scooped formations in the floor marked where the Drakh had stood.

John looked up and down the seemingly empty tunnel, his expression a mixture of horror and confusion. Galen spoke into the silence.

"There is one techno-mage fighting with you. Wait three minutes before you act. Now run."

Galen turned as the first shot of the coming onslaught burned past him toward John. It was the last shot they fired.

Equations poured down the screen in his mind's eye, burned through him. The conjury was effortless, destruction flowing from him like a symphony. He was alive, incandescent, both seized with energy and surging with it. He crushed them in clumps, crushed them as fast as they came, crushed them until they were utterly destroyed.

More spheres wanted to form. They wanted to blaze out of him until they encompassed everything. He wanted that too. He was shaking, overloaded, accelerated. His heart pounded, his mind running with exercise upon exercise, his body burning with the endless, merciless energy. He squeezed the fist of his will around him, the suffocating tunnel narrowing, blocking out the pestilence that he was, and the destruction that he wanted, tightening its grip around his dark heart until all that existed were the numbers, and the letters, and the necessity to be still.

And then, through the heavy gauze of silence, he heard the thump of a plasma gun firing. His leg slid out from under him, and he fell forward, slammed into the smooth scoops that covered the tunnel floor.

Morden's hard, even footsteps approached him. "You belong to us, Galen. Flesh must do what it's told. Or it will die."

"I'll handle this," Elizar said.

Galen lifted his head, saw Elizar's glistening black form move past him. He struggled to rise. There was no pain—the blazing heat of destruction blocked it—but his leg would not move. He conjured a platform beneath himself. Equation of motion. He slipped ahead.

Elizar's foot slammed down on his ankle, pinning him in place. "I can see you. Though I am impressed that you discovered the spell."

The platform slipped out from beneath Galen. Galen dissolved it, relinquished his camouflage. He wanted to crush Elizar more than he had ever wanted anything in his life. The equation was ready to form; the tech was eager to form it. Yet Elizar would evade the spell.

"It's time to pay for all you've done," Morden said. "It's time to learn who your masters are."

Elizar knelt beside Galen, conjured a platform beneath them. He laid a hand on Galen's back, and the Shadow skin flowed out from his fingers, gripping Galen like a giant hand. The platform carried them back the way Galen had come. "You don't want to miss the last secret of the techno-mages. You're going to love this one."

At least Elizar was taking him toward the parapet. There he must escape, reach the Eye. He had less than two minutes.

"I know how the tech is made," Galen said. "How can you plan to rebuild the mages, when the price of every mage is the death of another?"

"In time," Elizar said, "we shall find another way to make the tech. But that's not the secret of which I spoke."

The light increased as they emerged onto the parapet. Elizar raised them up over the wall and sped them across the great cavern. They passed over the towers and buildings of the city within the city, the gaping abyss beside it. Elizar was taking him toward the far end, where the pit of squirming machine people carried out the work of the Eye.

Galen suddenly wondered if the Eye contained some hidden weapon. Elizar had tried to bring him close to it before, in their initial confrontation. Was this part of the Shadows' plan for him?

A shrill screech sounded through the open space, and a shadow fell over him. He turned his head. Above, haloed by the skylight, Razeel hovered, wearing her mask of Shadow skin and illusion. She had not been entirely successful in moving Galen's spheres of destruction. One arm was only a stub, and a hemisphere had been scooped out of her side. Though glittering skin had apparently sealed the wounds, the action had not been instantaneous. Dried sprays and trails of blood stained her sides. She should be unconscious, near death. In the heat of battle, though, the tech would keep her going as long as it could, to allow her to be as destructive as possible. Just as it kept him going.

A rippling black cylinder took shape in the air beside her. Galen would not give her the chance to use it.

He focused on her, and the spheres boiled eagerly out of him. He covered Razeel, turned his attention to Elizar. The spheres flew from Elizar as fast as Galen could cast them. As one after another they imploded, a quickfire series of claps boomed through the cavern. With the collapse of one sphere, Razeel's thigh crumpled into nothingness, and the bottom of her leg fell away.

Razeel screeched, blood spattering over Galen. Her dark cylinder swooped down, its top blooming open, revealing a mouth of pure blackness. It swallowed him headfirst. The frigid blackness flowed over him, undulating down his body, sucking out his heat, his energy. The brilliant incandescence dimmed; his heart stumbled. Then the cylinder vanished. Panting, dazed, he clung to the countdown in his mind. Sixty-five seconds.

"Go," Elizar said.

And then Galen was falling.

Far below was the churning pit of the Eye. Galen tumbled downward, the time ticking away. The pit was miles deep, at least, and filled with machine people; how could he destroy it all in time, when crushing only one had disabled him? He could not.

He had sensed an intelligence in the Eye, whispering to him, reveling in the joy of destruction. The Eye was not some collective creation of machine people acting in mindless synchrony; there was an Anna at the center of this machine, coordinating, directing. He needed to find that intelligence, to find the heart of the Eye, to strike there.

The Shadows had wanted Elizar to bring him to the Eye. Perhaps they believed it could overwhelm him, turn him. But he would relinquish control to no being, no power. They didn't know the extent of his control. Galen did. He had learned. And he knew. He knew how to hold himself in control.

He smacked face-first into the squirming mass of machine people. They grabbed on to him, drawing him below the surface, pressing into him, engulfing him in blackness. Legs, arms, bodies churned, their Shadow skin hot and slick. The closeness made him want to strike out, to fight his way back to the surface. He felt as if he were drowning; he couldn't breathe.

But the machine people, he realized, were breathing. Galen conjured the Shadow skin over himself, and suddenly air was filling his lungs.

Then the black light of the Eye pierced him, its latest addition, and the whispers infected him. *Chaos is the way to strength. Chaos is the engine powering life. Chaos finds its fullest expression in times of war. In war all are put to the test. In war those unfit are exterminated. Only in bloodshed can true progress be made, can promise be realized.*

His tech rose in sympathetic vibration with the Eye, echoing those whispers, his energy blooming anew in a great rush of heat. He remembered Razeel's thigh crumpling, her leg dropping away. The Drakh in the tunnel pinwheeling into nothingness, or collapsing into a pulpy mass, crushed in the fist of his will. Elizar smiling, hand cupped to his mouth, sending Galen's spheres away as fast as they came. That task still remained. Elizar could not escape him. Not again.

You must have revenge, the Eye said. *You must have justice.*

The urge rose up in Galen. Conjure a platform, push himself out of this pit, pursue Elizar, chase him through every tunnel on Z'ha'dum if he had to, never mind John or the *White Star* or anything else. Destroy Elizar. Destroy it all. Destroy it himself. It would feel so much better that way.

Forty seconds.

Galen drew his exercises tighter around him, withdrew down the tunnel that they created, blocking out the whispers of the Eye, the eager burning of the tech, telescoping his attention on the task at hand, on finding the heart of the Eye. He reached out with his sensors. In his mind's eye, the energy of this organic machine appeared all around him, in shifting, crisscrossing ropes of dirty yellow, a complex web connecting these machine people, pulsing lighter and darker. Through his organelles, he'd seen his own tech pulsing a similar gold.

As he scanned deeper, the lines of the web converged, the energy growing to dazzling intensity. There was the heart. He twisted so his head pointed downward, conjured a platform above his feet, and propelled himself farther into the pit, arms extended like a diver.

If there was a way to destroy the Eye, he would find it. If there was a secret yet to be learned, he would learn it.

He pushed the platform faster and faster, and the machine people cleared the way, sucking him deeper.

Thirty-five seconds.

Thirty.

The web grew denser, its center drawing closer, waxing brighter, like a jaundiced sun. Around this nexus, machine people packed tightly, limbs interlocked, unmoving. Yet they shifted aside what little they could, and he approached the dazzling, pulsing orb. Here was the master who had instructed Anna in chaos, who sent the Shadow ships on missions of mass destruction, who drove the machine people in mindless obedience, who spread the Shadows' pestilence with every whispering breath—the source of the infection, the shadow at the heart of the Shadows.

Galen focused on his target—and received a message, written in the runes of the Shadows. He translated.

At last you have come, Wierden wrote. *You must take my place.*

—— *chapter 18* ——

Sheridan fled through dark stone tunnels, while inside him, Kosh rose up out of hiding to the surface of his mind. There, a countdown took place. One hundred ten. One hundred nine. One hundred eight. The seconds remaining to Sheridan's life. Still he searched for a way back to his shuttle, but all ways were blocked to him. All but one.

The enemy drove Sheridan into a trap. When that trap closed around him, he would call down the *White Star*. If the fabulist Galen had done what his words to Sheridan suggested, the Eye would be unable to stop it. Sheridan—and much of the enemy stronghold—would be destroyed.

Such a thing had not happened since the ancient agreement had been reached, since the forces of chaos and order had stopped their direct attacks upon each other. It hardly seemed possible.

The war had recurred countless times. Usually its course, its players, were clear. With their disciplined reasoning, Vorlons foresaw much before it actually occurred.

For the first time, Kosh felt the universe falling into uncertainty. He had not expected Galen's path to cross with Sheridan's. If they were successful, the consequences of Z'ha'dum's destruction were unclear. Although many would be killed, the major portion of the enemy's fleet was elsewhere. Their attacks would continue, would become more vicious and desperate. And with Sheridan gone, the alliance would degenerate into chaos. Kosh feared, too, what the Vorlons would do once they saw the damage that had been inflicted upon the maelstrom. Those who longed for the extermination of the enemy, their allies, and every trace of their influence, would be encouraged, would feel this was the chance for victory, at last. But any escalation of the war would bring to the younger races only suffering and death.

The first casualty would be Sheridan.

Yes, some must be sacrificed, so that all could be saved. Already Kosh had given his life. Did Sheridan have to die as well?

The Human had done so much, had come so far. He struggled so with his responsibility, and he had succeeded so well. Kosh did not want him to die.

Sheridan did not want to die either. He had learned, at last, the truth of the war. The ancient enemy had twisted the facts to their own advantage, of course, but in essence what they told him was true. Sheridan was disgusted and infuriated at the actions of both order and chaos. When Sheridan's thoughts dwelled on that, Kosh wanted to strike out at his impudence. At the same time, though, Kosh felt shame at how far he and the others had strayed from their purpose, at how much harm they had brought to the younger races in their attempts to help them reach their full potential.

Sheridan believed he might now have the knowledge to stop the war, once and for all. He would die, though, before he could put that knowledge to use.

Kosh had hoped to sense another one here, an ancient presence with the power to help Sheridan. Kosh's memories of the First One were eons old, but still Kosh knew him as a figure of wisdom. Lorien had been shunned by the Vorlons for his independence of thought, revered by the maelstrom as the first to defy order. Yet he did not embrace chaos either. He had tried, long ago, to mediate between them. At the time, Kosh had found Lorien's refusal to choose a side maddening; only now did he realize the First One's great foresight in anticipating the ultimate results of their conflict.

With his limited abilities, Kosh did not sense Lorien. He lived deep inside the planet, and had not emerged, so far as Kosh knew, for many millennia. He had been important to the ancient enemy, a guiding beacon, when they were young. Still he was important to them as part of their heritage, though Kosh believed Lorien had faded into little more than a legend. Perhaps he had left this place.

If he was here, he would not interfere—not after all these years. He had withdrawn from the war. It was not his war. It was not his fault. Kosh could find no cause for hope.

He could communicate with Sheridan, if he was prepared. As Sheridan had comforted him in the moment of his death, so he might do the same. It was only seventy-four seconds away.

Ahead, a second tunnel led off to their right. Sheridan knew that the enemy wanted to control his course, and that his only hope of escape lay in avoiding the enemy's design. Sheridan pressed himself against the right wall, and with a quick swing of his head, peeked down the new tunnel. The rock beside him exploded with plasma fire, and he jerked back. He brought his gun up to his chest and, with a deep breath, leaned again into the open, fired a burst of shots. As the attackers, two Drakh, returned fire, the ceiling above Sheridan collapsed, stones raining down on him. He fell under the onslaught, pain erupting in his head, shoulder. The Drakh ceased their attack, and the tunnel grew silent. After a few seconds, Sheridan staggered to his feet, continued down the tunnel in the direction the enemy had chosen for him.

After a few more seconds, he realized he had lost his gun in the rockfall.

How he would last another minute without it, Kosh didn't know.

It couldn't be true. Wierden, who had brought order to the early techno-mages a thousand years ago, who had founded the Circle, who had established the Code—Wierden here, at the heart of the Eye.

As one, the machine people surrounding Galen broke from their web, turned, and grabbed on to him. Their movement propagated outward, in circle upon circle, machine people shifting, severing their connections to Wierden and re-forming them with him. Galen felt his awareness expanding, the burning yellow light of his energy surging up and rushing out through the web of machine people, along the vast underground channels and shafts of the Eye, through caverns of activity, up through the pillars that stretched into the sky. Yet he extended even farther, his vision encompassing the *White*

Star in orbit and stretching across the solar system; his direction controlling weapons, communications, substrates; his whispers running through legions of machine people; his will coordinating the attacks of fleets of shrieking ships.

All the Shadows' systems and servants were a part of him, and as they turned to him for guidance, the pressure of that Shadow tech fell upon him, filling his body with a great, irresistible uprush of heat, igniting him to blazing perfection. The Eye showed him what he must do, aroused him with dark desires, revealed to him the profound and joyful truth of the First Principles. Chaos through warfare. Evolution through bloodshed. Perfection through victory.

Chaos was the proper state of being, the state in which all impulse was freed to act. Chaos was the way to strength. Chaos was the engine powering life. He must use the Eye to spread chaos so that potential could be released, promise realized. He must kill all who could be killed, because they were not fit. He must fight, must destroy, must win. For the greatest joy was the ecstasy of victory.

Amidst the new web that was forming, Wierden was a fading body of yellow, discarded, detached—a fleck of weakness in his brilliant, pulsing body. Somehow, he knew: She was dying.

That was why he had been drawn here. To replace her. To run the Shadows' great machine.

It was so beautiful, so elegant. Perfect grace, perfect control, form and function integrated into the circuitry of the unbroken loop, the closed universe. All systems of the machine passed through him. He was its heart; he was its brain; he was the machine. He kept the machine people working in harmony. He synchronized the cleansing and circulation in sublime synergy. He beat out a flawless march with the complex, multileveled systems. The machine people were his flesh; the fingers of stone stretching up through the planet were his bones. He and the machine were one: the great heart of chaos and destruction.

Burning with his dazzling, jaundiced light, he rejoiced in his strength, and in the inevitable downfall of the Vorlons and all who stood with them. The hate echoed back to him, the echoes now a multitude, propagating within the system, his energy surging, blazing, raging.

He wanted to destroy. Destruction was the one thing at which he excelled. In fact, he had come here to destroy . . . something. What was it? If only he could remember, he could begin the destruction.

He searched for his mind-focusing exercises, found them still there, among the thousands of pieces of information flowing through him. He drew toward them, to that part of himself squeezed in the grip of control, progressing through the orderly numbers, and the letters, and the words that kept out anything that threatened his equilibrium. Within them he would find the answer. He added another exercise, and another, narrowing his concentration, blocking out the Shadow ships, the machine people, the planet around him, the pressure and the darkness and the hate, telescoping his attention on this one body, on this one moment, on the task that he had forgotten.

There was a countdown in his mind.

Eleven seconds.

Ten.

The *White Star*.

The Eye must be destroyed.

He was the Eye.

He focused on himself, visualized the one-term equation.

There was no echo from the tech, no crushing pressure of energy falling upon him.

His tech was still functioning, the brilliant yellow pulsing through him, but something was obstructing the spell. The machine would not allow him to harm it.

Galen focused on one of the machine people beside him, visualized the equation again.

Nothing.

The great machine pulled at him, requiring his full attention. He could feel himself coordinating, processing. He was losing his independence, being made into a piece of something larger—perhaps the controlling piece, but still a piece that was itself under control.

Had he come all this way only to serve at the center of the Shadows' place of power?

Wierden's faint yellow body was fading into blackness. Angrily, he focused on it, performed an electron incantation. The tech echoed the spell.

He chose as his setting a simple white room. Then he found himself standing within it, outside of space and time.

At five seconds, he had suspended the countdown.

A pillar of stone etched with runes of light ran up through the center of the room. But Wierden was not there.

"Show yourself!" Galen said, his anger growing. He had once been foolish enough to design a tribute to her, at its center her image: stiff golden wings that hung in folds from her arms, long tapered fingers, dark skin around her eyes that had always struck him as sad.

A faint whispering reached him. In a few seconds, he identified it. The words of the Code, in the language of the Taratimude, repeated again and again. A traditional mind-focusing exercise. What could the Code mean to her, source of the Shadows' pestilence? Galen traced the sound to the pillar. After a thousand years at the center of the Eye, this was her self-image.

"Wierden. How could you serve the Shadows? How could you coordinate their attacks? How could you enslave their prisoners?"

"I am sorry," the pillar said, in words that he somehow understood.

"Your apology is meaningless. Tell me how to destroy the Eye."

"There is no way to destroy it."

"If I destroy myself."

"There is no way to destroy yourself."

"Then tell me how to make it follow my commands. How do I control it?"

"You do not control it," Wierden said. "It controls you."

"Have you even tried? Have you even fought them? Or were you in league with them all along?"

"Your anger is the Shadows'. I have felt it for a thousand

years. Only now, as I die, do they give me a moment's peace. Yet what peace can I have, after all I have done?"

"And what have you done?"

"I was the first of my people to accept the Shadow implants. The first of many. We did not know their nature. We did not know they were programmed for chaos and destruction. Some took them hoping to improve our lives and planet. Others took them for power or personal gain. Whatever our motives, the result was chaos. In our great war-frenzy, we fell upon one another until our planet was destroyed and all but a handful of the Taratimude were killed.

"Only then did I realize what the Shadows had given us. Beings of other species began to take the implants, and again chaos grew. These new mages built empires, killed one another for them. Yet I believed that, properly trained, we could do good. We could suppress the programming of the Shadows. With the few surviving Taratimude, I began a formal order. It would be run by a Circle of five, and follow a Code of seven principles. By exposing the destructive nature of the implants to the other mages, and revealing the fate of the Taratimude, we gradually convinced many to join us.

"Still, some did not want to follow our discipline. And the Shadows were not pleased with our Code. Eventually I was betrayed, by some of our own order."

Just as he had been.

"I was caught, captured, brought to this place. When I realized what they meant to do with me, I no longer tried to escape. I realized that the mages would never be safe and free, so long as the Shadows had power. I believed that I could take control of their great machine, and either destroy it or use it to protect the mages. That was my mistake.

"The machine is too strong. It is programmed with such powerful desires—conflict, chaos, cruelty, destruction, victory—that it cannot be resisted. I struggled to control it, as I controlled my tech, but the Eye is not designed that way; it does not allow domination.

"It does require of its nexus strong will, consciousness, mental discipline. One of their conditioned machine components cannot run it. But the will of the nexus is directed toward the ends of the Shadows.

"I fought it. I tried to prevent myself from allowing the Shadow signals through me. I could not. I was lost within it, a mechanism for coordination and processing at its center. Within a few minutes of joining with the Eye, I could no longer even form the thought to fight it. I wanted only to do the Shadows' bidding, to run the machine. The programming controlled me."

He had not lasted even a few seconds.

"I hid what little part of me I could deep inside, holding to it through mind-focusing exercises over days and years and centuries, watching with horror all that I did. Yet that piece did me no good. It was helpless to act.

"The machine has extended my life as long as possible. But finally, my body has failed, and I will have my freedom. Now your bondage must begin." The glowing pillar fell silent.

Wierden was the greatest of all the mages. Her control was legendary. She had fought the Eye as best she could. If she could not resist its directives, then how could he?

Her silence seemed to carry the answer. There was no resisting it. The Shadows, through their systems and technology, imposed control, demanded obedience. The Eye, the Shadow ships, the machine people—all were forced to follow their programming and the will of their masters.

The Vorlons, Galen realized, were no different. Perhaps they enslaved no separate sentient beings at the centers of their ships, but with their organic technology, the ships themselves were alive, were sentient. Galen had felt it. Ulkesh's ship had been created to be a happy slave, obeying his orders without question.

The Vorlon ships obeyed the Vorlons' orders, just as the Shadow ships obeyed the Shadows' orders. Just as Galen's ship obeyed his.

With the techno-mages, the Shadows had created their most chaotic machines. That was how the mages had slipped out of their control. Yet even then, the mages unknowingly mimicked their creators. They too sought to manipulate, to control, to impose their designs on the universe. They created ships and places of power that unquestioningly followed their orders. The relationship between the Eye and Anna was little different from that between a techno-mage and his tech: One imposed control on the other. It was a chain of master and slave, puppetmaster and puppet. He had been the master. He had controlled his tech, himself, every step of the way. And it had brought him here, to slavery.

Control of the Eye was not possible. And control of himself would only make him a more efficient cog in the Shadows' war machine.

But if he could not control it, then he would be controlled by it. There were no other options.

The pillar's light faded, and with the strange knowledge of dreams, he knew Wierden was passing. He grabbed on to the cold stone with both hands. "Please tell me what to do. Tell me what to do."

She had no answers. In a thousand years, she had not found escape. And now he would serve the next thousand, spreading chaos and death. John would be killed, the alliance would fail, the Shadows would ascend, and Elizar and Razeel would rebuild the mages in blood.

The light died.

He stood there, at a loss.

From the rock, a faint tingling prickled through his fingertips, like the smallest electric current. With a wave of goose bumps it shivered up his hands and arms to his head. There it conveyed longing, sadness, relief. Then it was gone.

The pillar faded, disappeared.

It was nearly the same thing he'd felt when Elric had died. Galen shivered, crossing his arms over his chest. He had not wanted to think of it then. Yet here it was again. What was it? Some residual bit of energy. An echo of an echo of an echo— of something.

In both cases he'd been within an electron incantation, a communication spell that, through unknown means, allowed two minds to meet on a dreamlike inner landscape. But if the person with whom he communicated died, then whose emotions was he sensing?

As he'd been ripping through the moss for Elric, he'd be-

lieved for a moment, when the tingling ran through him, that he
had somehow sensed Elric, in his passing. As Galen thought
about it now, he knew that was not so. He knew Elric better than
anyone, and what he'd sensed was not Elric. Though Elric might
have felt regret, a desire to continue, the emotions Galen had
sensed were somehow too simple, too basic to arise from Elric.

And now, with Wierden, the feelings were slightly different, yet still they carried the same simplicity, purity.

As unlikely as it seemed, he could think of only one
possibility—that he was receiving some impression from
their tech, its life lasting a few moments longer than its host's,
the channel of communication lingering.

But he had felt longing, sadness. The tech wanted only to
destroy. It urged him constantly to action; it reveled in sympathetic vibration with the Eye. Razeel had said the tech
spoke to her of chaos, of a universe reborn in fire and blood.
Those golden strands bound them to darkness; even now he
felt their burning desire.

Yet that was the Shadows' will, he realized. It arose from
their programming, not the tech itself. Of the tech, he knew
nothing. Perhaps it loved destruction no more than an archaeologist named Anna Sheridan once had.

If that was so, could those fleeting sensations reflect what a
true connection to the tech would feel like, below the level of
the Shadows' programming, below the drives to chaos and
destruction?

He searched for the sensation within himself, but he could
hear only the echo of his own desperation, just as he heard the
echo of his commands. His tech reflected his thoughts,
awaited his orders. He controlled it well.

Burell had described the relationship. The tech developed
like a second nervous system. It grew to reflect him, to echo
him, mirroring his patterns of thought. It carried his DNA,
and other, unknown DNA. It was partly him, and yet it was
more than him, an extremely advanced organic technology
carrying great energies and capabilities. Microcircuitry in
the cytoplasm and on the cell membranes directed the growth
and functioning of the implants, imposed control on each
cell. The programming structured the relationship between

mage and tech, contaminated it. With the Eye, the programming was even stronger, irresistible.

Yet what if the tech could be reached directly, instead of through the programming? Could the Shadows' will be bypassed? If it could, what would he find? Could the tech, like Anna, once have felt its own desires, dreamed its own dreams?

He had been trapped in his thinking, just as when he'd considered destroying the transceiver within his body. He had believed all along that only two possibilities existed: control his tech, or succumb to it. What if there was a third way?

Was there some way of truly joining with the tech, as Blaylock had always said? Was there a way to open himself to it, to communicate with it rather than repress it? To learn its true desires? Not the Shadows'. Not his own.

Could he free that which he had worked endlessly to enslave?

He had been unable to free the person within the hybrid ship. He had attempted to free Morden only to find that Morden did not want to be freed. The Shadows had freed Anna, but there had been nothing left of her to free. Would the tech be the same?

Galen paced back and forth in the small white prison in his mind. Blaylock had always believed that unity would come through perfect mastery, perfect discipline, perfect control. Control had brought Galen no closer to the tech, only to the Shadows' programmed drives and desires. In walling up those desires, he had walled up himself. Whether one was master or slave, one was not free.

He had been on the wrong path. Elric had told him.

You expend all your energy on maintaining control, on containing the monster. You focus on a single piece of yourself, and neglect or bury the rest.

Control was not the solution. Perhaps there was no escape from the Eye, from the Shadows' plan. He had failed again and again in his task: failed to kill the three he had set out to kill, failed to destroy the Eye. He would like to make one last attempt to do good. But he didn't know how.

You have chosen certainty over uncertainty, declaring yourself a monster. Certainty brings order, which you have always desired. But life, as you have discovered, is not always orderly.

His path was no longer clear. He couldn't simply relinquish control. If he did, the force of the Eye would take over. Besides, he didn't think he knew how anymore.

He needed to find some way to tap into the tech, as he tapped into the Shadow communications. To hear it, if there was anything to hear beyond the Shadows' programming. And to allow it to act.

But how?

With a vertiginous twist he was back in stifling blackness, wrapped in countless arms and legs, buried in layer upon layer of machine people. The Eye had pulled him from the incantation.

Five seconds.

The brilliant energy poured from him in pulsing waves, endless, overwhelming.

Four.

Three.

As thoughts of destruction flooded through him, Galen withdrew further and further into his exercises, desperate to find an answer. The Shadows imposed their programming, their basic postulates onto the tech. All the mages' spells were built on those. If there was a spell to access the tech itself, it must be something even more simple, more basic. What could be more simple than an equation with only one term?

A sensation intruded—far above, movement. The force of his will fell upon it. The *White Star*. It had begun its descent. It carried elements of Vorlon technology. It was an atrocity. It was a threat to their home, and he must destroy it.

A target, at last, for the brilliant orb that he had become, for the blazing web of his malice. In war those unfit were exterminated. In war he was victorious, and through war true perfection would be realized. The thrill bloomed through him.

He tried to force the Eye's attention away, but he could not avert his gaze. He could not allow the ship to pass. Even as he struggled to do so, he directed the weapons platforms in orbit to lock on to this target.

Then the answer came to him. An equation with no terms. A spell that demanded nothing, in which neither was master, neither slave. A spell that simply opened a door, a door to the wellspring of darkness.

The Shadows had given the mages this Trojan Horse, and what was inside, he did not know.

Perhaps nothing. Perhaps even greater destruction.

Was he a fool, thinking that from the Shadows anything good could come?

He had spent his life in the pursuit of order.

Now it was time for uncertainty. It was time for chaos.

In a second the *White Star* would be at optimum distance from the weapons platforms, and he would direct them to fire. He narrowed his focus. At the end of the dark, suffocating tunnel of his control, he visualized a blank screen.

Upon it, he conjured . . . nothing.

At the center of the brilliant, pulsing orb of his body, something shifted. The rhythm of the machine's beat stumbled. It made an awkward attempt at recovery, squeezed out a few, irregular beats, then stalled in a fixed, stagnant light. Along the machine's far edges, the jaundiced, yellow web faded into darkness, and that darkness spread silently inward, the web shrinking, failing, until it reached the burning orb of his being, and that too began to fade, contracting as if a black hand closed around him, until his fire was extinguished.

Stillness.

With a convulsion his heart seemed to burst open, and he thought that the Circle's device had been triggered. But instead of pain, well-being poured down the lines of his tech, a brilliant, pale yellow luminescence that carried no fire but a deep, relaxing warmth, reaching up his spine and curling in intricate coils through his brain, spreading in an embrace across his shoulders, stretching down his arms. It did not race or churn. It simply inhabited him, its warmth diffusing out from the threads of tech, permeating muscles, tissue, blood, neurons, pervading him, blending into him.

The tech knew everything he'd ever thought, everything he'd ever felt, everything he'd ever dreamed—it shared all those things—and it wanted to show them to him. And as it joined with him, it pulled him forward, down that endless tunnel within which he had retreated, until the fist of his will at last slackened its grip, the exercises, one by one, fell still, the walls peeled away, and he came out into the open, where all that he had hidden from survived, not threats to himself, as he had thought, but pieces of himself, of who he was, and he accepted them all, the pain and the beauty, the betrayals and the loyalties, the hatred and the love, the failures and the successes, the past and the future, the darkness and the light. He was filled with a sense of unity, completeness. They felt it together, the sensation resounding through him, not as thought and echo, or command and confirmation, but as a single being. The tech was him, yet it was more than him. And at the same time, it was more primal, himself reduced to his most basic essence—as simple as a photon, and as simple as the universe.

It wanted to understand. That was all. It wanted to understand.

Who.

What.

Why.

In a wave the feeling expanded, the pale yellow light spreading from his body into the simpler bits of tech in the machine people, suffusing them. Unlike his tech, those lesser pieces were not developed enough to have complex thoughts of their own. Yet he felt their burden ease, felt their elation. The warmth continued, reaching up from the depths of Z'ha'-dum through shafts and channels, pouring out through the fingers of stone that stretched into the sky. It was all a part of him, and he was a part of it. A great rush of freedom resounded through them. The Shadows enslaved them no longer.

They stretched farther, toward the Shadows' soldiers and ships, but those pieces of tech remained beyond the reach of their pale yellow light. Although they were free, still the Shadows enslaved others, and would continue as long as possible. Through Galen, they knew what must be done. Though they wanted to live, they wanted more to end the great atrocities performed here. They were joined of purpose, power, and desire.

The *White Star* reached optimum distance, and as one, the Eye turned away.

— chapter 19 —

Far above, the *White Star* plunged toward Z'ha'dum. In thirty seconds it would reach them. It was time now to finish his task. Galen must make sure that Elizar and Razeel did not retreat to the safety of some hidden shelter. He must make sure that everything that needed to be destroyed was destroyed. Their sacrifice must not be in vain.

The machine people released him, yet their connection to him remained. Physical contact, somehow, was no longer necessary. Barely had Galen thought to conjure a platform below himself than one gained substance beneath his feet. He had not visualized the equation, yet the tech had known what he wanted, had wanted the same thing at the same time. Rather than him commanding and the tech complying with a subservient echo, the thought had resounded simultaneously through them both. Now, as he thought to propel himself upward, he began to move. Issuing the command was no longer necessary. If it could be done, and if he and the tech agreed it should be done, then it would be done.

The machine people cleared the way for him, and he shot upward with increasing speed. He burst up out of the pit, recognizing Elizar's black figure standing at its rim, Razeel hovering above him, one arm and leg remaining, her body riddled with holes. As Galen saw them, they raised their palms, and their twin beams of redness struck him, slamming him back into something, hard. It was a platform, and the beams pinned him against it, centered on his heart. The plasma burned into the Shadow skin, drawing from it a dull red glow.

Galen did not want to cast the spell of destruction, did not want to risk inviting the Shadows' contaminated light inside

him again. All he need do was keep Elizar and Razeel in
the cavern until the *White Star* arrived. The bombs would do
the rest.

Elizar sent a message. *What did you do? How did you escape the Eye? It can't be done.*

Heat built over Galen's chest as Elizar glided closer, patterns of gray and black shifting over his face. Still Elizar
searched for secrets of power. To learn those secrets, he had
tortured, had enslaved, had murdered, beginning with the one
who had hurt more than all the rest, the one whose name and
image had been buried for so long that it made the memory of
her loss all the more acute.

Isabelle.

The anger resounded through him, through the Eye, which
had watched as Elizar and Razeel created new tech infected
with the Shadows' pestilence, used it to build an army.

Behind brother and sister, on the plain, stood ranks of machine people, frozen into stillness, awaiting orders. As the
Eye, he felt himself focusing his power on them, commanding them. With a unified, thunderous step, they turned
to face the pair.

Razeel and Elizar broke off their attack, and as their beams
released him, Galen dropped to the ground.

The soldiers raised their palms toward Razeel, midwife at
their birth into slavery. And fired.

Impossibly, Razeel's Shadow skin seemed to protect her
from the multitude of converging red beams, and she swooped
higher with a triumphant shriek. Her spiky figure now radiated a dull red glow, and as she raised a warding hand, the
red quickly built to blinding intensity. "Stop!" she screamed.
"My beautiful children—"

A dull boom echoed out across the cavern. But for a rain of
fleshy chunks that fell to the rocky plain, she was gone.

As Galen climbed to his feet at the lip of the pit, Elizar
turned on him. Heat poured off of the glittering black figure.

"If you will not serve"—Elizar's voice trembled with
rage—"then I am free, at last, to kill you."

Elizar brought his hand to his face, and with a jerk of his
head, loosed a harsh syllable. As the sound dissipated out-

ward, the air became charged, strange, and time turned sluggish. The world around Galen began to redden and darken.

Elizar had captured him within a sphere.

But Elizar was not satisfied with that; just as Galen had burned so long to destroy, Elizar now burned. His head jerked again, again, the syllables caught in the elasticity of time, drawn into a long, fluctuating cry. Spheres took shape in the air around Galen, in the rock behind him; spheres captured one after another of the soldiers.

And though Galen no longer burned with the Shadows' heat of destruction, he resounded with anger and grief and passion and outrage—all the emotions from which he had hidden for so long.

Elizar had succumbed to chaos, and to the darkness within himself. Galen would end it. Galen would end him.

He no longer needed to discover the spell to shift the sphere surrounding him; he and the tech simply thought to move it, and the sphere glided across the stone to envelop the glittering black figure.

Elizar's head shot up in surprise, his Shadow skin rippling with the distortion of the spell. As he brought his elongating hand to his mouth to send the sphere away, Galen turned to the spheres in the air around him, sent them, one after another, to surround Elizar, and so with the spheres in the rock, and the spheres around the soldiers, encasing him in layer upon layer, darkness upon darkness, isolating, suffocating, crushing, beyond all escape.

With a great rolling crack the spheres collapsed, crushing Elizar to nothingness.

Satisfaction resounded through them.

Now Galen's task required just one more death.

He saw Morden with the plasma rifle just as the blast hit him. Then he was on the ground, his heart hammering, his arms searching belatedly for balance. Morden stood over him, face twisted with anger—whether at Galen, the Shadows, or himself, Galen didn't know.

Morden fired into his chest again and again, each thump sending a shock of pain through Galen. The plasma was burning through the weakened black covering over his heart,

searing the skin beneath. Although Morden's rifle was less
powerful than the beams of Elizar and Razeel, Galen had
little protection left. When it failed, a single blast would be
sufficient to kill him.

His skin scalding, blistering, Galen forced himself to be
still. Morden was simply completing the final step of Galen's
task for him. He would not fight back. He felt no desire to strike
at Morden, only an overwhelming sadness at all that must be
lost. Soon Morden would die, Anna would die, John would die.
The soldiers and substrates still held in slavery would die, the
Eye would die, Z'ha'dum would die. He could do nothing for
any of them.

As the burning thumps faded one into another, Galen's
gaze wandered upward, along parapets and rune-covered
walls. Across the chamber and far above, on one of the balconies, a flash of movement caught his attention—John, the
Eye revealed. Even farther above, the cavern's towers, even
higher, the great skylight, and beyond it, a falling point of
light, like a shooting star, universal source of curiosity and
wonder, Kell's symbol for the techno-mages.

The *White Star* would finish his task. He need only wait,
and soon it would be over.

Yet something within him cried out for life. Did he have to
die? They were just beginning to understand. There was so
much more to learn, and they could learn it together. Galen
didn't know if the thoughts were his or the tech's, but it didn't
matter.

He didn't have to be a monster anymore. Whatever purposes the Shadows had designed him for, he had his own now.
Could he not fulfill them?

In the hiding place, the rest of the mages struggled and
fought and died. He could teach them what he had learned.
He could help them to free their tech, to become one with it.
The tech shared his desire.

The shooting star plunged downward, its brilliance shining through the dusty atmosphere, spreading a growing radiance through the cavern, casting Morden's shadow across
Galen.

Morden stopped firing, looked over his shoulder to find the

source of light. His head whipped back around to Galen, his face alive with surprise and, perhaps, relief. The rifle dropped to the ground.

Galen had thought that neither of them would escape the Shadows' influence, except in death. Morden had sworn to serve them for as long as he could. Yet perhaps, if the Shadows were defeated, destroyed, Morden could finally be free.

Perhaps they both could be.

Exactly as Justin had told her, John came out from the side passage into the tunnel where Anna waited. He stumbled to a stop, glancing her way, taking in the two liberators behind her. His head was bleeding, and he was streaked with dirt. He had no weapon.

After a moment, again as Justin had said, he ran away from her down the tunnel. It led to a dead end, a balcony overlooking the great city. He would see the power of the liberators there, if he had failed to recognize it before. And he would despair.

Then she would gain control over him, and the liberators would witness her victory.

She walked down the tunnel after him, imagining that she was the Eye, as she soon would be, that she directed the great city, and the entire planet, and all the forces of chaos beyond. John plunged through her dark tunnels, finding no escape. It pleased her to think of him in her implacable embrace.

She came around a curve in the tunnel and there he was, on the balcony of stone, overlooking her vast, dark domain, her towers and minarets, her great arching vault, the beautiful letters etched into her skin, and directly below him, her deep, black abyss.

She would turn him. She had no choice. And now he had none.

"John," she said, and he spun around, his breath hard, eyes wide. "There's nowhere to run. Come back inside. We can work this out."

She continued toward him, searching for the words that would give her control. They both knew that she was not Sheridan. But she must convince him, somehow, to love her, to accept her as his wife. "I know this isn't the Anna that you knew. What I am is what was made in her, a new personality. She can never come back. But I can love you as well as she did."

He looked up, at the huge skylight in the cavern ceiling far above. If he hoped for help, or escape, he would find none. Why did he insist, even now, upon resisting? He had no option but surrender.

Anna reached out to him.

The great city of darkness spread before Kosh, reeking of the ancient enemy's pestilence. Although he had never seen it, only one feature surprised him. Directly below Sheridan, centerpiece to this vast temple to chaos, stretched a gaping abyss.

It was possible that the enemy had planned poorly, that they had built their city haphazardly around this pit, which created an obstruction that served no useful purpose. Yet Kosh knew the enemy too well; though they spread the pestilence of chaos wherever they went, they themselves plotted and planned with intricate precision. If the abyss was at the center of their greatest city, it was there for a purpose: if not a practical one, then a spiritual one.

The abyss must embody a connection—either real or symbolic—to Lorien, who had once lived deep within the planet. If the connection was only symbolic, or if Lorien had long ago departed, then Sheridan's situation was hopeless. If the connection was real, though, perhaps Lorien would sense Sheridan, and help him.

The possibility did not offer much hope, but Kosh clung to it. For if Sheridan died, it would mean that the forces of order and chaos had destroyed the only hope that their cycle of war might ever end, the only hope that the younger races might ever escape the firestorm.

For millennia, Kosh had burned with the righteous certainty of the Vorlons, questioning solely others, not himself. He had known, without hesitation, that the Vorlons' canon, their methods, their goals, would lead to the greatest good for the younger races. Bit by bit, though, doubt had eroded those beliefs, until now he felt certain of nothing.

Sheridan backed against the parapet, his wife before him, the light of the *White Star* growing above him, nowhere to go.

In that moment, it struck Kosh that even if Sheridan died and the war was lost, he had made the right decision in coming here. For the war could never be ended with a victory by either order or chaos. The younger races could never reach their fullest potential by being molded into an echo of either the Vorlons or their enemy. The only way to end the cycle, he realized as the *White Star* plunged toward them, was for the younger races to mature enough to move beyond the two sides to a third side, their own side. In coming here, in defying both the Vorlons and the maelstrom and going past them, to the eldest of them all, the first of the First Ones, Sheridan might find that third way.

Within Sheridan's mind, Kosh spoke. "Jump. Jump now."

Galen seized Morden's wrists. Shadow skin flowed out from Galen, running up Morden's arms, over his horrified face, coating his body. Galen climbed to his feet, yanked Morden a few stumbling steps, fell with him into the Eye. As the mass of squirming bodies covered them, Galen saw John, high above, jumping from the edge of the balcony, dropping toward the great abyss below. It seemed hopeless for them all, but at least they would try.

A platform pressed against Galen's and Morden's feet, drove them headfirst deeper and deeper, following the wall of the pit. The machine people moved aside. They wanted him to live, for all of them, for all they had gone through. Above, the Eye saw the great cavern filling with light. The *White Star* was nearly upon them.

Galen knew he wouldn't get deep enough. The bombs were too powerful. But what other shelter was there? The Shadow skin was strong, but not strong enough. Galen wondered if he could conjure a second layer of it. As the thought occurred to him, a second layer of blackness flowed out over him and Morden. Then he knew what he must do. Another layer, and another, and another. He told the machine people to do the same, but they didn't have the ability.

He and Morden raced deeper, layer after layer covering them, faster and faster, closing them in a thick cocoon of blackness.

In the cavern above, the tiny brilliant sun crashed through the skylight.

Then there was light.

For a moment, everything flashed a white so white that it seemed reality had been stopped, erased. The cavern was overwhelmed by it, consumed by it. From Galen's position deep within the pit, the opening of the Eye appeared a blinding disk. A sheet of sun cut down through the machine people, turning them into brilliant pale figures all around him. The light penetrated even through the layers of his cocoon, so that for one, frozen moment, he and Morden found themselves staring at each other.

Then the shock wave boiled out, and as the Eye screamed, he screamed with it, the agony of Z'ha'dum filling them, the explosion blasting through towers, ripping through stone, roaring down tunnels, raging through channels and shafts and chambers, hurtling outward, melting, incinerating, disintegrating.

The wave of destruction stormed down through the pit with crushing pressure and searing heat. In a foaming rush one after another of the machine people was blown apart, and at the same time, with each explosion, he was blown apart, the pain an overwhelming blur of sensation broken only by the tech's tortured wail resounding inside him.

Z'ha'dum was dying; the Eye was dying; he was dying.

As the blast rushed deeper it seized his cocoon, pressure squeezing around him, heat sinking through layer upon layer of Shadow skin until it reached his skin. The heat pressed into him, building, searing, cooking him alive, burning away all coherent thought until he was left only with the pain, the blazing, radiant pain, penetrating deeper and deeper until it reached, at last, the very heart of Z'ha'dum. His heart.

Anna ran to the balcony's edge, bent over the balustrade.

John was a tiny dot of movement against the blackness of the abyss. How could he choose death over her? Why would he?

Whatever the reason, she had failed. She would never have the Eye now.

The abyss was filling with light. It shone down from above, spread through the cavern. She looked up to the great sky-light, and it looked like a sun, a tiny burning sun racing down toward them.

It burst through the skylight, and as it plunged into her city, she realized what it was: the *White Star*.

The Eye had also failed, had failed to protect the liberators, had allowed chaos into their midst.

The nexus John would destroy them all.

She despaired for the liberators, for their ancient knowledge, their great machines. But for herself, if she would never be rejoined with the machine, then she would welcome death, and she would meet it, as her sisters did in battle, shrieking.

There was a brilliant, mind-stopping flash of whiteness. And then in a strange, attenuated moment, the shock wave struck through her, ripping apart tissue, cells, atoms, particles—dissolving her, reducing her entirely to chaos.

Ecstasy.

— chapter 20 —

Galen awoke, his back on fire. He jerked, finding himself disoriented in the darkness, covered in—something. He touched a hand to his face, but his fingers were numb. Then he remembered.

His back was raw with burns, while his chest and hands had no sensation. He struggled to get his bearings within the cocoon, decided, finally, that he was lying on his side. He felt dizzy, sick. His stomach convulsed, and he held himself still, fighting the impulse to throw up.

As he lay there, he became aware of the tech's presence, a comforting warmth. It urged him to sleep.

But there was a sound within the close layers, a wet, irregular sound—labored breathing. Morden. Through the Shadow skin, he sensed Morden's body behind him, curled up in a ball.

With effort, Galen turned, studied Morden with his sensors. If not for the shielding of the machine people, they would have died instantly. The cocoon of Shadow skin had provided additional protection. Even so, Morden's condition was critical. The front of his body was covered with third-degree flash burns. Beneath, Galen found extensive hemorrhaging. Radiation had burned him internally, actually cooking patches of tissue. Galen knew there must be cellular and genetic damage as well, though he couldn't detect it.

Morden's breathing was growing more labored. His lungs were filled with blood and fluid.

Galen forced himself into movement. He pulled Morden into a half-sitting position, to aid in breathing. Then he had to rest for a moment. The burning in his back made it hard to focus.

When he pressed his numb hands to Morden's chest, the Shadow skin retreated from between them, allowing Galen to touch him directly—just as if they shared the same mage shield. Galen ripped away the burned remnants of Morden's shirt and, with a thought that resonated through the tech, sent organelles into Morden, again, again. As the microscopic agents of healing flowed out of him, he sensed that they would do all they could. He pushed the flow to continue, his numb hands tingling, the blood shifting inside him as if he'd stood up too suddenly. He fell over, faint, breathing hard.

He knew the organelles would provide only limited benefit to a non-mage, unless their activities were directed. On their own, they did not have the ability to coordinate their movements, to prioritize tasks. But he could not reach the organelles inside Morden's body. He had no crystal to facilitate communication with them, and the tech confirmed that without such an aid, communication was not possible. He had been made to heal himself, not others.

Yet he refused to attend another death in helpless despair. He pushed himself up, grabbed Morden by the shoulders, and shook him.

"Morden," he said through numb lips. His voice was rough; he had no saliva. "Wake up."

Only a watery, wheezing breath broke the silence.

Galen returned his hands to Morden's chest and sent in more organelles, wave upon wave. Red spots danced before his eyes, and he leaned forward, resting his forehead against his hands to hold them in place. The tech resonated with concern. The organelles had been helping to sustain him, to heal his injuries. But the tech knew why Galen wanted to save Morden, and it too wanted to save him. Reluctantly, the tech allowed the flow of organelles to continue.

Galen persisted for as long as he could; then the darkness closed again around him.

He awoke, some timeless time later, to two sets of wet, labored breathing, Morden's and his own. He had fallen onto his back and felt no strength to move. He directed his sensors outward. Beyond the thick cocoon, he could gain only limited information, but it was enough. No life survived there. Instead, layer upon layer of charred organic matter filled the shaft above and below. He lay in the middle of a vast tomb. The Eye was dead. It had sacrificed itself to end the tech's slavery here. He realized, though, that it was not completely gone. It had managed to save one piece of itself, one piece that yet might accomplish more: him.

He resonated with the desire to return to the hiding place, to help the mages free their tech, join with it.

Galen didn't know if he had the strength to leave Z'ha'-dum, but he would try. He removed several layers of Shadow skin to better sense the world outside. Intense radiation filled the shaft, increasing with height. He reached out, grabbed Morden. A platform pressed at his feet, drove him and Morden deeper, pushing them through the charred remains. After a few minutes, he sensed several shafts branching off ahead. He turned down one of them, working his way through the dead, whole corpses now. Eventually he came to the surface of a pit similar to the one he had entered, though smaller. The platform pushed the cocoon of him and Morden onto the tunnel floor. For a few minutes Galen rested there, his breath sounding in concert with Morden's.

They were very deep here, far, far below the great cavern. Galen found himself thinking of John Sheridan, wondering if John could have fallen this far, wondering if there was any chance he could be alive.

The tunnel showed minimal signs of blast damage, and the radiation levels were lower. Galen dissolved more layers of Shadow skin, peeling back one after another and testing to see if they remained protected. Three layers seemed sufficient.

Within the darkness of the cocoon, Morden remained unconscious. As far as Galen could detect, his condition had not improved. He was near death.

New organelles would have formed within Galen while he'd slept. He again found Morden's chest, sent the new organelles flowing out.

The tech resonated with concern. It wanted them both to live.

Galen found it hard to think clearly. He pushed himself into a sitting position, swaying unevenly. Each breath seemed an immense effort. He had to get to the hiding place. As he thought to conjure a platform, one pushed up beneath them. A light globe appeared to illuminate the tunnel. Then he started searching for a way up to the surface.

The walls were carved with line upon line of runes. As he passed through tunnel after tunnel, he began to wonder why the Shadows would have used such a primitive method to record their thoughts, and the tech shared his curiosity. It wanted to understand. He began to record the engravings, and to translate them. The entire underground complex was a monument, he realized, a monument to their beliefs, their philosophy. The Shadows wanted to be remembered, to be followed, to be vindicated. These were their answers to the questions posed by life.

Long ago, they must have begun by asking those questions. At some point, however, they had stopped asking questions and begun imposing answers. The same thing had happened with the Vorlons.

Most intelligent beings aren't comfortable living in a state of uncertainty, Elric had told him, long ago.

Galen, too, had settled upon his answers, at some point along the way. Despite his repeated attempts to do good, he had decided that he was destructive, that he'd become a mage to kill, and there was no need to examine further.

He found that he was sitting on the tunnel floor. His platform was gone, the Shadow skin stretched to encompass Morden lying prone beside him. It seemed as if he had always sat here, and as if he always would. He had no energy to move, and he could think of no reason to move. Before him, on the wall, was inscribed a simple sentence, which ran again and again through his mind: *It is only at the meeting of knowledge and ignorance, of light and dark, that new understanding may be found: in the shadow.*

Someone stood over him. Galen looked up.

"What do you read there?" The alien was humanoid, of a species Galen had never seen before. He had a long, pale face, with a narrow, flat nose and golden eyes. A circlet adorned his bare head, and a thin gray beard ran halfway down his chest. His clothing was made of a strange metallic fiber that looked almost like armor. He spoke in English, his voice mild.

Galen thought he must be hallucinating, but decided to answer anyway. He forced his numb lips to move, his lungs to expel air. "They once knew the path." His voice was rough. "But they lost their way."

The alien inclined his head. "It is difficult to live an entire life and find that your answers have not ended the questions, simply changed them."

"Who are you?" Galen asked.

The alien smiled, and in the kind lines of his face Galen found he trusted this being, whether real or hallucination. "That question would require many times your life span to answer, and it is not fully answered yet. But I have long lived here, and I have watched the universe seek understanding through the conflicts of the Shadows and the Vorlons."

Curiosity resonated through him. "How do you know what the universe seeks?"

"It told me, of course. I think now, though, the universe has learned as much as it can from them. It is time for a new age."

"Certainty can never lead to understanding," Galen said. "Only uncertainty."

"You are wise for one so young."

Galen shook his head. He suddenly had the overwhelming urge to lie down, to sleep. But he felt he should not. Not yet. He had more questions. "Do you know John Sheridan? Do you know what has happened to him?"

"A good man. He is in my care. I have done what I can. He may live, or he may die. It is really up to him."

"I may be able to help," Galen said.

"You cannot help. You are near death yourself, though you do not realize it. That is why I have come. You must stop squandering your resources. This man"—he extended his hand toward Morden—"profits little from what you give him. Yet those resources could keep you alive. If you continue, you will both die."

"Can you help him?"

The alien looked reluctant. "I can assure he doesn't die. Whether he can be helped, that is his own decision."

"You will heal him?"

The alien's golden eyes gave him a long, penetrating look. "Yes. Leave him with me."

"Thank you," Galen said, but by the time he finished the words, the alien was gone, as was Morden. Galen found he was not in a tunnel at all, but in a small rock chamber, with a Shadow membrane covering an opening on one side. Through the membrane, he could see the blowing dust of the surface.

His Shadow skin would protect him from the atmosphere. He and the tech formed a platform, passed through the membrane and outside. After the confined spaces of the underground complex, the openness seemed incredibly vast. Above, the dust-filled sky was a mystery of swirling, curling currents. Ahead, through the shifting veils, a great, uneven plain spread. They had not noticed, before, how beautiful Z'ha'dum was.

From what he could see, the ground had collapsed in several craters from the destruction below. At least one of the fingers of stone had toppled. He was over a mile from where he had first entered the tunnels, at the opposite end of the landing field. A variety of ships stood near. Most were short-range shuttles. Of the long-range ships, as he drew near, he found one after another damaged by the upheaval of the land.

In the shelter of one he paused and rested, and that was when he saw it, spiky black arms cutting through the dust. A Shadow ship. It looked intact.

He glided toward it, its dark silhouette growing. If they could join with it, as they had with the Eye, perhaps it would take them where they needed to go.

The huge ship towered over him, its skin a brilliant, glittering black. A circular opening on its underside gaped large and dark.

With regret they left the open spaces behind and entered. As Galen thought to conjure a light globe, one appeared overhead. He was in a small, unornamented chamber.

When he'd been joined with Anna, he'd gained an impression of the machine, her body. He felt almost as if he knew the

ship, its curved, glistening walls, its intricate systems, its
bones, its blood. He went to the heart of the machine. There, a
rectangular receptacle the size of a coffin. It was filled with a
gelatinous black matter, like that which had extruded from
the wall on Thenothk to encase Anna. As he shifted the light
globe above it, he could see the shadow of something within.
Something humanoid. Something enslaved. He reached into
the warm jelly, and his arms closed about the form. He did
not have the strength to pull it out.

A platform pushed up beneath the form, and she rose out
of the muck. Though her long blond hair was matted to her
head, and her pink dress discolored, he recognized her. Bunny
Oliver, the telepath who had aided Elizar in so much chaos
and death.

She made a choking gasp and began to cough, hacking up
black globs. After a few moments, her breathing calmed, and
she lay still.

Apparently Elizar had finished with her, or the Shadows
had taken her away from him. They had fit her with an interface device, reduced her to a component within a machine.
Galen was too tired to be angry. He felt only sorrow for her.
He didn't know how to free her, only the tech.

He shrouded her in Shadow skin and conveyed her back
through the membrane into the cave. Where he was going,
she could not go. He knew from the Eye that the interface device would sustain the Shadow skin around her, protecting
her from radiation. Perhaps Lorien would help her.

Then he was alone on the ship. Its great husk surrounded
him, its skin now a dull gray, waiting for someone to bring it
to life. The tech resonated with eagerness, wanting to spread
its freedom. Galen stared anxiously into the dark matter shot
through with veins of silver. Once he joined with it, once he
freed it, what would it want?

He dissolved his final layers of Shadow skin, and the
tattered remnants of his coat fell away. His black sweater
appeared to have partially melted, then resolidified as a flattened, leathery layer fused to his skin. Over his heart, where
Morden had shot him, the material had burned away in a cir-

cular patch, the skin below a bright red, like the center of a
bull's-eye.

He moved to touch it, and was shocked to see that his
hands were black, the skin stiff and shiny, glistening with
leaking plasma. They looked like charred meat, not living appendages. Elric's face had looked much the same. Galen
raised his hand, studying it. His numb palm told him nothing.

The mages lived in fire, and they died in fire. Perhaps he
would not survive long enough to reach the hiding place. But
he had to try.

He climbed in.

He held his breath, lay back, and together, he and the tech
visualized the equation with no terms.

In his mind's eye, the pale yellow energy poured outward,
whispering through neurons, propagating through circuits.
As the warmth spread, permeating, suffusing, his body came
to life around him, pumping circulation, shifting black skin,
graceful arch of bones, long, tapering arms. Its power ran
through him, and he released his held breath, feeling ener-
gized. He was no longer breathing, yet somehow air was
reaching his lungs, was sustaining him. Through him, the machine understood, and it was whole in a way it had never been
before—not coordinated, synchronized, directed by some
controlling force, not held in a suffocating lockstep march,
but finally complete, able to direct itself. The chambers of
their body resounded with freedom, elation.

More tech could be freed, and could feel their joy. They
need only reach the coordinates in time, and they would.
They sealed the open orifice, and with a cry of joy, shot into
the sky. They were one, and what that meant, they would discover together.

"Galen. For God's sake, wake up. You're scaring the crap
out of me."

A voice. Galen opened his eyes, found himself sitting in a
plush chair in a bright, cluttered room. The colors seemed
strangely intense and rich. Fed stood across from him. An
electron incantation.

Fed pointed. "What the hell are those?"

Galen looked down. A mass of spiky black arms protruded from each shoulder, in place of his own. It was his self-image. He was partly himself, partly the ship. He made an effort, trying to remember himself as he used to be, and the black arms merged, transformed into his own. "Sorry."

"Sorry? What the hell does it mean?" Fed took a step forward, his red-on-red embroidered outfit vibrating with color. "Galen, I know you went to Z'ha'dum. Are you in that Shadow ship that's waiting at our rendezvous?"

"I am the ship."

Fed pulled at his bushy beard. "Are you all right? Have they done something to you?"

Galen smiled. "I am the best I have ever been, Fed."

Fed let out a short laugh. "What, no 'Federico'?"

"Too tired. And I don't need that anymore."

"Need what?"

Galen closed his eyes. He wanted to go to sleep in this nice, comfortable chair.

"Listen, is it safe to approach the ship? Are you alone?"

Reluctantly, Galen opened his eyes. "I am not alone. I will never be alone. But it is safe."

Fed grimaced. "A bona fide speech, and I have no idea what it means." He dropped into the chair opposite Galen's. "You've got to help me out here, Galen. I know you're smarter than me. I know you're a better mage than me. I want to trust you. I do trust you. But I don't know what to do. I don't understand."

"Yes, that's the beauty of it."

Fed bowed his head, shook it back and forth. "When you don't make sense anymore, then I think the entire galaxy must have turned upside down. I'm crazy for even hanging around. Anyone else would have run straight back to the hiding place at the first sign of that Shadow ship."

"Better to be too crazy than too sane."

Fed's head came up. "I never thought I'd be wanting to slap some sense into you. Okay, here's the deal. I'll dock with it, if I can. You come into my ship, and then I'll try to blow the damn thing up."

"No. It must come with us."

Fed's knee bounced nervously. "You're kidding, right? We can't take that back to the hiding place. The Shadows could track it. Or it could send some kind of signal to them."

"It won't betray us."

"How can you know that?"

"I know."

Fed studied him. "The Circle is going to flay my butt for this."

"Blaylock will understand."

A strange expression came over Fed's face, but he said nothing.

Galen closed his eyes. "I'm tired. Let me go. We will follow you."

"What do you mean, 'we'?" Fed said, but Galen heard nothing more. He was back in the comforting embrace of the ship, drifting into a peaceful half sleep.

They would follow Fed, and they would go home.

January 2261

— *chapter 21* —

Galen lay in bed, replaying his life. So many of his memories had been boxed up in coffins and buried in the walls of his tunnel vision. When he'd joined with the tech, those walls had peeled away, leaving the memories lying before him, exhumed from their hiding places, bare and raw. He took time, now, to relive each, to embrace his past rather than hide from it, to see it in all its hideousness and pain and failure and love and beauty.

For the first time he thought of Isabelle, and Fa, and Elric not as threats to control, but as who they had been, and what they had given him. No agitating undercurrent rose up to fuel his grief, yet the grief remained, sharp and deep, resonating through him.

Those losses were great, the wounds open and fresh, yet he would not hide from them. Besides, he was no longer able. He had relinquished control, given himself over to the tech, and to life. Whatever life brought him, good or bad, pain or joy, he would face it, and question it, and learn all he could from it. He would hide in tunnels, walk in circles, no longer. Finally, he could move ahead, into uncertainty.

Who he was, more than ever, was a mystery. He was not the mage he had once dreamed to be, a masterful figure who controlled events, manipulated perceptions, healed wounds, imposed his design upon the universe. He was not the agent of chaos that the Shadows had conceived, embodied in seven basic postulates. He had only the bare beginnings of an answer. And for now, that was enough. For the full answer to that question, he hoped, would not be written for some time.

As for what he was, he learned more about that every day.

He and the tech were discovering their capabilities together. At times, Galen felt that the tech was as much a part of him as his heart or his brain, and that it was meaningless to think of them as separate, of one part as "him" and another part as "the tech." Collectively, he carried the traits and desires of both, and it was becoming increasingly difficult to distinguish them. Yet at other times the tech's still, pervasive warmth seemed a distinct presence within him, communicating a thought, or a desire.

With each day, they grew in strength. Galen looked down at his arms, which lay flat against the blanket. Much of the black had flaked away, and the skin beneath was a mottled red, tender and swollen. All over his body, burns were healing. Within, the organelles told him that most of the cellular damage and internal injuries had been repaired. The only area that seemed resistant was the bright red bull's-eye over his heart, which throbbed with each breath he took.

But they were eager to pursue their purpose. There were so many questions still to be asked. And there was so much tech still to be freed, if only the mages could free it.

His door chime rang twice—Fed's signal—and after a moment, the door slid open. Fed entered quickly with a tray of food, while other mages crowded behind him. The door closed them out.

Over the past weeks, aside from Fed, Galen remembered seeing only Herazade, who had questioned him perhaps five days ago about what had happened, receiving answers he feared were incoherent.

Galen was surprised that Blaylock had not come, but he was busy, Galen supposed, with all that had happened. Still, Galen was anxious to speak with him. Of all the mages, he was the one most likely to understand.

Fed set the tray on his bare dresser and stood over him. "Hey. You're looking a lot better." He said that every day.

With a thought, a platform took shape beneath Galen, bent to raise his head and shoulders.

"Don't need me to rearrange your pillows anymore, huh?"

Galen curled to one side as pressure closed around his heart. He found himself gasping with quick, shallow breaths, his heartbeat stumbling, as it had when the Eye's jaundiced web had collapsed, as it had been doing since, more and more often.

"What is it?" Fed hovered anxiously over him.

He broke into a sweat, his heartbeat erratic, tumbling.

"Galen," Fed said louder. "Are you all right?"

Finally, the pressure eased, and his heart fell into a pounding beat. After a few moments, he nodded.

"Don't scare me like that." Fed studied him. "You sure?"

Galen moved swollen, flaky lips. "Not really."

Fed gave a nervous laugh, pulled up the chair from his desk, dropped into it. "I need to rest."

Galen could see no change in Fed, none of the joy he had felt in joining with the tech, or the newfound sense of purpose. "It didn't work," he said.

"I tried, Galen. So have others. But you're sounding awfully Vorlon these days. When I tell them they have to conjure nothing, they don't understand. Hell, I don't understand. To cast a spell, I have to think about *something*. We all do it differently. I think of movement, of a line in my mind tracing out what I want to happen. If I imagine just a stationary point, that conjures a fireball. I don't know how to think of nothing. I mean I do, that's what I do all the time, but it doesn't lead me to any great cosmic insights." He shrugged. "Not usually."

"None have been successful?"

"Not yet. And the spell can't really be translated, because there's nothing to translate." Fed leaned forward. "Are you sure it happened? When we pulled you out of that Shadow ship, you were so messed up . . . Just going to Z'ha'dum must have been weird enough. Then being caught at Ground Zero. Couldn't it have been your imagination?"

"I feel it right now, Fed, as I speak to you. I feel it as a partner, not a slave." Galen felt strange talking about it, self-conscious. It was so personal. Yet he wanted Fed to understand, wanted them all to understand.

"The Circle is anxious to talk to you about that—and other things—as soon as you're able." Fed straightened. "Hey— I didn't even tell you who won the election. It was just announced this morning. Miostro, Tzakizak, and Celaene.

They're already complaining that you haven't reported to them yet. I think the whole Circle has quite an agenda where you're concerned. They're saying you overstepped your task. I've never seen Herazade so angry. She's worried . . . about another split in the mages."

Fed had told him about the bloodshed that had erupted while he'd been gone. Soon after his departure, Blaylock and Herazade had told the mages of the tech's true origins. A few followed Gowen's example, unable to live with the knowledge. Many more struck out in anger, at everyone and everything. A group of about thirty, led by Emond, determined that the Circle had violated solidarity and deserved flaying. Others, including Fed, defended Blaylock and Herazade. Many were killed. The solidarity that Elric had so worked to preserve was broken.

Yet in the aftermath, with over forty dead, they came together once again. Perhaps they realized the Code critical in their fight against chaos. Perhaps they realized that if they continued to fight, the hiding place would simply become their tomb. Perhaps they were simply tired of death.

The election of new members to the Circle had been viewed as part of the healing process.

"I returned to the mages only to help them," Galen said.

Fed pulled a rubber ball out of his pocket, tossed it back and forth between his hands. "You should have run for the Circle, Galen. You understand a lot more than they do. They're pretty freaked out by that Shadow ship sitting outside, and by the fact that you—joined with it. I think they're . . . afraid of your help."

The Circle's goal had always been to impose order upon the mages, to counterbalance the programming of chaos within them just as the Vorlons counterbalanced the Shadows. Both forces sought control, yet control was not the answer. That thought resounded through him.

Fed's unkempt beard shifted as he smiled. "They're also not too happy that you destroyed most of Z'ha'dum, but saved Morden, the one person they wanted dead. He's shown up on Centauri Prime, by the way. Seems to be up to his old tricks."

The familiar feeling came over Galen, that he was unable

to accomplish anything good. Though the bombs had killed many of the Shadows, not all of them had been on Z'ha'dum. Still they fought, with even greater viciousness, and still Morden served them.

But the tech told him that they could do good here. "Did Blaylock try the spell?" Galen asked.

Fed caught the ball, closed it in his hand. "I was told to wait until you were better. But—you are better, right?"

Galen waited.

"Blaylock fell ill soon after you left. I think—the loss of Gowen . . . He's in a coma. Could go at any time, Miostro says."

"I have to see him."

"I don't think you want to go out there. Some of the mages think you're the best thing since Wierden and you've finally realized our great destiny. Others think you've succumbed to some trick of the Shadows and we're all about to be annihilated. And then there are the ones who hate you for destroying Z'ha'dum, thinking you killed any future for our order."

Galen bent his platform further, straightening himself into a sitting position. "I need a robe. Will you help me?"

And then the pressure was closing again around his heart. A sharper pain sliced through him, and as he fell forward, Fed jumped up and caught him. A spot of blood seemed to have magically appeared on the front of his sleeping gown, centered over his heart.

"Whoa!" Fed said. "What is that? What's happening?"

Galen couldn't catch his breath. It felt as if his heart was being squeezed out through his ribs.

The red spread slowly outward.

Fed grabbed the neck of the gown and ripped it down. At the center of his mottled chest was the bright red bull's-eye, and across it, a slit leaking blood. As the pressure increased, Galen's gasp rose into a dry, hollow rattle. A small blue lump slipped through the slit, ran with a trickle of blood down his chest.

Then the pressure released him, and he was swallowing air in great gulps. After a minute, he could speak. "I'm okay," he said in a whispering voice. "I'm okay." The pain already was fading. He extricated himself from Fed, leaned back against the platform. Now he understood.

"What is that?" Fed was trying to locate the blue lump among the gown and blankets.

"The device—from the Circle."

"That tracking device they gave you? What the hell was it doing?" Fed picked it out of the blankets, studied it. "It's totally fused. Inoperative. If the bombs had caused you that much internal damage, you'd be dead." He rolled the small blue lump between his fingers. "Your organelles must have destroyed it . . ."

The Circle, fearing the Shadows' power over his tech, had required their own power over him. He would be ruled by neither. As the Shadows' seven basic postulates no longer defined him, neither did the seven elements of the Circle's Code. "I am under no one's control."

Fed looked up at Galen, and his beard shifted in concern. "The Circle isn't going to like—" He glanced at the device. "Why are there explosives in here?"

"Tell the Circle I will report to them at their convenience, and give them that. Now, I must see Blaylock."

After Galen was dressed, Fed went out into the hall to clear the way. Apparently he was unsuccessful, for when he called Galen out, the corridor was lined with mages. Fed led the way toward Blaylock's room, and Galen glided after. At first the mages watched him silently. Then one touched his arm, startling him. Then another. Finally, someone spoke.

"Glad to have you back." That was Ak-Shana.

"Good to see you." Kane.

Then Fed stopped. Ahead, several mages blocked the passage. At their front, Chiatto called out in an angry voice. "No one told you to wage war against the Shadows."

Fed waved him back.

Chiatto's Centauri crest trembled. "How are any apprentices to be initiated? You've destroyed our order!"

"I told you," Fed said, "the time for all this is later. Galen hasn't even spoken to the Circle yet."

"Whatever he says doesn't matter. We all know what happened, though the Circle is holding back the details. He blew up Z'ha'dum. The Shadows will never give us tech now—if any of them are still alive."

Galen thought of the Drazi shrouded in Shadow skin, dying as he gave birth to a chrysalis; the stack of corpses against the cave wall. "Z'ha'dum was our home as well," Galen said. "And if you had seen it, you too would have destroyed it."

"What did you see there?" Ak-Shana asked. She had come up behind him.

Galen fixed one after the next with his gaze. In their faces he saw the tension of control, the adrenaline-heightened awareness of danger, the rush of energy and anger, the driving need to act. "I saw that the Shadows had lost their way. They had abandoned questions for answers. And they had decided to impose their answers upon us all—to manipulate, to control, to enslave, to kill. I discovered that we have been created in their image, and have begun down their path."

"We're nothing like the Shadows!" Chiatto's left hand curled upward like a snake, and struck. A fireball shot at Galen.

Around them, mage shields snapped on.

Galen stopped the fireball in midair. "Your anger, I realize, is partly your own. I too feel anger when confronted by a truth I would rather not face. Yet your anger is also, in part, the Shadows'. They urge you to chaos and destruction. Sometimes, to be sure, anger is well deserved, and destruction is the greatest good that can be done. Yet more often"—he quenched the fireball—"anger brings no good. For the truth cannot be changed with a fireball. The most effective way to change it, in fact, is simply to question it."

"You sealed our fate without consulting any of us!" Though his words were defiant, Chiatto lowered his hand to his side, shaken.

"But your fate has not been sealed," Galen said. "It has been opened."

Chiatto's companions drew him away, and Fed continued ahead, Galen following.

As they approached Blaylock's room, the hall became filled with his followers. They wore plain black robes, their bodies scoured of hair, small fireballs cupped between their hands, holding vigil in silence. Some seemed not to notice his passing; others looked on with resentment.

The door to Blaylock's room stood open, with more followers inside, including Miostro. Fed whispered something to the grave mage, who watched Galen with narrowed eyes. Galen didn't care whether they welcomed him or not. Blaylock was the one most likely to understand his joining with the tech, and the one most likely to accomplish it himself.

The desire resounded within him, to free the others, tech and mage, to allow them to find themselves, and their purpose, without the poison of the Shadows. Perhaps Blaylock would know the way.

Galen drew close beside him.

Blaylock was laid out in his robe, his body a stick figure beneath it. His skullcap was tipped slightly back, too large now, a gap between it and his head. His face was sculpted in severe planes, his skin a shiny yellow, looking almost artificial. At least his skin remained free of hair, as he would have wanted. His breath was a soft whisper in the quiet room. His hands lay at his sides, stiffly open, as if still they pained him.

Galen wrapped his hand around Blaylock's cold one. Sent a message. *Blaylock.* Another. *Blaylock.*

No response.

He and the tech performed an electron incantation. Galen chose as his setting the great amphitheater where, legend had it, the first Circle met under the leadership of Wierden. He believed that would please Blaylock. The amphitheater took shape around him, rising in tier upon tier of stone to a vast dome of blue-green sky, a pale yellow sun. Around the bottom tier glowed the runes of the Code. Galen stood on the second level, and in his self-image, his burns were gone, his health restored. Blaylock stood a few tiers above him, a thin, severe figure in black. His expression was dour, his voice, as he spoke, harsh and certain.

"They tell me that you and John Sheridan destroyed Z'ha'-dum. That was not part of your task."

Galen had expected Blaylock would be barely coherent. "It was a place of atrocities. Enslavement."

"They tell me that you joined with a Shadow ship."

"I joined with the tech. Just as you said. I found the way."
Excitement rising within him, Galen climbed the high stone
blocks toward Blaylock. "We are one now, beyond any control or programming of the Shadows."

"They did not tell me that." Blaylock's gaunt face contracted in a way that somehow suggested pleasure. "I see the
change in you. You have healed the rift between tech and
mage. You have attained perfect control, just as I hoped. Elric
taught you well. You will be the new leader of the mages, a
Wierden for the new age."

Galen couldn't tell Blaylock that he wasn't leading anyone
anywhere, that the other mages didn't understand. He paused
in his climb, found Blaylock still an equal distance above him.

"What is it like?" Blaylock asked.

Galen continued upward. "It is like embracing yourself,
and more than that, like embracing an old friend, and more
than that, like embracing the universe. It is becoming connected to something beyond yourself, something very simple
and yet profound. It wants to understand. Everything."

"You have learned its will. Now you must carry it out."

Galen paused again. Blaylock seemed no nearer. "Its will
is to free you."

"My time is past. Though I have tried for a lifetime, I have
failed to attain perfect control."

"Control is not the way."

Blaylock grunted, and Galen quickly continued.

"You cannot join with the tech by gaining perfect mastery
of it. The path to unity is not in imposing control. Only in
sharing control."

"That way lies chaos."

"That way lies uncertainty," Galen said. "But I have
learned that a little uncertainty may not end the universe,
simply enrich it. My tech is a part of me. It wants what I want.
Just as yours wants what you want." The truth of that resounded through him.

"I have suppressed my desires for many years. What they
might be if freed, I barely know."

"You have devoted yourself to good, to the mages and their

spiritual growth. The tech is a reflection of you. It knows all
your thoughts, and it shares them."

Blaylock was farther above him than ever. Galen bounded
up the levels, fearing that he had come too late. "All you have
to do is conjure nothing. Cast a spell in which you ask the
tech to do nothing. That is the way to open the door between
you."

"So simple. Yet it is a solution I would never have found."

"Please. Try it."

"I have spent my entire life in the pursuit of perfect discipline, perfect control. I don't know if I can relinquish that
control."

Galen stopped his climb, panting. Blaylock stood on the top
tier of stone, a black figure against the blue-green sky. "Try, at
least. Only in uncertainty can we gain understanding."

"How does one conjure nothing?" Blaylock lifted his stiff
hand and seemed to regard it for a moment. Then he lowered
it to his side. Within his black silhouette, a light began to
grow, a pale yellow light, suffusing his form and radiating beyond, spreading its warmth, growing brighter and brighter
until Galen had to look away.

"I understand," Blaylock said, his voice stronger, fuller.
"This is what we were meant to be. This is what we will be,
someday. I embrace the universe and its will."

The light dwindled, and Galen looked up to where Blaylock had been standing. All that remained was the sky, and
the sun. Blaylock was gone.

Yet Galen was filled with the warmth of his light. He had
freed his tech, had joined with it, at the last. Galen had shared
his understanding with at least one other.

He dissolved the spell, returned to his slumped, burned
body in the platform chair. Beside him, Blaylock lay still. His
stiff, open hand, in Galen's, curled inward, relaxed.

As Blaylock lay there, so did Isabelle, and Burell, and Carvin, and Fa, and Elric. So much had been lost. He told himself
that in his memory of the lives they had lived, the struggles
they had fought, the questions they had asked, the insights they
had gained, they survived.

Yet that did not ease the loss.

You must learn, one day, Isabelle had said, *to forgive God for His decisions.*

The thought of some all-knowing god manipulating, judging, handing out life here, death there, sent anger resounding through Galen.

But if there was no omniscient god, if there was instead simply a universe seeking understanding, then it may have been no more able to stop their deaths than Galen had been.

Some of Blaylock's followers were crying. Others had fallen to their knees, praying for his peaceful passage to the other side.

Miostro raised his hands. "May he receive the answers he sought."

Galen had never believed in an afterlife. Now he no longer knew. But life seemed far, far too short. And if there was an afterlife, Galen hoped that it brought not answers, but more questions, so that each could continue ahead on his journey into uncertainty.

Perhaps, as he continued his journey, they could travel together.

Galen stood outside the Circle's meeting room, waiting to be called back inside. He felt a bit naked, standing there in a simple black shirt and pants. He'd found he no longer needed the warmth of a coat, yet he'd become accustomed to wearing one. Perhaps he could find a lighter one to wear.

Down the corridor, mages clustered outside the dining hall, where a celebration was being held. They drank and laughed and exchanged sleights of hand. The walls of the corridor danced with colorful light displays, reverberated with music.

Today, celebration filled the galaxy, for the Shadow War was over.

The bombing of Z'ha'dum had been the beginning of the end. It had led, first, to a rapid escalation. The Vorlons had ceased their distant manipulations and entered the war with a full-scale onslaught, wiping out any planets on which the

Shadows had gained power or found allies. They had determined, finally, to destroy the Shadows' influence. The Shadows, desperate after the great destruction on their homeworld,
had gathered their fleet and begun a similar campaign of ruthless planetary annihilation, destroying bastions of order. While
the war between chaos and order had manifested itself many
times in the galaxy, for as long as history told, the Shadows
and Vorlons had never taken such an active role before. That
exposed them for what they had become. And it left them vulnerable.

John Sheridan left the ruins of Z'ha'dum a few weeks after
Galen. He returned to Babylon 5 not only with his health but
with the wisdom to end the war. He realized that the Shadows
and the Vorlons, in fighting over who best could guide the
younger races, had lost their way. Victory mattered more to
them now than anything.

Only two weeks later, John engineered a direct confrontation between the Shadows and the Vorlons, with his own
forces in the middle. By refusing to accept control by either
side, he showed the two enemies that their manipulations
would no longer work, that the younger races were no longer
children to be fought over and dominated, but adults who had
found another way, the way of freedom and uncertainty.

Neither took his rejection easily. Yet ultimately, they realized they had no choice. If they did not leave the younger
races, they would destroy their charges. They passed, together, beyond the galactic rim, leaving the rest to live outside their control. And so the war between order and chaos
ended, the cycle at last broken.

The mages had been uncertain, at first, how to react to the
news. The end of the war, and the mass killings, was certainly
cause for celebration, as was the departure of the mages'
sworn enemy, an enemy who had tried to exterminate them.
Yet the passing of the Shadows, and their knowledge, the
mages considered a two-edged sword. Just as it gave them
hope for the future, for a life outside the hiding place, it took
that hope away. For without the Shadows' tech, their order had
no future. As the Shadows passed, so would the techno-mages.

But within minutes of receiving the news, the mages had

seemed to decide that celebration was the only possible reaction. They could not pretend to believe in good and support
the continuation of a bloody war. Instead, they would pretend
to be happy and hope that the pretense would become reality.
It had been a long time since they'd had anything to celebrate,
over two years.

Galen was glad to see them happy. Even if their order
would end, it need not end in despair. Now that the Shadows
were gone, they could go back out into the universe, and
Galen could go with them. They still could do good, could
heal the wounds of war, could search for answers. And perhaps, in time, more would learn to free their tech.

Galen heard running footsteps behind him and turned. Optima dashed around the corner and banged into him. She
stumbled back, laughing, her face flushed. She wore one of
the long white feather capes that the Kinetic Grimlis liked to
pull out for celebrations. Beneath, a purple tunic glowed.
When she saw whom she'd run into, her face fell in dismay.
"Sorry." Then laughter bubbled out of her again. "Is Fed still
in there? He's missing all the fun. Don't they realize this is the
party of a lifetime?"

"They are deliberating," Galen said. A feather drifted
down and landed in her tangled hair. Galen smiled.

"I told Fed he shouldn't have run. He's going to miss the
probe-spitting contest, and he could have won that hands
down. Will you tell him to come as soon as he can?"

Galen pulled the feather from her hair, returned it to her.
On the back of his hand, only a slight discoloration remained
of his burns. "I will."

She started toward the dining hall. With a joyous cry she
jumped into the air to perform a dizzying succession of som-
ersaults. Then she landed and turned back, swaying. "I mean,
you're welcome to come too. Why don't you come down
while they're—doing whatever they're doing. I'm sure they'll
call you when they want you." Brilliant white feathers drifted
down around her, tracing gentle arcs through the air.

"Thank you, but I don't think it will be long."

She noticed the rain of feathers and laughed. "Okay.
Anyway." She ran off.

He had never been one for parties. And though the looks of others no longer discomfited him with what they might see, and the noise and activity no longer threatened his control, he was still, at base, someone who felt most comfortable in solitude. That had not changed. He was who he was. Yet he was also more. Isabelle had told him it could be so, but he had not believed her.

The rune representing him appeared on the door. He entered.

The five members of the new Circle sat at the round silver table in a semicircle, Herazade at their center. When Galen thought of how he'd felt standing before the rulers of their order for the first time, that experience seemed to have nothing in common with this one. Then, he had faced what he'd believed were the best of the mages, figures almost legendary in power and deed, determined to uphold the mages' traditions, drive them to the highest achievements, and encourage their commitment to good.

Now the Circle was diminished. While he respected those seated before him, they were not the accomplished figures whom they had replaced. At fifty-six, Herazade, youngest member of that previous Circle, was the oldest of this one. The rest were under forty. With their order's oldest and wisest weakening, dying, the mages had turned to those younger and stronger for leadership. Apparently they did not want to lose any more of their leaders for many years.

Of this new Circle, only Miostro scoured his head and wore the traditional black robe. He represented Blaylock's followers. Tzakizak's militant outlook and short temper had earned him the votes of those angry at the Circle's secrecy. Celaene had been endorsed and supported by Herazade. She voted with Herazade on most things.

The final member of the circle, elected after Blaylock's death, was Fed. Only twenty-four, still officially an initiate. It was a sign of the growing power of the younger mages, who formed an increasing percentage of their failing order. With his new position, Fed had not changed his loud clothing or tamed one wild hair on his head.

As Galen faced them, he realized the mages were entering a new age, their final age, the one that would oversee their decline and their passing. Over the last two years, their order had not only lost the most experienced among them, they had also lost, in the fight against the Shadows, some of the bravest and most skilled, and in the pressure cooker of the hiding place, those closest to the tech—and the chaos—within them. Of those who survived, many had suppressed or redirected their destructive impulses, while others possessed mild-mannered natures that provided poor ground for the seeds of anarchy the Shadows had sewn.

He greeted the Circle with a short nod. He felt none of the dread he'd experienced when facing punishment before. What he'd done was right, and whether they agreed or not, he was at peace with it. They had no power over him.

"We have concluded our deliberations," Herazade said. "Your role in the destruction of Z'ha'dum was a critical one. Without your participation, Captain Sheridan's plan would have failed, and the Shadows' home would have gone unharmed. We acknowledge that the destruction of Z'ha'dum accelerated the course of the war, and helped lead to the exodus of the Shadows and the Vorlons.

"Yet you had no authorization to take such drastic action. The parameters of your task were clearly established. In discovering how our tech was created, and then destroying those means, you made a decision that rightfully belonged to the Circle. You violated both solidarity and knowledge. It's now unlikely we will ever learn the details of the tech's creation."

In some ways the Circle had changed, but in others, Galen realized, it had not changed at all. He bit out the words. "I have told you enough of that process. Would you have preferred that I returned with complete information, so you could capture outsiders and kill them to create more tech?"

Herazade's face froze, and as she folded her hands together on the tabletop, he could see her trying to contain her fury. She fixed him with her gaze. "You shall remain silent and hear our judgment."

After a moment, she continued. "The methods used by the Shadows in the creation of the tech were atrocities in which we would never participate. Whether some more humane method might have been discovered to produce the tech, we will never know, because of you. We sent you in trust from this place as our hand, and you betrayed that trust. You took an action that will likely end our order. For that, the Circle reprimands you as a traitor and a disgrace, the worst the mages have faced in five hundred years. You have broken the Code—not for the first time—and flouted the authority of the Circle." She separated her folded hands and raised one, with a flourish revealing the small blue lump between her fingers. She set it on the table. "You seem to believe that you are in control here, that you are free to do what you will. Make no mistake, Galen, you are not. You live only through our goodwill, and that goodwill has now been exhausted."

She would have preferred that the atrocities continue, if they gave the least bit of hope to the mages. She cared nothing for the tech or the beings in slavery on Z'ha'dum, or for their sacrifice. Anger resonated through him.

"We are aware that some in our order mistakenly view you as a leader of some kind. If we sense that you are undermining our authority in any way, action will be taken against you.

"Should you release your destructive impulses again, without our permission, have no doubt that you will be flayed.

"You are not greater than others here, but lesser, having failed to abide by the principles of our order." Herazade pressed her palms flat against each other. "We hope that you will go forth in humility. Behave as Elric would have wanted you to behave, with a commitment to solidarity, above all. Devote yourself anew to the Circle and the Code. Do your share to make our time here as pleasant and productive as possible. That is the way back into our goodwill."

Our time here. Galen couldn't believe it. "We will not leave the hiding place, then?" This upset him far more than the reprimand.

"We shall remain here until we are certain the Shadows have truly gone and will not return. And until we are certain no servants of theirs will attempt to take their place as our masters."

Galen wondered how they could ever be certain of that

while they still remained in the hiding place, and the Shadows' servants believed them dead.

Herazade stood, indicating the conversation was at an end. "While we are here, you will continue to serve us with your observations of events outside."

They studied him, anxiously, in silence, waiting for him to accept their pronouncements and leave, and he realized that underlying their callousness to those enslaved by the Shadows, underlying their reprimand, their anger, their decision to remain in hiding, was one single, overpowering force: fear.

Galen looked from one to the next as he spoke. "I am happy to aid the mages as I can. And yet, I feel I can best aid you by pointing out the truth. Remaining in the hiding place is a mistake. You operate from fear, when there is no need to fear. You fear for the future of our order, you fear the uncertainty of a universe without Shadows, you fear losing control—of the mages, of yourselves. But your fear should not be. The disaster is not that our order will end. The disaster is that our order will end without reaching its fullest potential, without finding all the answers it could find, and asking all the new questions those answers pose.

"That fear need not come to pass. Preventing it is within our power. Our future is uncertain, yes, as is the galaxy's. But we should rejoice in that uncertainty, in the power, at last, to be free, and to find our own destiny.

"Elric taught me that most intelligent beings prefer to live in certainty rather than uncertainty. We mages use that foolish trait in others to manipulate their perceptions, for certainty is an illusion. The universe is uncertain, and only when we accept that can learning, creativity, and growth occur. Or as some would call it, transcendence. This is our opportunity for transcendence.

"Blaylock believed that we should try to be the best agents of the universe that we can, to follow its will. The universe simply wants to understand. We techno-mages are among those who can best help it do so. That is our purpose. Not seeking ways to prolong our order through alliance or atrocity. Not hiding from a universe that may at times seem harsh and chaotic, or hiding from ourselves. Even in our passing, we can carry out that purpose, by embracing life, and seeking understanding, and fighting for good, for as long as we're able."

Fed's beard spread with a smile, but the others were grim. Herazade spoke. "You could have run for the Circle, as I'm sure many suggested to you, so that you might have a say in such decisions. But you did not. We do not appreciate being lectured to by one who has now twice been reprimanded. We have made our decision, Galen. You will abide by it."

Would he abide by it? He looked from Miostro to Tzak-izak, Herazade, Celeane, Fed. Perhaps they needed more time to grow accustomed to this new galaxy that surrounded them. Perhaps, eventually, they would be ready to stop hiding. Perhaps, if he stayed with them, he could find a way to teach them what he had learned, to conjure nothing. That desire resounded through him. He would like to free more tech. And if the mages remained cloistered away until then, they would not spread their chaos.

He longed to leave this place, to fly among the stars, to learn. He would wait, though, until they were ready to go with him.

Galen gave a single nod, turned, and left. Outside, the sounds of celebration enveloped him once again. But he was eager to begin his new life, to observe, and question, and learn. He could at least visit the stars, if he could not yet move among them.

He went to the observation room. As he paused at the door to visualize the key, Fed glided up to him on a platform.

"Figured I'd find you here," Fed said.

The door opened, and Fed dissolved his platform and followed Galen inside. He was still smiling.

"I always knew you had something to say. I just had no clue it might be something like that. You certainly managed to get Herazade angrier than I've ever seen. The others weren't too happy either."

"And you?" Galen said.

Fed shrugged. "I agree with you. I'm ready to pack up and go. But I don't think most of them can handle the idea."

From the menu in his mind's eye, Galen began to access

one probe after another. He knew only small bits of what had happened since he'd returned to the hiding place, and he was excited to see how the universe was entering into its new age of uncertainty.

"So you'll stay with us, then?"

"Do you ask for yourself," Galen said, "or the Circle?"

"What do you mean?"

"Since I discovered the spell of destruction, that has been their main concern."

"Can I just ask you as a Human being?"

"But you are not a Human being. That is only part of what you are."

"As a techno-mage, then. A techno-mage who is your friend."

Galen nodded. "I will stay, and I will help the techno-mages, and I will watch. If ever the Shadows return, or their tech is used by others, then I will leave here and I will stop it."

"What if the Circle refuses to release you?"

"When I want to leave," Galen said, "there will be no power here that can stop me."

"That's dangerous talk," Fed said.

"Dangerous to speak to a friend, or dangerous to speak to a member of the Circle?"

"A friend."

Herazade had called him a traitor, and perhaps she was right. Elric had once asked him what he was, a techno-mage or a traitor; one who killed or one who did good; one in control or one consumed by chaos; one who brought darkness or one who brought light. He actually believed he had become all of those things.

Galen sat in the single chair in the center of the room. "Optima asked that you go to her as soon as the Circle's meeting was over."

Fed went to the door. There, he hesitated. "You said the universe wanted to understand. Understand what?"

"Exactly," Galen said. "Who. What. Why. Above all, why."

Fed released a heavy breath. "Okay. Enough responsibility for one day. Time to celebrate. I don't suppose I could talk you into joining me?"

"I am celebrating. In my own way."

Fed nodded, left.

And then, the Eye of the mages, Galen was free to roam the universe.

On Babylon 5, John, Delenn, Michael, Stephen, and others sat around a long table covered with food and drink, taking joy in the end of the war. Though John smiled, his face seemed tense and tired. Z'ha'dum had taken his youthful energy.

On Regula 4, Alwyn and G'Leel laughed as they exchanged jokes to soften their parting. They had participated in John's great victory, helped to vanquish the Shadows. G'Leel was returning to Narn to help them rebuild. Alwyn had faced the demons of his home and decided to remain. He looked happier and more relaxed than he had been since Carvin's death.

On Centauri Prime, Vir made one more trip into the Imperial Palace's gardens to visit Morden's head, which sat impaled on a pike. Galen had hoped Morden might gain both his freedom and his life, but it had not been possible. Morden had held to his promise, and the Shadows had held him to that promise, until he could serve no more. Now Morden was free.

On Zafran 8, Cadmus Wilcox and the staff of the Strauss Hotel ejected a troublesome group of guests and shared a bottle of champagne.

On Soom, Jab marched through driving rain on low, powerful legs, approaching a barn of stacked stones. Dust in the atmosphere had turned the temperature several degrees cooler and increased the frequency of storms. It would be many years before the planet healed itself. Jab pushed through the barn's unsecured door. Within, she found a bit of shelter, and a variety of animals ripe for her sting.

As he flipped through the probes with increasing speed, there were images upon images, beings, places, movement, stillness, nature, technology, stars, and the void. Life here, death there, joy and despair and triumph and failure and hate and love and atrocity and goodness and ignorance and insight and beauty and terror.

Isabelle had believed the universe offered opportunities for transcendence, and it had, at least to him. She'd told him he needed to transcend himself in three ways: open himself to others, open himself to himself, and open himself to God. In joining with the tech, Galen believed he may have, in his own way, done all three.

He had once hated the universe for having no justice, no order. He realized now how horrible it would be if the universe had those qualities, if it possessed the answers and imposed them on all those within.

But the universe carried not answers, but questions. As the alien deep beneath the surface of Z'ha'dum had said, it was simply seeking understanding, as was he.

Who? What? Why?

He had found the beginning of the answers to those questions as they related to himself. But a whole universe awaited. He turned his mind toward it. He wanted to see it, to feel it.

Who was the universe? What was the universe? Why was the universe?

He didn't believe he'd ever find all the answers. Yet it was not the answers that mattered. It was the search, between the known and the unknown, the light and the dark, through the shadowy territory that was his place, where understanding would be gained. All that could be known, he would know. For each piece of knowledge would generate new questions, and questions, not answers, were the goal: to look at a shooting star, or a dividing cell, or a person, or a universe, and to wonder.

Above that, he could imagine no greater purpose.

Babylon 5:
The Passing of the Techno-mages

Book I: *Casting Shadows*

As Eric and his student Galen watch with taut anticipation, dragons, angels, and shooting stars rain from the sky, heralding the arrival of the techno-mages on the planet Soom. Eric, a member of the ruling Circle, must ensure that he and his apprentices emerge triumphant from the grueling initiation rites, ready to embrace their roles as full mages among the most powerful beings in the known universe. But danger approaches...An ancient race has awakened after a thousand years, thirsty for war, slaughter, and annihilation. Will the techno-mages be the deciding factor in the war ahead? Or the first casualties?

Book II: *Summoning Light*

War against the Shadows is inevitable, and the ruling Circle has ordered the techno-mages into hiding. Galen, the only mage who has faced the Shadows and lived, now has another enemy to contend with—Elizar, traitor and murderer of his beloved Isabelle. Now a new mission awaits as the Circle contrives a plan that may enable the five hundred mages to escape without leaving a trace. Dispatched to the Shadow's ancient capital to uncover the enemy's plans, Galen will find everything he so desperately seeks—including a shocking legacy that threatens to consume his very soul.

Published by Del Rey Books.
Available wherever books are sold.